T0196246

ARKADIA

F R A N K   S H E R R Y

ARKADIA

iUniverse books may be ordered through booksellers or by contacting:

iUniverse
1663 Liberty Drive
Bloomington, IN 47403
www.iuniverse.com
1-800-Authors (1-800-288-4677)

ISBN: 978-1-4917-7173-0 (sc)
ISBN: 978-1-4917-7174-7 (hc)
ISBN: 978-1-4917-7172-3 (e)

Library of Congress Control Number: 2015912237

Print information available on the last page.

iUniverse rev. date: 08/04/2015

Also by Frank Sherry
Raiders and Rebels
Pacific Passions

The Devils Captain
Eternity Falls
Talar
The Pucka-man's Odyssey
Mysteriad
Lust, Loathing, Lunacy

This book is for Stephen and Diana, together.

DREAD
SOVEREIGN

"There is no Theos, no benevolent Creator, no power of Good. There is only the power of Evil, the Dread Sovereign of all that exists." Seraph, the Golden Face

PART ONE

ARKADIA

PROLOGUE

According to Tradition—for we Arkadians lack any genuine history—the First Founders of Arkadia were aristocratic mercenary warriors who were members of a military fraternity known as "The Ten Thousand."

Tradition says that the mercenaries of The Ten Thousand having fought for the losing side in a war far from their own country found themselves alone and surrounded by enemies in an alien and hostile land.

Relying on their own courage and discipline The Ten Thousand resolved to march back to their homeland taking with them not only their loot but also a throng of captives, servants, concubines, and camp-followers who had attached themselves to these military adventurers.

As The Ten Thousand fought their arduous way through the mountains that towered everywhere around them, one of their formations—perhaps a thousand warriors in all—became separated from the main body. These lost warriors, accompanied by their own ragged and bewildered camp followers, then undertook a rambling march through labyrinthine mountains in an effort to reunite with their brethren of The Ten Thousand.

At last, their search having proved fruitless, the wanderers, now near starvation, stumbled out of a mountain pass into the fair land they were later to name "Arkadia." Here they rested on the southern bank of a slow-flowing river they called the "Bradys" and they refreshed themselves with the abundant game and fish they found there. They also decided to remain temporarily in this smiling land in order to plant and harvest a crop before resuming their search for their companions for this Arkadia seemed empty of habitation.

One night, however, undetected by sentries, a host of wild barbarians who called themselves "the Bem" appeared on the north bank of the River Bradys and fell with screams of fury on the unwary strangers encamped across the river on the south bank. Caught by surprise, our ancestors fought back bravely escaping annihilation only when the Bem savages, apparently satisfied with their night's work, withdrew across the Bradys again.

Though all but exterminated in the Bem assault these "First Founders" of Arkadia resolved that rather than flee once more to the mountains where their lack of supplies and depleted numbers would almost certainly lead to their utter destruction they would cling in desperation to this new land which their fallen comrades had already seasoned with their blood.

In a second battle with the Bem, our vastly outnumbered First Founders managed by some prodigy of arms, never explained in the Traditional accounts, to rout a Bem force even more numerous than their earlier host.

Following that victory our triumphant forebears now claimed their Arkadia by right of conquest. The Bem, however, refused to accept the presence of our early ancestors anywhere in their land but especially in the vicinity of the River Bradys which (as our forebears discovered only after the passage of many years) the Bem regarded as their sacred waterway. For it was on the north bank of the Bradys that the Bem were accustomed to sacrifice to their mad god, Dis, Lord of the Chaos that, according to Bem shamans underlay all the world. It was also on the north bank of the Bradys that the Bem cremated their dead, consulted their Oracle the so-called "Vessel of Dis", and practiced their various rites. Hence they regarded the proximity of our ancestors as an intolerable pollution and an abomination. And so the Bem, seething with hatred for the intruders on their lands, launched a perpetual war against our forebears.

Despite being always greatly outnumbered by the Bem savages, Arkadia's first generation warriors won battle after battle against these foes until they finally succeeded in driving the Bem barbarians from the River Bradys thus securing the fairest regions of Arkadia for themselves and future generations.

But despite their steady diet of defeat Bem hatred continued unabated and gave rise to what became a never-ending campaign of terror launched clandestinely from the north bank of the Bradys by "boy-gangs" who called themselves "Witnesses for Dis." These vicious young men sought glory in murdering the most defenseless of our ancestors: women, children, and the elderly, taking as trophies the severed hands, feet, and plucked-out eyes of the murdered. As a sideline the boy-gangs would often capture "Arkie" children and torture them before eventually selling them to slave merchants from unknown foreign lands.

These manifestations of Bem savagery soon provoked so much rage in our ancestors that many of them began calling for extermination of the "barbos" (the derisive name our forebears applied to the Bem and which is still in use as slang today.) In urging the eradication of the entire tribe of Bem our infuriated ancestors cited the fact that unless caught and killed at the scene of their crimes the frenzied Bem killers were almost always able to escape into the vastness of the great region of grasslands now known as the "Bemgrass."

Instead of attempting the impossible and, of course, immoral task of eradicating all the Bem people the leaders of an Arkadia now growing rich and powerful sent "punishment" detachments of warriors to hunt down Bem killers in the Bemgrass.

When that tactic failed the Arkadian leadership (by this time known as "The Hegemony") tried for decades to effect some kind of peace with Arkadia's intractable enemies. These attempts only met with scorn from Bem clan leaders who regarded all such efforts as evidence that "Arkie" (their slang for Arkadians) will to fight was weakening.

Finally, more than a century ago, the Hegemony constructed what was called a "Forbidden Zone" along the entire north bank of the River Bradys from its source at Mt. Phobys to its confluence with the Tachys River at Mill Point where the two streams formed the turbulent Pelorys. This Forbidden Zone—from which all Bem were to be excluded—eventually expanded to a strip of territory fifteen miles deep and approximately three hundred miles long. Military posts—towers and stockades—were established at twenty-mile intervals. Manned by companies of slingers and squadrons of cavalry, the Zone was patrolled night and day.

By denying the Bem access to the Bradys in this manner the Forbidden Zone formed an effective barrier between what was now called Arkadia to the south and the Bemgrass to the north. Murderous incidents diminished although some "Witnesses for Dis" bent on "holy suicide" did manage to penetrate the Zone to carry out their missions of death. For the most part, however, the Zone fulfilled its purpose for Arkadians. For the Bem, on the other hand, it was both a constant reminder of their "lost" land and a further goad to their hatred. Still, only a few Arkadians thought much about Bem sensibilities as long as the Forbidden Zone kept most of them out of Arkadia.

One who did think about such matters was our current Hegemon, Agathon the Fifth. When he was elevated to the High Bench as ruler of Arkadia more than thirty years ago at this writing the Forbidden Zone had been in existence for years and the Bem were thought by most of us Arkadians to be thoroughly demoralized, even tamed. But Agathon saw little evidence of it. What he did see was a hostile Bem nation which, though temporarily cowed, was actually a cauldron seething as never before with hatred. Recognizing the ultimate futility of the Forbidden Zone Agathon sought some means of mitigating at least to some degree Bem enmity and so perhaps opening the door (eventually) to the possibility of making peace between the two antagonistic peoples.

Toward this end Agathon using his power as Hegemon established a yearly ritual called "The Passing of the Bem into the Forbidden Zone." Under this dispensation the Bem clans were permitted to "pass" into the Zone during the "Month of Low Water" each year. Once camped within the Zone they were free for a period of ten days as long as they kept the peace to erect their huts and to renew their ancient practices with the exception of human sacrifice.

Under Agathon's rules for the "Passings", the Bem men might turn their ponies out to graze while they fished and hunted along the River Bradys. The tribal women were at liberty to gather from the riverbed the peculiar stones they valued. In addition, the clans were granted license to frequent again their age-old shrines on the river's islands and even to consult their oracular "Vessel of Dis." Moreover, Agathon made it a point to turn a blind eye to rough-edged Bem "religious" rites such as the burning of their dead and the scattering of their ashes in the river. He also refused to investigate rumors of human sacrifices for he considered it essential for the sake of any possible future peace that the Bem come to realize that his Hegemony did not seek to impose Arkadian laws on them so long as they refrained from acts of violence.

In brief then, during the ten days of the Passing, the Bem might do as they chose so long as they did it peaceably—and so long as none of them crossed the river to the south bank where Arkadia proper began.

So far the annual Passing ceremonies, even after thirty years, have not produced Agathon's hoped-for peace but apparently the annual event has become a fixture in Bem life and may yet achieve the Hegemon's aim. After all, Hegemon Agathon has stated often that the conflict that the Bem first forced on our ancestors has persisted ever since our First Founders camped along the Bradys—a span of thirty generations—and that one must not expect an easy end to it.

At this point in my narrative, I must pause to observe that in spite of the intractable malevolence of the Bem, we Arkadians have flourished generation after generation. We have also changed greatly. For example, the camp followers of our First Founders became skilled artisans and merchants eventually forming a powerful social class called the "Koinars." At the same time the descendants of the warriors of our First Founders became the aristocracy of Arkadia. Today they constitute the wealthy landowner and warrior castes called "Megars" and "Riders."

With the further passage of time, even the original language of our First Founders—the language of their lost homeland—slowly fell into disuse replaced by the more supple tongue of Koinar speech. Also abandoned were the ancient customs, gods, games, and burial rites of our First Founders. Instead, Arkadians of all social classes, Megars, Riders, and Koinars alike, embraced a new source of moral and spiritual strength: the "Logos."

This Revered Artifact, whose origin and enigmatic powers remain as much a mystery today as generations ago, was at first an "Object of Veneration" only to Koinars but was eventually accepted as such by all Arkadians. And so, in spite of the unending hatred of the Bem, our blessed Arkadia has prospered beyond all expectation.

This, then, is the brief tale of Arkadia according to our Tradition. And yet this account falls far short of a complete history for our Tradition. While certainly not a mere fiction, it is flawed by large gaps in the early narrative, where plain fact is absent and, by a resort to assumptions, where explanations are lacking.

Hence, despite the passage of those thirty generations since the Founding, questions persist about many of the great transitions that marked the progress of our people. Who, exactly, were our warrior-forebears from The Ten Thousand? What was their country? Their language? Their customs? How, after their initial defeat and near-eradication by the Bem, did they contrive to defeat the barbarian host and then drive them from this beloved land? By what means—philosophy? coercion? exhortation?—did our Arkadia flourish as it did—and still does? And what impelled—compelled—the Arkadian elite eventually to abandon their own ancient language and familiar customs in order to adopt not only the tongue of the Koinars but also their devotion to the Logos? And exactly what is the Logos? What was its origin and from what does it derive its strange power? And by what means did the camp followers of our First Founders transform themselves into the Koinar caste of Arkadia?

These are some of the questions left unanswered in the Tradition. Perhaps they will remain unanswered forever unless Fate favors us with some unexpected illumination to light up the darker spaces of our past. If that prodigious light should ever fall upon us, perhaps we shall obtain the answer to the most profound questions of all: What is Arkadia itself? An enchantment? A dream? Some grand illusion? Does our Arkadia exist as part of a larger, more real world? Or might it be the creation of beings—divine? demonic?—beyond our small comprehension?

Until some event, discovery, or force, unimaginable now, emerges from the darkness of the past to enlighten us, these great questions must go unanswered leaving us to flounder in mystery as we always have. May the Logos guide us now and always.

From: *"Traditional Arkadia: A Meditation on the Beginning, the Middle, and the Present"*—written at Ten Turrets by Megistes the Logofant

I

PASSINGS

ONE

U nder the chaste brilliance of a summer sky a glittering body of heavily armed and superbly disciplined warriors—the proud "Array of Arkadia"—awaited the annual appearance of the clans of the Bem barbarians, a population of forty thousand all of them pledged to eternal hatred of the Arkadian people.

To receive this host the Arkadian Array composed of twenty-thousand horsemen known as "The Riders of the Realm", and one thousand pike-men called "The Phalanx", as well as numerous slinger auxiliaries, was drawn up along the north bank of the River Bradys within the strip of territory known as "The Forbidden Zone"—from which the Bem were ordinarily barred.

On any other day the approaching Bem would have encountered the Arkadian Array columns of mounted warriors and heavy infantry prepared to bar the Bem horde by force from the "Zone" and access to the river. But this was not any other day; this was the day of the annual "Passing" ritual when the Bem clans were to receive permission from the Arkadian ruler, the Hegemon, to enter the Zone for a period of ten days during which time they would be free to engage in their sacred rites at their old holy sites along the bank of the Bradys. Thus the day of the Passing was designated a ceremonial occasion.

Accordingly, the Arkadian troopers, though fully armed as a contingency measure, were positioned more for display than for battle, that is, they were assembled on the north bank in a long line only two ranks deep—Riders on the left wing, Phalanx and auxiliaries on the right. Moreover, the troopers were placed so they were facing away from the river and towards the expanse of the Zone itself. Although their formation was suited well-enough for the parade grounds it made the Array's young soldiers nervous for they understood how quickly some insignificant act or word could incite the Bem to violence. True, no serious outbreaks had occurred during any of the previous Passings but the Arkadian soldiers knew that fact was no guarantee that the Bem would keep the peace today. Also contributing to the disquiet in the Array was the realization that, in another perilous deviation from normal practice, the Hegemon's white and gold royal war chariot was stationed in the open well in front of the Riders' line instead of occupying its customary position behind the pike-men of the Phalanx. Further, in a truly extraordinary act of the self-imposed daring that he always accepted as part of these Passings, the Hegemon himself stood motionless along with his driver within his fragile chariot. Thus Agathon, the fifth Hegemon of Arkadia to bear that name, was not only in full view of his own worried troops he would also be in full view and within easy reach of the oncoming throngs of barbarians when they arrived.

This Hegemon, Agathon by name, was a man of fifty, gravely handsome and beardless. A mane of white hair fell in waves down his back. Attired in the white robes of his office and wearing across his brow the plain gold circlet which denoted his rank, Agathon was acutely conscious of his obligation to uphold the dignity of the Hegemony. For this reason he betrayed no fear as he waited, though he was aware that every barbarian who would soon appear at the entrance to the Forbidden Zone would rejoice to see him dead and Arkadia destroyed. Agathon also knew, however, that should he manifest even the slightest uneasiness to the oncoming barbarian throng, it might invite them to attack. A retaliatory massacre by the Array would then follow, inevitably demolishing, perhaps forever, all Agathon's hopes for a future era of peace between Arkadia and her perennial foe. And so Agathon maintained a rigid immobility even when his charioteer, clutching the reins tightly in both hands, gave them a tug from time to time along with a murmured *s-s-s-s-s* to control the restlessness of his pair of spirited grays.

Few of those beholding the Hegemon of Arkadia on that radiant afternoon could have imagined that Agathon's iconic public demeanor was in fact so foreign to his natural inclination toward merriment and good-fellowship that he privately lamented the necessity of it. Nevertheless he had long ago realized that the pose was necessary not only to impress the Bem but also to retain the confidence of his people. Hence the Hegemon of Arkadia had to appear knowing and imperturbable at all times, had to seem more than a mere man, though a mere man was what Agathon knew himself to be.

Always sensitive to the mood of the young men of the Array, Agathon perceived the anxiety that they always felt at these Passings because of the risky nature of the event and to the peril to their Hegemon. But this year the level of disquiet struck Agathon as even higher than previous years. The reason for this seemed obvious to him. It was the presence at the Passing for the first time of Agathon's sixteen-year-old son, Milo, heir to the High Bench of Arkadia.

Milo, the elder of Agathon's two sons, was a handsome boy with curls of bright yellow hair. Garbed in the white leather tunic and blue cape of a Cadet of the Rider Regiment, Milo was mounted on a well-behaved white mare and posted on the left side of the royal chariot where he was doing his best to emulate the poised dignity of his superb father. Milo himself was also acutely mindful of the fact that three others, each an important figure in his life, were nearby and closely observing his deportment. These three were, in descending order of his affections, his much-admired best friend, sixteen-year-old Phylax, his aged tutor, Megistes, and his irritating younger brother, twelve-year-old Darden, who was also present for the first time, by special dispensation, at this potentially dangerous assembly.

Both Phylax and Darden were mounted on frisky palfreys, while ancient Megistes squirmed on a soft-back mare especially chosen in the hope of sparing the old man's aged bones. Milo was also aware that, although Phylax and Darden had been cautioned by Megistes, their tutor, to keep themselves inconspicuous among their slinger guards, he had only to look back over his shoulder to spot his best friend Phylax at once, definitely conspicuous by virtue of his height and bearing among the slinger-guards. Furthermore, Milo did not doubt that if he looked back at them, he would find that Darden and Megistes, and Phylax, too, of course, would have their attention focused on him to check the behavior of the heir making his first important public appearance. Good old Phylax, Milo knew, would be wishing him well. Megistes would be swelling with pride in his royal pupil. Runty Darden, of course, would be scowling with jealousy.

Suddenly Milo felt a strong urge to cast a glance back at the trio behind him just to verify his assessment of their interest in his conduct. Milo managed to fend off the temptation, however, when he realized that to succumb might shatter the solemnity of the rite in which he was still to play a notable part that would be his first public act of responsibility as heir to the great Agathon. Accordingly, Milo forced himself to continue staring ahead in order to maintain his own version of his father's imperturbable appearance. Milo's strong young heart, however, was beating in his ears like a pike-man's signal drum. Nor could he help but wonder again and again: *Where are the barbo warriors? When will they get here?* Milo's unuttered questions were what every other Arkadian was also asking himself for every man was eager for the hate-sodden Bem to appear so that this yearly ordeal could commence at last. *Soonest begun, soonest ended*, was a saying caroming in many a mind.

In order to maintain his own grave posture during this seemingly endless interval of expectation, Agathon occupied himself by rehearsing once more in his mind the steps by which the ritual was to unfold assuming all went as planned.

First, the Bem cavalcade was to proceed slowly and under the watchful eyes of the Array until the vanguard of their procession reached the vicinity of the royal chariot. Here the Bem throng was to halt while their chiefs and shamans asked for the Hegemon's leave to advance completely into the Zone. When formally granted permission to "Pass On!" the Bem were to continue past the Array, into their former sacred ground. Once the ceremonial part of the Passing was complete and the clans peacefully within the Zone, most of the Array led by Agathon himself would withdraw from the Zone to the river's south bank. There the troopers, having already established an elaborate tented camp called a "Komai" to use the military term, would bivouac for the duration of the Bem presence across the river.

Settled behind the temporary mud-brick wall which always surrounded any Arkadian Komai the young men of the Array would be considered off-duty and so at liberty to indulge in games, gambling, feasting, drinking, and—above all—in frolicking with the paid women who always seemed to find their way to the tents of soldiers. Despite the Komai's festive debauchery—which Agathon surreptitiously encouraged by ignoring it—the Array would maintain an alert discipline outside the Komai's wall. Sentries would be posted on the south bank day and night to keep watch on the river always fordable at this season. In addition, small contingents of Riders and slinger auxiliaries would remain in the north bank outposts. Their task would remind the excitable Bem clans that they were present in the Zone only by the indulgence of the Hegemon of Arkadia.

Yes, thought Agathon, *that was the way it was supposed to happen and that was the way it would happen, unless, by some mischance the Bem hatred of Arkadia exploded this time into violence. But it was better not to dwell on that possibility, and instead focus on the good that the Passing might be accomplishing for future generations of both Bem and Arkadians.*

Agathon was well aware that many of his own people regarded the Passings as wasted effort. To these skeptics any hope of achieving harmony with Arkadia's intractable enemy was a delusion. And perhaps, Agathon had to admit to himself, the doubters would be proven right in the end. Still, the experiment had to go on for the sake of those unborn generations. Besides Agathon realized, as the skeptics did not, the Passings achieved two practical results, not often visible to casual eyes.

First, every Passing forced the unruly and even bellicose young men of the Bem, all of whom had been inculcated with such slogans as "Death to the Logos!", "Kill for Lord Dis!", and "Destroy the Arkie Demons!" to recognize, however briefly, the reality that they lived only by the sufferance of Arkadia, that the military power of the Array could crush any outbreak of Bem violence at any time or place.

Second, the Passings demonstrated to new recruits in the Arkadian Array the perverse nature of their enemy who would joyfully slay every Arkadian man, woman, and child had they the power to do so. Nevertheless, for Agathon the main goal of these Passings was always the same: to find a way to reconcile Arkie and Bem. It was in pursuit of that end, after all, that he was forcing himself on this scintillating afternoon to endure still as a sunstone carving in the royal chariot while his young sons and the men of the Array stirred in restless anticipation of the advent of the enemy. *Yes and where were the Bem?*

Abruptly a blast of trumpets sounded from the hills beyond the Zone. This signal, announcing the approach, finally of the Bem caravans, blew away Agathon's skein of wandering thoughts. *Time now for duty.* Agathon drew himself up to full height and prepared to receive the enemy with the dignity befitting the Hegemon of the Arkadians.

Soon trumpets and drums began sounding all along the lines of the Array answering earlier signals, sending forth new ones. The warhorses of the Arkadian Riders tossed their plumed heads. The Riders lowered the visors of their helmets. The men of the Arkadian Phalanx closed ranks smartly with a *clang* of armor and hefted their pikes for possible action. The slingers weighed in their hands bags of the iron pellets that they used as ammunition.

"They come, Strategat," announced Agathon's charioteer unnecessarily. The dark-visaged charioteer tightened his hold on his reins lest his restive team forget who was in charge of them.

The first of the Bem, a single warrior-scout mounted on a long-haired pony, appeared at the brow of the hilly road leading to the Zone's entrance. Here the Bem warrior paused as if taking in the now-alert Array below.

Mounted on his smallish long-haired pony the Bem fighter sat his tough steed without the help of saddle or stirrup. He controlled his pony with his bridle and his knees just as his ancestors had done. The warrior himself a man of indeterminate age wore a stiff leather jerkin painted in the pale blue color of his clan and bearing signs holy to his people. The man's sun-darkened face was grim with fetish tattoos. A tangle of black hair, not cut since childhood, hung down his back and was crowned with the universal mark of the Bem warrior: a horned leather helmet dyed with the color of his clan. In his right hand this lone harbinger of the approaching Bem carried a long spear with a head of razor-sharp flint affixed to it.

The Bem warriors, thought Agathon, *never altered in appearance or attitude even after thirty generations of conflict. This man could have ridden with the Horned Host that had almost destroyed the First Founders of Arkadia among whom Agathon's own ancestors could be found.*

The single Bem warrior now began to descend the hill. Behind him followed the first carts and wagons of a disorderly barbo mob that straggled for miles behind. This year's Passing of the Bem was underway.

TWO

ourteen-year-old Milo mounted on a fine white mare kept rigidly to his station at the left side of his father's chariot although he had to clench his jaw lest he betray his excitement at the arrival of the Bem. *At last!*

As the barbo cavalcade crested the hill in the wake of their single scout, however, Milo began to experience an odd but definite disappointment. Instead of the proudly ferocious wild nation he had expected to greet with stern curiosity what he saw emerging from attendant clouds of trail dust was a gasping herd of pathetic folk weak with hunger, sickness, and long fatigue. Many of these women and children for the most part lolled in their ox-drawn wagons and two-wheeled carts just staring big-eyed at nothing as they jolted through the entrance to the Zone. To Milo this humble rabble seemed so sunk in despair as to be indifferent to any fate that might befall them. Even the warriors goading their exhausted ponies alongside the mass of Bem looked as if bent under a weight of hopelessness despite the absurd attempts at bravado manifest in their variously-colored facial tattoos, horned helmets, and leather surcoats. Adding to the dispirited aspect of the Bem was the dust that clung to them. People, beasts, and rickety carts all lay under a coat of yellow grit from the trail. *The Bem,* thought Milo, *looked as he supposed a routed army might look after a devastating defeat in battle.*

And then, borne on the yellow scud churned up in the Passing a vile stench assailed Milo's nostrils. He knew at once that this had to be the notorious Bem stink so often alluded to by Arkadians whose duty or business took them into any proximity with the barbos. Composed of a blend of foul odors—long dead corpses awaiting cremation at the river, thousands of unwashed living bodies, human feces left to lie in wagons and carts where they had been excreted, as well as spilled blood, rotted meat, animal dung being dried for fuel, and generations of sweat—the Bem stink struck Milo as every bit as revolting as he had heard.

. Soon the stench evoked in him waves of barely controlled nausea. It also wiped from his consciousness those streamlets of sympathy which had started forming in his young heart at his initial look at these undisciplined creatures as they crowded into the Zone. Instead of compassion he was now experiencing an access of disgust for these woebegone barbarians who carried their pestilential miasma with them wherever they went. *Why didn't they at least clean their filthy skins as a mark of respect for the Hegemon of Arkadia to whom they ought to show gratitude for this indulgence of the Passing?*

All at once Milo felt a powerful urge to make some gesture to express his revulsion for this contemptible mob who would soon be pitching their dirty huts on Arkadian soil. Abruptly it came to him how he might communicate his revulsion: He needed only to twist around slightly in his saddle and look back to where his friend Phylax was stationed along with their old tutor, Megistes, and Milo's pesky twelve-year-old brother, Darden. Then, as Milo imagined it, he would hold his nose and grin back at Phylax who would certainly appreciate the jape. In fact, Phylax and he might even add it to the list of their memorable pranks. *Oh, how they would laugh together later at such effrontery!* Milo even conjured Phylax's admiration as the two of them might speak of it afterwards: *"I never thought you'd have the nerve to pull off a joke like that and at the Passing too!"* On further reflection, however, Milo realized that Phylax being Phylax and thus respectful of tradition would probably not laugh at all, would instead exercise his principled self-discipline to sustain the solemn mask considered appropriate for this occasion of the Passing. On the other hand, Darden would certainly seize the chance to let loose with those giggles he resorted to whenever he judged that his elder brother had committed an error of any kind. *But Darden's stupid reaction didn't count,* thought Milo. Of course old Megistes certainly would fall into a spitting rage if Milo breached decorum with such a jest. And, in retaliation the old man would surely lay into Milo's ass with his stick at the first opportunity. How Darden would giggle at that! On the whole, Milo now concluded, he would do better to keep a straight face.

Only after making this decision did Milo recognize the best reason of all for abandoning his joke idea: It would make his father ashamed of him. Milo took a deep breath realizing that he had just avoided making a terrible mistake—a child's mistake—in full view of the Array. *It was a mistake,* he told himself, *that Phylax would never make.* Thus—and not for the first time—Milo admonished himself to grow up, to become more like Phylax, less like Darden or he might never be accepted into the White Angel Regiment of Riders which was his fondest wish. With this resolve Milo drew himself taut in the saddle and focused his full attention once more upon the Bem who were now pushing like stupid sheep into the Zone. Soon the odorous multitude had pressed its way to a point in close proximity to the five alert regiments of Riders, each looking superb.

Eventually the Bem horde, carrying its stink with it, reached the place where the imposing Hegemon and Milo, looking suitably grave, turned to face them as the ritual required. At once the barbo mob halted in their tracks. A hush fell over the scene as the squeaking wheels of Bem carts and wagons ceased their turning. The only sounds Milo could now detect were the clinking of chain mail and the unnerving scraping of swords being drawn from scabbards as the nearest company of Riders stood up in their stirrups in response to the nearness of the Bem to the person of the Hegemon and his son, both of whom (Milo trembling a little) remained erect and vulnerable as they awaited the next movement in the ritual.

That action came almost immediately as four Bem elders in accord with the protocol of the Passing dismounted from their ponies. These graybeards, each attired in warrior's dress adorned with the colors and markings of his clan, were the chiefs—*Kapits* in their own language—of the Bem clans. The quartet of abject Kapits spread their arms wide to signify that they carried no weapons and then hobbled forward together causing a further reflexive stir among the nervous Riders and slinger auxiliaries nearby. The Kapits then kneeled before the Royal Chariot.

As Milo watched the servile Bem Kapits with their bald heads, the tattoos marking their weathered faces, their artificially elongated earlobes stretched with weights since childhood, Milo could not help but think they looked no more dangerous than the discarded husks of locusts that crackled to dust if you trod on them. Still Milo understood, as did every man in the Array from the proudest lancer to the humblest slinger, that every Bem man, woman, or child blamed their misery on Arkadian "greed, cruelty, and injustice" and so lived in an unending boil of hatred.

Accordingly, every Arkadian—young Milo among them—recognized that if they dared and if they possessed the means the Bem would happily slit the throats of every adult Arkadian and then sell their children into slavery. *It was no wonder then,* Milo reflected, *that with the Bem so near, the men of the Array were betraying some uneasiness for they were convinced that Bem treachery and desperation would erupt into a suicidal onslaught some day and suppose that day turned out to be this day?*

At this moment the noble Hegemon, Milo's father, Agathon, drew his heavy sword and extended its point toward the kneeling Kapits. Milo, remembering his instructions from old Megistes drew his own much lighter weapon. According to the rite of the Passing, this gesture on the part of the Hegemon and his son was intended to remind the Bem leaders that their people must behave peacefully during their stay in the Zone or face serious consequences. Now Agathon pointed his gleaming blade downriver thus indicating where the Bem were to go.

Meanwhile Milo's skinny boy's arm was beginning to throb with the weight of his own extended sword. He felt the sweat running down his ribs from his armpits. He longed to replace his blade in its scabbard but he knew he had to endure, must not waver or falter, despite the tremulous ache along his arm from shoulder to wrist. Moreover, he had to continue as best he could to keep a warrior's scowl on his beardless face lest some observant Megar officer or Rider think him weak or, even worse, lest he appear feeble to the watching Bem. *No,* Milo admonished himself, *he must hold on, must let everyone see him as worthy to succeed the great Agathon on the High Bench of Arkadia. Hold on. Hold on,* he commanded himself inwardly.

The quartet of kneeling Kapits, acting in unison as required by ritual, now scooped up handfuls of Arkadian soil and lowering their heads to kiss the ground let the sand and grit trickle over their hairless pates as a sign of submission. At this the unsmiling Agathon slid his sword back into its scabbard. Milo did the same with his own blade grateful beyond measure to have withstood the ordeal as the Hegemon's son ought. *No, as the Hegemon's son must*, Milo corrected himself, feeling the first pricklings of pride that he had comported himself well so far at least. *But hold on*, he admonished himself recalling that there was more to come.

The Kapits still on their knees, their arms again widespread, were staring up at a grave Agathon apparently awaiting some additional sign. The Hegemon, however, only continued to frown in silence. Had something gone awry in the ceremony? A shiver of alarm ran through Milo and he sensed it ran through the entire Array as well. Though not a single man betrayed his unease all must be wondering, as Milo was as well, how to interpret the ongoing silence of the Hegemon. Had Agathon detected some evidence of impending Bem treachery? Was he about to break his longstanding custom by commanding the Array to annihilate the disgusting Bem once and for all? *Certainly*, Milo reflected, *many among the troopers would rejoice at such an order.* It did not come, however, though Agathon's silence persisted. Clearly on the edge of panic at the Hegemon's unprecedented behavior, the quartet of Bem Kapits, still on their knees, rapidly began to repeat their abasement ritual, the heads lowered to kiss the soil, the dirt over the bald scalps as if in their cloudy minds a repetition would repair some dangerous misstep in procedure, an oversight they could not recall but which must have happened. And now in a confusion matching that of the smelly Bem chiefs young Milo glanced over at his frowning father who nodded down at him and then toward the suppliant Kapits. At once Milo understood. His father wished him to make the necessary final gesture of the Passing ceremony.

His heart near bursting with pride, Milo rose in his stirrups and in his light boy's voice shouted out the required command: "Pass on!"

The Bem Kapits rose. They bowed to Milo as the visible author of their passage. Then, in unison, they backed away gesturing to their waiting people that they had obtained the Hegemon's permission to enter the Zone.

With a sound much like a collective sigh of relief, the tension drained from the men of the Array. Drums began to thunder down the line of warriors. Warhorses stamped and snorted. The trumpets of the Phalanx sounded an accompaniment to the drums.

Though always protective of his Hegemonic dignity, Agathon allowed a brief smile to play over his lips so that his son could see his approval of the boy's quick acceptance of a role he had not expected to play. Further, in an act that pleased Milo almost as much as his father's smile, the charioteer, who had never even looked at Milo before this moment, broke his customary statue-like posture to lean over towards Milo and growl: "Well done, Strategat. Well done."

Strategat. Austere Karou had addressed him with the word reserved for the rulers of Arkadia. Milo surged with renewed determination to make himself a worthy successor to his father. *This Passing of the Bem,* he reflected, *was already an event he would remember forever.*

Once again, as the muddled cavalcade of Bem clans began to plod past the Array into their old holy haunts, the Arkadian troopers, now growing impatient at the prospect of the disorderly procession still to be monitored and endured, Milo was tempted to twist around to find his friend Phylax in the ranks of the Riders and give him a swift smile of triumph. *Surely,* Milo told himself, *when even a stickler like his father's charioteer could bend the rules to say "well done" to the son of the Hegemon and even call him "Strategat", the recipient of that praise could be allowed to send a quick little greeting to his best friend.*

With this in mind and before second thoughts again intervened Milo turned in his saddle, spotted Phylax at once, and gave him an enormous grin. This time Phylax nodded and returned the grin as if to say, "I'm proud of you, friend."

At once, Milo turned back to resume his observation of the Bem passage. His father glanced at him briefly but Milo detected no disapproval in Agathon's stern face at his son's minor infraction with Phylax. Now, though keeping his eye soberly fixed on the Bem, Milo found himself thinking of other matters that interested him more, namely, the feast to follow when the Passing was complete. It was there that he would tell Phylax that the charioteer whom Phylax admired greatly had addressed him as "Strategat". How Phylax would marvel at that! *Strategat!*

White bearded Megistes, tutor to the two sons of the Hegemon as well as Chief Keeper of the Logos—his official title was "Logofant"—also had seen the exchange of grins between Milo and his great friend Phylax. However, Megistes intended to ignore that breach of discipline. *No harm done, after all. Let the boys savor their little mischief.* As for the Passing, Megistes was pleased that it was going well or at least appeared to be going well. And he was more than pleased—he was delighted—that his young charge Milo was playing his part so well. Megistes would say as much to the boy at the evening feast. *In the meantime,* Megistes reflected with some rue, *he had no choice but to suffer with as much dignity as he could muster through the remainder of this wretched parade of barbarians, his aged bones and unpadded behind protesting all the way.*

An old man, Megistes grumbled to himself, *especially if he happened to be the Logofant of Arkadia, should not be required to mount any animal, not even one as sway backed and docile as the superannuated nag that had been afflicting his poor backside for hours now. Still,* the old man reminded himself, *it's always best not to dwell on one's misery. Instead one must fight it by letting the mind fly free. In other words,* he had to find something other than an aching backside to think about. *Detach the mind from the imprisoning carcass.*

Megistes, now in his eighty-ninth year—a long life even by the standards of the long-lived Arkadians—had been attending these ritual Passings in the company of his dear friend Agathon, ever since the great Hegemon (himself once a pupil of Megistes) had instituted them after his elevation to the High Bench. In the early years of his observance of the entry of the wretched Bem into the blessed land of Arkadia, or more accurately into the Forbidden Zone, Megistes had often felt his heart melting at the sight of the sick and starved children staring out from the stinking wagons of the Bem cavalcade. He had wept at the sight of the ignored old folk left to wither and die slowly of hunger and neglect. He had raged to behold the Bem women from little girls to ancient crones crippled from the ankle bonds they were forced to wear all their lives from puberty to death. These fetters said to be pleasing to Dis consisted of leather cuffs fitted about each ankle and then attached to each other by a short strip of hempen rope that limited the stride of the wearer making it impossible to run or even to walk except by adopting a gait cruelly unnatural for anyone but a small child. Megistes had never erased from his mind his first appalled sight of cowed women forced to hobble about their chores as their god supposedly demanded.

Even after so many years the practice still filled Megistes with loathing for the cruel god whose worship had brought nothing but misery to the Bem people. Megistes used to ask why the Bem clung to their so-called Lord of Chaos, their Dis. *Why,* he wondered, *couldn't they be persuaded to abandon their vicious deity and thus be welcomed into the benevolent realm that was Arkadia?* With the passage of the years, however, Megistes had concluded reluctantly that the Bem were willfully blind to all such truths.

Of course, for the boys in his charge, Milo, Darden, and Phylax, the Passing now taking place before them was the first they had been allowed to attend and so as Megistes well knew they were probably overflowing with compassion for the downtrodden Bem despite the avoidable stench and misery that the cavalcade exuded. This sympathetic reaction Megistes felt was undoubtedly strongest in young Darden whose fine mind already obvious at the tender age of twelve was linked to a heart acutely sensitive to the misfortunes of others. Megistes, however, did not worry overmuch about Darden's boyish pity for the barbarian clans for he believed that Darden like himself would eventually come to recognize that the misery of the Bem was almost entirely self-inflicted. It was the Bem, after all, who embraced terror, scorned peace, and chose to grub along on the brink of starvation, rather than admit Arkadia's right to exist. It was for the sake of this stubborn enmity that the Bem sold their children to clandestine slave traders, let their babies die of diseases that any Arkadian physician could easily cure, and ruthlessly abandoned their lame and infirm, both children and the elderly, to wander the Bemgrass until their wasted carcasses were devoured by beasts. In spite of their self-imposed misery the Bem continued to refuse the peace they could have at any time preferring to rejoice whenever one of theirs managed to commit an atrocity against Arkadians. Such intractable rejection of reason not only puzzled Megistes it revolted him as well. *If the Bem could despise the great Agathon, who was their only hope for bettering their lot,* thought Megistes, *then the barbarians were doomed and perhaps Arkadia was doomed as well for he could see no way out of the mire except by a war of extermination which—if it ever came to pass—would surely destroy not only the Bem but also the spiritual basis of Arkadia itself.*

Megistes abruptly broke off these gloomy reflections when his attention was caught by the arrival in the Bem cavalcade of a gaudily decorated wooden building mounted on two attached wagons and drawn by six teams of oxen. Megistes immediately recognized this structure as the "House on Wheels" as the Bem called it that was the residence of the Supreme Oracle of all the clans. This personage, seldom seen by ordinary Bem, was known as "The Vessel of Dis" because he supposedly carried within him the essence of "Divine Chaos." Megistes knew from certain agents he maintained to report on the Bem that the Vessel himself (it was always a male) emerged from his House on Wheels only on sacred occasions or in certain "Holy Places" such as "demon caves" and "dream places" venerated or feared by the Bem.

The Vessel's chief function was to divine and then reveal "the will of Dis." The Vessel was also consulted on all important matters and was called upon to conduct required sacrifices, including so it was said, human sacrifices. Because the Vessel embodied the Essence of Chaos he was thought immortal. His House on Wheels, an icon itself, always accompanied the Bem on their migrations and, according to the shamans, would do so until the "Final Chaos" put an end to time itself.

Nothing could better illustrate the cultural gulf between the Bem and Arkadians, Megistes mused, than the honor paid to this barbarian fraud, this "Vessel." *In truth,* Megistes reflected, *the Bem people subscribed to a mad belief that the cosmos was created by and for Chaos and that Chaos would spin the visible Creation out of existence unless held in check by spells, ancient practices, and rituals. For crazed spirits and demons—servants of Chaos—swarmed everywhere and had to be propitiated lest they do ever-increasing harm. Thus Dis,* the unknowable Lord of Chaos, had to be mollified though he could never be understood.

In direct contrast to the irrational beliefs of the benighted Bem, Megistes reflected, *the Arkadians trusted in customs and laws which the people had made for themselves and which rested for the most part on human "reason" that virtually all Arkadians recognized as the source of their nation's greatness.*

As the Vessel's House on Wheels finally lumbered away past the last companies of the Arkadian soldiery, Megistes permitted himself a sigh of exasperation for what was beginning to seem an interminable parade of the pitiful Bem. Megistes hoped that it would not last much longer. And then as if in answer to his plea he saw turning into the

Zone the gaggle of priests and shamans together with their warrior escorts that invariably formed the final contingent of the Bem mob. *Soon,* Megistes reassured himself, *he would be free to dismount from his perch aboard his patient nag and what bliss it would be then to rub some feeling back into his skinny backside!*

Attended by a guard of renowned fighters chosen from their clans, a troop of shamans, each mounted on an exhausted pony and each accompanied by an apprentice version of himself, approached the Royal Chariot. Here, as the ceremony required, the shamans, apprentices, and warriors halted. Leaving some thirty yards of open ground between themselves and the Hegemon's chariot they awaited permission to dismount for the final act of the Passing. To the Arkadians who beheld them, these priests of Dis and their attendant juniors offered a far from impressive appearance. Each of them— priest and apprentice alike—wore a tattered gown of rough-spun brown wool secured by a rope cincture about the waist. This garment made up the entire wardrobe of these "Servants of Chaos" as they styled themselves for they also went unshod. In fact, according to the rule of their fraternity, the brown robe was never to be removed for any reason, was never to be washed or repaired any more than the priest's own body was. As a consequence the passage of time turned each brown habit into a construction of shredded rags as could be discerned from even a cursory look at the shamans awaiting Agathon's permission to dismount.

In other ways, too, the priests of Dis fell far short of an Arkadian's conception of a decent appearance. Each priest as well as his assigned apprentice displayed a shaved scalp marked by self-inflicted cuts. Most of the shamans and apprentices were visibly pierced—belly, ears, nose, ankle, and, presumably, the unseen private parts as well— with metal slivers, shards of glass, and a variety of pins and studs. And all of these bits and pieces were left to hang from the skin. Most of the adult priests also bore old scars no doubt also self-inflicted on their faces. A few tottered on crooked legs or carried a crippled arm the result of having allowed broken bones to knit together without proper care.

Among the young apprentices there was one who was hunchbacked. This tyro's right leg was also shorter than his left one which caused him to limp noticeably. This same youth had a face so disfigured apparently by fire that the scar tissue had grown over his left eye leaving it sightless. In spite of these deformities this young man was shown a certain deference by his fellow apprentices who nodded and touched his ravaged face if he happened to look in their direction. This behavior was apparently because to the Bem the young man's deformities marked him as one beloved of the Lord of Chaos and thus a source of the peculiar form of "grace" imagined by barbaric Bem minds.

Such were the Bem shamans who now humbly waited for great Agathon's sign that they might dismount and as the ritual dictated bow in unison to the Ruler of Arkadia who would then acknowledge their submission whereupon the shamans, aided by their junior servants, would mount again and together with their warrior escorts move off in the wake of the Bem cavalcade which had now preceded them. This was the final act of the Passing for after the shamans and their escorts moved past the last company of the Phalanx the trumpets of the Array would sound the all clear. Only then would the Passing of the Bem be finished for another year. And no man in the Arkadian Array would be sorry.

So, as this final Bem group stood before the royal chariot awaiting permission to dismount and make their obeisance, a barely detectable but nevertheless irrepressible slackness, born of relief that the Passing was nearly done for this year and the troopers' celebration was soon to start, undulated down the line of the Arkadian Array like a subtle wave. It was at this moment that the strikingly deformed Bem apprentice, whom no observer could have failed to remark among the Bem priesthood, deserted the side of his still mounted master and began to hobble forward as fast as he could manage toward the royal chariot.

The audacity of the act caught every onlooker—Arkadian and Bem alike—by surprise. Agathon himself seemed amazed at the crippled youth's effrontery. Even the Riders nearest the Hegemon as well as the shamans' own escort of Bem warriors seemed frozen with shock, unsure of how to react to what was happening before their eyes. Only when the maimed young man having hauled himself to within twenty paces of the Hegemon halted as if exhausted from his exertions did anyone respond to the danger implicit in his act. The Royal Charioteer placed his own body in front of Agathon as a shield against what he judged to be an imminent attack on his master. The Bem apprentice, however, made no further aggressive move toward the Hegemon. Instead he began to shout at Agathon in labored Arkadian phrases. "Oh, most unjust Kapit of oppressing race, hear from my mouth the curse that comes to you from Dis."

At last, recovering from their initial startled confusion, several troopers from the Rider line flung themselves from their saddles and in a fury derived largely from shame at their failure to provide proper protection to their Hegemon, drew back their javelins to strike down the crippled Bem lunatic. But just in time Agathon himself forestalled them with a roared command that astonished all at the scene: "Do him no harm! Only hold him!" The troopers obeyed though it was plain that they would much rather have skewered their bent and half-blind prisoner.

After clapping his hand on his charioteer's shoulder in a public display of gratitude for the man's valor in shielding him from possible assassination, Agathon instructed his intrepid driver to move closer to "this servant of Dis". The charioteer did as he was told although the stench of the apprentice shaman caused his high-strung team to start and stamp irritably. Agathon, however, took no notice. Instead, from the height of his chariot he inspected this bent youth who presumed to threaten him in the name of his non-existent deity.

From his perusal, Agathon quickly concluded that the fellow, who kept his one wild eye fixed on the Hegemon, had been the recipient of much ill-treatment in his short life and that he was also perversely proud of the rags and scraps he wore as well as the bits of metal embedded in his filthy hide. *All for the glory of Dis, I suppose,* Agathon thought. Finished with his examination Agathon looked back to see how his son, Milo, was reacting to this singular interruption in the Passing ceremony. The boy was still seated on his mare though his face had gone white as milk from the shock of encountering Bem hostility at such close quarters. *Well,* thought Agathon, *let the boy see what a Hegemon must do if we of Arkadia are ever to overcome our own history. And now,* he asked himself, *what can I do of a practical nature to extract some good from this event?*

Agathon looked across at the Bem shamans and the warrior escorts who accompanied them. He sensed that, although they were few in number and in a state of shock, the priests and their warriors fully expected that the Arkadian Hegemon, tall and immaculate in his white and gold garment, his jeweled circlet of office gleaming on his severe forehead, would now order their daring but foolhardy apprentice beheaded as a lesson to all such recalcitrant servants of Dis. Agathon also sensed that Bem warriors, frozen with indecision only yards away, also were sure that the Arkadian Kapit, as they called Agathon, would order a general massacre of the compliant Bem so forcing them into a hopeless fight with the Arkadian Array—a fight that must inevitably spread and result in the slaughter of hundreds of Bem.

Yet the Bem warriors on the scene made no move to initiate such a fight themselves though there were undoubtedly a few among them who sick with humiliation and self-loathing actually hoped that Agathon would have the lamed young shaman executed so granting them the boon of launching themselves against the Arkie tyrant so that they might die with a death song on their lips and Arkie blood in their long hair as a true Bem warrior should.

Agathon, however, had no intention of satisfying the bloodlust rampant on both sides. Instead, he issued a command to his burly Riders who still gripped the Bem madman in iron hands. "Bring that young fool closer so I can get a better look at him."

The Riders, who would have much preferred to decapitate their captive "barbo dung ball," obeyed, dragging the Bem apprentice to a spot less than ten yards from Agathon's chariot, halting only when Milo rode forward to his father's side in a gesture the Riders considered both brave and foolish.

After a smile for his son, Agathon addressed himself to the disfigured Bem youth, but in a voice that could be heard by all in the vicinity. "Can you understand my words?"

Though shaking with uncontrollable fear and fury, and obviously anticipating death at any moment, the captive replied with temerity. "I speak good you language, Kapit of Arkadia, and so me understand enough."

Agathon nodded. "Well then, let me hear again what you were shouting as you limped so foolishly toward my chariot. Well? Cry it

29

forth for all present to hear: my sons, my soldiers, your own people. Let them hear what you dared to scream at the Hegemon of Arkadia who holds your life and the lives of your people in his hands. Let us all hear it!"

The youth keeping his half-blind and scarred face fixed on Agathon suddenly howled out with all his strength: "I cry out a warning, Kapit. Dis will punish you. You do crimes on the Bem people! I lay on you and you peoples the curse of mighty Dis!"

With this the youth hung his battered head as if awaiting the retaliation that now must surely fall on him. But Agathon still frowning deeply only posed a question. "What is your name?" The maimed young man looked up at the Hegemon again. "I am call Seraph." *Was there defiance in that answer?* "Who gave you that name?'

"I give name myself."

"Did you? Well then, hear this, Seraph. I, too, believe in punishment for crimes and so I think it would be a genuine crime to permit you, out of some twisted cunning or madness, to bring undeserved further sorrow to the Bem people whom you call your people. And so, Seraph, the self-anointed, though you clearly care more to provoke a memorable death for yourself than you care for the welfare of these people, I will not bestow martyrdom on you today. I will not make you another stupid witness for Dis. I scorn your threats as well as your Dis. So I give you your wretched life. You are free to continue in the chains of ignorance which you have affixed to your spirit. So limp back to your people little fool and try to deny that Agathon of Arkadia showed you mercy. A hero, you are not."

Released from the grip of his captors the half-blind apprentice shaman covered in confusion shouted out more of his anguish. "Where be you souls? Arkie peoples got no souls."

"Go, hero, go!"

Agathon began to laugh.

The lame Seraph, not knowing what else to do hobbled back to rejoin his fellow Servants of Dis and was received into the rough arms of two dismounted Bem warriors. One of these a man capable of uttering some primitive phrases in the Arkadian tongue cried out some words that seemed to be an offer to execute this Seraph "if it would please the Great Kapit".

Agathon responded with a few words in the Bem language which he spoke well enough to make himself understood. "No punishment.

But look at this Seraph among your people and remember that mercy can be a medicine for bad feelings. Now all of you proceed into the Zone—quickly—and tell your people what mercy the Hegemon of Arkadia did here today. Go!"

After a moment of hesitation the ragged collection of Bem warriors, shamans, and apprentices fled pell-mell into the Zone. In the clouds of dust raised by their flight a lone figure could be seen limping painfully after them until the hanging dust obscured him.

Minutes after the trumpets sounded the "all clear" the Arkadian Array began its planned withdrawal to the south bank of the River Bradys leaving behind a force of slingers to man the line of Arkadian guard-towers in the Zone, and a contingent of Riders to patrol them. Within another hour the Array, now in column formation with Agathon at its head, was on the march to the festive Komai encampment already prepared for them on the high ground across the river from the Bem campsites. Here, waiting for their arrival were viands and strong drink as well as bards and various entertainers and musicians. Also awaiting them were assorted dancing girls and the whores whose presence Agathon always managed to overlook. At the Komai the young soldiers of the Array would feast and frolic while the Bem went about their strange rites across the river.

Usually on this approach to the festival part of the Passing, the men of the Array would be in good humor, singing and looking forward to the rough pleasures which young men, especially soldiers, favored. On this particular march, however, the spirits of the Array seemed eerily and uncharacteristically subdued.

Megistes, now ensconced in a comfortable, more or less, wagon while his three young charges trotted alongside on fresh mounts, attributed the less than festive mood of the column to the earlier incident of the Bem cripple's confrontation with Agathon. Although the bizarre occurrence had resulted in no serious consequences, every man of the Array knew that the outcome could have been very different; their beloved Hegemon might have been wounded or worse, and all because the troopers had let down their guard for a moment. Agathon, of course, had not blamed anyone for he knew it was enough that his young men blamed themselves. In any case, Megistes felt sure, good spirits would return with the advent of good drink, good food, good music, good dancing, and above all good sport with girls who were not good at all. Like the ache in his behind that Megistes had endured all afternoon, the bad mood of the troops would disappear when massaged the right way by the wrong girl.

Thinking of girls and drink reminded Megistes that the festival ahead would be the first such experience of the male dark-side to be seen up close by any of his three pupils. Megistes himself would find it interesting to observe their reactions. Milo, at fourteen, and Phylax at sixteen and already a strapping young man would probably enjoy themselves immensely. However, Darden, though an exceedingly intelligent twelve-year-old, was in Megistes' judgment, still too young to see, much less participate in, the "ardent sport" at the Komai. Therefore, Megistes decided to impose his customary curfew on Darden to get the lad away from the most egregious behaviors. The curfew would also provide an excuse for Megistes himself to seek his tent at a relatively early hour. The truth was that he had never approved of the roughest of male pursuits though he seemed to recall that he had joined in with the best of them in his long-ago youth, evidence, if any was needed, that even the most abstemious of men might easily succumb to temptations of the flesh. These days, however, Megistes had put aside all that. Besides, he had his dignity to uphold. Yes, the tutor of the Hegemon's sons had best be abed when the lovely bad girls and sultry courtesans began prancing about later in the night.

As he stretched out more or less at ease in the bed of the wagon that was jolting him on toward the Komai celebration, Megistes could not help but reflect on lame Seraph's outburst directed at Agathon. *The young Bem's curse,* thought Megistes, *had amounted to a perfect expression of the unquenchable hatred that every living Bem felt for every living Arkie. Hatred, pure and simple. That was what underlay every act of this mad Bem nation from their self-destructive seeking of unnecessary suffering to their immovable rejection of even the smallest gesture toward peace. Bem hatred—intractable and eternal—was the cause of all the agony though Agathon the good, refused to accept such a simple—and evil—explanation. And then one still had to ask: what was the source of Bem hatred?*

Based on his own observations, on meditation, and, of course, on the reports of his network of agents among the Bem, Megistes had formulated his own theory about the origin and profound nature of Bem hatred. Admittedly, Bem malignity was, to some degree, a result of the conviction general among the Bem that the Arkies had stolen "their" land. But the real cause of their hatred and the inevitable obstacle to any meeting of minds between Arkie and barbo was the Logos of Arkadia. For barbarians, addicted to the magical worship of their god Dis and forever drowning in a tide of daily chaos, the nondescript little object that was the physical Logos could only seem an incomprehensible and thus sinister instrument whose hidden power the Arkies had used to "steal" the land from the Bem, to maintain a baleful ascendancy over the faithful servants of Dis, and worst of all to guide them through a cosmos which was incomprehensible to the Bem.

For the Bem, the Logos-thing that somehow endowed the Arkies with a fearsome "understanding" which allowed them to make their own rules instead of appeasing the ever-present mad chaos of the Creation was not only an outrageous insult to Dis but also to generations of Bem ancestors. It also gave rise to the general belief among the Bem that, as Seraph had declared at the Passing, Arkies had no souls, were perhaps not even part of the Created world. How else to account for the horrifying orderliness of the Arkie domain?

When the Arkies claimed that their Logos-thing permitted them to deny the almighty power of Chaos and to reject the magic of Dis which alone could provide some margin of safety for vulnerable mankind, the assertion seemed to the barbarians not only profane, but disgusting, for how could a piece of dirty leather wrapped around what appeared to be a metal spike possess such power? Recognizing that it could not, the Bem came to believe with the passion of the self-anointed oppressed that in some time yet to come the Logos abomination must fail. Then the Bem Faithful and Dis would triumph. The Arkies would die in agony and the land they stole would belong to the Bem again. So Justice would be accomplished. Such were the ingrained Bem misconceptions about the Logos.

As always, Megistes could only wonder how Agathon and the Arkadian people for whom the Logos was the very soul of existence could persuade the Bem to peace in the face of such cultural revulsion to the Logos. What corrective truth could prevail against such primitive hatred? How could you ever expect such indurate minds to recognize the efficacy of a crude metal cylinder encased in ancient leather and very like the handle of a dagger? After all was the Logos not above all else a mystery, even to Arkadians? And yet, as Megistes himself believed with all his heart did it not somehow contain within it the essence of thought, the abstract shapes of all existence, the design of rules for conduct, for speech, for numbers, and the latent images of things not yet devised. The soul of Arkadia lay within that cylinder that so repelled the Bem. And no one had ever grasped its nature or its mystery although many a fine mind had ruined itself trying to do so.

Even the Koinars, the most numerous and influential though still the lowest ranking order of Arkadian society, quailed from attempts to comprehend the Logos. Yet it was from those builders of the now-defunct Koinar state-within-the-state that the Logos and its language had originated. Moreover, although the Koinars had by now discarded their old separate existence in favor of participation in Arkadian life as evidenced, for example, by their service today as auxiliaries and slingers in the Array, they continued truthfully, Megistes believed, to disavow any special knowledge of, or affinity for, the Revered Object that they themselves had introduced into Arkadia. And so the Logos mystery still defied understanding even as it lay like a barricade across the road to peace with the Barbarians.

In order to study the Logos—as well as to honor its place in Arkadian life—the Hegemony long ago had decided to house it in a shrine-complex known as the "Logofane". Built on Mt. Hierys, deep in a heavily-wooded district, the Logofane had expanded over the generations into an institute devoted to the study of all aspects of the Logos, from its history, to its obvious ability to shape Arkadia in ways not yet understood, to its often-mystical effects on the human mind. By long-established law the Logofane was set up to operate under the direction of a highly-respected scholar called the "Logofant". For many years now, Megistes was proud to say, he himself had held that office. He was never happier than when he could devote his whole mind to studying what he called the "Mysteries of the Logos".

In recent years, however, he had been unable to spend as much time as he would have liked in his study at the Logofane for Agathon had needed him to oversee the education of his two sons and their close companion, Phylax. Because he could never refuse Agathon anything and could never approach any task half-heartedly Megistes these days found himself spending more of his time as tutor to the boys than as Logofant of the Realm. Oh, how he longed to return to his work at the Logofane! Ah, well, he assured himself, he'd get back to his chief work as soon as Agathon designated either young Milo or Darden as his successor.

Megistes felt certain that that day could not be more than two or three years away. Moreover, it was becoming more and more likely that the Hegemon would choose Milo at least judging from the honor shown Milo earlier that day. Until the choice was made, however, Megistes himself would continue to cling to his sustaining faith that old as he was he would live long enough to solve at least some of the mysteries of the Logos.

With this comforting thought in mind the sage dozed off despite the miserable jolting of the wagon carrying his ancient bones.

THREE

Upon his return to the royal pavilions which had been as always deliberately erected well away from the site where the Feast of the Passing was to take place a weary and dust-laden Agathon had soaked himself in a hot bath, drunk a cup of unmixed wine, and had himself barbered and shaved. Refreshed he had then dressed in an elegant cloak of white linen worked with designs in gold thread—a costume fit for the Hegemon of Arkadia.

Now, as full darkness engulfed the world and the torches were being lit in and around the royal compound, Agathon allowed himself to become aware of the strains of music that were beginning to emanate from the parade ground where the men of the Array were starting to gather. *It was a good sign that music,* Agathon thought, *for it meant that the earlier somber mood of the Array was brightening now as was only to be expected when virile young men assembled to wallow in license for a few days. Still,* Agathon told himself, *he was honestly glad that those same virile young men and their officers felt shame at having let their guard down enough that afternoon for that Bem fellow, that Seraph, to get dangerously close to their Hegemon. A dose of shame would be good for these lads,* Agathon reflected, *would brace them tighter than ever to their duty. Still, he was sure the lesson had already sunk in.*

Later, when the feast was well underway but before the women entered the scene Agathon would make his own appearance and even have Karou drive the chariot right into the center of the feast. The young men would really cheer that unorthodox touch though fussy Karou would no doubt frown. *Well, let him frown; the Hegemon of Arkadia was entitled to a little fun of his own occasionally, was he not?*

As he imagined the scene Agathon pictured his chariot surrounded by the lads. Then, as always, he would address them from the chariot.

He would heap praise on them, would not dwell over-much on the incident of the Bem madman, and he would make it clear that he still loved every one of his troopers. Then, as usual, instead of lingering further, he would have himself driven off from the feast lest his presence dampen the merrymaking.

Still another more compelling reason for removing himself from the party so precipitously lay in the fact that he did not wish to be made officially aware of the drunkenness so rampant at the festivities. Nor did he want to see any behavior that might force him to discipline the perpetrators. *Better to see nothing and hear nothing,* he told himself, *so that once-a-year license could reign untrammeled as a guarantee of stringent self-discipline for the rest of the year.*

Sighing with a weariness that seemed to be always with him these days, Agathon poured another cup of strong wine. He reclined on a nearby couch to sip it at leisure, and in peace. It was at moments like this, he reflected, that he felt most keenly the loneliness that had turned his true self—his hidden self—bleak as a winter forest. Agathon recognized that most of his loneliness was inescapable: the price he had to pay for the power he wielded as Hegemon. He had few friends, for friendship required mutual understanding. And who, even among those he respected and admired, could comprehend the weight of self-doubt and obligation that had to be borne as the accompaniment to every decision he had to make? Agathon did not expect to be understood and he did expect to be lonely. Yet he could not deny that it was hard to live so alone.

It had not always been so for he had had *her* until Fate had snatched her away. Agathon tried not to think of her anymore for even the memory of her still caused a painful tightening of his throat—as now. His "Dark Princess" he had called her, a silly name she scoffed at even though Agathon knew that privately she loved it. She was the only woman he had ever loved with his whole heart.

Agathon had not loved Melissa, his wife, though no one except Melissa and he knew it. Having wed as a matter of state they had lived together contentedly enough. Now dead these six years, Melissa had been a good and loving mother to Milo and Darden. Agathon remembered her with fond affection. Still, it was the other he had truly loved, though they had to love in secrecy. She, too, was gone now and with her was gone the passion and tenderness he had experienced only with her: his Dark Princess. It was impossible to forget her, impossible also to remember her without a stinging of the eyes. Yes, he was bleak with loneliness both as Hegemon and as a man.

Abruptly shattering Agathon's reverie, a pair of aged kitchen servants, Tellus and Doros by name, men who had served in his father's household as well, entered with trays.

"Supper, Strategat," murmured Tellus, the senior of the two.

Grateful for the distraction, Agathon nodded and the trays were placed on a low table of carved wood. The servants withdrew. On each of the trays were wine, olives, freshly baked bread, soft cheese, and dates. Agathon always ate sparingly and usually alone except for state occasions. This evening, however, he had invited Megistes to join him, not only for the company but also to hear his old companion's thoughts about the day's events. Moments later Doros, the lesser of the two servants, showed Megistes into the Hegemon's quarters, unobtrusively lit a bowl of incense, and noiselessly withdrew again.

Wine cup in hand Agathon rose and greeted his guest with a smile and gestured for Megistes to take one of the couches arranged around the table that bore the evening's repast. Neither man spoke as they ate for it was their custom to reserve conversation until the post-prandial cup.

Agathon noted that Megistes dressed tonight in one of the worn robes, this one a faded blue that he favored, ate and drank even more sparingly than did the Hegemon himself. No doubt, Agathon reflected, this abstemious bent was why the elderly Logofant had lived so long and why he would surely live for many more years to come.

Not for the first time Agathon found himself marveling at the stamina of his aged friend. As Hegemon he himself had spent the long hours of the Passing on his feet. He had been supremely weary when at last the Array had reached the Komai site where he could rest and refresh himself in the Royal Pavilion.

Megistes, too, thought Agathon, *must have felt near exhaustion after his long and uncomfortable day in the saddle. Yet, the aged tutor, almost forty years older than Agathon, exhibited no signs of excessive fatigue, though unlike the Hegemon's, the old man's quarters in camp offered few amenities with which to revive a tired body and mind. Perhaps,* Agathon mused, *the old man did possess extraordinary powers as many suggested. Had he developed those powers, such as his remarkable stamina, as a by-product of his devotion to the Logos? One day, Agathon resolved, he would pose that question directly to Megistes but not tonight when more immediate matters were pressing both of them.*

When the table was cleared and the servers dismissed for the evening, Agathon himself poured more of the well-watered wine and broached the subject most on his mind.

"Now, old friend, what do you make of this afternoon's incident with that mad young Bem shaman?"

Megistes had been expecting the query for his long association with Agathon both as teacher and as advisor had rendered him sensitive to much of the Hegemon's inner self. Accordingly, Megistes suspected that despite his imperturbable surface Agathon had been shaken by the episode with the lame Bem.

"Aside from its being a courageous though ignorant deed," said Megistes, "the young fool's act was a demonstration, if one was needed, that Bem malevolence toward Arkadia has not ebbed in the least."

"Yes," Agathon said with a smile, "And if you will pardon the metaphorical flourish the young zealot's single eye seemed aflame with his malignity. I presume you realized Megistes that I spoke to the fellow as I did in the hope that he might understand that though I had the power to have him executed I forbore because I, too, am human and prefer peace over malignity."

"I doubt that he got the message."

"Probably not. Still, why not? Surely that fellow must have seen that I am not cruel, that Arkadians are not beasts. Surely that truth must eventually occur to him, or to those Bem looking on."

"More than likely that young man and the others as well saw your mild words only as evidence of weakness."

Megistes' pessimism no doubt closer to reality than his own too-often forced optimism elicited a surge of frustration in Agathon.

"By the Logos, old friend, their stubborn ignorance sometimes infuriates me! Why can't they see that they can have peace with us if they will have it? How long will they continue to send young terrorists to die in useless pursuit of the unattainable? Why do they refuse to take the hand of those who can help them feed their hungry, cure their sick, and build their state?"

"You already know the answer," Megistes said softly. "Hatred makes men mad and blind to their own self-interest as well as to the welfare of their children."

Agathon sighed.

"Yes, but I continue to hope that sooner or later reality must prevail. Neither the Bem nor we can continue this conflict forever. At some point Arkadia's own zealots, though few right now, may gain the upper hand in our Hegemony and launch that war of extermination they clamor for. What then?"

Megistes made no answer for though he feared that horror as much as the Hegemon did he could see no solution to the Arkadian dilemma.

Agathon poured more wine. "I remember something you said, Megistes, when I was still a very young student at your Logofane Academy."

"What was that?" Megistes said, adding, "You know I often spoke foolishly in those early days when I was so sure that law and reason would always win."

"You said that it is culture not mere power that determines the destiny of a society. I took those words to heart, old friend. Those words of yours explain why I have spent so much of my time as Hegemon seeking a road to peace with the Bem."

"You may yet find it, Agathon. Who knows what the future might bring?"

In fact Megistes was one of the few men in the Hegemony who knew the full extent of Agathon's efforts to reach the Bem. Apart from his founding of the Passings Agathon had authorized Megistes to set up and supervise an "intelligence network" among the Bem with the dual purpose of uncovering information about terror groups and of "turning" certain Bem Kapits toward peace.

The network was composed entirely of dissident Arkadian Koinars, members of a small but self-righteous sect that called itself the "Pious Koinars." These Pious Koinars had rejected the doctrine, accepted by the vast majority of Koinars, that their Logos was meant for all Arkadians not just for Koinars. The Pious rather than embrace that view had withdrawn to small enclaves in the most out-of-the-way region of Arkadia: the eastern bank of the River Pelorys. From this far-off place nominally under the control of the Hegemony, the Pious carried on a secret, and illegal, trade in contraband goods, which surely included slaves, with Bem renegades and certain criminal merchants. All efforts on the part of the Hegemony to suppress these Pious outlaws had failed for as soon as any Rider patrols appeared in the vicinity of their settlements, the Pious would flee to the Bem side of the River Pelorys where regulations forbade the Riders to follow and the fugitives would disappear into the impenetrable Bemgrass.

With the Hegemony apparently unable to quell the outlawry of the Pious Koinars although efforts to do so continued intermittently, Megistes had conceived the idea of enlisting a select few of them at the price of overlooking their illegal activities to act as his eyes, ears, and occasional voice among the Bem. Though they excelled at such work Megistes had to admit that his agents had not yet turned up a single advocate of peace among the barbarians.

Agathon had also had it in mind to offer "sanctuary" and with it education in the "Way of the Logos" to any Bem courageous enough to choose the benefits of peace. Agathon had also, by way of Megistes' network let it be known that Arkadia would give refuge to the abandoned Bem children known as "throwaways" as well as to discarded Bem wives for under current circumstances most of these children as well as women either died in misery on the Bemgrass or, as Megistes suspected though he could not prove it, fell into the hands of slave traders.

So far, not one of these throwaways, child or woman, had had the benefit of the Hegemon's generosity. Still, thought Megistes, *despite lack of success the effort had to continue.*

"We ought not give up," said Megistes. "Who knows when the road to peace might open up against all odds?"

Agathon smiled wanly.

"Yes, who knows? But I feel my time is growing short, old friend. I yearn to achieve at least some small gains before I go."

Both men fell silent. What more was there to say on the subject?

It was Agathon who broke the silence.

"I wonder how that crazy boy, Seraph, wasn't that what he called himself, learned how to speak Arkadian."

"He didn't speak it all that well," Megistes remarked.

"I understood him well enough," said Agathon with a smile, "but who taught him? What do you think?"

Megistes said, "It's an old story among the Bem, Strategat. The boy was born lame. Thus he was probably considered useless and abandoned on the Bemgrass—a throwaway. But he must have been lucky if you want to call it that. He was picked up by one of our own Pious Koinar lawbreakers who probably intended to work the child to death. The boy, however, managed to survive his tenure with the outlaw absorbing shreds of our language in the process. And then, somehow, he managed to escape and make his way back to his clan."

"Where he also managed to make himself an apprentice shaman," said Agathon. "Thus it would seem our young shaman must be not only courageous but uncommonly intelligent as well."

"Perhaps."

The boy had not seemed particularly intelligent to Megistes.

Another interval of silence ensued. Again Agathon was first to shatter it.

"Might we not make good use of this Seraph? I know he hates me or says he does but one must make use of whatever tool comes to hand. We must find some way to begin the necessary journey to peace. Someone must be first, why not this Seraph? Why could he not become our agent of peace?"

"He hates you, Agathon."

"Yes, yes, I know, but couldn't we change all that if we went about it the right way?"

Agathon paused and Megistes could sense enthusiasm now building within this peace-loving man so willing to give himself to the cause in which he believed.

Agathon, suddenly smiling broadly, said, "Here is the plan Megistes: As soon as possible, preferably while the Bem are still encamped within reach across the river, you will send some of those clever agents of yours to find this Seraph—clandestinely of course—and bring him to Ten Turrets where we will convert him, show him the light. He's intelligent. Perhaps he will understand the advantages to his own people of a sincere amity with us."

"Assuming we do turn him, what then?"

"We'll send him back to his people as our ambassador. We should not refuse to adopt unorthodox methods to break the cultural impasse that now binds us. I won't claim that this proposal of mine will accomplish anything much but I am convinced we must try it."

Though skeptical, Megistes agreed that the idea was worth the attempt and he said as much to Agathon but then added, "But why use my Pious but unreliable Koinar underground for the job? Why not just send a squadron of Riders across the river tonight right into the Bem encampment and seize the quarry? Do the job right."

Agathon shook his head ruefully.

"That would be a violation of my standing pledge at the Passings, old friend. Have I not promised the Bem for thirty years that they may remain for ten days in the Zone without molestation so long as they behave peacefully? If I break that pledge by seizing this Seraph it would prove to the Bem that I cannot be trusted, that Arkadian peace is a sham. No, no, it must be your Pious Koinars, my friend. Agreed?"

"I will set it in motion."

"Excellent."

Agathon, satisfied, poured another cup of wine for himself. Megistes refused the offered flagon.

Having now resolved, at least temporarily, one of the subjects that had been troubling him, Agathon, as was his habit, immediately turned his agile mind to another.

"In your opinion did my son perform satisfactorily during the Passing? It was, after all, his first exposure to public scrutiny, a most important step in my plan of succession for the Hegemony."

Megistes knew that Agathon's term "my son" referred to young Milo not to the even younger Darden for in the Hegemon's mind Darden hardly counted except as a possible substitute for Milo should tragedy strike down the heir apparent.

"I thought Milo did very well indeed," said Megistes, "especially because his first time out also included that untoward incident with our friend Seraph. Still, it gave Milo a chance to experience Bem hatred at close quarters."

"I agree with your assessment," said Agathon, "though I sensed the boy's shock when Seraph began his antics."

"We were all shocked," Megistes pointed out.

"Yet Milo came forward to stand by my chariot when he thought me threatened. That shows good instincts for the necessary public bearing of a Hegemon. Wouldn't you agree?"

"Certainly. Milo is a fine young man. Thankfully, he is much under the influence of your example Hegemon. Like you, my friend, Milo has cultivated, even at his tender age, a commendable skepticism about the flattery that constantly assails him as your apparent heir. At the same time he is properly conscious of his high potential and of the responsibilities that may lie ahead. He is understandably sometimes nervous about his ability to govern as Hegemon but he is eager to prepare himself for that task. I think he could make a just and capable Hegemon."

"I am glad to hear you say so. Is he a good student?"

"Good enough. Better than fair but he was not made to be a scholar."

In his private mind Megistes regarded Milo as a little spoiled, a little too free with himself sometimes, a little too stiff at other times, but also one, who with guidance, would probably achieve a sensible balance. Furthermore, Milo's sense of honor and dignity was already well developed. He would have to guard against a too-quick temper perhaps, especially if he perceived any kind of threat to his honor and dignity. For example, Megistes could easily imagine Milo had he been Hegemon this afternoon ordering the insolent Seraph whipped for his insulting words. Still, Megistes had spoken his true assessment of Milo to his father: The boy would do honor to the High Bench. He might never light up the sky as Agathon himself had but he would do his duty to the Arkadian people. Megistes himself, a Megar by virtue of his status as Logofant and thus a member of the Grand Council would gladly cast his vote to confirm Milo as Hegemon when, and if, that time came.

"I'll soon have to nominate an Anax, I suppose."

This was Agathon ruminating aloud.

Megistes said, "Surely not yet. It can wait for three or four years."

"Best to begin contemplating it, however," said Agathon. "The Hegemony has been too long without an Anax."

The office of Anax, by tradition filled by the Hegemon's designated successor who also acted as titular and often actual Commander of the Array, had been empty for the past fifteen years, since Agathon's own younger brother had been killed in a hunting accident. Hence Megistes could understand Agathon's anxiety to fill it as soon as possible now that Milo was nearing an appropriate age. But Milo was not yet ready for even titular responsibility.

"The boy still needs to learn his role," Megistes said. "He is still a lad."

Agathon sighed.

"I know you are right but I would be grateful if you would accelerate his education."

"I will do my best."

Another sigh from Agathon, then, "What is your opinion of that Koinar lad, that companion of Milo's?"

Megistes smiled for Agathon persisted in referring to young Phylax, who was in truth only partly of Koinar blood, as "that Koinar lad" though he certainly knew the boy's name for it was Agathon himself who, apparently acting on a whim, had plucked Phylax from obscurity to serve as companion to his elder son.

"Phylax is Phylax," said Megistes enigmatically hoping to deflect Agathon from forcing an evaluation of Phylax that would only diminish Milo by contrast.

Agathon was not to be put off.

"Might this Phylax be exercising too much influence over Milo?"

"Not at all," said Megistes. "Besides, any influence Phylax wields is to Milo's benefit I assure you."

Agathon gave a wry smile.

"Is the Koinar boy such a paragon?"

"I would not go that far in describing him but from my own observations I can say this much: Even at sixteen, Phylax is an accomplished athlete, brawny, well beyond his age. He also shows definite promise as a soldier. Already he can ride like a trooper, handle a javelin, and brandish a sword as well as most veterans of the Rider Regiments. On top of that the boy is brave, even reckless. I have seen him jump a ditch astride a warhorse. Shall I go on? Yes? Very well then. In addition to his physical attributes I can tell you that Phylax is also loyal, an excellent friend to Milo. In fact the boys call each other *del* which as you know is the latest soldier slang for 'best friend.' Above all, Phylax is a faithful servant to the Hegemony, an uncomplicated young man, he reveres his own honor as well as the honor of his Hegemon. Still, he can laugh. He's no scholar, however, though he is a good student when the subject interests him. There! Have I described a paragon?"

Agathon laughed.

"Indeed, I would say so, my friend. Perhaps I should nominate this Koinar lad to be our next Anax!"

Megistes, too, laughed at the patent absurdity of the Hegemon's facetious remark. In the private chambers of his own thoughts, however, Megistes had often lamented that a young man in possession of Phylax's attributes was barred by the accident of birth from holding an office for which he was eminently qualified. Megistes regarded it as a major weakness of the Hegemony, this custom of basing the Succession to the High Bench on so fickle a determinant as ancestry. *One day,* he feared, *the practice would extract a high price from the Hegemony.*

Aloud, however, in response to Agathon's jocular allusion to Phylax as a possible Anax, Megistes said. "Phylax would make an excellent Anax." Then he added the obvious. "Of course the Council would never approve a Koinar in that role."

Agathon signified his agreement with a nod.

"Besides," Megistes went on, "though Phylax would probably make a fine Anax where resolution and courage count most he probably would not make a very good Hegemon, an office that requires good judgment and strategic thought above all else. Milo, on the other hand, might very well flounder as Anax but bloom as Hegemon."

"I hope you are right, old friend and glad that the Koinar lad stands so high in your estimation."

In fact, though he considered it well to keep it to himself, Megistes' estimate of Phylax was even higher than he had revealed to Agathon. The whole truth was that during his tutelage of Phylax, Megistes had developed a strong affection for the boy. Although he was fond, in varying degrees, of each of the three boys in his charge, it was dark-haired, sinewy Phylax that Megistes would have liked to have for his own son for Megistes sensed that Phylax had even more in him than the aged tutor had let on to Agathon. Despite his youth, usually an impediment to serious understanding of obligation, Phylax could be trusted to keep his word. With time, Megistes hoped, Phylax would grow more supple in wit and more profound in wisdom. But more important, in his opinion, Phylax would rise to challenges. He would develop that rare capacity among men: the ability to find in himself whatever he required to do his duty. In the end, Megistes was sure Phylax would turn out to be the best man among his three charges even if the world of lesser men never knew it.

All this evaluation of Phylax—as if he was a prize racing colt at auction—brought back to Megistes memories of the bizarre, but certainly fortunate, circumstances that surrounded the boy's advent into Megistes' own life, as well as the lad's later advancement to the Hegemon's household.

The skein of events had commenced when a Koinar woman of surpassing beauty and grace, though apparently impoverished, had brought the boy—an intelligent and wide-eyed five-year-old—to Megistes, then very much committed to his role as Logofant. The woman, who had refused to reveal her name or place of origin, had told a story that was not uncommon: she had borne a child by a high-ranking Megar, whom she also refused to identify. She had fled from her lover because he wished to take the boy from her to be raised as a Megar. She and the child, Phylax, had taken refuge with a Koinar family who lived in a secluded Koinar community. Now, she told Megistes, she was fatally ill and she wanted to provide for her son by dedicating him to the study of the Logos at the Logofane Academy. A "dedication" of this kind was then a fairly widespread practice among Koinars.

As Logofant, Megistes had taken the boy in. Three years later, on one of his infrequent inspection visits to the Logofane Shrine, the Hegemon Agathon had spotted the eight-year-old Phylax and, on impulse, had asked that he be sent to the Hegemonic household to be companion to his sons, Milo and Darden. So Phylax had begun his journey to whatever destiny lay before him.

"And what of Darden, my friend? What can you tell me of my son, Darden, eh?"

The Hegemon's question at once brought Megistes back to the present in the Royal Pavilion.

"Ah, yes, Darden," said Megistes. "The truth without equivocation?"

Agathon frowned. "When have I ever asked you for equivocation?"

"Never, of course, it was an unworthy remark. I apologize. Well then, about Darden."

Megistes paused. *Here,* he thought, *he would have to tread carefully.*

There was much about Darden that the boy's austere father might easily misconstrue, for Darden was, after all, still a rather delicate twelve-year-old with a soft heart and an even softer head, so far. Often frail, Darden, also yellow-haired, looked at one through mild blue eyes like those of a sweet girl. Unlike his big brother and Phylax little Darden evinced no interest in sport or games of any kind preferring to read and dream. For this reason he was seldom included in the activities of Phylax and Milo and when he was, he invariably fell short. He was quick to take offense but quick of mind as well, quick to question, slow to enjoy.

"Darden is still so young," Megistes now said aloud, "and still so unformed that I hesitate to draw any definite conclusions about him."

Agathon frowned as always impatient with hesitation from his advisors.

"But surely you must have made some judgments: the boy's character, his interests, his inclinations? I confess *I* can't fathom him at all; he only mumbles in my presence and takes himself away from me as soon as he can. He irritates me and I know I have neglected him because of it. I need to know something of a son who might one day, if fate is unkind, be called upon to mount the High Bench."

Now it was Megistes' turn to frown for it was hard for him to imagine Darden as the Hegemon of Arkadia yet it could happen. Hence, struggling not to say too much or too little, the old tutor gave his assessment still tentative, though not now presented as such, to the Hegemon.

"I think Darden, though something of a dreamer and often too sensitive for his own good, is the most intelligent, certainly the best student, of the three boys you have entrusted to me. He is imaginative, but thorough, and already possesses a deep sense of justice. He will be a man of many talents and some excellent qualities. If destiny calls him to the High Bench, however, I doubt that he will acquit himself well for there is already a little too much of the tyrant in his heart."

"Yes, I, too, detect some of that in the boy. Well then tell me this: If, as I fervently hope, Darden is not called to the High bench, what other role can you see him playing in the Hegemony?'

Now, here was a question Megistes himself had often considered and so he answered this time without hesitation.

"He would make a decent poet and artist but an even better scholar of the Logos. I could imagine him carrying on my work at the Logofane."

"As Logofant?"

The Hegemon seemed astonished at the old man's reply.

"Eventually, yes," said Megistes. "The post of Logofant, I think, would suit him, spirit and mind."

Agathon, adopting a characteristic pose when considering possibilities, leaned forward and cupped his chin in his left hand. Megistes fell silent to allow the Hegemon whatever time he needed to ponder the idea of Darden as Logofant of Arkadia.

In truth it was a suggestion the aged tutor had intended to keep to himself for a while, though he had been contemplating it for some time now as a means of diverting Darden from his tendency to think too often and too deeply about matters that ought not to trouble one so young. In his private mind, Megistes had begun to fear that Darden would be liable in the near future to spring to incorrect conclusions even embrace philosophies of which he had little understanding. And what if, after Megistes' stint as tutor ended, young Darden fell under the influence of some stronger personality? It was because of his concern for this aspect of the boy's character that Megistes was always very willing to show respect for Darden's intelligence, make time to answer the boy's often-naive inquiries, and even engage in gentle debate all to keep Darden from stumbling into some philosophical swamp deleterious for him and for Arkadia as well.

In brief, Megistes accepted it as his task to deal seriously with Darden's lonely mental and spiritual anxieties lest he go astray. Megistes also recognized that he had to carry out this task in secret for he knew that Agathon would have no patience with his son's "childish nonsense" as the Hegemon would surely call Darden's current inclinations.

The old sage recollected that only this afternoon after the Passing of the Bem was finished and the Array was returning to the Komai encampment, Megistes, finally dismounted and resting his rattling bones in the wagon commandeered for him, had detected the sullen look on Darden's pretty face that almost always signaled that he was troubled in his mind. Though, for the sake of his weary body, Megistes would have preferred to ignore for once Darden's need for succor, he managed to rise to his self-imposed duty with regard to the sensitive boy. He called Darden to ride beside his wagon. The exuberant Phylax and Milo had previously received the tutor's permission to ride at the head of the column with the Royal Chariot.

"A long face, Darden," Megistes had asked to begin the process.

The boy appeared to be in a sulk. He often sulked at and even more often scorned what he didn't understand or couldn't control.

Guessing what was eating at Darden this time, Megistes said: "Now that you've seen the Bem what do you think of them?"

Of the three boys Darden had shown the most interest when his father had announced that the lads under Megistes' tutelage would be allowed to attend the Passing to observe the mysterious Bem at first hand. Now, after the Passing, Darden was moping. Why? Megistes pressed him. "Well, what do you think of the Bem?

Darden answered hesitantly.

"They were dirty."

"Yes."

"And they looked sick, a lot of them."

"They *are* sick, most of them."

"They look hungry too. Even the warriors' ponies looked scrawny."

Megistes nodded.

"Dirty, sick, and hungry. An apt description, Darden."

Darden then burst forth with the genuine question that was troubling him.

"But why? Why do we have so much and they have so little? I feel sorry for them. It's not fair."

"Fair?" repeated Megistes, "What would be fair, Darden?'

"They should have as much as we have," the boy declared his face flushing as if with indignation. "They should have equality."

Megistes sighed. Equality. Was this not the daemon that tortured the moral conscience of youth and fools in every generation? That it should surface in Darden's twelve-year-old mind testified to the boy's tender nature and swift intellect but it also warned Megistes that the boy was indeed beginning to wander into the quicksand of good and evil. Megistes cautioned himself to proceed carefully from here on.

Fortunately, however, at this moment Phylax riding pell-mell aboard a black war-stallion that he took wild joy in controlling came thundering up to Megistes' wagon and reigned in. He immediately cast a good-natured gibe at Darden.

"Talking about the Bem, right? They weren't exactly an Arkadian Phalanx on parade, were they? No wonder the barbos can't fight us, hey?"

Darden, suddenly red-faced with fury, said, "You shouldn't call them barbos."

"Is that so? The troopers call them that."

Megistes intervened.

"Darden's right Phylax. That term is just coarse soldier-slang. I don't want to hear you talking like a grumpy trooper."

"Sorry, Master. It just slipped out."

Darden, as so often, now spoke when silence would have served him better.

"You ought to mind your manners, Phylax."

The older boy shot Darden a look of utter contempt.

Megistes cut in.

"All right, that's enough." Then Megistes asked Phylax, "Where did you leave Milo?"

Phylax grinned.

"By my thick stick oops, sorry again, Master I forgot my manners. Anyway, the Hegemon sent me back to fetch Darden to ride up front with him and Milo and me. We're almost at the Komai."

With this, Phylax thundered away on his charger.

Megistes said, "Go up to the front, Darden. You and I will talk again later. Go. Don't say anything about our talk to your father. Not yet."

Megistes had watched Darden canter off and resolved that he would do his utmost to rescue Darden from the morass of good intentions that so obviously threatened to engulf him. True, this boy was often selfish, unlovable, stubborn, proud, but he was also lonely and in need of a friendly guiding hand. Megistes had accepted the fact that he had to be Darden's guiding hand.

Agathon again re-called Megistes to the present moment in the Royal Tent.

"Can you really imagine Darden as Logofant, old friend?"

Agathon, with a half-skeptical grimace on his handsome face, then continued.

"I find it hard to visualize Darden in any responsible post. Still, I suppose wonders take place constantly in Arkadia, eh? Well, well, old friend, when it comes to Darden I must defer to your judgment for I confess the boy baffles me."

With this Agathon emitted a little groan, stretched, and rose to his feet. Megistes followed suit.

"So, we've had a fruitful exchange, old friend," said the Hegemon, "but now I must prepare to make my appearance at the feast, which

51

is—I presume—well underway by now." Agathon made a wry face, which Megistes recognized as a silent expression of distaste for the "annual debauchery" as Agathon termed his soldiers' Komai celebrations.

In fact neither Agathon nor Megistes approved of the Komai feasts. Nothing edifying or beautiful took place at them. Nevertheless, both men recognized that these carnal affairs had value as a kind of safety valve, a means of quickly releasing the nervous energy of young men pent-up after long-term mental pressure in the time period before and during the Passing season. Of course Agathon—and Megistes even more—would have preferred a course of meditation as the means of discharging tensions. But both the Hegemon and his Logofant saw the value in allowing the troopers to indulge in intensely licentious behavior for a limited length of time. It brought the desired results. And by now it had become rooted in military custom and culture. One might even say that the Komai feast was, for the Array, their own Passing into a Forbidden Zone of sorts.

Needing to say none of this to each other the two men embraced. Unexpectedly Agathon spoke again, this time in the soft voice he reserved for exchanges with his few intimates.

"Dear old Megistes, how grateful I am to you for your invaluable work with the boys entrusted to you. I know you would rather be back at your Logofane, poring over your books and charts, your endless searching, always trying to solve the mystery of our strange Arkadia, eh? I promise, my friend, I shall not forget your services when you retire to your studies. In the meantime what can I do to lighten your burden?"

Megistes almost asked to be relieved of the task of seizing the Bem apprentice Seraph for, upon reflection, he found that he now doubted that the business would accomplish any movement toward peace. Still, the Hegemon was resolved on it and only he, Megistes, could pull it off. Thus, he replied lightly to Agathon's offer.

"I am content with your friendship, Strategat."

Agathon's eyes rose in surprise.

"Strategat? There is no *Strategat* between us."

Megistes nodded.

The Hegemon withdrew to his private chambers. Megistes went out into the night, now pleasantly fresh as it neared the tenth hour.

Megistes had instructed his three charges to wait for him at the feast at the places designated for the sons of the Hegemon.

They had better be there—all three—or anyone missing would get a serious warming of the behind.

Meanwhile, across the slick flow of the River Bradys in the disorganized camp of the Bem, Seraph the Lame, brooded as he limped distractedly among the wretched huts and the dung fires of his people. Across the river he could see the lights of the Arkadia encampment—torches in neat rows and horses tethered, well-fed, and watered. From time to time Seraph caught strains of music and masculine singing. By Dis, he hated them, these evil Arkies, proud and superior as they celebrated their latest humiliation of the hopeless Bem! How he longed to bring them low!

Abruptly, his leg and hip aching, he halted to watch as the hobbled women, most of them limping as painfully as he did himself, went about preparing the stinking corpses of the their dead with oil and salt for the funeral fires that would soon devour them.

As Seraph looked upon this ritual activity he became aware that the women were glancing—furtively—at him as well, as were the nearby men, many of them warriors lazing in the firelight. In truth he had been aware of this sneaky observation everywhere his restlessness carried him in the camp that night. It had not taken him long to recognize that the scrutiny he was receiving was an expression of awe and admiration, part of a general, and mistaken, belief that he had somehow inflicted a defeat on the Arkies when he had confronted their big chief earlier at the Passing. In reality, of course, Seraph knew it had been the other way around. Yet, these stupid folk, the women, now beginning to wail their grief as they dragged their stinking bodies to the pyres, and the recumbent warriors boastful in their paint and feathers, all of them were too ignorant to comprehend that it was not the Arkie Kapit but the Bem would-be hero himself who had failed.

All at once Seraph was filled with disgust for the entire scene: the wailing women, the rotting dead, the warriors sunk in self-deception about their "prowess". *Was this really what Dis craved from his people?*

If so, then Dis was stupid too. But of course Dis was stupid. How could it be otherwise? Was Dis not the very "Kapit of Chaos"?

Refusing to meet the worshipful eyes that turned to him as he hauled himself past them, Seraph continued his agitated patrol of the camp. Again and again the vision of his fumbling collapse before the Arkie Chieftain caused his soul to cringe within the body that had repulsed him for most of his own stupid life. Seraph had planned his confrontation with the Arkie chief with great care, aiming to shock the oppressors at their own derisive "Passing" show by demonstrating that one of the despised barbos possessed sufficient brain and courage to stand up before the Chief Oppressor himself to proclaim by word and deed: *I am Bem and proud and you should fear me!* Seraph had hoped—and half-expected—that his bold action would so confound Arkie arrogance that confusion would spread among them, would inflict, on some of them at least a wound in the mind, an unforgettable never-healing wound that would fester and spread its poison among them like the plague sowing terror into their clean skins. Surely, Seraph had convinced himself, the Arkie tyrants would not be able to endure the knowledge that one of the "despised" had succeeded in crying forth the curse of the lowest Bem upon the highest Arkie. Surely, so Seraph had hoped and expected, his blow would crack the shield of Arkie self-assurance and plant in their bloodless Arkie hearts the chancre of fear of the lowly Bem. Fear, so Seraph had hoped, would then breed madness, the madness of Dis in them, for surely, after Seraph's unthinkable act the Logos-lovers would have to acknowledge that the cosmos even the Arkie slice of it was at bottom a heap of incomprehensible shit.

It had begun well, Seraph's act of defiance. Brazenly, he had dragged his shit-stained body before the Great Enemy. He had delivered the curse that he had so carefully prepared. He had done that much hadn't he? Or was he now dreaming it in his muddled head? At first the Arkies had quailed, hadn't they? At first they had felt in their hearts, yes, even in their Kapit's imperious heart, the magical power of the curse. Surely their Kapit had at first felt the cosmic blow delivered to him. Hadn't the other Arkies for an instant also glimpsed their doom in Seraph's bold words? But then it had come apart somehow. He, Seraph the gimp, had trusted that the Arkies would kill him, at once, that he would die as a Witness for Dis. In this way he, Seraph the bold gimp, alone among all Bem martyrs, would have succeeded in planting in the enemy heart a seed of doubt that would grow and spread, becoming at last the parasite that would devour their pride for they surely did not possess souls these contemptuous Arkies. He, Seraph the Lame, had understood that if only one Bem—himself—showed his own contempt to the contemptuous oppressors, it would be the spark to ignite their rotten Arkadia like the flash of Dis lightning that sets the whole of the grasslands ablaze. The curse of Seraph the Lame would turn the vile Arkie State to charred grass for, though he expected they would kill him, his curse would ring forever, unanswerable in their inner parts. But they had not killed him. And here the memory caused him to cringe in shame. Instead they had seized him as easily as a dire-cat seizes a Bem child and their arrogant Kapit had played with him as a dire-cat plays with his prey.

Seraph the Lame had been unable to think of words to add to his curse. Instead, reduced by the Arkie chieftain's imperturbable disdain, intimidated by his eyes, his tall presence, his white robes, Seraph the Lame had felt his curse diminished, made a "nonsense." Dis had been exposed as a fraud and as despised as were the Bem people.

Looking back, Seraph the Lame could only blame himself. *Why had he failed to meet the oppressor Chieftain's eyes? Why had he failed to reveal further his contempt for the Arkies and their Chief? Why had he hung his head? He had hung his head, hadn't he? Why had he succumbed to the Arkie chief's questions delivered so smoothly with a natural malevolence for a scorned barbo captive? Why hadn't Seraph the Lame screamed his Bem fury to the sky? Why hadn't he struggled in the arms of his captors? Why had he meekly accepted their "merciful" dismissal of him when they had finished with him? Why had Dis failed him?*

Only in the aftermath of his cowardly collapse when he had reached the safety of the Bem camp which existed only by sufferance of the tyrants across the river had the would-be champion, Seraph the Lame, perceived the reason for his ignominious bowing to the Arkies: It was because he was no champion but merely contemptible Seraph and every bit as despicable as the Arkies thought him. This was the reason why instead of planting his curse and then defending his brave act with holy intransigence he had embraced the humiliation that he deserved—that Dis deserved, that the Bem nation itself deserved. How else could he now explain the admiring glances that the despicable Bem had been bestowing upon him since his return to camp?

Though covered in shame at the botch of his mission, Seraph had not been permitted to hide himself in the stinking darkness of his master shaman's hut as he longed to do. No, his master had insisted that he show himself among the people. As ignorant accounts of the lame and half-blind Bem youth's curse of the Arkie Kapit had spread, the Bem folk had refused to regard it as the humiliation it truly was, humiliation for the fraudulent Dis and his people as well as for lame Seraph. Instead they had insisted on reckoning his fiasco as a "feat" an act that when falsified sufficiently provided the forever-humbled Bem still another reason to hate the Arkie tyrants. Even now, as he sought among the cook fires and huts for some dark place where he might find the solitude to weep undisturbed, Seraph felt the eyes of these witless brutes—his people—upon him. *Were the Bem really the builders of their own miserable existence as some Arkie missionaries held?* And then, as sudden as a lightning strike on the plain, a question he had never considered before entered his head: *If the Arkies disappeared tomorrow in what way would the lives of the beastly Bem improve? Would these women and girls who cooked and carried; who wove and worked; who even now laboring by firelight to prepare for the pyres the corpses of males; who in life had beaten them senseless after taking pleasure in their bodies; how would their lives be different if there were no Arkies? Would these enslaved women be free of the shackles that now crippled them until death released them? Would these same women stop tossing their unwanted infants to the predators of the Bemgrass or selling their older children for a skinful of drink? And without their common hatred of the Arkies to force a semblance of unity upon them would not these drunken self-inflated "warriors" immediately revive the senseless warfare of one color-clan against all others? Was not such behavior the true life of the Bem whether or not the Arkies were there to tyrannize them? And of what use was Dis to such an abject people except as a lie that only increased their misery? In short were the Bem not vile himself among them? Did they not deserve their wretched life?*

In truth, Seraph saw he hated his own people as much as he hated the Arkies. Perhaps more, for even as he observed them here all around him, he was acutely aware of how they wallowed in filth, howled with hunger, and quarreled among themselves as they set up their huts. He was also aware that later, when drunk and angry enough, the men—the so-called warriors—would fuck the women, their wives, or any others they could get. Then after beating both wives and any unwary daughters, these heroes would fall into a stupor. Perhaps two or three would be drunk enough to drown in their own vomit. *They disgusted him, his people. They deserved their wretched life as they deserved their impotent god.*

His mind focused on such bitter thoughts, Seraph hauled himself away from the dung fires, the shouts, and the wailing that pervaded the camp. Suddenly, he felt his stomach tighten with fear. *Better not to think how much his people revolted him,* he told himself, *for such thinking must inevitably lead him to question whether he wished to live any longer among such a people.*

At that moment Seraph felt a powerful hand seize his wrist halting his labored progress through the chaotic encampment. The hand belonged to his Master, the Shaman Darst of the Green Clan.

"Stay, boy. I have been looking everywhere for you."

"Pardon, master. I was showing myself as you bade me. I was walking."

The shaman sneered.

"So? You call it walking that humping gait of yours?"

Seraph said nothing for he knew Darst was incapable of any kindness and must be endured.

"Come with me, gimp-leg," said the master shaman, a man who gloried in his own rotted teeth, pierced nipples, and the ulcerated sores he wore here and there on his skin.

"Come," he repeated.

Still gripping Seraph's wrist in his strong hand, Darst commenced to pull a stumbling Seraph after him through the disorder until they emerged at the quiet place where the "House on Wheels", the home of the Vessel, chief oracle of Dis, stood alone in a cleared area. No light was visible from within.

Darst seated himself on the damp ground and pulled Seraph down beside him. In silence, for Seraph knew better than to speak before his master did, the two, master shaman and ragged apprentice, stared at the Vessel's lightless House on Wheels.

Darst, as if on impulse, now, ran his hands over Seraph's ravaged face, looked at him, and said: "Yes, Dis has surely put his mark on your face."

Seraph had heard this many times from many people even in his childhood when he'd first been found, a lost child wandering on the Bemgrass. It was the Mark of Dis, his ugliness that had brought Seraph to his apprenticeship with Darst.

Darst began speaking in an excited whisper as if divulging a powerful spell to his apprentice.

"I have heard that the Vessel now asleep in that House on Wheels will soon receive his flight to Dis. You know what that means, gimp?"

Seraph knew:

The Vessel was soon to be sacrificed upon the Sacred Stones.

Darst continued.

"Because of your stupid but much regarded denunciation of the Arkie Kapit you may be chosen as the next Vessel."

Appalled at the very thought, Seraph burst out, "I am not worthy, Master!"

"Shut up! You are worthy if I say so!"

Seraph obeyed lest his master strike him on his blind eye as he so often did. Seraph, the failed champion, had no wish to pretend to know the "Will of Dis" and then pass it on to people too stupid to recognize a lie when told to them. He had no wish to pretend to serve a non-existent god that he had already renounced in his own mind.

Moreover, Seraph shrank from having to live the rest of his wretched life entombed in the Vessel's decorated House on Wheels. He would go mad in that House of Horror as every Vessel probably did sooner or later. But how was he to avoid this fate that Darst seemed to be preparing for him? Seraph was too cowardly to kill himself. And if he uttered the truth: that he no longer believed in Dis, he would suffer the caress of the torturer before the shamans finally put an end to his life. He was trapped.

Darst spoke again in his excited whisper. "You will do as I say, Gimp-leg or I shall take the light from your other eye, understand?"

Seraph nodded. His master was cruel enough to carry out the threat.

"Come to my hut within the hour," Darst commanded. "I shall present you to the Kapits of the Colors who are encamped here and to certain others. You understand?"

"Yes, Master."

If only he had his legs, Seraph thought, *he would run. Or would he, coward that he was?*

Darst rose.

"In one hour, Gimp, at my hut. In the meantime look well on yon Vessel's house. In a day or two it may be yours, or rather it may be ours."

The shaman strode off to arrange the promised meeting.

Seraph found himself staring at the House on Wheels. *Did the madman within it suspect that he was facing his doom?* For a moment Seraph considered the possibility of warning the imprisoned Vessel of his peril.

But how? Besides it would probably prove a useless act for even if he knew how to deliver such a warning, the Vessel—the servant of Dis— would scoff, or perhaps, in his madness, welcome a death by sacrifice on the rocks. However the Vessel might receive Seraph's warning, it was certain that Seraph himself would suffer deadly consequences.

All at once a shrill sound like nothing Seraph had ever heard before—part scream of horror and part hysterical giggle—erupted from within the Vessel's gaudy prison. *Was the Vessel calling for mercy in there or was he cursing Dis the fraud?*

Unable to endure a repetition of that terrible cry, Seraph struggled to his feet and limped away, covering his ears. He managed to get himself to the crest of a low hill nearby. From this vantage point he could no longer hear the cries of the Vessel. Also from here he was able not only to look back on the wretched huts of the Bem but also to look down on the river and across to the walled Arkie bivouac with its lights and faint sounds of music.

Trapped, Seraph told himself.

Behind him lay a living death as the Vessel. Ahead were the river and the Arkies who would gladly remove his ugly head from his scrawny neck. With this thought it came to him how he might escape the Vessel's fate and at the same time redeem at least in his own mind his failed effort at the Passing: he would cross the Bradys and boldly spy on the Arkies as they rejoiced in still another triumphant humiliation of the Bem.

Lest second thoughts erase his resolve, Seraph limped as fast as he could—but actually slowly and painfully—to where a line of docile ponies were negligently tethered. He took one of the beasts from the line and struggled onto its patient back. In a leather bag tied onto the animal's shaggy mane he found a good flint knife as well as an assortment of Dis fetish charms, all of which the pony's owner no doubt considered protection against the theft of his mount. Seraph slipped the knife into his ragged cloak. He threw the charm bag into the night. *So much for Dis the Guardian against thieves.* Now, his heart beating madly, Seraph rode the pony down to a place he knew on the river where the shallow flow made an easy ford. He crossed, reaching the south bank, forbidden to all Bem. Seraph urged the pony on.

The Arkies, Seraph knew, soon would find him and kill him. *Good. He would try to use his knife to take one or two of them down with him. He would not hide from them. Instead he would ride boldly toward their torchlight in this way seeking a proper end to his wretched and worthless existence.*

FOUR

T he great celebration of the Passing set up in the sprawling central plaza of the Komai had reached that stage when the more than three thousand off-duty troopers of the Array, plus Auxiliaries, servants, and grooms had had their fill of roasted meat, sweet cakes, and beer. Not yet drunk or as rowdy as they hoped to get as the hour wore on toward midnight, the men of the Array lounged like mountain wolves after feeding on fat prey. Musicians wandered among the celebrants making merry tunes with harp and reed pipe. From time to time groups of veterans would roar forth bawdy songs with verses such as: *"The Bem he has no cock! The Bem he has no balls! The Bem he drinks the vilest piss and lies just where he falls! Oh, the barbo! The barbo! We kills 'em when we can! But the cowards run away from us, for the Bem is not a man."*

Since the founding of Arkadia, a thousand variations of such doggerel had been sung around the campfires of the Array. Soon, anticipating the barrels of wine still to come this night, as well as the girls yet to appear from their tents, the men would begin with chants such as: *"Bring on the ladies, let their tits be like cream, make them round in the belly and broad in the beam!"*

That "second act" of the feast, however, had yet to get underway. For this reason Agathon chose this interim when appetites for food and drink were satisfied and other appetites weren't yet gnawing at youthful lust to make his traditional and always brief appearance at this often-unruly celebration.

Announced by a blast of trumpets, the Royal Chariot, Karou frowning as always at the reins, drove slowly into the crowd of happy soldiers with the tall and smiling figure of Agathon aboard. At the sight of their chief, resplendent in a spotless white and gold robe, his circlet gleaming on his brow, the young men burst into roars of acclaim and applause, much of it produced by pounding their shields with their fists.

As arranged, Karou halted the chariot in the midst of the throng. The Hegemon acknowledged the plaudits by recognizing with a wave of his hand, or a salute, various troopers known to him by sight. At last Agathon had to hold up his hands in a plea for silence. The shouting gradually fell away until silence prevailed. Employing the urgent voice audible everywhere that he always employed when addressing the Array, Agathon began speaking to his men.

"It is my duty tonight," Agathon cried, "as well as my pleasure, to salute the steadfastness of the Arkadian warrior!"

At this the troopers burst into new cheers.

Agathon, silencing the cheering, continued.

"I know that many of you lads probably felt a bit of chagrin when your Hegemon appeared to be in danger from that Bem priest this afternoon."

The silence was thick in the crowd as the men of the Array anticipated a possible rebuke from their beloved commander. Agathon, however, knew the hearts of his men.

In the silence, he declared in his resonant voice, "But I tell you, lads, I never felt in danger for a moment for I knew that the men of the Array were with me!"

A new burst of cheering ensued.

Quickly, Agathon went on. "Your Hegemon also knew that the glittering presence of the invincible warriors of Arkadia had already paralyzed the hostility of the Bem and may it always be so!"

Explosive cheers.

Agathon again.

"As long as the Array stands Arkadia will stand!"

More explosive cheers.

"And so those comrades of the Array who are not with us tonight because they must stand guard in the Forbidden Zone deserve our special thanks as do all of you!"

Agathon let the exuberance continue for almost a minute as he smiled down on the young men who served the Hegemony, the young men who knew that their commander meant every word of praise he had bestowed on them, thus relieving them of the guilt they experienced when they had failed to strike down the crippled Bem at once this afternoon.

Agathon, however, had some more to say and held up his hand until the shouting subsided.

"And now, before I leave you to enjoy the festivities you have so much deserved from your grateful country, I want all of you to acknowledge my young son Milo, who stood with all of us this afternoon."

Agathon pointed to a cluster of seated figures at the rear of the throng: three young boys and the old man who was known to the soldiers as "the Keeper."

"Stand up, my son," shouted Agathon, "and show yourself to the men of Arkadia whose ranks you will soon enter."

The handsome yellow haired boy, abashed, slim, and dressed in a white tunic much like his father's, slowly got to his feet and was greeted by an ocean of applause.

The boy, Milo, smiled shyly and in a gesture habitual with him brushed the fine hair from his eyes. Another boy seated with him, dark and older was grinning with impish delight. Suddenly Milo lifted his hand to his brow in a salute to his father, the Hegemon, at which the cheering of the troopers reached a thunderous crescendo.

Seizing upon this fortuitous gesture of Milo's, *the boy obviously possessed a natural public presence,* thought his delighted father, as the perfect climax to his visit to his troops Agathon immediately ordered Karou to drive out of the crowd and back to the Royal Pavilion. There the Hegemon intended to seclude himself while the young men of the Array enjoyed strong drink and the lusty favors of women both pleasures ordinarily denied to them.

Flushed with pride at his father's public praise though he modestly tried not to show the joy that was in his heart Milo, who had already imbibed a sizeable and, of course, surreptitious goblet of unmixed wine, simply could not stop grinning at everyone—soldier or servant—who caught his eye, even the Old Stick, Megistes. Milo saw happily that everyone was smiling back at him, except Darden who had gone into one of his dim sulks because their father had failed to honor him as well as Milo. *But, by the Logos,* Milo groused to himself, *what had Darden done to deserve any honors before the Array? Nothing, that's what! The little purse-mouth was only good for one thing: kissing Megistes' wrinkly ass.*

Thinking of Megistes, Milo now openly regarded the old man: As usual the tutor had little to say in the way of praise for his student. Still, his occasional grim smile told Milo that the Old Stick was certainly proud of him tonight. So, tonight at least, Megistes really wasn't such an Old Stick.

It was Phylax, however, whose response to the Hegemon's commendation pleased Milo the most for Phylax overflowed with jokey delight at Milo's success: "Good job, *del*, you're sure to be named Anax now."

In all that crowd only Megistes knew that the word *del*, soldier's slang often used between Phylax and Milo to denote their close friendship, was in fact some kind of derivative from the lost language of the First Founders.

"I'm not Anax yet," Milo said in reply to Phylax's good wishes. In truth he was reluctant to anticipate an event that, after all, might not happen lest it offend Fate.

"Well, you'll be Anax in a couple of years," Phylax persisted, his grin now spreading even wider than Milo's own. "It has to be you, Milo. No worry about that. The Hegemon practically announced it tonight. And when it happens remember your friend Phylax, right? Hey, when you're Anax will I have to address you as Strategat?"

"Maybe," said Milo, replying in kind to the absurd question. "Or maybe I'll just make you kneel in my presence."

At once it came to Milo that Phylax was more his brother than broody Darden could ever be. This thought, he felt, needed to be uttered aloud. "Brothers, forever, Phy, right?"

"Brothers, forever," said Phylax abruptly serious. "And Milo, you did really well today. No joking. Really."

Milo went red in the face. That Phylax could approve of him so directly was almost as important to him as his father's approval. Still, he must avoid any semblance of boasting. Milo said, "I didn't do anything much, Phy, except stay at the Hegemon's side."

Phylax, still grave, said, "What else is an Anax supposed to do? It's his duty to be at the Hegemon's side. You did your job, *del*. Really."

Both boys went back to grinning at each other.

By now pairs of dancing girls, veiled and barefoot with bells attached to their ankles and wrists, had appeared. One girl in each pair would dance with sinuous grace while the other plucked the strings of a lyre. Other women, too, had begun making their way into the throng. These, their long hair loosed, were older and bolder than the more girlish dancers. The eyes of these women were ringed with kohl and their lips were colored in audacious shades of red. Most of them also wore heavy gold necklaces and armlets, and were garbed in sheer veil-gowns that left no doubt about the shape of the female body they covered. These heavily-scented carnal beauties now commenced drinking draughts of unmixed wine with the soldiers—wine from barrels that had somehow appeared immediately after the Hegemon's departure from the premises. Given the numbers of dancing girls, lyre-players, and wanton whores, soldiers who were not too drunk to do so soon began to find whatever kind of "action" they desired.

Clearly, Megistes realized, most of this "action" was of the kind that fascinated a gaping Phylax and Milo. Darden on the other hand seemed perhaps understandably in view of his youth aloof from and even bemused by the activities beginning to swirl around him. Interrupting the tutor's train of thought, Phylax suddenly begged permission to "go and watch the dancers". Megistes found himself considering the request, for Phylax though only sixteen looked older, was older in many ways both physically and mentally. Phylax was in fact on the brink of manhood. So, after a brief hesitation, Megistes nodded his permission. Upon this to Megistes' astonishment a whooping Phylax grasped fourteen-year-old Milo's arm and dragged the younger boy with him into the crowd.

"Not Milo!" Megistes called after them. But they didn't hear or more likely they feigned not hearing. Megistes could only hope that Milo would come to no harm. *No*, he told himself, *Phylax would see to his safety. Ah, well, no use worrying about it.*

The noise of the party, mostly music and shrill female laughter, was growing louder by the minute. It soon became more than Megistes could tolerate. *In any case, it was time to get Darden out of the melee lest he observe something he might find disturbing though in fact Darden seemed only bored by the spectacle.*

"Time for bed," said Megistes. "Let's go to our tent, lad."

"I'm not tired," said Darden petulantly.

"That's as may be, but I'm exhausted. Come."

Megistes led the boy out of the parade ground past tents from which were now emanating the lusty groans and cries of men and women at sexual play. The Sage and the boy also went past dimly-lit places where girlish dancers and soldiers in tight embrace slowly swayed against each other pelvis to pelvis.

Finally, Megistes extricated Darden, and himself from the over-heated atmosphere of the camp. In the welcome cool of the night Megistes and Darden could see across the river the smoldering pyres and torches of the Bem all reflected in the slow water. Darden spoke, "May we walk a while, Master? Along the river path?"

The night air was reviving Megistes. He decided he could postpone bed for a while for he could see that Darden, as usual more sensitive than was good for him, was still as troubled in his mind as he had been earlier during the Array's withdrawal to the Komai. Megistes had assured Darden then that they would resume their talk at the first opportunity. Despite the lateness of the hour Megistes reckoned that in Darden's mind the promised "first opportunity" had arrived. The aged tutor had long ago learned that if one wished to retain the respect of the young one had better keep one's promises to them however inconvenient. With a sigh, Megistes said, "Let's hear what's on your mind, Darden. Best to get it out."

Darden pointed to the fires across the river. "Those poor people," he said. "It isn't fair."

Megistes shivered in his worn robe not because of the evening's chill for it was still warm enough even for his creaky bones but because Darden had used the word "fair," a conception that like a parasite always found a home in the spongy mind of youth to whom utopian fantasy seemed the veriest truth easily obtained if only people would be "good." The aged tutor could almost predict the well-worn abstract path that Darden now would follow during their talk. Resigned to it, Megistes had to ask the required question: "What do you mean by fair, Darden?"

"People ought to be equal."

"I presume you mean to say that the Bem ought to be equal to the Arkadians."

"Yes. They should have as much as we have."

"It may surprise you, Darden, to hear that I agree with your idea as do most thinking folk in Arkadia."

Megistes smiled. The sensitive young were always astonished when he said that. The Hegemon's young son was no exception. Then Megistes sent up the intellectual balloon. "Why do you think the Bem don't have even as much as the poorest Arkadian herdsman has?"

Darden frowned. "Because we won't let them have anything. Because we look down on them. We call them barbos, and we say they stink."

"They do stink. Facts are facts and we must at least acknowledge that fact. People who don't bathe smell pretty bad after a while. And, if you've forgotten, let me remind you, they call us Arkies. They hate us, Darden. They want to kill us just because we are Arkadians. Their oracle tells them that their god demands the obliteration of Arkadia. You must admit few Arkadians hate them that much."

"Maybe. But if they hate us, it's because we stole their land. That's why Arkadia is so rich."

"If we are rich and that is a term that means different things to different people we owe it to the fact that, under the rule of the Logos, every Arkadian is free to follow his own path so long as he respects the Laws he helped to make. You might not grasp the full implications of this reality at your age, but freedom is what unleashed a flood of talents and energy in Arkadia. Freedom and the Logos that's what made Arkadia great, not stolen land."

Darden put on a stubborn face. "Even if what you say is true, Master, the Bem don't have either freedom or the Logos."

Megistes replied patiently.

"They could have both, Darden if they would but accept them. The Logos is for all, and with it comes guaranteed rights—that is freedom."

"What do you mean?"

Darden was frowning, a sign in him of skeptical confusion.

"I mean that the Bem could share in what we have in Arkadia. We could teach them how to feed their hungry, care for their sick, and embrace the rights that come with the Logos, all they need to do is stop trying to kill us. But they would rather hate us and let their people suffer."

Megistes paused to allow the boy to absorb these ideas if he could.

"You may not be aware of it, Darden," Megistes continued, "but your father has been trying for thirty years to convince the Bem that it's in their interest to make peace with us but to no avail. Well, you were there this afternoon; you saw that young Bem shaman who cursed your father. That's hatred, Darden. That's invariably the response we get."

They walked on in silence, Megistes letting Darden stew. When, after a while they came to a stone bench placed to overlook the placid Bradys they sat. Megistes had to admit that he was now too tired to continue either the talk or the walk. Darden, too, was showing fatigue though he tried to stifle his yawns for Darden was one of those who fought a nightly fight against sleep.

Megistes stared across the river at the Bem fires. He supposed they were funeral pyres judging by the odor of roasting meat faint but unmistakable. *Equality,* Megistes reflected scornfully. *Even if such a concept was achievable—as it was not—among men and women of good will, what could such an idea possibly mean to the Bem, a people who adored chaos, who believed their very existence depended on magical incantations?*

Megistes heard Darden speak again.

"If I were ever to become Hegemon I would help the Bem and I would find a way to make peace too. Somehow."

When Megistes did not respond the boy heaved a sigh that verged on a sob.

"But I will never be Hegemon, will I, Master?"

"Probably not. You must prepare yourself for that."

Another sigh-sob.

"I know it. I'll never be Anax either, will I?"

"No."

They sat together in the silent darkness both weary of talking, Megistes now longing for his bed. Suddenly his eyes caught the movement of three figures nearby. He immediately identified two of the figures as Phylax and a dancing girl. They were strolling and kissing as they did so. The third figure trailing behind Phylax and the girl he now recognized as Milo. The three went on oblivious of Megistes and Darden on the bench.

All at once Darden uttered a harsh whisper. "That Phylax is disgusting and Milo looks drunk."

He paused.

"Aren't you going to stop them, Master?"

"No. And you are to say nothing about this now or later. Do you understand?"

Megistes thought it very likely that Milo unused to unmixed wine was a bit tipsy and was trailing after his good *del*, Phylax, because he couldn't recall how to get back to his quarters. As for Phylax, that young man seemed to be experiencing with the girl-dancer the kind of rapture that could but more likely would not turn into an important event in his unfolding life. And so, it was an experience that Megistes refused to disrupt. At the proper time, if it presented itself, Megistes would have a word with both Phylax and Milo. Right now, however, it was long past his and Darden's bedtime. Accordingly, Megistes stood up.

"Let's go, Darden. Bedtime."

As they retraced their route slowly and in silence back towards the Komai, Megistes found himself musing on this talk with Darden. Of course he hadn't convinced the boy; he hadn't expected to do so. Long acquaintance with young idealists had taught Megistes that the best he might expect from Darden was that as the boy grew older and learned to view life with greater clarity he would recollect this talk with his old tutor and recognize the truth proffered to him on this cool night of the Passing.

Seraph lay prone upon a mound of sandy soil. From the top of this peculiarly elevated pile of dirt Seraph had a clear view over the mud wall of the Arkie camp. Though he did not know it the heap of earth he lay on was the remnant of a large latrine dug by the Arkies, and then, after much use, filled in again. Seraph, however, knew nothing of latrines. Nor was he disturbed by the lingering odors seeping from the pile for such smells were rampant among the Bem. He was used to them. For Seraph then, the mound was only a convenient location from which he could observe undetected the often-incomprehensible activities now unfolding before his good eye in the Arkie camp. Even from the modest height of this vantage point he could see down into most of the open parade ground where Arkie warriors were busily pleasing themselves with their repugnant females and their filthy drink, their "wine" as they called it.

Seraph had been occupying his spy-place for more than an hour though such an Arkie way of marking time was as foreign to him as the idea of a designated place for shitting and pissing, and so far to his astonishment he had escaped detection. In truth, his invasion of this so-called "Komai" of the Arkies had proven not at all as difficult as he had supposed for after fording the holy river on his stolen pony, while holding his stolen knife ready for use, Seraph had ridden with deliberate carelessness along the south bank teeming with Arkies.

Heedless of his wretched life after his humiliation at the hands of the Arkie Kapit, Seraph had been determined to display his defiance of the Arkie rule prohibiting Bem trespass on their stolen south bank. And so, as he had ridden on so incautiously he had expected to encounter an Arkie patrol at any moment, had expected guards to seize him and take off his ugly head with their gleaming metal swords. Seraph was prepared for that and prepared to use his flint knife to send at least one Arkie to eternal Chaos.

No sentinels or patrol had accosted him, however. Seraph had finally decided to attribute this temporary good fortune to an arrogant Arkie certainty that no mere barbo would dare to defy their rules. Or perhaps and this soon had seemed a likelier explanation, the Arkies did not know of the ford that Seraph had used to cross, and so they had seen no reason to set guards over it.

With his mood of furious daring beginning to be tinged with a dollop of scorn for the inattentive enemy, Seraph had kicked his pony on toward a glow readily visible in the night. Surely, Seraph thought, this was light from the torches and fires of the Arkie Komai. Though he had continued to make no attempt to hide from any sentries who might be about, he encountered no one.

After a time, with the glow ever-brightening in his single seeing eye and the sounds of Arkie music and laughter in his ears, Seraph had come upon the mound that unknown to him covered an abandoned latrine. Recognizing at once that this pile of sandy earth much like a small hill would afford him an excellent vantage-point from which to view the Arkies at play something he suddenly wanted very much to do and do without interference from any alert guard, he decided to climb the little hill.

With this in mind, Seraph had used his hands to lift his lame leg over the withers of the pony and slid to the ground. After tethering his mount to a nearby bush to crop the grass, Seraph, employing his flint blade to gain purchase on the easy slope of the dirt pile, hauled himself foot by foot to the summit of the hillock.

Below him the Arkie camp seemed to boil like a pot of stewed meat. *What was happening down there?* He felt dizzy with the effort to focus his eye on the variety of movements and foreign sounds that assaulted him. Only with the passage of several minutes had he begun to gain a general impression of what he was seeing below him: Fires were everywhere, and everywhere, too, were displays of Arkie wealth and power. At one point his eye had fixed on a series of sword contests between individual warriors. And then he had watched in amazement as other warriors, these mounted on their magnificent war-horses, hurled javelins at targets, one after the other with wonderful skill. Seraph could not help but admire these swordsmen and horsemen. No Bem warrior he realized with sinking heart could match such skill let alone such marvelous weapons. Seraph found himself wondering where these Arkies had come from. *How had such creatures perhaps more than men come to the land of the Bem? Had their sinister Logos-thing led them to this land that was not theirs in order to destroy the Bem? Were these Arkies even human? Or, since they had no souls, were they creatures of the sky?* All such questions always ended for Seraph in a storm of uncertainty. If any god knew the answers, which Seraph doubted, he refused to share his knowledge. As for the Bem shamans they really knew nothing whatever of the Arkies. Still they boasted of their magic powers which they surely did not possess claiming that their arts would someday bring down the "enemies of Dis."

Picturing the proud Arkie chieftain who had so easily shamed him that afternoon, Seraph suddenly understood that to bring down these Arkie tyrants it would be necessary first to know them. If he survived this night, admittedly an unlikely outcome, Seraph promised himself he would devote his strength to understanding the Arkie nature. *With understanding would come power over them.* Or so he hoped.

All at once Seraph's eye caught the abrupt appearance of Arkie females who soon thronged among the men. Brazen creatures with unfettered ankles, they went freely about. Such behavior was an arrogance that, despite his sympathy for the burdened women and girls of the Bem Colors, Seraph found himself unable to accept in reality. These female beings, lacking all modesty displayed their bodies indecently in the thin veils of their gowns in fabric so tenuous that the female shape, disgustingly blatant, showed plainly through in a manner as wicked as it was repellent. Moreover, these Arkie females not only flaunted the hair of their head in colors—gold, russet, blue, never seen among the Bem—but also paraded the secret fleece of the body for all to view as they pleased. They also freely offered their heavy breasts and painted mouths to any who drew near and they did this, not by the command of their husbands or their men as was the custom among the Bem, but at the whim of these females themselves! And yet Seraph felt his blood stir as he studied them even though his throat closed in revulsion at their confident assertiveness. It was as if these females claimed to have possession of their own bodies! *Indecent Arkie females! How he hated them as they opened the hidden gardens of their bodies to this man or that, as they chose! And yes, the wine they poured on breasts and belly for any man to drink—that wine drove them mad too!*

Nor could Seraph endure the shrieks that reached his ears when these mad females were mounted. Their cries, and sometimes laughter, rattled like stones in a gourd, or rose like the howling of a dire-cat on the prowl for a mate. No Bem woman would have dared such effrontery. Instead she would have humbly received whatever second or third warrior her lord bestowed on her. She would have accepted all with thanks even after taking blows for she would always be aware of her own native inferiority. These Arkie females, however, flung themselves about, cried out, and laughed, as they pleased. And the males who sank themselves into all this gleaming flesh, who seemed willing to enslave themselves to it, who laughed and cried with what looked like mad desire to hold these creatures against them, surely these were not warriors! Surely not!

It came to Seraph that perhaps the female beings he was seeing were demons, loosed from some demonic region of Creation to please the contorted desires of young Arkies at this time when their dark natures came to the fore and demanded satisfaction. *Yes,* thought Seraph, *that might explain the revolting spectacle. Or perhaps the Arkies lacking souls were depicting their true selves rampant in the scene below.*

And now Seraph noticed other women in his view as well. These were not as strident as the demonic ones though they too displayed their bodies in near-transparent veils and wore their hair loose. These, younger and slimmer than the demonic females, moved together, often in unison, as if impelled by the sounds that issued from reeds that some blew into or from the touch of clever fingers on stringed "instruments". Seraph supposed that these moving females were engaged in a sort of dancing though their motions were like no dance he had ever seen among the Bem. No, the "dance" of these creatures who were also indecently free of ankle fetters and constantly smiling as if offering themselves to the enraptured men who beheld them, bore no resemblance to the stamping thunder of a Bem warrior's dance.

As he continued to watch, Seraph began to sense in the sinuous bodies glistening in the torchlight something deeply baleful, something that was reaching out, seeking him, some force that meant to entwine him, to suck his spirit from him as perhaps the impious females below sucked dry the warrior essence of the Arkies who used their terrifying bodies. *Terrifying.* Yes, that was the feeling that was now overtaking Seraph. Terror. He had to get away from this fiery pit that boiled with the profane beauty of its demon-women.

All at once Seraph perceived that the demon-women were summoning him, for yes, yes, they were beautiful and yes he wanted them, though at the same time he wished just as much to destroy them, destroy all, everything in sight, Bem, Arkie and himself.

With his ears ringing with the urgent need to get away, Seraph began to drag himself back down the mound. He had to find his pony and then flee, as useless and ugly as he was, from the infamy he had just looked upon with horrific desire. Breathing hard from both fear (spiritual fear?) and from his exertions, Seraph reached the bottom of the dirt pile. He managed to force himself to a standing position. Suddenly, not fifty feet from where he stood, a torch appeared. Seraph, frozen in its glare, beheld an old Arkie man with a white beard, and clinging to the old man's arm, an Arkie boy, his eyes wide with fright. The old man began to call out wildly in a powerful voice that belied his apparent frailty.

"Guards! Guards! A barbo intruder here! Guards, come, help us, help! We have found a barbo intruder!"

Seraph, aware that his lame leg would make it impossible for him to escape clutched his knife against his chest and began to limp as best he could toward the old man and the frightened boy. Seraph thought *how much he would welcome the death that was surely only a minute or two away*—when some Arkie guard responded to the old man's call. *Still, he might be able to send a pair of Arkie oppressors to their doom while he yet lived.*

Megistes realized, as the barbo struggled toward him and Darden, that in truth they had little to fear from their would-be assailant for he recognized the fellow as the Bem apprentice shaman who had accosted Agathon near the end of the Passing ceremony earlier.

"I know who you are, Seraph," Megistes called in a now-calm voice to the ragged Bem priest. "I saw you at the Passing today and I reckon that you know that this boy with me is the Hegemon's son and I am the Logofant of Arkadia. Halt where you are and I will try to save your life."

Seraph halted.

"Yes, I am knowing you and the child," Seraph responded in stilted Arkadian but his voice big with the enormity of his loathing for all things Arkadian. "I do not wish to keep my life, old Arkie." With this he brandished his knife. "I wish to cut you neck, hey? Then boy's neck and then myself's neck."

Megistes felt the trembling hand of the stunned Darden grasp his.

"We are perfectly safe, Darden," he assured the lad. "We can easily avoid this crippled Bem until the guards come. Aye and here they are!"

Two dark figures both slim but one sturdier and taller than the other came into the light thus revealing themselves to Megistes' astonishment as a spear-carrying Phylax and an obviously-drunken Milo.

Phylax frowningly serious said, "We heard you call Master and ran to find you. In fact, we happened to be out looking for you. Lucky we found you when we did. *Hoo*, this barbo really stinks, doesn't he?"

Megistes said, "Good work, Phylax, and I thank you, but I don't think this fellow Seraph is a genuine threat to anyone but himself."

Phylax despite his youth already a formidable figure said, "That may be Master but he's in prohibited territory. As Rider cadets, Milo and I have to do our duty."

Megistes smiled over at Milo who seemed too befuddled by his first exposure to excessive wine drinking to do more than wobble and stare about him. Phylax spoke again.

"Master, regulations say we have to disarm this barbo first of all."

With this Phylax confidently advanced and pried the knife from the disfigured Bem's hand.

Near-helpless Seraph only glowered rigidly ahead as if awaiting the worst.

Megistes found himself wondering what had possessed this deformed young Bem to risk himself so stupidly as to trespass in Arkadia itself. *Was the fool seeking some sort of "glorious" death? Did he hate himself as well as Arkadians? Perhaps Bem hatred was so venomous that it poisoned its carrier as well as its object.*

Darden, his face white with shock, his piping boy-voice shrill, addressed himself to Phylax. "What will you do with him now?"

Phylax, determined to act as a cadet of a Rider regiment should, answered without taking his eyes off his captive.

"Regulations say I have to escort this barbo to the nearest guard house. They'll take it from there."

"No!" cried Darden. "They'll kill him for fun, Phylax. You know it!"

The older boy, whom Megistes could not help but admire for his sense of responsibility, flushed red with wrath.

"Listen here, you soft-boy, I've got to do my duty and it's a lie that troopers kill barbos for sport so shut up for once when you don't know what you're talking about!"

Darden appealed to Megistes.

"Look at the barbo, Master. All bent over. He can barely see. What harm can he do? Save him, Master! Please save him!"

Darden burst into tears then uttered a near-hysterical threat.

"I'll kill myself if you don't save him!"

In one respect, at least, Megistes found himself in agreement with the tenderhearted Darden. *Despite his malevolence, the disfigured Seraph was clearly incapable of doing much harm. Certainly he had violated the law but it was, after all, a law that ought not to apply to a disabled and perhaps crazed young Bem still a boy himself. Moreover,* Megistes reflected, *given his sympathetic nature Darden might actually destroy his young life in an explosion of grief for the suffering barbo or he might do something almost as terrible in Megistes' estimation: he might renounce all affection and respect for Megistes himself. And what, after all, was to be gained by allowing Phylax to do his duty? Besides, hadn't Agathon himself spoken however vaguely of recruiting this same Bem shaman to the ranks of the Logos? It occurred to Megistes that he might satisfy Phylax's sense of duty and at the same time soothe Darden's outrage simply by carrying out—here and now—Agathon's directive to spirit this Seraph away from the Bem. All he had to do was to order Phylax to seize the young Bem and turn him over to the guards to be held, not punished, in accordance with the Hegemon's wishes. Simple. Bring down two birds with one stone. On second thought, however, Megistes reckoned that capturing the Bem lad so openly would probably displease Agathon who wanted the matter handled with no obvious link to the Hegemony. Clearly then the best course at this moment was to get rid of the problem by sending this troublesome apprentice shaman back across the river to the Bem encampment. In any case it was growing late, near the mid-point of the night. Megistes wanted his bed, and wanted to keep Darden's esteem. Hence, he decided to employ his authority both as tutor and as Logofant to over-rule Phylax.*

"This barbo boy who certainly does stink as much as you say, Phylax, must have a pony tethered somewhere nearby. He could not have walked across the river. Take him to his animal, Phylax, and send him on his way. That is an order, lad, an order. I mean it. And, if it makes you feel better about this business you may give this fellow a stroke with your spear handle to remind him not to come back. I'll make it clear to anyone who asks that it was I who ordered you to do this."

Phylax did not protest.

"You always know best, Master." To the cowering Bem Phylax said: "Get going you." He laid a stroke of his spear on the back of the Bem's good leg.

Seraph showed no gratitude despite his amazement at having escaped death for a second time that day. Though his heart was pounding, he no longer feared for his life for he was certain that his Arkie escort would not dare to disobey the old bearded one. That was the way Arkies acted.

Seraph limped away in silence to find the place where he had left his pony. Behind him he heard the boy Arkie say to the old man: "Thank you, Master, thank you."

If the old man made any reply, Seraph could not hear it, but his throat was suddenly choked with a surge of renewed loathing. He could only hope that the day would come when he could repay that tearful Arkie boy, whose face was like a girl's, and the kindly old man as they deserved with a knife in the heart.

When Seraph and his big Arkie guard reached the place where the pony waited the guard said, "Mount up, barbo."

Without a word, Seraph struggled onto the pony's back.

His captor, this robust young Arkie called Phylax, said in a voice meant to be menacing: "You have twice offended your betters today, barbo. Once, by daring to accost our great and merciful Agathon, and again tonight by invading Arkadian space. A third try will prove fatal. I promise you."

Seraph felt a need to reply whatever the consequences.

"Offended betters have I, Arkie? No. I not see any Arkie better than my own self today only see Arkie thieves and they filthy females."

Ignoring the jibe, Phylax only said contemptuously, "Here this is yours."

Seraph took the knife from the Arkie's hand and immediately rode off into the river's low water. Phylax watched him go. *"Queer little barbo,"* he thought, *"not much fight in him."*

In truth Phylax felt somewhat disappointed that the barbo had just gone off accepting his luck as it came to him. Phylax had rather hoped that the barbo would attack him when he got his knife back and thus provide an honorable excuse to rid the world of one more accursed barbo terrorist. Still, Megistes and surely that weepy little soft-boy Darden would be happy to hear that the barbo had gotten off with no further damage to his misshapen body. "Good riddance to him, then," muttered Phylax to himself.

Phylax turned away intending first to put Milo to bed—and then to go back to the party. *Maybe he'd find that pretty little dancer again if she hadn't yet gone off with some older fellow.*

As a midnight moon nearly full rose over the Bemgrass Seraph rode on in silence. He let the pony take him where it would. As he rode he watched flashes of lightning play across the northern horizon too far away for its thunder to reach his ears. *What*, he wondered, *lay out there?* The Bemgrass, it was said, stretched to the northern sea—the "Onyx" as the Arkies called it—and to the vast mountains so far away that a man could spend his life trying to reach them. *But why not try?*

Seraph could no longer bear to live among the Bem. *So why not ride on forever?*

Suddenly Seraph felt an urge to do so.

Yes, why not lose himself in the boundless emptiness where, according to lore, even warrior hunting parties had left their bones to bleach in the immensity? And if fortune allowed might he not eventually find a way to carry out the resolve he'd made earlier: to learn the secrets of the Arkies and so gain power over them? Yes, he had to ride on in search of that knowing. Clearly, Seraph reflected, *the rush of events on this day of the Passing had altered something deep in him. Just what that something might be he could not say but he knew that he no longer possessed a home anywhere.*

This recognition filled Seraph with surprising exaltation. *He would ride, and ride again*, he told himself, *a wanderer forever on the endless grassland, until he somehow contrived to die or to glorify his twisted life.*

With this thought Seraph kicked his pony into a trot to begin the necessary journey.

Across the wild Bemgrass in a place still unknown to Seraph, a place of fire and shadows, the goddess Eris, the last of her kind, stirred.

II

JOURNEYS

FIVE

K ala Aristaia, the ravishingly lovely sixteen-year-old daughter
of Arkadia's wealthiest and most distinguished Megar family
the Aristids of Richland Hall, had never made a journey of
any kind until now. Though she knew several girls her age who had
traveled as far as The Mills at the confluence of the Tachys and the
River Bradys and a few others who had fared as far as Northfair
always with their parents none of those girls had ever laid eyes on
Ten Turrets which was not only the Capital of Arkadia and the very
center of Arkadian life but also Kala's current destination. *Besides,*
she reflected with an inward smile of satisfaction, *even if any of her*
girlfriends should ever have occasion to visit Ten Turrets it would
certainly not be for a "Ceremony of Betrothal" to the future Hegemon
of Arkadia. That enormous honor, Kala reminded herself happily,
belonged to her alone unless she somehow bungled the betrothal ritual
something she was determined not to do. So, unless this young heir to
the High Bench of Arkadia, this "Milo", whom of course she had not yet
met, turned out to be unreasonably ugly, or a conspicuous fool, or a
base vulgarian of some kind, Kala would become his "Intended Bride"
in two days' time.

Milo, at least judging by the miniature painting sent to her father
who had then presented it to Kala for approval, was definitely not ugly.
Nor did he seem an obvious fool or a bad sort of any kind. Retrieving
the neat little painting from her personal kit Kala examined it for
what seemed to her the thousandth time. As on all those previous
perusals the fortunate Milo with his loose mane of tousled blond hair,
his vivid eyes blue as Bradys' river stones and his shy smile seemed
altogether appealing to Kala. She could not imagine that his open
face quite handsome hid any mental flaws or character faults. No, in

Kala's mind Milo was burdened with only one slight deficiency as her "Intended Groom"—his age.

The young Milo, at fifteen, was almost a year younger than Kala a fact that she knew was of no consequence in a dynastic union such as hers was to be with the future Hegemon of Arkadia. But in her private mind Kala also longed for her marriage to be a "love match" and she could not help but worry that Milo's younger age might prove a serious handicap to developing that aspect of their relationship. After all, as Kala had often been told, girls as a rule matured earlier than boys. *Accordingly, she thought, Milo would be in certain important ways too young for her, a reality that the picture she was looking at seemed to confirm.*

Kala also recalled that when she had expressed to her mother her concern about the age aspect of her approaching Betrothal her mother had assured her that "boys who grow up in the shadow of the High Bench" did in fact reach maturity much faster than ordinary boys. "Besides," said Kala's mother, the still exquisite Lady Chryse, "when you and Milo actually wed, my darling, two years will have passed. By then both you and he will have formed a strong attachment to each other into which age will not enter. More important, both of you will then fully understand what it means to share both a dynastic marriage, as well as, I hope, a love match." Kala had been much assured by her magnificent mother's words although, truth be told, she was still uncertain about their full significance.

Thinking of her absent mother, Kala felt a pain much like a pang of hunger under her breast. *Oh, how much she missed her mother! Oh, how she wished that the Lady Chryse could be here with her in this grand coach as it rumbled on closer and closer to Ten Turrets with every minute that passed!*

But this wish, she reminded herself, was childish and she must purge all such juvenile emotions from her heart, for this journey to the Citadel of Arkadia was meant to be the start of her final passage into womanhood. Kala was expected to conduct herself, not only during this journey to Ten Turrets, but also during her subsequent two-year sojourn at her new home, with the independence, dignity, and grace possessed by all Megar women, but especially to be found in the women of the House of Aristid.

In recognition of this fact, Kala was traveling without her usual attendants in this enormous ceremonial coach that had been used by generations of Aristid men and women. The coach drawn by three pairs of "Arkadian Grays" bred only at Richland Hall was being driven by only one pair of experienced coachmen: Old Gregor and his half-Koinar son, Adon. Though, as the Heir's Betrothed-to-be and thus considered adult enough to make this trip virtually alone, Kala was grateful that her father had insisted that she not travel entirely by herself and had ordered her three older brothers to escort her coach until she was safely delivered to the Hegemon's residence at Ten Turrets. Kala had to admit, if only to herself, that the presence of her brothers in their Hilltopper Regiment regalia and riding on their warhorses ahead of the coach relieved her of any concern that some mad Bem terrorist might take it into his head to attack her vehicle on the road to Ten Turrets.

As her companion within the coach, custom dictated that she might have only one, Kala had received her mother's elderly Koinar maid, "Faithful Mina" as she was called at home. Mina was not much company on the road for she and Kala had little in common to talk about and Mina, as now, often dozed off waking only when a jolt of the coach shook her from sleep.

Although not acknowledged openly, Kala understood that Mina was really chosen to accompany her to Ten Turrets because many at Richland Hall regarded the old nurse as a wise woman. This reputation rested on the fact that, like most Koinars, Mina possessed an unquenchable thirst for learning. In pursuit of knowledge she had taught herself to read and had devoted herself over her many years of service with the Aristid family to imbibing a great many books resident in the library at Richland Hall. In this way Mina had developed a supple vocabulary as well as a nimbleness of mind that made her a valuable, if usually clandestine, counselor to her Lady Chryse and even to the Master of Richland Hall himself.

Inevitably, word of Mina's gifts became generally known. Though she insisted with becoming modesty that her learning was in no way extraordinary, her repute as a wise woman became so firmly established at Richland that many at the Hall made it a practice to seek her advice on a variety of public and private matters.

Thus Kala, on her way to the first important event in her life, felt confident that she could count on Mina not only to guard her from any untoward breaches of form but also to guide her gently through the brief but daunting ceremony awaiting her at Ten Turrets.

Kala looked again at Milo's picture. This time she studied and admired the anonymous artist's technique. In fact, Kala herself was more than adequate at chalk renderings though few knew it at home in Richland Hall and she intended to keep it that way when she arrived at Ten Turrets for her ability with her chalks was too precious and too personal to share or to discuss even with her mother or Mina.

Moreover, though she could not explain why exactly Kala sometimes found herself troubled about what her eye and hand caused the chalks to produce on the blank surface. *Best not to think too much of that,* she reflected, *best just to accept the gifts of her sometimes disturbing muse.*

On impulse Kala touched her lips to the little painting of Milo and returned it to her private kit. *I'm being childish,* she admonished herself, *childish to kiss a painting.* Irritated with herself for making such a silly gesture she turned her attention as she had so often on this journey to the scene passing outside the window of the carriage.

The day beyond the glass was bright with the benevolent sun of Arkadia, the sky a celestial tent of unmarred azure that stretched clear to the horizon where the golden grain fields of the gentle Katoran foothills melded into the endless grasslands. Far off in the yellow fields Kala could make out the speck-like figures of men and women wielding scythes while other specks bundled the decapitated stalks into sheaves and tossed them onto waiting wagons. *The harvest was well underway,* she thought. *And, oh how bountiful and glorious it was, this Arkadia!*

Mina, the wise woman and nurse detailed to watch over her young charge, lay asleep across from Kala on the cushioned bench provided for passengers. A sudden jolt wrenched Mina from a pleasant dream that seemed to have been about picking apples on the banks of a river—the Tachys?—where she had dwelt as a girl. *An odd dream,* Mina thought, *and a trifling one as well.* Still it was somehow quite agreeable, a dream she might like to resume. The persistent bumping and thumping of the carriage, however, *had they reached a bad stretch of road?,* made a return to her dream impossible. Through slitted eyes Mina let her gaze fall on Kala Aristaia, who was staring out the window opposite as if entranced by the scene that rolled past as the coach rolled forward. *How near perfect this girl is,* Mina mused, still feigning sleep lest her young mistress give her some task to perform when she would rather laze about on her comfortable bench.

Continuing to observe Kala Aristaia surreptitiously and feeling much like a dozing cat on a hearth, Mina fell to admiring her youthful charge in detail as she might admire a work of art, if she actually possessed a work of art. As usual when she contemplated Kala's loveliness Mina was drawn first to an appreciation of the girl's extraordinary crown of aureate curls which flowed like a molten stream over her shoulders to the small of her back. That splendid flood of gold complemented skin as pale as alabaster and as smooth as the creamiest silk. That resplendent flow also framed a face that, by its very oddity, banished all prevailing ideas of "prettiness" putting in its place an "other" beauty, exotic and novel, that belonged to Kala Aristaia alone.

At first glance, Mina knew, a casual and ignorant observer weaned on "prettiness" might even regard Kala's face as "flawed." After all, so this fool might think, the girl's nose was not of the popular "snub" variety; her lips were rose not red, and her lower lip was fuller than her upper one. That fool might also cluck over the fact that Kala's cheekbones were higher than the usual idea of "prettiness" allowed. As for Kala's eyes the fool would see at once that they deviated greatly from the ordinary for those eyes were not blue as one might expect in so pale a blonde girl nor were they shaped or spaced as "symmetry" dictated. They were instead, more slanted than they "ought" to be and spaced further apart than fashion required. Furthermore, those extraordinary eyes were of a mysterious hue that seemed to alter with the light that struck them. Set under lush black brows and surrounded with thick lashes equally black, the color of Kala's prodigious eyes appeared most often to hover in a range between umber and an emerald shot with specks of gold dust. And yet even the fool, probably to his own consternation, would be forced to confess from the evidence of his own vision that Kala Aristaia possessed a magnificent, if mysterious, beauty beyond compare and beyond explanation. As for the girl's body which Mina had had several occasions to observe in the bath prior to this journey to Ten Turrets, even the fool could only conclude that with its well-shaped breasts and narrow waist

Kala's body was already lovely though not quite fully formed, not quite "womanly".

Of course, Mina reflected with some amusement, Kala's bodily attractiveness was far from obvious to anyone at this moment given the sensible traveling costume in which Mina herself had dressed the girl that morning: a voluminous ankle-length skirt of plain brown wool and a loose long-sleeved jacket of tan cotton. *Time enough for Kala to don fine clothes when she was settled in and rested in her quarters at Ten Turrets,* thought Mina. Till then, plain brown would suffice. At least it didn't show the dust that got into the coach despite all efforts to keep it out. *In spite of her unflattering dress today,* Mina thought, *Kala's almost supernatural beauty shone forth like a little sun. And yet how placidly she bore the considerable weight of that loveliness of hers!*

In this as in many other ways, Mina reflected, Kala Aristaia differed greatly from her mother, Mina's own "Little Chryse" of years long past. That glorious girl had borne the burden of her own beauty so dark, where Kala's was so gold and white, with much fret and fear. Chryse, as Mina recalled, had lived most of her youth in terror that Fate would deprive her of her external grace if she ever left it unattended for an instant. That constantly worried young girl, whom Mina had privately called "Poor Chryse" back then, had since become "Lucky Chryse" in Mina's mind, for in one of Mina's favorite ironies that dark-haired fretful Chryse had grown into a lustrous woman no longer enslaved by the beauty that had tormented her youth but finally at liberty in body and soul to chart her own rewarding course in the world. Further, as if Destiny too loved irony, Chryse had become the mother of a beauty altogether different from herself not only physically but in spirit as well for Kala Aristaia, so like a goddess and so completely unlike her mother, never doubted her own attributes. Nor did she value them enough to fear their loss. Instead, Kala believed, as every superb creature does, that she was made as nature intended and that was sufficient attention to the subject.

Mina herself had already decided that for ordinary ducks like her and most others the presence of a Kala Aristaia in the pond amounted to a sort of proof that the ever-silent Creator occasionally fashioned a Kala in order to demonstrate what he could do for his favored children if so inclined. Or so Mina, the Wise Woman of Richland, preferred to believe for she stubbornly refused to accept what sometimes seemed obvious: that chance and bitter struggle ruled the world.

Oblivious to Mina's surreptitious scrutiny of her, Kala was still gazing dreamily out the coach window at a landscape which appeared to consist only of endless fields of ripe grain that fell toward the far off grasslands in steps like a Titan's stairway covered with saffron carpeting. From time to time Kala could still see even further off the harvesters at work on the yellow stairway. From this distance the workers looked like miniscule black crows pecking at the ground. How little this scene resembled her own home! The thought abruptly called forth a deluge of memories—images rather—of Richland the immense estate in the Katoran Hills that bordered the wild River Tachys and the serene forest streams that emptied into that river.

Kala's family, first among the Megars, had lived on their land since the very Founding of Arkadia. From childhood she had trod its thick forests and its groves of fruit trees—apples, peaches and pears mostly. She had watched the men at their furnaces and forges as they extracted the iron ore from the red earth that abounded in the Katoran meadows where sheep grazed unfazed despite the hammering at the nearby forges. Even as a child Kala had understood that it was this iron ore beaten into ingots that had brought such great wealth to the Aristids. A Rich Land, indeed!

And the Hall itself—Richland Hall—how she loved that ancient stone edifice! The Hall sprawled as if a wild growth itself though in fact its sprawl was the result of generations of rebuilding, adding on and tearing down, in the process so altering the shape and size of the Hall that no Aristid of Kala's generation could locate any remnant of the original stones. As boys Kala's three boisterous brothers had searched doggedly for those original stones but had finally admitted defeat at least to little sister Kala, if not to each other.

Kala had not searched for the lost parts of the hall. She was content with the existing dark rooms of her suite and with her sunlit studio where she drew her pictures. She was already missing all of it she realized. But most of all she was missing her mother so calm whatever happened, and her lofty father whom she loved dearly.

Like no other in the household, Kala thought with a smile, *she could see through her father's stern façade to the sweet papa he really was at least to Kala whom she had always sensed he cherished even more than her mother or even Richland Hall.* Such memories and images brought tears to Kala's eyes. She stifled them, however, for she knew well enough that she had no real cause to cry as if she were still a girl-child. No, her father had explained everything to her: He had arranged this betrothal at the urging of the great Hegemon Agathon himself who wished to unite the Aristids to his ruling dynasty. Kala's betrothal to Milo, her father had told her gently, was therefore a great dignity not only for her but for the family as well. It was also an opportunity for Kala to do honor to her mother and father, her brothers, and all the Aristids. So, no tears she admonished herself. Kala was about to enter into a Megar woman's full estate. In two years if all went well she would wed Milo. After that when Fate decreed she would become the Lady of the Hegemon Milo. Such was her duty. She would do it. And no tears.

All at once like the shifting of a scene in a theater the view beyond her window was transformed: Instead of the Titanic vistas of ripe grain Kala now saw that the coach was passing through a considerable village. Beyond the glass were clusters of cottages, muddy lanes, larger structures that might have been marketplaces or public buildings and people gathered along the road as her coach passed. Among these folks Kala noted burly straw-hatted men in muddy boots. All the men seemed to be burnt red from the sun. Also in the assemblage were scampering barefoot boys in knee britches and women and girls wearing plain dresses much like the one Kala herself was wearing.

All these people were smiling and waving their hands apparently in greeting as Kala's grand coach, moving slowly now—Gregor and Adon having reined in the horses to avoid collisions with excited pedestrians—proceeded along the main thoroughfare of the village. Clearly these folk knew that the gleaming coach was bearing "the Megar girl" to be betrothed to the son of their "Great Agathon" and they were welcoming her with open hearts.

Kala, touched that folk who had never laid eyes on her until now, should welcome her so warmly, fell to returning their greetings with dazzling smiles of her own and with graceful waves of her hand. Her response elicited a cheering that caused Kala to flush with pleasure.

How fine it was that the people, the "pegs and nails" that held together the structure that was Arkadia as her father used to say so often, wanted her!

Mina, no longer pretending to sleep, joined Kala at the window.

"They love you already," Mina said.

I hope so, thought Kala continuing to smile and wave. Aloud she replied to Mina, "I will love them, too."

Soon the coach rumbled through another even larger village. Here the cheering drowned out the thunder of the vehicle's passing. Mina had to shout to be heard over the tumult.

"We are nearing Ten Turrets, my darling! There it is, see?"

Mina was pointing to some sight beyond the window.

With her heart beating with a rapidity she'd never experienced before Kala peered in the direction the wise woman indicated. There, silhouetted at the apex of a flat-topped eminence appeared what Kala first took to be a gigantic building. Her immediate impression was of a blank surface that reared against the sky like a red cliff. As the coach came closer, however, she realized that the "cliff" was made of bricks—millions of them certainly—and was not part of an edifice but a section of the exterior wall of the fortress-capital of Arkadia.

Continuing to stare as the carriage went on Kala's amazement grew as she gradually realized that the actual height and thickness of the façade of aureate brick was more than her eye could measure accurately. Moreover, this gigantic surface slanted backward as it climbed toward an imposing round tower also built of aureate brick that crowned the summit of this part of the immense wall. *No doubt,* thought Kala, though she could not tell from her limited vantage-point, *an additional nine such towers were to be seen at other strategic places on the wall which she reckoned, must stretch for miles on every side. There had to be Ten Turrets in all, of course.*

How strange it seemed this fortress bigger than any man-made thing Kala had ever seen or dreamed of! How intimidating! Surely no army of Bem Colors let alone any terror-band could ever threaten much less conquer this Ten Turrets. Kala found herself shivering with apprehension at the prospect of her own imminent entry into this daunting seat of Arkadian power and glory.

At this moment the coachmen Gregor and Adon, apparently in response to a signal, reined up the horses, bringing their vehicle to an abrupt stop.

In the unwonted quiet Kala said: "What's happening?"

The thought crossed Kala's mind that the Hegemon might have changed his mind about her betrothal to his son. Perhaps he had ordered the coach to stop because he was going to send her back to Richland Hall. At this moment such an eventuality did not strike Kala as completely unwelcome.

Mina who had pulled open the window and struck her head outside to see what was going on now resumed her seat at Kala's side.

"It's a guard of honor sent to escort you to the Hegemon's Residence."

"A guard of honor? How am I supposed to behave before a crowd of soldiers?"

Mina smiled and patted Kala's hand.

"Don't worry. It's nothing outrageous just some Rider Cadets sent to greet you I suppose on behalf of Milo. Young fellows, they are. All you need do is smile and wave charmingly."

"Charmingly?"

"Just the way you've been doing it so far, darling. The boys will fall on their faces when you smile, I assure you."

Kala heard trumpets and the unmistakable thudding of hoof beats from outside. Without warning a dozen or so young men all mounted on white chargers appeared beyond the glass. All of them wore resplendent blue and white uniforms complete with shining helmets and ceremonial swords. Two of them were carrying trumpets. The others except for their leaders who were unencumbered were flaunting blue and white pennants apparently emblematic of their Rider Regiment the identity of which was unknown to Kala who had never cared a whit for military pomp of any sort. Kala was interested, however, in seeing how her three brothers, who were garbed in uniforms that differed from the blue and whites, were receiving the glittering newcomers for Kala was always fascinated by the behavior of males especially those who were not her brothers and who thus presented novel facets of masculine comportment to her eager eyes.

In the present instance which Kala was unobtrusively watching from her carriage it was obvious that her brothers and the cadet guards of honor none of whom seemed aware of Kala's observation of them knew one another already for, after exchanging salutations, her brothers and the leaders of the blue and whites immediately commenced the good natured chaffing and posturing that Kala recognized but did not understand as part of a masculine greeting ritual. Her brothers and the chiefs of the new boys loudly scoffed and boasted to one another all the while bumping horse to horse. The play reminded Kala of dogs sniffing one another under the tail: not charming but apparently necessary for a proper expression of good will.

There was one young man among the blue and whites, however, who struck Kala as rather more sensible than the others including her brothers. He was clearly the Commander of the blue and whites perhaps the Cadet Colonel himself. *And quite handsome too,* she thought, *with the kind of dark Koinar looks that she found most attractive and manly too, she could think of no other word. Here was a youth whom she might have considered more appropriate for her than young Milo.*

No sooner had this notion made its way into Kala's mind, however, than the young man in question seemed to realize with a visible blush that Kala and Mina were watching the rather juvenile horse-play outside their halted coach. Clearly abashed, the Cadet Colonel, for surely so fine a figure must hold at least that rank, called his Riders to order. He then looked at Kala full in the face and smiled.

Feeling her own face flood with warmth Kala turned away from the window. *What was she thinking in letting her attention dwell on anyone other than Milo however handsome that anyone might be? She was going to her betrothal! She must never forget that. She must be sure to maintain her dignity at all times from now on.*

Abruptly the coach lurched forward again. The trumpets sounded up ahead. Kala's guard of honor was now where it ought to be, in front. Kala took a deep breath and stole a glance at Mina. *Had the Wise Woman noticed her momentary lapse when the Cadet Colonel had smiled at her? It didn't seem likely for Mina was once again looking out the window watching where the coach was heading which was toward an enormous gate now opening ahead. Like a dragon's mouth,* thought Kala.

Passing through this portal the coach entered a kind of unlit tunnel that led through the fortress wall. And then, breaking from the tunnel, Kala found herself again in the glory of the sun and within the magnificent citadel of Ten Turrets. *My new home,* she thought, with a quiver of excitement.

Led by the honor guard of Cadets as well as her brothers all now stiff with dignity on their prancing steeds the coach bearing Kala Aristaia the chosen future bride of the probable next Hegemon of Arkadia proceeded at a stately pace along the broad central thoroughfare of Ten Turrets. This roadway, known as the "Dromon" was wide enough to accommodate side by side at least six vehicles as large as Kala's. It was used for ceremonial purposes such as this one known to the people as "The "Megar Girl's Arrival," as well as horse and chariot races. Thus the Dromon ran in a straight line from the East Gate through which Kala had entered to its terminus at the Hegemon's Residence where Kala's own journey was to end.

The seven-tiered Residence, Kala knew having seen pictures, was constructed of gleaming alabaster and red-veined black marble and was the tallest building not only in Ten Turrets but in all Arkadia as well. It was said that the summit of the Residence, a pyramid of cut porphyry, was visible from everywhere in Ten Turrets and could be seen for miles outside the fortress walls. Kala was eager to behold the famous edifice up close. Admittedly, however, she was much less eager to dwell within it.

Mindful that she must not gawk like a country girl Kala resisted the temptation to stare not just at the Residence but also at the temples and other grand structures which rose on both sides of the Dromon and which were among the glories of this citadel-city. Kala had, of course, heard much about these famous buildings that she had seen only in pictures. Reminding herself that she would have much time in the future to acquaint herself fully with Ten Turrets Kala now turned her attention to the throngs that lined the Dromon to shout their joy at her arrival. Instinct told Kala that these welcoming crowds wanted only to love her as she wished to love them in turn and that when she smiled and waved at them they felt a happiness which astonished her for she was only Kala Aristaia. Kala was glad to bestow her smiles and waves, however, even though her cheeks were beginning to ache from so much smiling and her wrists were growing numb with the incessant waving.

"Keep it up, Darling," Mina said. "We are almost there."

Kala obeyed.

Kala was starting to suspect what her chief duty would amount to as Milo's betrothed: to smile and wave unto perishing. At last, after what had come to seem an interminable smile-fest the coach passed through the main gate of the Hegemon's Residence and into an extensive courtyard in which fountains of silvery water played over flower gardens in bloom. Here the coach came to a final, and most welcome, stop.

Kala's eldest brother, Ruben, grim with self-importance dismounted and then opened the door to the coach. Kala appeared in the door with Mina hovering behind. A gasp rose from the various functionaries gathered in the garden-courtyard to receive the new arrival as they beheld the girl's beauty with their own eyes and realized that reports of her unusual loveliness were, if anything, understated and that drawings they had seen had failed completely to depict the real girl. Following their collective gasp at the sight of Kala at the door of the coach the greeters in the courtyard, women as well as men, broke into spontaneous applause as brother Ruben offered his arm to help Kala alight from the coach.

Kala's other brothers, silent Ibram and hulking Jost, respectively the middle and the youngest of the three, then helped Mina out of the carriage all the while stealing prideful glances at their little sister now on her way to becoming a great lady much to their never-to-be-admitted surprise.

No sooner did Kala's dainty feet touch the gravel of the gardens than she was surrounded by officials and wives of diverse rank all jostling to extend their best wishes to her. Kala, who had never seen these people before and knew nothing of their position or lack thereof in the hierarchy of the Hegemon's Household, relied on Mina who was well-acquainted with such protocol to guide her through the press that surrounded her. At Mina's prompting, therefore, Kala found herself accepting from a swarm of overdressed women and men a storm of bows and curtsies as well as an onslaught of perfumey kisses on her cheek. Kala even found herself extending her limp hand to be nuzzled by strange men who invariably mumbled words she could not hear as they bent over her numb fingers.

At one point in the flurry of welcomes Kala spied the handsome Cadet Colonel of her mounted escort standing easy and alone at the fringe of the well-wishers. He seemed to be regarding her with a smile of what might have been sympathy but which she rather thought betokened interest of an altogether different kind. As she more or less covertly returned his gaze she could not help but note how tall he was. Even though dismounted now, he still appeared to overtop everyone else like a tree among bushes. *Or a god*, she thought. Why, she suddenly realized, this self-assured fellow had to be more than a head taller than she was! Again Kala found herself flushing at such inappropriate fancies and she once again cautioned herself that she must guard her dignity scrupulously now that she was in Ten Turrets. Besides, it was surely insolence in this tall Koinar youth to look at her in his uncouth way. Accordingly, she turned her back to him and would have stamped her foot to indicate her vexation with him and with herself as well if the crowd around her had allowed her room to do so. Finally, it was finished.

The Chief Steward of the Household a man whose upright and confident bearing testified to his importance in the Residence hierarchy came forward together with an epicene under-steward and a red-faced maid, and smoothly separated Kala and Mina from the remnant of the welcoming celebrants. With Mina trotting behind them the Chief Steward and his assistants guided Kala to her quarters in the Residence. This turned out to be a suite of rooms much grander than any such apartment at Richland Hall. This was to be her home the Chief Steward explained until permanent quarters could be arranged for her. There were servants on call he assured her to provide whatever she wished. She or Mina had only to pull the indicated cord to summon them. Wishing her good fortune and happiness, the Chief Steward with his company withdrew.

Alone with Mina at last Kala in a fog of fatigue felt too tired even to listen to her Wise Woman's appraisal of the extremely long day just passed. Instead Kala found her bedroom which was as big as the reception hall at Richland and threw herself on the silk-canopied bed. Exhausted, she fell asleep at once.

In the late afternoon of the following day exactly as scheduled the Betrothal Ceremony took place in the Family Quarters of the Hegemon's Residence. Among the few invited guests was the Sage

Megistes, Logofant of Arkadia. As he watched the unfolding of this first meeting between the Megar girl, Kala Aristaia, and his own still quite young pupil, Milo Agathonson, Megistes reflected not for the first time on the simplicity of this traditional ceremony which was not in fact a true ceremony at all at least not in the ordinary sense.

First of all, unlike for example a Hegemonic wedding, or funeral, or the investiture of a new Anax, all of which were public events, the traditional betrothal "ceremony" was completely private. It always took place in the family quarters. Always present were, of course, the two young people themselves, the Hegemon and his family— in this case the "family" meant only Agathon and his younger son Darden as well as invited guests of the principals. Custom dictated that the parents of the girl in question were excluded from the meeting-ceremony in order, so it was said, that the girl might more quickly and easily understand and accept that her former life was over that she was now to take her place as an adult member of the Hegemonic family. However, lest the girl feel uncomfortably isolated as she undertook her new life she was always allowed to invite other members of her "old" family if she wished, as well as any friends she might wish to be present. With this in mind Megistes reckoned the Megar girl, Kala, had invited her brothers and an older woman who was said to be her counselor. This was a short guest-list to be sure. Still, Megistes reflected, the girl had apparently spent most of her life in relative isolation at her home at Richland and perhaps preferred sparse company. As for Milo, Megistes saw that the boy had invited his long-time *del*, Phylax, now at seventeen Cadet Commander of the White Angels Regiment of the Riders to which both young men belonged. A few other White Angels were also on hand.

Agathon's guests, in addition to Megistes himself, included such military and political luminaries as the Chiefs of the Riders and of the Phalanx and the leaders of the State Council including some outstanding Koinars. None of those Agathon had invited were known to Megistes, except by name and rank.

As for the "ceremony" itself it was to be carried out with the traditional simplicity. Basically it would consist of introducing the two principals to each other after which they would be seated together in order to "get to know each other" as the phrase went. They would then receive the congratulations of the invited. A brief period of music, dancing, and wine drinking would follow and the event would come to a close. The newly-betrothed couple was expected to participate in this celebratory climax after which they were to "part company" until brought together on a series of such scheduled occasions thereafter.

All in all Megistes considered the betrothal system well founded. It usually had the effect of impressing the boy and girl principals with the fact that they now had a duty to the Hegemony and to each other to keep the promises made at this private initiation into public life. At the same time the system wisely provided for a two-year wait from betrothal to wedding day, an interim during which either or both of the principals might withdraw from any pledges made. This provision, Megistes knew from old records, had come into play only twice and those instances had occurred more than two hundred years ago. In Megistes' view the system also had the advantage of allowing for the kindling of genuine love between the boy and girl while at the same time precluding the derangements so often occasioned by childish expectations of unrealistic attraction.

Although the fathers of the boy and girl anxious to ward off romance always chose the couple based on compatibility of class and interests foolish fancies did sometimes seize the couple, upsetting matters temporarily. Nevertheless, it was generally held that genuine love did blossom from time to time from the seeds planted at a Betrothal. In fact Megistes himself believed he had seen it happen between Agathon and his Lady Melissa, now long deceased, at their betrothal ceremony some forty years ago. Of course no one not even the Logofant of Arkadia could ever be sure how the subsequent marriage between Agathon and Melissa had actually developed. Their Betrothal, however, had seemed to foretell happiness. Megistes could only hope that Milo and the Megar girl would experience similar tender emotions at their first meeting which was only minutes away now.

Moments later when the ceremony got underway Megistes, still sharp-eyed despite his almost ninety years, observed with keen interest as the girl, Kala Aristaia, entering first, curtsied to Agathon and then nodded a smiling greeting to the gathered guests. *The girl was certainly a beauty,* thought Megistes. Indeed, she was superb, incomparable. In truth he could think of no adequate word to describe the effect she was having on the audience in the chamber. All eyes were fixed on her. And yet Megistes perceived nothing consciously seductive in her behavior. In fact, he could discern no artifice whatever in her demeanor for even though she wore one of the recently-fashionable gauzy gowns (this one creamy white) that revealed so much of the female body, young Kala seemed not the least bit coy or brazen about having her breasts (and other parts) displayed in this manner. Fashion, after all, had to be served Megistes reckoned and in his experience most women donned "the latest thing" without a blink of hesitation as long as it was "in style". In this respect, at least, Kala Aristaia marched in perfect step with her sisters.

All at once it came to Megistes that the girl's glorious beauty obvious to all, coupled with her high intelligence attested to by Agathon himself, could prove an overwhelming—even deadly— combination if, as Megistes suspected, her character also included more than a little innocence. This Kala Aristaia would bear some discreet scrutiny Megistes told himself lest she innocently put her foot wrong.

At this point Milo entered the chamber. His stark blue eyes and loose blond hair gave him at least in Megistes' view a rather hectic look as he bowed to his father and guests and then turned to Kala Aristaia whom he was seeing for the first time. The boy immediately blanched, seemingly stunned at this initial sight of his betrothed. Mouth slightly agape Milo hesitated for several long moments before recovering himself sufficiently to approach Kala and clasp her extended hands in his as custom required.

Following established procedure Agathon then rose and formally introduced the young couple to each other. They embraced and exchanged a chaste kiss. Agathon then presented them, still hand in hand, to the guests who applauded them enthusiastically. Milo and Kala sat together on a small sofa. Holding hands they fell to talking to each other (about what? Megistes wondered) and grinning gamely. It was clear at least to Megistes that both Milo and Kala for all their smiling and chatting were—understandably—more than a little uneasy with each other although Kala appeared less so than Milo who occasionally forgot to maintain a mask of happiness on his face and sometimes even hung his head as if unable to look into the eyes of his beautiful betrothed. Only when a guest approached to offer congratulations or rose to make a toast to the new couple did Milo manage to achieve the more or less happy expression expected of him.

Megistes attributed Milo's less than joyous manner to his lack of familiarity with the female sex. Besides, the old man mused, what young fellow would not feel at least a little intimidated by Kala Aristaia? After all, Megistes judged, she was not only dazzling, she also appeared to be considerably nearer to womanhood than Milo was to manhood. Still, Megistes saw nothing to worry about in Milo's diffidence with Kala; time and further acquaintance with her would eventually cure his shyness. Besides, the old sage felt sure that Kala also sensed Milo's perplexity and would soon find ways to alleviate it. Until then, however, Milo would just have to muddle through. The boy's difficulties were, after all, part of growing up, obstacles to be overcome on the road to adulthood. Megistes certainly did not intend to interfere in any way in Milo's budding love-life unless circumstances, which he could not now imagine, forced him to do so.

Later, when the musicians (harpers, pipers, flutists, and a lone drummer) struck up for the dancing, Megistes who cared little for dancing and even less for music watched with amusement as the White Angel Cadets as well as Kala Aristaia's trio of brothers raced to choose partners from among the daughters and the younger wives of the invited guests. Within moments, or so it seemed to Megistes, all the young folk present were twirling, whirling, and gyrating in what he regarded as one of the tribal rites necessary to youth. Even the betrothed couple had joined in, Kala managing to look cool and graceful despite Milo's stiff ineptitude at the art of dancing. Even Darden was dancing with a Household Officer's tolerant wife who seemed much amused by the boy's boldness in picking her as his partner.

As he continued to look on from his post at the far edge of the hilarity Megistes found himself reflecting on some of the fundamental differences between these privileged youngsters among whom he noted Megars, Riders, and even a Koinar lad or two and the more ordinary and far more numerous youth of Arkadia who worked the land, studied for the professions, and attended schools with their peers. These dancers before him, he mused, did not appear to deviate much from their generation's norms. If one did not know their rank one could easily mistake them for well-mannered and attractive ordinary juveniles, charming adolescents with an aura of innocence still clinging to them. These juveniles, however, had come to an early blossoming having been planted and then carefully cultivated in a garden replete with mature blooms and fertilized with the exercise of power, its joys and its demands. Hence, although young and probably somewhat innocent still, the dancers before him, Megistes knew, already understood the rules of their garden especially what was required of them, requirements of judgment that their co-evals would not face for years to come, if at all.

And so it was that the gorgeous Kala Aristaia though nominally only a sixteen-year-old girl already possessed what seemed remarkable maturity that would stand her in good stead for her future in the Hegemony unless she dragged too much residual innocence with her into her new life. Megistes abruptly abandoned further meditation along these lines when he realized that Phylax had not joined in the dancing. *Why not? Where had that young man, usually to be found in the front of all such activities taken himself?* Megistes soon located him.

Though turned out in his glittering dress uniform and looking darkly dashing as always Phylax nevertheless exuded at least to Megistes' practiced eye an uncharacteristically glum air today. Slouched against a convenient wall with a sour cast on his countenance the much-admired Colonel of Cadets seemed to have sunk into a profound sulk as his eyes tracked the whirling dancers around the room. *Why this sullen look? Had Phylax imbibed too much wine?* Then, tracing the trajectory of Phylax's sullen stare, Megistes understood: The young man was sick with desire for his *del's* betrothed, the forbidden Kala Aristaia. *This is bad,* thought Megistes *very bad.* Even worse, however, he soon realized, was the subtle way that beauteous Kala, graceful Kala, intelligent Kala—betrothed Kala—furtively returned quick glances to her lovesick admirer huddled against his wall. *Here was most certainly trouble,* Megistes thought. *Here was a trap that must never be sprung.* He resolved to have a serious talk with Phylax as soon as possible. More important still, he decided, he must arrange a private, discreet—but above all honest—audience with Kala Aristaia to discover what lay in her heart. Innocence? If so, he must find the means to drain that sweetness from her for such sweetness was poison in the hot-house world she had just entered. Bad, the old man reflected, bad all around unless stopped. And soon.

"Well, what did you think of the betrothal?"

"I thought it went quite well," Megistes said.

At Agathon's request Megistes had come to the Hegemon's private quarters for a late night cup of wine and some talk. Although they were alone and Agathon, in dressing gown and sandals, was trying to seem at ease, Megistes sensed some agitation under the Hegemon's apparent calm.

"And the girl?" said Agathon. "What was your impression of her?"

"Kala?"

"Of course, Kala, who else would I ask about?"

The Hegemon let a rare frown of irritability cross his face.

Certainly something is disturbing him, Megistes thought. *Had Agathon perhaps also detected the glances passing between the girl and Phylax?* Aloud Megistes said: "Kala is a magnificent beauty."

"And intelligent too? I want your opinion."

"Only time will tell, but she certainly seems intelligent."

"I wish she hadn't worn that dress," groused Agathon.

"Why? All the ladies were wearing that kind of dress," Megistes pointed out. "It's the fashion, my friend. If Kala had not worn such a dress the ladies of your Household would be criticizing her now as dowdy, too rustic, not sophisticated enough for the Hegemon's Household."

"I suppose so, but I just can't get accustomed to girls parading around the Residence showing off their breasts so blatantly."

Megistes smiled into his cup.

"Get used to it my dear Agathon. Even the Hegemon can't dictate the fashions."

Was this what was roiling him, Kala's dress? No. Too trivial. But Agathon seemed unable to let it go.

"The girl looks older than sixteen. She looks as if she's already prepared for the marriage bed."

Another Hegemonic frown.

Megistes wondered if he should make an allusion here to the admittedly very tentative show of attraction between Kala and Phylax. He thought it better to say nothing yet however at least until he'd had a chance to sound out the girl and Phylax. To Agathon he said, "I agree that Kala appears to be physically advanced my friend but I fear she may be much less advanced in other ways."

"What do you mean?"

Agathon frowned suspiciously?

Megistes shrugged and returned a bland reply lest he inadvertently and maybe unjustly feed any ill will that Agathon might be starting to harbor against the girl.

"To answer your question, my friend, I meant only that Kala may still have much to learn about what is now expected of her."

"I see."

A pause.

"I wasn't very happy with Milo's behavior either today. The boy looked awkward, very shy"

"He'll get over it. Give him time."

"There's only so much time, Megistes. I have to name an Anax soon. After today I worry."

"That he's shy with Kala Aristaia? Nature will cure that, don't worry."

Agathon took a deep breath. "Is Milo up to it? Not just the girl but all that's ahead of him. Can he handle all that's coming to him? That's my worry."

"You have to trust in the blood."

"I suppose," Agathon sighed. "Still, I feel there's something not quite right with Milo. In this past year he seems to have changed. He doesn't seem to be the same enthusiastic boy he was at last year's Passing of the Bem. I had expected that as he grew older he'd become more capable, more sure of himself. But it seems to me now that last year, at fourteen, Milo exhibited more fitness for his future role than he does now at fifteen. Something's changed in him. During this year's Passing he seemed to me to have lost his—I don't know—his exuberance perhaps. I can't put my finger on it but it bothers me." The Hegemon gave another puzzled sigh then added: "Well Milo had better be up to the tasks ahead of him. We have no other for the job."

"There's Darden," Megistes said with a brief sardonic smile.

"Out of the question, as you well know."

The two men fell silent each sipping his wine, each wrapped in his own thoughts.

Finally Agathon broke the silence.

"By the way, Megistes, speaking of this last Passing reminds me to ask if your Pious Koinar agents ever made any progress in finding that Bem priestling—what was his name?"

"Seraph," said Megistes. "I'm sorry that I haven't reported on this before but there's been nothing to tell. The fellow appears to have vanished. My people say he hasn't been seen or heard of for more than a year. He never returned to the Bem camp after that incident when he cursed you. My fellows are still on the lookout for him, of course, if he should show up again but it's my opinion that he hobbled off into the Bemgrass that night and got himself eaten by the dire cats."

"Too bad," said Agathon. "I hoped he might be the one Bem we might bring to see the truth. Now we'll never know."

And thanks be to the Fates for that Megistes told himself for he believed that Seraph would have proved himself more a wolf cub than a converted lamb had he been taken into the bosom of the Hegemony.

Six

S lumped over his pony's drooping neck Seraph the Lame allowed the long-suffering animal to carry him where it would through the dark hours on the Bemgrass. Only with the coming of dawn would Seraph the Lame interrupt his aimless nightly journeying in order to conceal himself and his precious pony during the dangerous daylight hours until the fall of darkness summoned him once again to resume his nocturnal pilgrimage. How many nights had Seraph the Lame spent wandering as now over this wild emptiness? Five hundred? A thousand? Was he condemned to go on forever like this, a near delirious figure mounted on a beast so used up that his ribs showed and his shaggy head hung low as he plodded dumbly onward? How many more nights like this one still lay ahead of him dark hours of directionless rambling without design or system? Was he now only a derelict doomed to perish out here his bones fit only to nourish the wilderness? Yet he persisted. For what purpose? That he no longer knew. And yet he persisted for some residual knowledge clung to his mind like a dusty memory of a once-glimpsed face which had faded beyond recognition. Still it told him against all reason that there was some "thing" out here in this everlasting expanse of grass that he had to find. What it might be, however, or where he might discover it that he knew not. And so he roamed the night a pilgrim after "Something" that was also "Nothing."

All at once the night was filled with the yowling of the great dire-cats causing Seraph's pony in spite of his exhaustion to shy and whinny an expression of his instinctive equine terror of the cats. Unlike his steed, however, Seraph had learned not to dread the packs of dire-cats that hunted the Bemgrass every night. He had gotten accustomed to their appalling roars and howls in the darkness as they ran down the terrified deer and lost wild-ox calves that were their preferred meat and then in a snarling heap of bloody maws and claws fought each other to gorge on the still-living flesh of their prey. Every night, as now, Seraph heard the packs of hunting cats all around him as they went about their business of pursuit, kill, and devour until at dawn the satiated cats, having left no scraps behind, invariably withdrew like Seraph himself to rest during the daylight and to wait for the next night's chase after prey. Even after so much experience of their hunting habits Seraph would still find himself wondering why the dire-cats did not seem interested in making a meal of him and his pony for these creatures possessed of such keen senses must surely have become quickly aware of him as soon as he began dragging himself through the nights. Yet, from the beginning, they had ignored him and the pony. Even when, from time to time, Seraph would come upon several pairs of yellow eyes gleaming at him in the dark, they always turned away again—so far at least.

Puzzled by the cats' behavior toward him and his pony Seraph finally had concluded that the great beasts were put off perhaps even disgusted by his putrid bodily scent an odor that even Seraph himself thought repellent. Perhaps his appearance also inhibited their predatory instincts for he realized that after so long adrift in the emptiness he resembled nothing that the cats could welcome as prey. And even less, he surmised, did he look like anything human. His hair had grown into a shaggy tangle of curls, filthy with sweat and dirt. He was naked except for the remaining shreds of his shaman's robe which he had fixed around his waist by means of a cincture of woven grass. The bones of his starved body were visible under the hanging folds of his empty skin. Only one aspect of his being had remained mostly unchanged: his mutilated face. Because of the scars that disfigured his jaw, cheeks, and throat only a few wisps of beard had sprouted there and so he would still be recognizable by any Bem at least as the fugitive shaman apprentice who had fled from his people and their Dis. He was still, therefore, Seraph the Lame. It suddenly occurred to him that perhaps he had run to the Bemgrass in order to rid himself somehow of Seraph the Lame. If so he had not yet succeeded in doing so. Maybe only death could release him from that burden and that eventuality could not be far off. And yet he persisted.

At this moment he became aware that a profound silence had descended over the Bemgrass a sign that the dire-cats in anticipation of the dawn had retreated into the thickest growth to spend the daylight hours. Accordingly Seraph, emulating the cats, began to search in what was now turning into the first gray light of day for a suitable place in which to hide himself and his pony until nightfall made it once again safe to resume his wandering existence.

The threat that made it necessary for Seraph to conceal himself by day came from the Bem hunting parties he so often heard yipping and howling under the sun as they pursued the wild oxen that were their favorite prey for, in addition to their meat, the ferocious wild ox furnished the hunters with sport, hides, bones, and even their sinew all useful to the Bem. Seraph knew that these Bem hunters and even the scattered shepherds guarding their flocks of sheep and goats were his deadly enemies, much to be feared, not because they would kill him a fate he might welcome by now but because, if they found him, they would without hesitation haul him back to his former master, Darst, who would certainly devise such "chastisements" for him as would make death even more desirable than one of those yellow-haired harlots that Seraph had observed at the Arkie camp after the Passing—how long ago now?

As the new day bloomed ever nearer to full light, Seraph feeling pressed for time located a thicket of low bushes that, while not ideal, would have to do. Quickly he dismounted and let the pony drink from a nearby puddle of water. These small pools of muddy water usually no more than an inch or two "deep" were apparently formed naturally and could usually be found as this one was near the copses of bushes that dotted the grasslands here and there. Though unpalatable the puddle-water was drinkable, at least Seraph and his pony thought so. Moving as fast as his twisted leg allowed Seraph hobbled the pony to one of "his" bushes and then crawled on his belly into the thicket.

Breathing deeply at last within the uncertain safety of the bushes Seraph, visited again by the demon of intractable hunger, spotted a small snake coiled only inches from his face. Instantly he seized the reptile and killed it by biting through its head. He gulped it down, head and all, an offering to the famished demon in his gut. The demon, however, cried for more but there was no more.

Deep in his thicket with the newly-risen sun aflame in a cloudless sky and the long-suffering but astonishingly hardy pony nearby cropping whatever green it could locate in the mostly desiccated grass Seraph now sought sleep despite the hunger still gnawing in his guts. But sleep, as usual, would not come in spite of or maybe because of the insuperable fatigue that continually seethed in his body and mind.

Seraph had resigned himself to the likelihood that he would never again achieve genuine sleep but only a fugue state in which faces and forms at once familiar and foreign hung in front of his single fossil eye to mix doubtful memory with the certain recollection of past terrors. *Who was this woman he beheld so often when trying to sleep? Who was she whose never-ending rage moved her to smash a boy's face repeatedly with a rock despite his screams of pain which matched her own screams of fury? Who was this boy he saw so often—this lame child of no use to anyone—who fell blind and begging for mercy while the rock was pulverizing his face?*

Seraph, dreaming, reliving memory, knew them both, did he not? Or was it delusion, this scene? A vision brought on by unremitting hunger and a starved brain? No, no, he knew those faces. His fossil eye had seen all of it, recorded all of it. The woman had she not been the one he longed to call "mother" then? The boy was he not his own child-self destroyed on the Bemgrass by the one he had wished only to love? Had she not embraced him from time to time? No, never had she embraced him, nor kissed him either except for the swift kiss of her leather strap on his shrunken boy-body when his shortened leg caused him to fall behind the cart. Her voice surely she had whispered sweetly to him some time? No. Never. She had no voice except when screaming her rage as she smashed his face with her rock. With that ruin accomplished had she not abandoned that boy on the Bemgrass for the dire-cats to feed on? Delusion? Any of it? No, for had he not wakened alone, blind, with the blood dried on his ruined face? Oh, let it not be so. But it was so. The boy knew it at once. Or was that act of murder an act of love? Oh, let it be so. But it was not so. The boy had known it. And now the survivor Seraph in a demi-dream in a Bemgrass thicket with his pony, Seraph the fugitive, he knew it too though he must have always known it in the caves of his wretched mind. Murder-love?

A throw-away Bem child, Seraph had wished then to perish into the peace, if it existed, of the dead. He had not perished then, however, and now again a throw-away but by his own choice, Seraph discovered that he did not wish to perish after all. Instead he longed to avenge his shattered face and wasted body. No mere wish that, but a desire fierce as the hunger throbbing in his belly.

Slowly, minute by minute, as the day melted into sheltering night he emerged from the phantom realm of delusion and memory where more and more often his wounded spirit rambled even as his weakening body persisted on the Bemgrass in search of—what?

Awake, or mostly so, Seraph lay still after his failed search for true sleep. He was waiting for the dusk to deepen enough to permit him to return to his pilgrimage. As he waited for the night a new flash of memories showed Seraph a series of hitherto unknown pictures. First he beheld a man and woman: both surely Koinars. Had he ever known them? He thought so. Yes, the conviction seized him that in fact he had killed both of them. At that instant, however, he could bear no more of recollection. Better to defend himself by resuming his meandering journey. With the advent of the dark, therefore, Seraph struggled again onto the back of his patient mount and rode once more into the deep Bemgrass.

Alone in his private quarters after returning from another wearisome reception for him and Kala Aristaia the third such since their betrothal, Milo lit a lamp and drew the heavy drapes over the window that looked out over the busy Dromon below. Cut off from the world outside, Milo stripped off his Cadet uniform whose stark white and blue prissiness he was beginning to detest and flung himself naked on his bed. Now he could rest and unbend and think things through, or try to anyway. And maybe later he might play again with the Eye of Isis. Perhaps with the help of the Eye he might be able to stave off a new bout of the "Dims" for he could sense a "darkening" coming on.

In the meantime Milo found it soothing to stare up at the ceiling where streams of blackness, shadows cast upward by the lamp, wavered, melded, and broke apart again in patterns that created a murky kaleidoscope in which swam pictures recalled from the hours just passed.

Milo saw the girl, now his Betrothed, wearing another gown of white. She had been as beautiful tonight as she had been three weeks ago at their stupid Betrothal but she also had been more intimidating yet sweet as well trying to please him though she knew not how to please him and so infuriated him instead for nothing could please him anymore except the Eye of Isis his beloved "Treasure". Yes, there lay his pleasure now. Milo saw again his father's painful smile as he, Milo the Heir, had danced woodenly with his Betrothed and laughed stiffly at the good-natured jibes of his cadet-mates. Only Phylax had refrained from the joking choosing instead to glower at him. *Probably ashamed of me*, thought Milo.

Milo didn't wonder that his father was disappointed in him for he had fared no better this evening than he had at the Betrothal itself. He couldn't even unsnarl his tongue to speak to his own Betrothed! He possessed no wit or courage. No wonder no one liked him. Of course he knew that these were small things but he also knew better than anyone else that they were also just the tip of the skunk's lifted tail.

Alone in his chambers Milo was well acquainted with the whole skunk. He knew that his shyness was really cowardice, his clumsiness really dullness of mind. He even lacked what Megistes called "first principles." Milo didn't genuinely believe in anything. Not even the Logos. He knew better than everyone else that he was completely unworthy to be Anax. Much less was he worthy to be Hegemon. This was his secret heart—his true heart.

Milo fervently wished that his betrothal had never taken place. Even more fervently he hoped that the wedding would not happen. He didn't deserve that lovely girl as much as he covertly desired her. She was a companion fit for a Hegemon but Milo saw clearly that he was not fit for her. *The Hegemon Milo Agathonson? Absurd.*

Yet it was his Destiny, inescapable: Milo was to be the next Anax and then Hegemon of Arkadia. He did not dare to disgrace his father. He had to accept with agonizing pretense all that was still to come: the wedding, the advance to Anax, the inevitable elevation to the High Bench where his failings would surely bring harm to many of the innocent. He had to go through with all of it for he had no stomach to kill himself an act that would not only disgrace him but also his father, the Hegemony, and all of Arkadia.

Milo was trapped. He had to proceed according to custom. It would hurt too many people not to do so and Milo was discovering just how much he hated to hurt anyone. He wanted everyone to like him. A childish desire, he admitted, but it was the most genuine emotion besides self-loathing that he was capable of feeling. Milo suddenly realized that despite his naked state he was sweating lavishly and his gut was going into spasm. Was he about to suffer an attack of the Dims? *Relief,* he thought. *He needed relief.*

Milo went to his private chest, unlocked it, and opened it. The milky globe, big enough that it took two hands to hold it securely, reposed in its nest of black velvet. "My sweet Eye of Isis", Milo whispered to himself, "My own Beloved Treasure, my Marvel."

Milo lifted the nearly weightless globe filled with swirls of pale smoke and at once experienced the familiar thrill of well-being that the Eye occasioned in him. "My Treasure," he whispered again.

Willing the ecstasy to swell within him, Milo thought, *"Come to me."*

The response—the mysterious response—was immediate.

"My Treasure," he murmured.

Milo could not deny the enormous good the Eye had already done him especially in holding off the Dims. Nor, as he looked back over the long year since he had discovered the Eye, could he doubt that it was Fate that had arranged the seemingly random events that had led him to his darling treasure. That skein of inevitabilities had begun when Phylax, to celebrate his then recent promotion to Colonel of Cadets, had embarked on one of his typically daring escapades and had insisted that Milo, share the adventure with him.

Accordingly, Phylax and Milo, disguised as young members of the so-called Pious Koinar Sect had set out without leave and against all Regimental Regulations for a "wild weekend" in Northfair.

"A last lark," Phylax had called it, "before we grow decrepit with responsibility, right?"

Not having visited the notorious port before and so unfamiliar with its heralded, though illicit, delights Phylax and Milo had rambled through the city with no certain objective in mind except to enjoy whatever this exotic enclave within Arkadian territory offered them. For two days, sleepless most of the time, the boys had wandered the waterfront market where they goggled at the outlandishly-garbed merchants and their alien goods from across the Onyx Sea and stared in awe at the great ships, the first they had ever seen, at anchor in the harbor.

Intent on pleasure the young "Koinars" freely imbibed the strong drink of Northfair imported from lands across the salt water. They also spent two long nights as patrons of several famous "Slave Brothels" so clandestinely celebrated among Arkadian youth. In one of these a young woman with a black skin, a phenomenon neither of the boys had encountered before, had relieved Milo of the intolerable burden of his virginity, a burden that seventeen-year-old Phylax had long ago disposed of for himself back in Arkadia. In the end, near exhaustion from their exertions, the stripling adventurers who had now begun to regard the city as more grimly sleazy than wickedly exciting agreed that the time had come to head home.

Before leaving, however, Milo had visited one of the port's ubiquitous "magic stalls" while Phylax went to retrieve their horses from the inn where they had been stabled. Milo's object in entering the magic stall was to purchase a souvenir of his sojourn in Northfair.

The shop had smelled powerfully of some sort of incense and was empty except for a gnome-like being who identified himself in a heavy whisper as "wizard and purveyor of the extraordinary".

Looking around at the jumble of shabby merchandise, the gnome at his side, Milo felt himself drawn to a small chest of highly varnished dark wood decorated with incised whorls and circles.

"What's in that box?"

The gnome had rubbed his hands together and smiled revealing teeth black with decay, and hissed a reply. "Ah, young master, it seems she has intrigued you."

"Who has?"

The gnome bowed.

"Isis. She whom I serve. She put it in your mind to inquire. The receptacle contains her most powerful talisman. The Eye."

Milo's curiosity now aroused said, "Show me."

Reverently the gnome laid the box on a nearby table.

"Before I open it, young master, I must first warn you that the Eye of Isis sees into secret places in order to satisfy hidden hungers. Isis is merciless in this aspect."

Milo, impatient with the gnome's sham pose, said, "Just open it."

The proprietor/wizard did so.

Inside, protected by a nest of black velvet, lay a large ball apparently made of milky white glass. Intrigued, Milo reached to pick it up but the gnome halted him with an abrupt grip of iron on his wrist.

"No, no. You must not touch it. Not yet. The Eye has not yet chosen you."

Milo grinned.

"The Eye chooses me, eh? That's how it works?"

"Precisely."

"How will I know if and when it chooses me?"

"You will know as I will also young master."

"So now what?"

"Look into the glass. Look hard but do not touch the Eye."

Milo had bent over till his gaze was only inches from the white glass. He tried to focus all his attention on the globe. After a brief period a minute perhaps no more the white blankness slowly thinned, then faded completely leaving only a flawless ball of transparent glass. *Remarkable, t*hought Milo, transfixed. But the globe was not yet done with displaying its remarkable qualities for a thick vapor—fog?—smoke?—now flowed into it from what source Milo could not tell. The smoke for that was how Milo saw it swirled hypnotically within the glass. He had found himself yearning to own this Eye of Isis, even if as he suspected its "magic" was more mischief than marvel. *How Phy would puzzle over this thing!*

"I want this thing," said Milo. "How much?"

"Good, young master, for it appears the Eye wants you as well. Price is of no consequence. Take it into your hands now and look deep and you will see the true power of Isis."

Though skeptical Milo had done what the gnome commanded.

As he held the globe warm as flesh in his palms, it seemed to have no weight at all, the smoke swirled away as if blown on a wind. To Milo's amazement the globe now contained in miniature a simulacrum of the black-skinned woman with whom he had spent the previous night. The figure naked within the glass was moving about, smiling, combing her hair, as if a projection of the real woman going about her business at this moment wherever she might be located and certainly unaware of Milo's lascivious eyes upon her. *Perhaps,* thought Milo his body stirring with desire as he gazed and remembered his excitement of the night before with this black beauty, *the gnome had spoken the truth when he warned that the Eye of Isis could see into secret places and satisfy hidden hungers. But was such a thing possible? No, of course not. It had to be a trick or some kind of spell although it was surely impossible for the gnome to know about the beautiful black-skinned harlot much less form a moving miniature image of her. Impossible, yet there she was within the glass globe.*

Whatever the truth about the Eye of Isis Milo knew he had to possess it for even if it was some kind of trickery it made him feel good, relaxed, but energetic, just to hold it in his hands as now. Reluctantly Milo replaced it in its velvet nest. Instantly it returned to its white opacity.

"I want to buy it," Milo had croaked. He was yearning to hold the thing again. "How does it work?"

The gnome only shrugged. "I don't really know, young fella," he said jauntily no longer pretending to be any form of wizard but now reverting to his genuine merchant-self. "I can't see into the thing. Only those chosen by the Eye get to see what Isis reveals or so I hear."

Milo remained skeptical. "Do you mean to say you couldn't see the woman in the globe?"

"Exactly right."

The gnome showed his rotting teeth in a sardonic grin.

"Only a few get that privilege, fella, and a lot of them end up not liking what they see after a while and they return the thing to me. I take it back for a modest fee, of course. It's yours, if you want it, though. Do you still want it?"

"It just seems too good to be true."

Unexpectedly the gnome clapped Milo on the back as if they were *dels*.

"Listen, young fella. I been over the Onyx Sea as far as the Desert Kingdoms and back and there's one thing I learned: the world's full of marvels and this here Eye of Isis is one of 'em. Even the Priests of the Sand can't or won't explain it. What do you say? Deal?"

Milo hesitated for, as much as he wanted the thing, he didn't want to be gulled either.

"I only wish I had a better idea how it works."

"Listen," said the gnome apparently growing a mite impatient with his customer, "when you get right down to it the Eye shows you what you want to see, right? You think of it. Isis shows it to you in her Eye. Anything you want to see. Even your girlfriend's twat, right?" He grinned.

In the end Milo offered to buy the Eye for sixty Certies all he had left from his "wild weekend" but a considerable sum for a magic trick or whatever it was. He also had to add his silver inlaid dagger to the offer before the gnome would part with his "Eye of Isis".

Though tempted more than once especially on the return trip from Northfair to tell Phylax about his purchase Milo kept the transaction to himself not only out of a fear of ridicule, but also because some instinct forbade any disclosures about an instrument whose powers, if any, he intended to explore and use for himself.

Upon his return from his Northfair excursion, which never came to the attention of any disciplinary body or official, Milo had placed the Eye, still in its box, in the locked chest where he kept his most valued private possessions. Since that time he had discovered much about and had experienced much with the Eye, now his Beloved Treasure.

In the first weeks of his possession of the Eye Milo hadn't really understood how to use it. Nor had he been fully convinced that it could produce again the exciting scene it had depicted in Northfair. Try as he would to summon into the globe the naked miniature of the black harlot, he had managed at first to evoke only shapeless vapors. Had it all been an illusion, he began to ask himself, some trick of his vision that day in Northfair? Probably. And yet there was no denying the intense pleasure he experienced even without the presence in the globe of a desirable miniature whenever he just took the Eye into his hands. There was no doubting the thrilling sensation in his groin on those occasions for his rod would quickly grow hard and demand the stroking of his hand until the liquid pearls flew from it and he fell back spent after the final shuddering paroxysm.

Soon this ritual masturbation with the Eye in his left hand and his straining rod in his right had become the event he cherished most in his life. In its aftermath he always felt soothed, his failings seemed less obvious. And when the Dims began to assail him he had quickly discovered that only the Eye, usually but not always accompanied by masturbation, could relieve the "darkening" that he felt throughout his being though it seemed to seep into him from no physical source.

As he struggled against the Dims secretly for he did not dare to reveal this new weakness even to Phylax, Milo had come to rely solely on the Eye to bring him out of the dark moods that afflicted him. Eventually he had begun to wonder, if given the Eye's palliative effect on the Dims, it might not also help him to overcome some of the character defects that plagued him. Thus, holding the Eye close to his beating heart Milo had tried to will himself to be brave. The experiment had failed completely. The Dims, however, seemed to have run their course at last and Milo had emerged gratefully from the abysmal Darkenings that accompanied them.

It was at this point that Milo had resolved to renounce his sessions with the Eye. In effect he meant to break a habit that even he realized was dominating his life. And so, in order to put himself in an environment distant from the Eye's influence, Milo had volunteered for a month-long tour of patrol duty in the Forbidden Zone along the north bank of the River Bradys. At the end of his stint militarily uneventful he had been assigned to the Hegemon's Residence at Ten Turrets in order to "become familiar with the Arkadian government" as his father put it. Feeling cleansed and alert, convinced that he had left behind both the Dims and his dependence on the Eye, Milo had thrown himself into his new tasks with unusual vigor. Clearly he had overcome the various bad behaviors that had encumbered him in the past. He felt certain that he had now found the right path. That judgment, however, soon proved itself as far from the truth as it could possibly be for the Dims, apparently having built up behind the barrier of his "good" behavior had suddenly smashed through their dam and washed over him nearly drowning him in a flood of darkling thoughts.

After a week of suffering Milo had decided that only a half-wit would put up with such horrible feelings when he could find relief in the box that lay in his private chest only an arm's length away. And so, on a night when the Dims were hammering like a hundred crazy blacksmiths inside his head, Milo had extracted the Eye from its hiding-place. How fine it felt to cup its smooth warmth in his hands again! How calming! How quickly it drove away misery and filled him with pleasure instead! Milo must have been out of his mind to turn his back on his darling Treasure. Never again would he betray himself in that way. *No, no! From now on,* he vowed, *he intended to devote himself to the one thing he truly loved in his stupid life.*

Having made that decision Milo then undertook a serious effort to discover all there was to know about the Eye in order to enjoy to the full every delight it was capable of providing. He was particularly bent on ascertaining the technique required to generate within the globe miniature beings such as his Northfair harlot. Accordingly, he had experimented night after night with the Eye: holding it this way and that, shaking it, caressing it, speaking to it, even kissing it and pleading with it to perform. In the course of these various trials Milo learned several additional methods for increasing the intensity of the ecstasies that his sweet Treasure could yield to him. Try as he might, however, the opaque smoke that swirled within the glass had stubbornly refused to depart and reveal the simulacrum that he was seeking.

One night, after still another failure, Milo had erupted in a surge of furious frustration not at his beloved Treasure but at the gnome who had sold the Eye to him. Hadn't that scrawny little fraud claimed that the Eye would show him whatever he wished to see? That had been a damned lie and he, being the fool he was, had swallowed it. *"Curse that gnome,"* thought Milo, *"I wish the bastard was here right now so I could break his bald head like an egg!"*

With the utterance of this angry desire, Milo, to his astonishment, saw the whorls of gray smoke within the Eye evaporate at once as if dispelled by a windstorm. Within the glass now he beheld a living homunculus the gnome himself in miniature. In stunned silence Milo had gazed upon the oblivious figure in the globe as the gnome went about his business—the creature was engrossed in shaving his face.

Why, Milo wondered, *after so much failure, had he finally succeeded at this particular moment? What had he done or thought that was different this time? And why of all the far more palatable possibilities had the Eye brought him the ugly gnome?*

All at once the perplexity in his mind blew off like the smoke in the globe and Milo had grasped the secret of the Eye.

Desire, the genuine full-throated wanting with all one's being, that was the key that moved the Eye. Passion, sexual hunger, or mere rage, it didn't matter. Strong feeling, that was what caused the Eye to perform at full power. Because Milo had felt and expressed such enormous wrath for the gnome the Eye had searched out the creature and had produced a simulacrum of him in the globe.

With joy billowing in every part of his interior Milo had hugged the globe to him murmuring, "My sweet Treasure, my own love."

Milo noted that the simulacrum of the gnome had now disappeared. Smoke once more filled the globe. Naturally, so Milo concluded, for he no longer desired the gnome for any purpose not even to crack his skull and so the creature's living image no longer occupied the globe.

Excitedly, to test his theory of how the Eye functioned, Milo had then pictured in his mind's eye the pretty young wife of a Residence guard. She had smiled at him one afternoon when he had encountered her in the garden. Her name was—what?—oh, yes, Dia. He wanted Dia right here before him and now at once for his rod was already beginning to swell at the memory of her.

The smoke evaporated. Dia had appeared. She was wearing a night dress and standing before a mirror brushing her russet hair as if readying herself for bed. Oh, how he wanted to see her naked! At once Dia left off brushing. Removing her night dress she had stretched out on her bed as if displaying herself to him although of course she could have no knowledge—the real Dia couldn't—that she was now languishing within the Eye of Isis while the Hegemon's son stared at her and stroked himself to a royal orgasm.

After that first "play" as Milo decided to call his episodes with the Eye it had become progressively easier to play the Eye. In fact it became a game to see which beauty he could next bring into the Eye as a prisoner, unknown to her, in the globe.

Subsequent experience had confirmed that the other, the object of the game as Milo thought of her, had to be someone he could desire even if he had never spoken to her or even met her. Nor as his skill in the play increased with practice did the object of the game have to fit any criteria of age, hair color, or style. All that mattered was that he could conjure up her image in his inner eye and that—imprisoned in miniature within the glass globe—she could engage his ardor long enough for his masturbatory fantasy to bring him to fervid orgasm. To further test his theory that desire was the driving force of the Eye Milo had attempted to bring Darden's image to the globe without success. An attempt to summon Phylax also failed. This was enough to confirm Milo in his theory: Desire—always sexual for him—actuated his play with the Eye of Isis.

After this insight Milo had flung himself unreservedly into "Eye-play" and if such games with his Treasure did not banish the Dims entirely they greatly ameliorated the worst of his Darkenings. Moreover, the Eye-games mysteriously produced in him, at least temporarily, an unaccustomed sense of superiority by suggesting that despite his many shortcomings he actually possessed hidden resources beyond the powers of others and that included Phylax too.

Of course he knew better than to divulge any information to anyone about his Eye-play for to do so would no doubt bring opprobrium from such as his father and Megistes as well as ridicule which would be far worse from Phylax. So Milo had guarded his secret closely.

In fact, the only one who possessed even the slightest intimation of Milo's underground life with the Eye was his younger brother, Darden. And that circumstance had come about inadvertently when Darden, as was his arrogant habit, had invaded Milo's quarters without knocking and had found his elder brother masturbating while clutching a glass globe. Darden had only snickered at the sight not because he had caught Milo so engaged for Darden had also begun to indulge in the practice occasionally but because his elder brother was clasping a glass ball as he did so, a ridiculous affectation even for Milo or so Darden had opined in his mocking voice.

Quite naturally Milo had been enraged by Darden's interruption but soon calmed down when upon reflection he realized that Darden actually could have seen nothing incriminating since Milo alone could behold in the Eye the miniature object of his fantasy. Hence Milo dismissed Darden as a threat; he was a nuisance nothing more.

Despite his perception of positive effects from his Eye-play Milo did find himself worrying from time to time that he might have to pay some kind of physical or mental price for the ecstasy his Treasure brought him. He defused such concerns, however, by assuring himself that if he ever did begin to experience ill effects and surely by now they would have made themselves felt he could halt his playing at once. After all, he didn't need to play; he just liked it. And so Milo played as often as the urge impelled him.

Since his betrothal, however, the sole occupant of the globe of the Eye had been a simulacrum of the magnificent Kala Aristaia.

Night after night Milo had slaked his insuperable though still unexpressed passion for her by staring at the diminutive simulation of her unclothed body as it moved before him in the enticing poses he dictated to the Eye. Milo was especially transfixed by those postures which allowed him to focus all his masturbatory attention on the golden silk of Kala's sex until orgasm ended the play. Sometimes in these sessions, prodded by the mere memory of her beauty which he coveted despite his snarled speech in her actual presence Milo would summon Kala Aristaia again to the Eye for a second round of play. There was no denying it: he lusted for her and she belonged to him by right of betrothal. Yet he shrank from the real Kala much to the obvious chagrin of his father, the apparent disgust of Phylax, and his own absolute self-loathing.

Making matters worse Milo had to acknowledge that for all its capacity to check the Dims even his play with the Eye could not efface the revulsion he felt for himself because of his incapacity as a man, his weak character, his stupidity, his cowardice, all of which made him unfit to rule in his father's place. Had he not once again demonstrated his general incompetence at the reception tendered only this afternoon for Kala and him? Wouldn't he always fail when it was necessary to succeed? How could such as he rise to the so-called Destiny that awaited him? The Eye could not answer that question. Nor could it cure him of himself.

All at once, alone in his quarters, Milo began to sense the Dims gathering around him, the Darkenings piling up higher and more oppressive than he'd experienced them in several weeks. To save himself Milo resorted to the only relief he had available: He took the globe of the Eye in his left hand, his limp sex in his right and pictured Kala Aristaia laughing gaily but with an undercurrent of strain as she had danced this afternoon. He pictured her naked body under her clothing and as if on cue she appeared naked ivory and gold in the globe of the Eye. Milo made her dance as she had danced earlier, a winged sprite in the arms of faceless others. His rod was hard now. Watching Kala in the Eye he initiated the play that would, he knew, at least drive off the immediate clamor of the Dims. Then a harsh boyish laugh rang out, dousing Milo's play.

Darden.

Milo shouted at him.

"Haven't I told you to knock before you come in here, Darden?"

"Did knock, brother. I guess you were too pre-occupied to hear my polite tapping at your door. Still playing with yourself I see. But I've been meaning to ask: what's the point of the glass ball? Some kind of fetish? How's it work? I might like to try it myself sometime."

"Shut up, Darden. What I do is none of your damned business. What do you want here, anyway?"

Darden walked over to the window and pulled back the draperies.

"Warm night out there," Darden said, his back to Milo. "What do I want, big brother? Nothing you can provide. I am here with a message from our father, the great Agathon."

"What's the message?'

Darden turned around to face Milo.

Darden's dark face though still that of a thirteen-year-old boy nevertheless wore a sardonic expression that ordinarily belonged to one much older. *How had Darden become so hard, so sure, so damned ready? How had he become so unlike me,* Milo wondered.

Grinning, Darden said, "Our beloved Hegemon of Arkadia has summoned the two of us to his private chambers to share another of his austere suppers of little food and no wine after which he will lecture both of us. You, Milo, for your obvious lack of enthusiasm for your exalted position me for too much enthusiasm for contrary argument. Old Megistes, I'm glad to say, will not be present tonight to shake his stick at us. That's the message. I have delivered it. Now shall we go or have you not yet finished with your poor rod and your silly glass ball?"

"If you ever mention to anybody what you've seen here, Darden, I'll kill you."

"Oh, I doubt you'd ever kill anyone, Milo. But don't worry your pitiful little secrets only bore me. I feel sorry for you Milo. I'll wait for you in the hallway."

Jauntily Darden took his leave.

That Darden felt sorry for him, Milo reflected, only underscored the truth that the putative heir to the Hegemony of Arkadia ought to be disqualified from succeeding to the High Bench because of spiritual infirmities so flagrant that even his nasty piss-ant little brother could see them plain.

"Nobody knows me," Milo muttered bitterly. "Nobody knows the real me."

The goddess Eris, Mistress of Strife and Rage, sister and lover of the war god, Ares, and purveyor of hatred throughout Creation, woke in a world beneath the world. Was this the realm of Hades? Had Father Zeus banished her to an Eternity where the only light came from pools of fire from within the earth? Had great Zeus damned her then? She could not remember. Nevertheless, though interred within this underworld she sent forth a plea: Father Zeus take pity. She received no response. She had not expected one.

Somewhere, perhaps from the Void itself, the goddess Eris felt what could only be a shifting of the cosmic tides. Even in this prison meant to impregnate the captive with unending despair the goddess felt the turning of the Cosmos. Even though she might have been asleep for a thousand years or perhaps for a minute only she detected the change at once. Some motion from outside—outside what?—had stirred the embers of her ashen soul starting a slow rekindling of her once furious will.

Eris rose from the sarcophagus that had cradled her during her sleep. As she did so, her long gown of white linen emblematic of her membership in the divine sorority of Olympian goddesses began to disintegrate in patches of decayed cloth until only a few ragged shreds continued to cling to her body. Feeling disoriented and vulnerable without the shield of the habitual raiment that proclaimed her divinity Eris set off to find an exit from this place of her confinement. Once free, she assured herself, she would don once more the draped costume which identified her as one of the Olympian race.

Encountering a pulsing curtain of un-natural flame that blocked what seemed to be the sole way out of this dungeon of rocky walls and vaulted domes Eris halted. In addition to the foul odor of Sulphur she detected another gas one far more pleasant containing within it the promise of pleasure. Or was this still another caprice of this Hades?

Eris strained to see over the hissing barrier of flame to ascertain what world might lay beyond but she gave up when, in this cavern of altered time, she sensed a boiling of hatred in the heart of some wandering mortal. The discovery of this mortal rage thrilled her for like all the immortal gods Eris required the worship or at least the attention of lesser mortal beings in order to maintain her own immortality. Eris perceived that such a one enraged and lost had appeared somewhere beyond the barricade of flames. She must call this mortal being to her. Fighting off the hopelessness that sought to paralyze her volition Eris sent forth signals of her presence.

Come to me mortal, come to Eris, Goddess of Strife, that I may feed thy fury.

Seven

Riding under a blanched quarter-moon Seraph gradually became aware of flashes of light to the east. He soon realized that these bursts of brightness were not the lightning so often attributed to mindless Dis but more probably a beacon of some kind. *Might that signal-fire be meant for him? Was it possible that some wandering god or goddess in sympathy with his heart's fury was abroad on the Bemgrass tonight? And was this grand being summoning him? Had Seraph the Lame discovered his journey's destination at last? Or had he stumbled into more delusion?*

The flashes continued from the east. Somehow Seraph knew that in the east a boisterous river churned toward the sea. The flashes, Seraph abruptly realized, came as regularly as the beating of his blood. *In fact did not each burst of brightness pierce the night in unison with each contraction of his heart as if the two were acting in harmony? Surely that was no delusion. No, no, some power must be abroad and calling him, drawing him on for even his pony unguided now turned its drooping head eastward toward the flashes of light and the mysterious river.*

Seraph rode on hunger and exhaustion his unrelenting tormentors. He longed to rest but he reckoned he had no choice but to obey the power calling him with its pulsing light. He would rest when the dawn still some hours off made it too perilous to travel further.

Soon as the pony plodded eastward Seraph fell once again into that fugue state in which delirium brought forth memory. *The river he was seeking might it be the one that the Arkies called Pelorys? He suddenly thought it likely. And he sensed that he had crossed that broad water before and often. But how? And when?*

As if exhumed from his past by these questions familiar pictures rose before his fossil-eye. In a swift swirl of memory Seraph beheld once again the face of the old Koinar woman, hair white as a wispy cloud, skin wrinkled and dark as a rotted grape, a toothless mouth that seemed to collapse on itself like an empty purse. She stooped, that aged Koinar female, when she walked, and she rasped like a crow when she spoke. She spoke seldom, however. Her man, also old, his scalp hairless and speckled with brown spots, was still vigorous. His arms were like tree trunks. His square teeth could crush a nut still in its shell. Unlike his woman, the old Koinar man could move with dispatch and strength when he chose. Dark of skin like all Koinars the man unlike his aged woman companion was far from taciturn for he talked often and loudly customarily issuing his orders by shouting. These two whose names Seraph never learned, although as he now recalled he had spent six years with them, had come upon him, a half-blind and half-murdered, Bem boy while they were foraging illegally across the River Pelorys in Bem territory. This aged Koinar couple Seraph was to learn later belonged to a settlement of Koinars who called themselves "The Pious" though why they bore that label Seraph never did discover. The Pious Koinar couple who had plucked him from the Bemgrass turned out to be, so Seraph remembered now, outlaw merchants who regularly broke their own Arkie laws to trade with any Bem willing to exchange goods with them.

It was while engaged in this enterprise that the Koinar couple each mounted on a broken-down Arkie nag had discovered the near-helpless Seraph. Clucking with sympathy they had carried him back from the Bemgrass across the river by means of a rope cable attached to a raft-ferry to their own hut which stood in the midst of corrals and storage shacks. There the old woman fighting off the half-dead boy's frantic attempts to resist her ministrations had nursed the throw-away.

In time the boy had healed sufficiently to grasp the obvious fact that the Koinars did not intend to harm him though he could not begin to fathom their purpose in rescuing him from his abandonment on the Bemgrass. When he had healed sufficiently to get about on his lame leg he would often go down to the river and stare across to the grasslands on the other side. At such times he would think how glad he was to have escaped that site of his suffering.

By degrees the boy-Seraph had realized that his Koinar benefactors eked out their sparse living by illegally trading Arkie wood and woven cloth—scarce items in the Bem lands—for salt, certain stones, and the animal skins coveted by the foreign merchants who visited them (also a forbidden practice under Arkie law) from their port city called Northfair located on the far-off Onyx Sea. All this Seraph learned slowly, piece by piece, during the years he served the renegade Koinar couple.

Eventually, too, but long before he perceived its full scope Seraph learned what service he was to render his Koinar owners for he found that he had been "rescued" only to become a slave. Speaking in a degraded form of the Bem tongue the old Koinars notified their slave that he was to take part in a new addition to their various enterprises. Specifically, he was to accompany them on their incursions into the Bemgrass where throwaway Bem children were often to be found. When one of these abandoned children was encountered Seraph was to approach the terrified child and speak soothingly to her (for girls were much the preferred prey) in her own Bem dialect and convince her to accompany him and his kind Koinar friends to a "refuge" across the Pelorys River. There, Seraph would assure his quarry, the throw-away, would receive in safety whatever food, care, and rest she required all without fear of the terrible dire-cats of the grasslands. Most of the little girls Seraph accosted in this way embraced the proffered aid with heartbreaking gratitude and readily went with him and his "benevolent" Koinar owners. Even when confronted with the frightening ordeal of having to cross the river in the basket-like raft-contraption the Koinars used for this purpose the trusting children took comfort from Seraph's reassurances that he had been rescued from abandonment and worse in just this way by these same kindly Koinars. Not all Arkies were hateful, he would say, at least not "Pious Koinar" folk.

Once arrived on the far bank of the river the old woman would take Seraph away to lock him in the hut while the old man without further artifice would drag the child, now screaming for Seraph to help her, to the cage where she was to remain until one of the Northfair slave-traders bought her. For whom the traders purchased her and for what purposes Seraph was never told.

For six years as he learned the language of the Arkies and grew in mental, if not physical prowess, Seraph had played his part in this vicious business. All the while, however, he was building up stores of venomous hatred for the Koinar couple and for himself as well for he calculated that he had lured more than two-hundred and fifty throw-aways, the overwhelming majority of them terrorized little girls of seven or eight, into the Pious Koinar cages. *How could he not hate himself for those deceptions? On the other hand,* he often thought, *did he not have every right to reject the guilt attendant on actions he was forced to carry out? And hadn't he himself suffered worse than any of these throw-aways?*

Seraph also consoled himself with the reflection that these girl-children, whatever their subsequent fate might be, would not have to perish in an agony of hunger on the grass thanks to the deceitful seizures he facilitated for his Koinar owners. Moreover, as slaves of the mysterious foreigners of Northfair, the captured girls would lose only a spurious freedom which as females of their clans they had never in fact possessed, nor ever would possess among the Bem. In truth, Seraph recalled, he had tried to tell himself that although he was luring these children from certain death to an unknown fate it was surely a better fate than they could expect as clan-wives. In this way he suppressed guilt even as he stoked ever higher the fires of furious resentment that burned in his heart for his own blind eye, broken body, and shattered face. With the passage of time resentment swelled into a monstrous hatred like a ball of pus in Seraph's soul not just for her who had maimed him but even more so for his Koinar owners and by extension for all Arkies whatever their station.

One day as had to happen eventually the pus ball in Seraph's soul had burst into an act at once liberating and horrific. Taking a long pointed metal bar from a shed he had made his way in darkness into the sleeping place of the Koinar couple. Standing over them as they slept he plunged the pointed bar through each gurgling old throat. Then, roaring with laughter he washed his ruined face in the blood that gushed from the torn arteries. He then sawed off the heads and threw them into the Pelorys to be carried, he hoped, to Northfair and then to the sea. After this satisfying action Seraph had stuffed both bodies into a single barrel. Neither of the dead Koinars weighed any more than the girl-children they had crammed into their slave cages to be sold along with their other illicit merchandise. Finally, Seraph set fire to the barrel as well as to the huts and sheds watching as the flames spewed a storm of sparks into the night sky. Then he rode one of the Koinar nags down to the river. There, frantic with fear that some others of the Pious might happen upon his crime, for the Pious from nearby settlements were accustomed to visit one another at whim, Seraph emulating his dead owners hooked the basket-raft to the rope and pulley device the Koinars had strung across the river in a place of calm water to transport themselves back and forth. In this way, Seraph managed though with enormous effort to ferry himself back to the Bemgrass.

Soon thereafter, no longer a throw-away child but a resourceful malefactor in spite of his infirmities Seraph stole a broken down horse from a careless Koinar outlaw-trader. Mounted well enough, he had then ridden across the Bemgrass away from the Pious Koinar outlaws to rejoin his people some of whom had hailed him as a "Son of Dis". The mother who had crushed his face and on whom he had both feared and longed to avenge himself was not among those who greeted his return for she had disappeared on the Bemgrass a throw-away herself in the end. With that punishment for his murderous mother, Seraph recalled, he had contented himself.

And here he was tonight years (he did not know how many years) after his slaughter of the Koinar couple again on the Bemgrass both a traitor to Dis and a fugitive from the Bem whom he now despised, a crippled seeker of what?—and riding toward the River Pelorys to answer a summons that he did not understand unless it was a response to the hatred in his heart.

At this moment, as if prompted by his earlier recollections, Seraph recalled the night of his flight into the Bemgrass and his desperate vow to bring down the Arkie state. This was his purpose, his chosen quest. All that had happened since that night of his vow— his suffering, his wandering—had been in preparation for this night of the flashing beacon and his recovered destiny. Grasping at this revelation Seraph hurled a plea into the night sky: "If you are a god calling me, come out! Help me!"

The flashing light only beat on in cadence with Seraph's heart. This seeming indifference inflamed Seraph. How could his divine summoner fail to respond, to perceive that he had undertaken a quest, that he had resolved one way or the other to bring down that hateful construction, Arkadia? As if in recognition of Seraph's disturbed spirit, the distant light began to flash rapidly, surely a throbbing acknowledgement of his quest. Seraph reined in his pony.

Picturing once more the Arkie Kapit who had so easily humiliated him on that day of the Passing Seraph threw his arms wide, tilted his head back, and cried out an oath in binding form to the serene stars: "I, gimp-leg Seraph, swear by the power of my hatred, the strength of my arm, and the cunning of my mind, to destroy utterly the arrogant entity that calls itself Arkadia. Only in victory or in death will my soul find peace! This I swear to any god who will hear me!"

In her cavern-prison across the far River Pelorys the goddess Eris thrilled at the mortal's blood-oath. How she longed to behold his fury! How she longed to aid him to achieve his vengeance! Blood, fury, and revenge—these were the arts of which she was mistress. She prayed to the unknown cosmos that the hate-soaked mortal possessed the necessary courage, cunning, and strength to come to her, to set her free of her prison. Only then could she guide him on the journey to evil that she knew he must yet make to achieve the destiny he craved.

Within the encircling walls of Ten Turrets, Kala Aristaia was also experiencing an unexpected visitation for Mina had just informed her but diffidently, as if reluctant to appear complicit in a scandal, that the Logofant Megistes had come unannounced to her darling girl's sequestered lodgings in the Residence. Mina now whispered a shocked elaboration. "He wishes to speak with you, in private, my darling."

Kala blinked in astonishment at Mina's news. She was, she realized, not only surprised, but even more she was immensely pleased though nervously so that this supreme scholar whose historical and philosophical meditations she had been reading (studying really, and puzzling over) for several years at home in Richland Hall deigned to visit her. It was a privilege she had not prepared for. Nevertheless, she now resolved she would make the most of the Logofant's fortuitous presence in her quarters for she could not help but reflect that his visit would afford her an opportunity to study (clandestinely, of course) his face for one of her chalk drawings. To Mina, she said, "Please show Master Megistes in." Was her voice trembling? She hoped not lest the great man think her merely a "country-girl" to use Mina's deprecating term.

Moments later Mina returned in company with the old Sage. Kala almost jumped to her feet in greeting but recalled just in time that protocol required the Betrothed of the Heir to remain seated when receiving visitors even one as distinguished as the Logofant of Arkadia.

"Welcome, Master," she said. Her voice she was relieved to find quavered not at all.

The old man gave a quick nod of his head, his version of a bow.

"Salutations, Kala Aristaia."

As if by mutual agreement the aged wise man and the youthful beauty paused to scrutinize each other face-to-face for until this moment each had observed the other only at the distance required at formal occasions. Now Kala saw before her a tall, bearded man with a crown of fine white hair which was bound in a circlet of silver. The face, with its pale white skin stretched like parchment over the skull beneath, seemed to Kala severe but also capable of much kindness. The eyes, stony blue, looked out unflinchingly from under thick white brows. He wore a spotless, though clearly much used, ankle-length gown of plain white wool. In his left hand he carried a staff of highly polished wood which reached to his shoulder and seemed to be decorated with incised words from the original and now lost language of the Founders of Arkadia.

For his part Megistes saw before him, seated alertly on a divan, a Megar woman who was certainly aware of her remarkable beauty but who unlike most Megar ladies of Megistes' acquaintance appeared to carry her loveliness as if it was merely a part of her, not her whole being. Kala Aristaia also seemed to be free of the usual haughtiness of Megar women. Dressed in a simple "at home" blue linen gown instead of the fashionable and revealing clothing she apparently donned only for formal occasions Kala Aristaia looked approachable, sensible, and even eager for conversation all signs of an open mind in Megistes' estimation. Furthermore, her wide smile as she looked up at him seemed to betoken a warm heart. At first glance at least he found her charming and he hoped he would soon find in her a genuine intelligence to match her charm for much depended on this girl's perception of her role in Arkadia's future.

At this moment, with mutual reconnaissance at an end, Mina, who had removed herself earlier, re-entered with a tray bearing sliced fruit and cups of light wine. She placed the tray on a low table and immediately withdrew. Kala indicated that Megistes should seat himself opposite her. He did so and availed himself at once of the wine, as Kala did also.

Kala Aristaia recalled that protocol dictated that she introduce their colloquy. Better to begin with light matters she told herself. Aloud she said with a shyness she did not often feel: "I have read your work, Master."

He gave her a surprised but kind smile.

"Surely not all of it?"

"No, no." Kala blushed; *he must think her a dolt.* "I have read your *'Thoughts on the Logos.'*"

"Hard going that one," Megistes said taking another sip of the wine which was too fruity for his taste.

"I also read *'What is Arkadia?'*," said Kala.

"Ah? What did you think of it?"

"I thought it brilliant."

Again Megistes smiled, clearly pleased.

"I see you are clever as well as charming and beautiful."

Kala understood that he was joking with her but she didn't mind. It meant he was also warming to her. Megistes' attitude encouraged her to reveal something that only Mina knew about her.

"If I hadn't somehow landed where I am now, Master, I should have liked to study at your Logofane Academy as one of your scholars."

She smiled.

Megistes found that he could not doubt the sincerity of her smile. But he seized upon her words as the opening that he needed in order to subtly raise his concerns about the danger inherent in the mixing of power and artlessness.

"We would have welcomed you at the Academy but Fate has placed you where you are, Lady. There can be no more important role for you than that of partner-wife to the next Anax and Hegemon of Arkadia."

"Yes," she replied erasing her smile. "And I am determined, Master Megistes, to be worthy of my place."

The sentiment as expressed struck Megistes as more rote than conviction. But did such a trite response truly reveal the kind of perilous innocence he dreaded to find in her? Megistes could not tell.

Hence, to get to the heart of the matter, he decided he had to probe further. In a deliberately emotionless voice Megistes said, "I think you should know that I have sent Phylax away to the Logofane for a while."

Megistes examined Kala's face for any sign of dismay. He saw nothing overt. Kala's dark eyebrows lifted, however, as if to express puzzlement.

"Phylax? Have I missed something, Master?"

Again Megistes was not sure how to interpret Kala's response. Was her question guileless or was it a more or less a clumsy attempt to deceive him? Either way it annoyed him.

"Please, let's put pretense aside, Lady. This is a serious matter."

Kala was unshaken. "I'm sure it is Master and I apologize for my ignorance."

Kala looked concerned but far from disconcerted. Megistes wondered if her apparent confusion arose from something so simple as her not knowing the name of her lovesick admirer. He would give her the benefit of the doubt, and so explained that "Phylax" was the name of the handsome Cadet Colonel whom she must have noticed at her betrothal ceremony and after.

"Ah!" she exclaimed, "Now I know who you mean. His name is Phylax? And you have sent him away? May I ask why?"

Megistes frowned, letting his irritation show briefly.

"Surely you know why, Lady."

Kala shook her head in bewilderment.

"Truly, I do not. Forgive me, please."

Megistes' heart sank for it was now clear that this girl had no pretense in her surely an indication of the fault he feared. Aloud he said, "I see that you are blameless in this matter and perhaps in other ways as well. I must tell you, Lady that innocence simply will not do in one of your rank."

Bewilderment did its best to crowd out the beauty of her face.

"I don't understand," she murmured. "Instruct me, Master. Please."

Megistes had every intention of doing so and without delay.

"First, Kala Aristaia, you must accept my word that where Fate has now placed you in the world the obvious innocence of your heart and mind which was once an ornament of your personality is now a wrong waiting to happen, a defect that can do unintentional injury to yourself and others even to the Hegemony itself. Therefore, it must be your portion from now on to learn all you can of your new place in the world in order to divest yourself of any past attitudes—even virtuous ones—that might impede your performance as the Betrothed of the next Hegemon."

Kala's intelligence came to the fore.

"You worry that I might, in my ignorance—"

Megistes interrupted. "Let us say innocence; it is a kinder word."

"But ignorance is the more accurate word, Master," Kala said. Then she continued her original thought. "As I say, Master, you worry that my ignorance wrapped in the simplicity I have always cherished as a strength and comfort will now lead me to do harm without my being aware of it."

"You have said it well," Megistes responded.

Clearly, Megistes reflected, the girl's innate goodness was of an impressively expansive kind so much so that it had led her almost instantly to grasp a difficult reality: that in the universe of duty and responsibility where she must live now the good might not be achieved by any simple act of conscience as heretofore but might require a hunt through a forest of complexities.

Quietly, her odd gold-flecked eyes fixed on the Logofant, Kala said, "Things here are often not as they seem. Is this what you wish me to understand?'

Megistes nodded. "And accept as well."

"Then you must guide me, Master."

"I will."

Megistes was feeling almost triumphant at her quick comprehension of his lesson. Still it might be well to test her further but gently. Accordingly, after letting a few more moments of silence pass, he said, "I sent Phylax to the Logofane on leave because he was sick with desire for you. I could not allow him to destroy himself—and you—for a passion that must not be. Do you understand, Kala?"

"I do. Thank you, Master Megistes."

Though she did not say so Kala felt more grateful to the Sage than she could easily express. Megistes had kept her from incurring a disgrace that would have destroyed her family for though she had not known his name she had indeed looked on this Phylax with a casually smoldering desire that (she realized this now) might well have burst eventually into a flaming conflagration beyond all controlling. Kala sensed that she did not need to speak of this to Megistes for she was sure he knew it already had known it before she did herself.

With a groan of effort the old man rose to his feet. Bending forward Megistes took Kala's hand in his and laid his dry lips against it.

"We shall be friends," Megistes said. Then he added a single but significant word: "Daughter."

Tears blurred Kala's eyes. Ignoring the protocol of the Residence, she also rose and in silent appreciation kissed the wise old man's desiccated cheek.

Later that night genuinely at ease for the first time since her arrival at Ten Turrets a state of well-being she attributed to the reassuring guidance she had received earlier from Megistes, Kala Aristaia decided to examine once again the chalk portrait she had made of her betrothed, Milo Agathonson. *Perhaps,* she told herself, *the picture that had troubled her so much upon completion would no longer seem so disturbing after her comforting talk with Megistes that afternoon.* Retrieving her portfolio from its place at her bedside Kala opened it to the depiction of Milo that she had done from memory, as she did all her portraits, only the day after her betrothal to him. She studied the face thus revealed.

There was no denying it. The Milo on the paper looked to be a soul in torment and not at all like the boyish face in the miniature that she had carried prior to meeting him at their betrothal. Kala hated the picture that she had made of the young man. But she knew better than to dismiss it as merely a failed attempt to portray a complex young man for she recognized that she had not failed as an artist but had delineated on the heavy paper a true picture of Milo's interior self. That the picture chilled Kala's heart when, as now, she peered at it, told her beyond a doubt that her husband to be, the future occupant of the High Bench of Arkadia, was in spiritual need. But what need? That was far from clear from the portrait. In an effort to unearth some clue Kala kept her attention fixed on the chalk surfaces while once again cataloging the anomalies that it continued to present to her eye.

First, the portrait possessed what she could only call an unsettling asymmetry as if the face was in some odd way out of focus—an impossibility of course, but there it was, undeniable. Moreover, the colors were, subtly, so far from the true that they gave the shape of the head a grotesquely indefinite outline—as though the subject was deformed. Or perhaps not quite there. Or perhaps he was trying not to be there, trying to evade the reality of his self. Even the eyes were wrong. Their blue was too pale, their pupils shrunken. Moreover, the face had a distinctly sly look, a "twisted" aspect, as if its owner was forever conscious of some secret vice that crushed him with shame—a shame he chose to shrink from, rather than confront. The picture, Kala knew, was—at its deepest level—a delineation of a concealed perversity. She could not doubt that this unsettling image crafted by her own eye and hand had laid bare Milo's true and disquieting interior self. For this, as Kala Aristaia had long ago discovered, was her mysterious gift and in some sense her affliction: that in some inexplicable manner she was compelled to use her chalks and pens not only to depict the physical appearance of her subjects but also in that process to shadow forth their agonies of soul.

Precisely how she achieved this effect Kala had no idea. From her very early childhood she had taken delight in drawing anything that caught her eye. As she got older, however, she had fastened on making splendid portrayals of faces in charcoal and colored chalks. She had done dozens of studies of her brothers, her father, and her mother and especially of Mina who, unlike the others, seemed to enjoy the chore of posing. Then, about four years ago, beginning with the onset of her monthly flow from which event she dated many important changes though she remained skeptical of any causality, Kala Aristaia, the artist, developed a predilection for drawing her subjects from memory instead of making them pose for her. The technique she devised for this approach called for her first to study her subject with her own eyes and without the subject's knowledge making sure to observe him or her in a variety of circumstances until she was satisfied with the conception that had gradually taken shape in her inner eye, only then, alone with her chalks, her pens, and the remembered image, would she swiftly transmit the recollected face to her paper.

The process exhilarated Kala, for drawing, at least for her, came down to just allowing her inner sight to move the hand plying the chalk with unimpeded, virtually automatic, motions. She described the process to herself as "letting the hands dance." Just as dancers speak of being "carried away" with music, of feet flying with the rhythm, so Kala thought of her art as hands being carried away with the "music" of her stored image until the portrait was complete on her paper. Though Kala herself experienced only joy from her new method some of her subjects had professed themselves repelled by her depictions of them.

At first, in reaction to such criticism, Kala had attempted to alter the "unsatisfactory" pictures to please her critics. She soon found, however, that even when she tried to "correct" a portrait her attempts failed. The portrayal stubbornly refused to change in any significant way. In some manner that puzzled Kala deeply it seemed to her that when one of her portraits was done it became unchangeable. It was wise Mina who had suggested the reason for this perplexing side of Kala's art.

"Darling girl, don't you see? Your drawings expose to the beholder the true face of your subjects. Many would rather pretend that you have missed the mark in depicting them when just the opposite is the case. They shrink from your unintended revelation of their soiled insides. There is an obvious reason why you are unable to change your portraits; it is because your subjects have to do the changing—of themselves—for only then will your inner eye be able to alter its view of their souls. Yes, you portray souls, my darling. It is a gift, you see? You must cultivate it like a vineyard for you produce a rare vintage, darling girl."

When Mina, who rarely wasted words, finished with this lengthy insight Kala had recognized its truth at once. She had also resolved to forego making judgments of others unless one of her portrayals revealed some truly disturbing aspects of a subject's inner self as her portrait of Milo did. Well, then, what now, she asked herself.

Kala's talk with Megistes had opened her eyes to the complexity and the demanding nature of her new responsibilities. Yet on one point at least she could now see her way clearly: she must somehow help Milo to extricate himself from whatever mysterious misery—as exposed in the portrait—held him in its grip. Kala had to begin that task by getting to know Milo's true heart and soul. Even before that, however, she had to show her portrait of Milo to Megistes for guidance.

Intuition told the goddess Eris that Time in the infernal realm in which she found herself was of an order like no other in the Creation. She gave it a name: *Meta-time.* It did not flow as time did beyond her imprisoning flames, that is, in a steady stream that was mortal time. No, this meta-time, she discerned, could roll forward or back. It could twist and turn to re-create the past or to show forth potential futures. Meta-time could stand still or keep pace with light itself for its nature belonged to the Cosmos not to the life of mortals, nor even to the gods.

With this astute apprehension of meta-time, Eris recognized that she could not know or even estimate when, if at all, the hate-hearted mortal who was ranging across the Bemgrass might reach her for he was tied to the rhythms of life-time while she, incarcerated in Hades, was bound by no such reckoning. Hence, the much desired advent of the mortal whose worship alone could restore Eris to divine freedom might take mere days or weeks to accomplish as the mortal experienced his time, but require generations to achieve in the meta-time that now confined her. Could it be done at all, her union with the mortal? Or was she doomed to wait forever for the faith of a believing mortal to validate her existence and so restore her? Such questions did not bear thinking about.

Rather than wait in fret, Eris decided to regard the mortal's arrival as certain though temporally indefinite. To assuage the anxiety she could not help feeling as the result of her situation she retreated from the wall of fire which denied her escape to the world beyond and, despite her near nakedness, set out to explore the interior of her prison. As she proceeded cautiously the delicate unshod feet of the goddess sank ankle-deep into the accumulated dust of uncounted ages. It was a dust that felt as oddly comfortable to her feet as if she were treading on the finest down. Stepping warily, the Goddess of Strife passed into the red-lit interior of her nether world.

Halting, she looked up into a soaring dome of shadows which Titans must have carved from living rock as if eviscerating the bowels of a mountain. Or were these caves not true caves at all but containers of an alien universe in which space—like time—could expand to infinity or contract to atoms at need? Such large thoughts made her shudder and she turned away from them focusing again on the great cavern in which she now found herself.

Strewn here and there in the dust that carpeted the floor Eris saw the bones of ancient sacrifices. Some of these bones were human and all of them were prettily crimsoned by the pools of fire that snarled and hissed here and there and threw up gouts of smoke throughout the enormous chamber.

As well as the scattered bones, the goddess came across sacrificial altars of white marble each stained with what looked to be generations of propitiatory blood. *To what deities had these sanguinary offerings been made? To the Olympians? Perhaps,* she thought, although she could discern no evidence in the reddened gloom that those prideful deities—her own tribe after all though most of them had disdained her—had ever held sway in this Hell. A moment later Eris noticed cut into the rock several passageways that seemed to lead from this hall even deeper into the mountain's heart. She chose one at random and entered.

Eris emerged in another domed chamber which at first seemed much like the one she had just left. Soon, however, she saw that this hall was chillingly different from the first although the dust that prevailed here as everywhere made for a general appearance of uniformity. In this chamber, however, no old bones or abandoned altars were to be seen. Instead, Eris with a heart suddenly seized by bitter grief beheld tenuous shapes, male and female, gliding among the mephitic fires and smoke clouds. These, as Eris well knew, were the shades of the dead. Aimless, empty-eyed, mute and bereft, they drifted, mere membranes, indifferent to power, and immune to desire. Eris at once identified these specters as the shades of the once-arrogant Olympian immortals, the gods of the land of Hellas her own native land. Eris supposed that these phantom gods, clearly not eternal after all, had been sentenced here by faithless mortals to evanesce at last into the eternal Cosmos.

In spite of their incorporeality and near-transparent presence Eris—always a lesser goddess of their order—recognized each of these condemned remnants. Here was great Zeus, blank-eyed and lost. Here was Aphrodite, her sexual beauty become a wretched mockery for who could now embrace her divine body? Here was Ares, lover of war, brother of Strife, who had loved Eris herself for a season or two. The fierce visage of Ares was now mashed to that of a dolt.

One by one, as they glided past her on their useless trajectories, Eris considered them. Here the Queen of Olympus, jealous Hera, trailed forlornly in search of her faithless husband, Zeus. And Artemis came after, fast fading, her hunting bow discarded. Then Hermes, no longer winged of foot, plodded past with downcast eyes. Apollo appeared—saddest of all for having lost the haughty effrontery that he used to consider his divine right. Majestic Athena, now crushed, hovered uncertainly, and passed, and then befuddled Poseidon, longing for his salt-water realm, his neglected beard unkempt as falling oak leaves floated past. Eris knew them at once, and recognized all the rest—some of them only pitiful demi-gods—who drifted past as well. Here they were all those who, during their reign of pride and power, had scorned Eris, Goddess of Strife, as a trifler, a mere trouble-maker. Now they were here, shades of themselves. Only Eris herself and one other had escaped the fate of these helpless Olympians. That other she reckoned by his absence was certainly Mad Dionysius who had practiced ecstasy with wine and poetry. Eris easily grasped the reason for the mad god's omission from the line of Olympian shadows: Dionysius, an illegitimate son of Zeus, had never been accepted by the Olympians as one of them and was therefore spared. More important, however, his absence from the sepulchral march of the doomed deities proclaimed that Mad Dionysius was still an object of mortal adoration. He had always been the god of cults. No doubt wild women continued to worship him at secret altars hidden in mountainous forests. There, at least, the ecstatic god endured.

But why had she, Eris, survived whatever calamity had caused the hammer of Fate to fall upon the great divinities of the long-lost land of Hellas? Why had Strife been spared in that catastrophe the history of which Eris could not recollect if she had ever heard it? The probable answer soon came to her: mortals, who had abandoned Zeus and company, had never been able to abandon Strife and so the Goddess of Strife still lived at least for now. Reminding herself that in Homer's underworld dead Achilles had been able to speak to a remorseful though still-living Odysseus, Eris attempted to address the Lord of the Olympians:

"Oh, Father Zeus, if I, Eris, was never your beloved daughter it was not for lack of wishing it but because unending rage afflicted me and afflicts me still for it is my nature to spread ill. I cannot help it. Yet I now desire to serve you, to do what lies in my power to restore the halcyon times of thy glory. So I implore you to speak; tell me how you and our tribe came to this pass so that I may help revive the Olympians. Or failing that, tell me how I might take vengeance on those traitor mortals who banished our family to this eternity, this Hades."

Thus, Eris, Goddess of Strife, familiar with the rhetorical forms necessary in a speech to the gods of Hellas, addressed herself to mighty Zeus. But he, blind and indifferent, passed by in silence. Upon this, the Goddess of Strife, overcome with sorrow and heedless of her near-naked body, flung herself to her knees. Covering her eyes with her hands she gave way to grief. Grieving, she wept into the dust of ages.

After a time—a meta-minute—a year—the Goddess Eris raised her tear-washed eyes and cried out: "Come to me mortal, before I too expire!"

EIGHT

Afer a long night of intermittent downpours—a rare occurrence on the Bemgrass—Seraph, his nearly naked body shivering with cold and his gut knotted with a hunger fiercer than any dire-cat, stumbled upon the remains of an abandoned hunter's camp.

It was the hour before dawn. The rain had ceased at last. Dismounting from his spent pony, Seraph crawled forward to examine the camp from a hiding-place in the tall grass. The camp was certainly deserted for there was no movement, only the soaked ashes of a long-dead fire, a scattering of bones picked clean by scavenger birds, and a lump of something covered by a heap of leaves and grass. This, he thought, might be a carcass so spoiled that the hunters had left it to rot when they departed to resume their hunt. Seraph, however, was too famished to turn up his nose at any meat however putrid or maggoty. Accordingly, his mouth watering, he crawled forward into the soggy mud of the camp and saw that under the pile of leaves and grass lay a body—a corpse. So much the better, he told himself, for the corpse would probably be at least a little fresher than a piece of old game. Better it should fill his belly rather than the gut of a prowling cat. Coming closer he took out his knife to cut a piece of rotted flesh from the dead body.

With a terrifyingly abrupt movement, however, the corpse sat up scattering its covering of leaves. Eyes wide with dread, it spoke in the rough dialect of the Bem: "Spare me."

Quickly recovering from his initial shock Seraph's first thought was to kill at once for he now realized that the "corpse" was a Bem woman not young, not old. Skinny as she was, Seraph thought, she was meat and fresh meat at that a commodity he had not dreamed of finding on the grasslands. Seraph's mouth now awash with saliva in anticipation of the warm taste of bloody flesh he raised his knife.

"Please," the woman pleaded, stricken with terror. "I have food. Take it. I can get more. I can help you."

Perhaps the woman could help him Seraph thought but it was meat he needed now.

"You have meat? Bring me meat."

Immediately the woman reached out her thin arm and brought forth from under a small pile of grass a charred chunk of ox only slightly foul.

Holding the seared meat with both hands Seraph tore at it as the woman watched with hopeful eyes. When, to his surprise his stomach cramped unable to accept more—at least for the moment—he knelt to drink from a muddy puddle left by that night's rain. But he stopped when the Bem woman proffered a gourd of water. Seraph drank deeply emptying the container. The water he realized had been mixed with the juice of certain relaxing herbs called "tunnik."

"Will you hurt me," the woman asked.

She was on her knees to him now her eyes seeming to bulge from her head with fear. Seraph noticed that she had covered herself against the night chill with the threadbare remnant of a woolen blanket.

"Give me your cloak," he rasped at her.

The woman stripped it off at once and handed it to him. Seraph saw that under the "cloak" she was wearing an ankle-length gown of some sort. Sewn together from scraps of ox-hide and stiff with old dried ox blood the garment reeked even worse than Seraph himself. Wrapping himself in the shreds of the woolen blanket the first "clothing" of any kind he'd had against his skin for many weeks Seraph almost smiled so grateful was he for even the little warmth it imparted.

The Bem woman spoke again in her pleading voice.

"Do not hurt me, I beg you. I can help you."

But Seraph was feeding again and the tunnik was also helping to calm his frenzied hunger and so he did not reply to her question. It occurred to him, however, that she might be deceiving him that the camp might not be abandoned after all but a glance around reassured him: the dead fire, the absence of pony dung and baled ox-hides—these said that the Bem hunters had gone some time ago.

No doubt they had abandoned the woman along with their camp. Seraph also saw that she was eyeing his lame leg. *Was she trying to estimate how much his leg would hamper his movements if she made an attempt to escape into the tall grass?* Then he remembered that like all Bem women, this one was surely bound at the ankles and that it was therefore unlikely that she could hobble away from him any faster than he could pursue her. *Why, after finding herself deserted,* he wondered, *hadn't the woman used a sharp stone to cut through her ankle restraints? How stupid the Bem were,* he thought, *especially the women.* And yet her predicament aroused his curiosity.

"Tell me how you came to be alone out here."

In a monotone carefully devoid of any expression of anger or resentment, after all, despite his infirmity her interrogator was a male and so a tyrant and a potential assailant, the Bem woman began to relate her story as Seraph continued, more slowly now, devouring the chunk of half-rotten ox meat.

The woman said she had been accompanying her husband, a Blue Color warrior she interjected with some pride as if her husband's idiotic pedigree would impress Seraph, on an ox-hunting expedition. The hunting party had also included three additional Blue warrior-friends of her husband as well as another woman who was wife to one of the other Blues. The warriors had brought the two women along to cook, to gather tunnik for the men to drink, to preserve the meat and hides, and above all to set up and break down the camps. The women, of course, were also to provide sexual services when needed.

How craven and stupid these Bem cows are Seraph could not help reflecting as the woman recounted her tale.

One night, said the Bem female, after a successful hunt that had resulted in six kills, her husband had given her to have sex with one of his friends as a reward for the man's prowess on the hunt that afternoon. She had complied according to custom but somehow she had angered the warrior who was very drunk on fermented tunnik. The furious man had struck her in the face with his fist sending her reeling into unconsciousness. When she came to herself again it was full daylight. She was lying on her back and she was alone. She knew at once that her husband had deliberately left her behind without a morsel of food or a drop of drink when he and his comrades had ridden off with only a single woman to serve them.

Seraph thought that this must have been the hunting party he had heard so close as he had lain hidden in the grass some days ago. He said to the woman, "Have you stayed here in this camp since the others left you?"

She nodded.

"But just before the sunrise I go to a place nearby to get water and the tunnik berries and to steal any meat the cats may have left there."

Seraph said, "But why do you remain here? Do you think your husband may come back?"

"No."

"Why don't you move on, then?"

"Where can I go?"

The Bem woman lifted the hem of her garment to show the ankle bonds she wore.

"I am afraid of the dire-cats. See? I cannot run or climb."

Seraph shook his head. Did the Bem lack even rudimentary intelligence?

"Remove those bonds, woman. Then you will be able to run if need be."

She frowned.

"Remove? How?"

Seraph replied in exasperation. "Use a sharp rock. Cut the rope."

Seraph saw the appalled expression that came over her face at the idea of freeing herself.

"I dare not."

The woman was, Seraph saw, still a prisoner in her mind and probably always would be. Angry at her stupidity, Seraph drew his flint knife still sharp as any Arkie blade of metal. In a single swift motion he severed the hemp cord that bound the woman's ankles to each other. His voice sharp with disgust at this Bem practice that hobbled both the body and the soul of Bem women, assuming that Bem women even possessed souls, Seraph said, "Now you are free. I'll cut off the rest of it later."

Seraph drank some more of the tunnik to help him swallow another chunk of the noxious meat.

The woman began weeping bitterly, her gnarled hands covering her face.

"Dis will punish me for this," she sobbed.

"Dis? Hah! Your Dis is as stupid as the people who worship him."

The woman uncovered her sooty face now streaked with tears. She stared at him her mouth open in awe and horror at his blasphemy. Seraph saw that her teeth like the teeth of all Bem women were stained and worn down by years of chewing ox hides and sinew to soften them. The teeth of Arkie women on the other hand, Seraph recalled, shone in their mouths like the white stones you sometimes found in the shallows of the River Bradys.

A remarkable idea abruptly bloomed in Seraph's mind. Now that he had removed her ankle hobbles might he not make use of this Bem woman to help him complete his journey to the Pelorys River? Specifically he envisioned her leading his worn-out pony forward each night while he rode on the poor beast's back carrying any supplies they might manage to scrape together. In other ways, too, she might prove helpful. For example, she could find water and such roots and berries that women knew about. And if she balked at his proposed arrangement? Then he would have no choice but to kill her and use her body for meat.

Seraph said, "What is your name?"

When she seemed hesitant about answering he flared again with irritation.

"I'm not going to use your name to cast a spell on you woman though I might just cut your throat and be done with you."

Seraph showed her his flint knife again.

The Bem woman divulged her name in a tremulous murmur.

"I am Rin, a wife of the Blue Clan".

"Very well Rin, here is my proposal."

Seraph explained his plan for them to travel together at night to the Pelorys. He saw her nervous hesitation and laid before her the alternative.

"If you refuse, I will kill you for meat."

When she still hesitated, he added: "Don't think that because I cannot move rapidly on my withered leg that I am feeble. Believe me, though weakened by hunger, I am strong enough to overcome you, Rin, and I am resolved to do so if I must. Say what you will do, Rin."

She nodded her agreement.

So she was not an absolute imbecile after all, thought Seraph, although the fact was that now that he had removed the last of her hobbles as promised she might very well escape him by running into the tall grass.

But this was a truth she would not dare to test. Ducking her head as if expecting a blow for her temerity she whispered again. "You will not leave me?"

Seraph tried to smile though he knew that with his ruined face his distorted smile looked more like a threatening grimace than an expression of reassurance.

"I shall not leave you, Rin," he said, "So long as you obey and serve me well."

She breathed a single word. "Yes."

"We shall rest by day," Seraph said, "but there is still an hour before dawn. You spoke earlier of a place nearby where you go for water and berries. Is it a good place to hide during the day?"

She nodded.

"Yes. There is a stream and a thicket of thorn bushes. Berries too, and wild onions. Sometimes birds and small animals come there to drink but the big cats come only in the darkness."

"Yes, a time when we shall be traveling onward," Seraph put in. "Well then, you will take me there, Rin. Now, before the dawn appears."

Seraph did not say that he also wished to make the move in order to test her ability and willingness to lead the pony in the dark.

"Now bring the pony to me, Rin."

Rin went off at once to fetch the beast.

The garden at the top of the Hegemon's Residence covered the entire roof except for a small and plain cubicle of white marble which stood in the very center of the garden. To this glistening structure that enclosed only a single room unadorned and furnished only with a few silken pillows and a suspended lamp fueled by fragrant oils the Hegemon Agathon was accustomed to retire to meditate.

Whenever the Hegemon made use of his "thought temple" as he called his white chamber all others were forbidden access to the Residence roof and to the glory of its garden famed for its profusion of blooms both ordinary (roses) and exotic (orchids from afar). The garden also was much-admired for the perfumes it breathed out so voluptuous that many a visitor found them too rich to endure for long.

On this particular afternoon of azure heaven, lenient sunlight, and sly puff-balls of air which mitigated somewhat the intensity of the garden fragrances the Hegemon was absent and the roof deserted except for two late visitors: the Sage Megistes and his pupil, Darden Agathonson.

The two had come to the roof-top for one of Darden's weekly tutorial sessions with Megistes for the Logofant had recently altered Darden's course of instruction to include excursions to a variety of venues where the boy and the old man were simply to talk to each other about any topic that came up. Under such rules it was only natural that their discussions usually rambled over a variety of topics from the highly personal to the abstract political.

By allowing Darden to speak without restraint in their sessions Megistes hoped the boy might reveal, even if inadvertently, the roots of the wrath that seemed to animate his otherwise excellent mind. So far nothing so salutary had occurred but Darden had presented his mentor with numerous opportunities to point out the profusion of errors in the boy's thinking. Still, Megistes did not delude himself that his arguments, however cogent, had persuaded Darden to abandon any of the opinions he was so bent on trumpeting to the world. Nevertheless, Megistes persisted in correcting his student for he had discovered in his long life that when it came to precocious youth, and Darden was certainly one of those, the effects of one's argumentation might lie dormant until for some unfathomable reason they suddenly spring to life—for good or ill let it be said—in the youthful mind often in the disguise of an original conception of the young thinker himself. And, of course, Megistes reflected, the long-suffering instructor would never know just what words of his had resulted in his pupil's "insight." It was precisely this kind of outcome that Megistes sought to achieve with Darden for the old man considered it his duty to protect his pupil as far as it might be possible from falling prey to the fashionable follies that continually bobbed up in every generation to beguile the young away from true wisdom.

On this fine day Megistes had taken Darden to the Residence roof garden not only because it offered a panoramic view of Ten Turrets and the Katoran hills beyond but also because he hoped the majesty of the scene would lodge in the boy's memory to surface one day and move him to a more just appreciation of his native land.

On this occasion Megistes himself was filled as always with admiration bordering on love as he beheld the citadel below him and the purple mist of the vineyards and the silver-green of olive orchards in the distance.

Darden, however, merely yawned ostentatiously as if displaying his contempt for the view.

"Be fair, Darden," said Megistes with a tolerant smile for the youngest and most intelligent of his charges, "Why not admit that what you're looking at is magnificent?"

The boy shrugged.

"Sorry, Master, I can't see what's so great about it. What does it mean, after all? When you think about it Ten Turrets is just a pile of rock and brick and junk that says, 'Look how powerful we Arkies are!' What's so magnificent about that? Sure those towers and walls keep the Bem out. So what? The Bem, as far as I can tell, don't want to get in here anyway. Maybe they never did. So to me Ten Turrets is just vanity."

Megistes said, "Well, Darden, I see a quite different scene down there—an architectural achievement, the product of a free people's fallible struggle to create a just society. I find it beautiful."

"No offense, Master," Darden said, "But don't you reckon that there are bigger, better, and certainly more beautiful cities elsewhere?"

"Oh? Where?"

Darden scowled.

"I don't know where. Some place. Maybe across the Onyx Sea. In Northfair they say that the world outside Arkadia is filled with all kinds of people, and all sorts of cities and temples and settlements."

Megistes made no comment for he harbored a secret fear that as Darden had so astutely speculated such peoples and cities did exist elsewhere and that true to the natural greed of human beings they would covet Arkadia for themselves if they learned of its existence something the Northfair merchant-cabal itself strove to avoid in order to protect its monopoly of trade with both the Bem and Arkadia.

As if his imagination was excitedly conjuring a world that both Megistes and the Northfair merchants would rather not picture,

146

Darden said, "Maybe the day will arrive when one of those Onyx Sea folk will come here and pull down those arrogant Arkadian walls and turrets. Probably be a good thing too."

Megistes was invariably puzzled by Darden's often-expressed dislike for the land of his birth. He would always seek the reason for it, if a genuine reason other than an ill disposition existed, by probing the young man with a taunt or two.

"Do you actually mean to say that you a self-proclaimed champion of peace and justice would welcome a foreign invasion of Arkadia? Surely you can see that the first victims of such an assault would be your poor Bem."

Stung by his teacher's barb Darden flushed, brushed a hank of his unruly hair back from his forehead, and cleared his throat. "Well, of course, I don't mean to be taken literally."

"No?" Still probing Megistes said, "Then how do you wish to be taken?"

"I just want to show how much I hate tyranny."

"Are you now saying that Arkadia is a tyranny?'

Megistes was not about to allow the boy to escape by editing his own thoughtless words.

"Maybe Arkadia's not a tyranny yet but we're heading that way."

Apparently the boy had decided to retreat no further.

"So, you're now claiming that Agathon is a tyrant?"

"Not yet, maybe, but he's heading in that direction."

The boy looked Megistes in the eye, defiant.

Megistes said with a sardonic smile, "We are speaking of your father, are we not? The Hegemon Agathon?"

"We are, yes."

Megistes frowned at Darden. He found the boy's attitude repellent even if it was mostly a pose.

"If you really reckon the Hegemon of Arkadia is a potential tyrant I must demand that you explain yourself."

Darden brushed his hair back again. When it fell once more he ignored it though it was plain it annoyed him.

In this brief pantomime Megistes detected what seemed to be the expression of a hitherto seldom noticed aspect of Darden's character: a capacity to plow through distraction in order to confront larger matters on his mind. Megistes regarded the little business with the irritating lock of hair as somehow a symbol of a quite formidable trait taking shape in the boy: Darden, already a most disagreeable acquaintance, was growing into an even more disagreeably dogged opponent.

Defiant, Darden said, "I will try to explain myself as best I can, Master."

"Please do," said Megistes.

Megistes looked forward with fascination to hearing Darden's "case" against his father.

"I believe," Darden began tentatively, apparently marshalling his thought, "that despite our current Hegemon's public and perhaps even sincere promotion of individual freedom, at least in Arkadia, he must inevitably end as a tyrant."

"And you make that judgment based on what evidence? Surely I've taught you better."

Darden ignored the jibe.

"I base my judgment on no so-called 'evidence' whatsoever but on observation of the differences between what is supposed to happen in our happy land, and what actually does happen."

The boy favored the Sage with an impudent grin.

Megistes frowned in response to the boy's insolence.

"Say your piece straight and plain, Darden. Surely you learned that much from me."

The impudent grin remained.

"You taught us well, Master. In fact, it's thanks to your instruction that I've come to my judgment of my dear father."

Megistes felt unaccustomed anger beginning to simmer in his entrails. *By the Logos! This supercilious boy was playing with him!*

Darden, the grin still clinging to his lips, continued.

"According to the lessons that Milo, and I, and Phylax learned from you, Master, the Hegemon is supposed to govern with the approval of the elected Grand Council, right?"

Megistes nodded but he thought he saw where Darden was headed. One could not deny the acuity of this juvenile's precocious intellect.

"But it doesn't work as it should does it?"

Darden's grin now twisted into a sneer of contempt.

"The Council is run by the Megar and Rider aristocrats who care only for their titles, and for ceremonies, and playing at soldier, and—oh yes—making sure that the elected Koinars in the Council never get to vote. And all that's just fine with the great Agathon as long as the Council does exactly what he tells it to do. No debate, no questions, and by the way, the aristocrats don't dare make even the simplest laws without Agathon's prior approval. Yet the 'Founder Laws' say that the Council is supposed to vote 'after public debate' to choose, both the Hegemon and the Anax. But there's never a debate these days. The Council doesn't even go through the motions; they just endorse the Hegemon's will. The Founder Laws also say that any citizen may put himself before the Council as a candidate for Anax or Hegemon. But nobody dares to do so lest he incur the wrath of the old men of the Council for such temerity. The result is that only members of one family, my family as it happens, have occupied the High Bench for as long as anyone can remember. And now it'll be my ridiculous brother who'll be raised to Anax and then to the High Bench. And if all this doesn't add up to tyranny—soft maybe, but tyranny nevertheless—then I don't know what tyranny is."

Having finished making his case at least for the moment Darden again brushed the unruly hair from his forehead and fixed challenging eyes on his teacher.

Nettled by the boy's ungracious manner Megistes replied with a touch of haughtiness of his own.

"What you have failed to grasp, Darden, probably due to your lack of experience, is the fact that genuine tyranny, the real thing, always—and mark me on this—ends up resorting to force. People obey because if they don't, they suffer. To my knowledge no Hegemon of Arkadia has ever used force to exert his will."

Darden shot back without a moment's hesitation.

"Except against the Bem who don't count I suppose. Plenty of force gets used against the Bem. And, forgive me for speculating, Master, but who's to say that the Hegemony will not use force in Arkadia if it is thwarted in any matter important to it?"

The insolent grin re-appeared.

Though irritated at Darden's rude manner and therefore tempted to strike back with a sarcastic comment, Megistes managed to hold his temper as well as his tongue for the truth was that he agreed, in part, with the young man's general complaint. Of course Darden, having little knowledge of the world as it really was, had greatly exaggerated the case when he charged his father as a potential tyrant even against the murderous Bem. Nevertheless, Megistes granted, that the boy had hit the mark in one respect: Too much power had accumulated over the generations in the hands of the Hegemony. But this had not come about by design; it was, rather, the result of the remarkably effective stewardship of a long line of Hegemons the latest of whom was Darden's own sire, the great Agathon. It was, Megistes recognized, a weakness in the Founder Laws that Arkadia's good government depended so much on men of outstanding character being chosen to conduct the public business. The unforeseen irony lay in the fact that a procession of wise and talented rulers had made it so, had also made it, apparently, unnecessary for other good but lesser men to devote themselves to the exercise of self-government.

At this moment of insight Megistes found himself reflecting on an axiom which he for all his supposed wisdom had not fully grasped until now though young Darden had comprehended it instinctively: "When the folk of a nation lose their grip on the Public Business by resigning their interests to others, they open the gates to the dire-cats of tyranny."

So far, thanks to a succession of excellent rulers, Arkadia had avoided those tyrannical dire-cats. Nevertheless, the nation now depended for its governance on a continuation of that line of wise and brilliant men. Was Milo the Heir such a man? Megistes recalled that at his last meeting with Agathon, sometime after Milo's betrothal to Kala Aristaia, the Hegemon had expressed some rather vague worry about Milo's response or lack thereof to his betrothed.

Though Megistes himself had also sensed some inchoate deficiencies in Milo he had attributed them to the boy's youth and had then, blithely and perhaps wrongly, re-assured Agathon that his Heir would right himself in time.

When he'd had his talk with Kala, the Sage now recalled, had he not detected in her some uneasiness about her future husband though Milo himself had not been the subject of their talk? And now Darden, too, had implied that Milo was in some serious way flawed even "ridiculous." Perhaps Darden was merely grousing, exposing a younger brother's jealousy of a favored elder brother. But one ought to make certain in these matters. With this in mind, Megistes addressed a stern question to Darden.

"What did you mean when you called Milo ridiculous?"

"I may have spoken too harshly. I meant to say that it's ridiculous the partiality shown to my brother. It's ridiculous that we must have the next Anax be 'of the blood' even though he's completely unqualified."

"In what way unqualified? Give me a straight answer, Darden."

The boy let a contemptuous smile play briefly over his lips.

"I'll just say that Milo's character leaves much to be desired."

"No," said Megistes. "I won't permit you to get away with easy innuendo. If you know something that would affect Milo as Anax it's your duty to spit it out."

Detecting the iron insistence in Megistes' query Darden met the old man's hard eyes with a grim face of his own.

"Very well, Master, I will say that the Milo I know is stupid and weak. He has disgusting habits. He fools with magic in his private quarters. I've seen it. He's addicted to playing with a kind of magical glass ball and that's all I'm going to say, Master, even to you. Let others confirm it, if they have the courage."

Megistes found himself stunned.

Milo? Magic? Some sort of secret debauchery?

"Does Kala Aristaia know about this," Megistes asked.

Had the girl played him for a fool, he wondered. *Had she and Milo formed a cabal of two?*

Darden emitted a bark of cruel laughter.

"Does Kala Aristaia know about Milo's little addiction? Hardly. That girl doesn't actually know anything, except how to look enticing in public. She's too spoiled to notice anyone but herself."

Darden grinned again then went on.

"Besides poor Milo doesn't want anyone to know about his dirty little vice, least of all the girl he's supposed to marry who incidentally scares the fool half to death."

Relieved to hear Kala inadvertently absolved of falsity by Darden, the aged tutor growled, "There's more to Kala than you know."

Darden only shrugged his contempt.

Still staggered by his pupil's revelations about Milo—assuming they were true—Megistes considered what action to take in order to deal with the situation for any problem concerning the Heir to the High Bench, assuming it was a problem and not some enlarged fantasy from the fertile brain of a resentful younger brother, had to be confronted. How to do it then?

Agathon, Megistes told himself, had best be kept in the dark for as long as necessary possibly forever if the "problem" could be solved without his participation. Yet Megistes recognized his own inadequacy in this matter for the complexities of human desires, guilts, and physical perversities often baffled him. Hence, he saw only one path open to him: to recruit Kala Aristaia as the instrument to free Milo from his addiction if it really existed. Megistes resolved to speak to her again as soon as it could be arranged. He would certainly make her understand that she would find no better way to serve Arkadia than to be the agent for the salvation of the nation's next Hegemon. Moreover, Megistes could think of no more certain means by which to test the young woman's devotion to her own new role as the Betrothed than to assign her to such an important task.

Darden, his face suddenly a glum mask, broke into Megistes' reflections.

"I never should have spoken of this stuff, Master, even to you, but it all seems so unfair!"

The boy's face reddened with the resentment he no longer could hide.

"I should be chosen Anax not Milo. I'm better than he is in every way and you know it, Master."

Megistes said nothing but in fact he thought Darden's character too unstable to rule in any capacity. Besides, how could Darden serve an Arkadia he professed to despise? Darden, however, had still more to say.

"I just want to have genuine purpose in my life, Master, but I know I'm doomed to be a nobody while Milo is given power he doesn't know how to use."

Said Megistes, "There are many posts you can fill to achieve a purpose."

"Like what? Enlist as a cadet in the Array? Become some kind of liaison between the Hegemony and the Council so I can be addressed as Strategat? No, thank you. I want to serve all people not just the Hegemony."

Hearing this youth speak of his hunger to "serve" Megistes reflected on how often such a hunger elided into a raging thirst to rule.

"You're talking about having power," said Megistes.

"Yes, certainly, you can only do good when you have the power to do it."

"And what would you actually do if you had power?"

Darden hesitated as if he'd never considered such a question. He frowned.

"I don't know, exactly. Not yet anyway. But I would want to change the way things work now; everything needs to change."

Megistes nodded.

"You'd give the people Justice, I suppose?"

"Exactly."

"Whatever the cost?"

"Certainly. Justice would be my first goal. Justice for all, including the Bem."

"Very admirable," said the Sage.

Megistes sighed wearily and noted that the sun was already touching the western mountains. A cool easterly breeze from the Bemgrass had begun blowing as well.

"It's getting late," Megistes said, "time we were off home."

As Megistes and Darden were making a wordless descent on the ramp from the roof garden there suddenly appeared in the tutor's mental eye a visual memory of Milo as he had been on that bright afternoon of his first attendance at a Passing Ceremony. How mischievous the boy had been then on his prancing steed! How proud he'd been then, how full of joyful anticipation of his future! Now, if Darden was to be believed, that Milo of the Passing was no more. What had happened to change him? Had Milo, as many of the young elite were wont to do, fallen into what Megistes conceived of as the "adolescent abyss"? Was he undergoing the tortures of self-doubt? Was he feeling the overwhelming tug of sexual desire that he knew not how to satisfy? Was he resenting the replacement of childhood freedom with the shackles of responsibility? Was he asking himself am I normal and finding no answers?

If these questions had produced a malaise in Milo, thought Megistes, *then time and sympathetic support would salvage him. But suppose something more sinister had seized Milo, some self-generated demon against which he felt helpless?* Megistes loosed a sigh. *Was he never to be allowed the tranquility he yearned after?*

At once Megistes put that thought from his mind for in addition to revealing his own perilous state Darden had presented him with a possible problem regarding Milo, a riddle which he, Megistes, was best equipped to unravel. In fact, he had already decided on how to begin the task of salvation for both Milo and Darden.

First, he would definitely try to enlist Kala Aristaia in an effort to discover the nature of Milo's malaise and then in a program to rescue him from any self-generated demons that might be threatening to possess him. And second, with regard to Darden, Megistes would prevail on Agathon to order the boy to spend some time at the Logofane where Phylax was presently in temporary quarantine as well. At the Logofane, Megistes himself, with the aid of the Logos, would attempt to purge Darden of the beautiful but poisonous illusions infesting the boy's brain and heart. Which of these two somehow intertwined tasks would prove the more difficult, that Megistes could not know. But he did know that both of them had to be accomplished for the sake of the free Arkadia he loved.

Within her underworld dungeon, Eris, Goddess of Strife, continued to shed bitter tears of grief over the demise of her family the Olympian gods. She knew that her weeping might continue through eternity or might halt at any moment for in these Meta-chron caverns she was experiencing meta-grief and irrigating it with meta-tears. Then a prodigious epiphany put a stop to her tears.

Before Eris' astonished vision a rough-edged circle of emptiness had become manifest, expansive enough for her to step through into—what? It seemed to Eris an orb of a blackness so pure that she could only conceive of it as "Nothing." Or perhaps it was an aperture to nothingness for beyond its threshold there existed no shape, dimension, or other measurable quality but only a lightless absence.

The circumference of the circle of Nothing throbbed like a wound in the integument of what passes for reality. Though a rent in the fabric of space and time, the manifestation, Eris knew, offered her no exit from her prison. Of that much she felt certain for it was wholly negative: a Nothing, Non, Not, a Never, a Naught. Yet she saw this Nullity plain before her eyes. All at once she understood its Nature.

Eris was looking into the *Antekosmos*—the black emptiness a billionth of an instant before the instant of Creation. That *Antekosmos*, she understood, contained in embryo all that was to explode into existence: all history, all science, all thought—everything to be. Compelled, she stepped across the threshold into the pregnant Nullity whereupon Eris ceased to exist or at least it seemed so to her for a moment or perhaps for a thousand years. Then she found herself once more alone within her hell. Gone was the *Antekosmos*. But now she knew and understood all that had happened in the land of Arkadia to cause the terrible fate of her tribe.

Under the weight of that fearful history, Eris knelt and scooped the acrid dust of the caverns onto her head. She washed her face in it. She wailed. To contain within her soul the tragic tale just revealed to her this was more than she could bear in silence. So Eris cried it forth so that the story might echo eternally among the fires and foul smokes of her hell.

Eris' narrative of the disastrous decline and fall of the Olympian gods from the Pantheon of Arkadia began with the mundane fact that when the mercenary warrior fraternity known as "The Ten Thousand" first departed their native soil of Hellas to fight for the Eastern King who had hired them, they naturally brought with them the worship of their Hellenic gods, the Olympians. Throughout their adventures in the East, the warriors of the Ten Thousand, but not their mob of foreign camp-followers, reverenced their deities, made sacrifice to them, and implored their aid. This veneration of the Olympian divinities became even more fervent when, after the defeat of their royal client, the Ten Thousand undertook their heroic march back to their homeland. Then the Great Separation had occurred when the warriors, destined to become the Founders of Arkadia, lost contact with the main body of The Ten Thousand.

Mistakenly regarding the separation as temporary, for not even the gods could see much less fight off Fate, the Hellenic Olympians— exercising the prerogatives of their divinity—decided to split themselves into two duplicate sets, each set replicating the other. Thus were formed dual divinities with each of the eternal Hellenic gods becoming indistinguishable from his or her new brother, or sister.

One set of the duplicate Olympians remained with the main body of the Ten Thousand and eventually found their way home to Hellas in triumph. The other set meanwhile obedient, though unknowingly, to Destiny, accompanied the lost battalions in their wanderings. These became the Olympian gods of the new land of Arkadia. Quite naturally they considered themselves, as did the First Founders of Arkadia, Hellenes, still native to Hellas the homeland of all who had made up the original Ten Thousand.

As the generations passed in Arkadia the divine twins of the gods of Hellas like the First Founders themselves had flourished in their new land. In substance, in powers, in all aspects of personality, the transplanted Arkadian Olympians remained the Olympians of Hellas just as the First Arkadians continued to be Hellenes though neither the transplanted gods nor their worshippers still inhabited their lost homeland.

For long swaths of mortal time then, the Arkadian Olympians had been honored and feared by the descendants of the aristocratic warrior caste of their lost Hellas. Although in their new land the displaced warriors of the Ten Thousand renamed themselves "Megars" and "Riders", they remained the dominant aristocracy of Arkadia and they made it a religious practice to preserve both the attitudes and customs of the homeland they would never see again but could not forget. Under these conditions the Arkadian branch of the Olympian gods lived in joy.

As immortal twins of their Hellenic selves the Arkadian deities practiced the same capricious manners that had characterized their behavior in Hellas, behavior that their Megar and Rider worshippers expected of them. That is to say that the Arkadian branch of Olympus clung to their old divine sensuality, cruelty, and ferocity toward those who both adored and feared them. Depending on their mood, the Arkadian Olympians would often indulge in grand oracular pronouncements, grant wishes, clarify confusion, and give courage to the fearful. Just as often, however, they might demand the building of brilliant new temples, insist on blood sacrifices, and drive their priests and priestesses to mad excess. Capricious Zeus, ever lusting for this beautiful mortal or that, would ravage any woman or boy he chose and he often did so while in bizarre disguise. Nor did Aphrodite harbor any qualms about driving mortals to distraction with lust. Nor did Apollo, despite his oft-stated reverence for mortal art shrink from flaying the skin from any mortal poets and artists too who failed to pay him proper deference. Nor did this same Lord of the Sun refrain from issuing teasing oracles, riddles really, when it pleased him to confuse his worshippers. In truth, none of the Arkadian gods, including Eris herself to her shame would shrink from any cruel mischief if it pleased them. Thus did the Arkadian gods who constantly squabbled among themselves display an ongoing distemper toward the mortals on whose faith their very existence depended. Yet, despite the cruelty with which the immortals too often treated them the Arkadian aristocrats clung to their Olympians for how else were mere mortals to cope with the mysteries and terrors of Fate in the hostile cosmos? For all their faults Arkadian aristocracy believed their deities essential: to explain, to protect, to legitimize, to carry out ceremonies of blessing.

Accordingly, the Megars and Riders of Arkadia with both fear and hope animating them paid tribute to their own Olympian deities by ceremonial piety and by erecting gleaming shrines to house grand statues, as well as by festivals, all to plead for the blessings of the gods. In addition, a literature of tales and wonders grew up to enshrine belief in the gods in each Arkadian heart. These were halcyon times for the gods. It was no wonder then that, in their arrogant confidence, the Olympians failed to notice the malignancy growing in the very midst of their felicity. In truth the course of the dark fate that would finally overtake the Olympians could be traced back to the cancer induced by one seemingly unimportant fact: namely that a mongrel throng had accompanied the Hellenic aristocrats and their Hellenic gods to Arkadia.

This polyglot mob composed of slaves, captives, whores, petty-merchants, thieves, uprooted hangers-on, refugees from barbarian tribes, and often enough concubines and their children had followed the lost battalions of the Ten Thousand through the mountains to the land that would be named Arkadia. Used to fending for themselves and left by the Megars and Riders to perish or survive by their own devices this unruly and half-starved rabble banded together more or less during their long trek to the new land. Once arrived in Arkadia and fearing the contemptuous power of their former Megar and Rider masters these poor folk continued to cling to one another as if by instinct. In this manner did the mongrel crowd to whom their betters gave the derisive name "Koinars." from the Hellenic word for common, form a community of their own kind.

During those long swaths of mortal time when the Arkadian aristocracy and their gods flourished these Koinars under the lash of necessity developed a common tongue from the many languages originally spoken among them. Largely ignored by their Megar and Rider neighbors the Koinars also formulated an agreed-upon set of rules to govern behavior within their multiplying and thriving communities. Most important, the Koinar entity unified by what soon became common values, tastes, and customs were also evolving a belief system and an agreed-upon history that had no roots in the land of Hellas for of course the Koinars had never laid eyes on the homeland of the wealthy Megars and Riders and so had little interest in it or in the Olympian gods of Arkadian aristocrats. Instead the Koinars spent their energies creating not only a supple language of their own and a body of internal laws but also a system of belief and behavior that relied on mortal reason to make moral decisions for individuals and rulers alike. As a symbol of their system the Koinars began to attribute certain powers to a somewhat shabby artifact, otherwise unidentifiable, which they called their "Logos" and which they revered as the mystical embodiment of their amalgamation of peoples and beliefs. As for the Olympians gods, the Koinars scoffed at them or ignored them.

The gods, in turn, mocked the Koinar Logos—a name the Olympians pointed out to each other with gleeful scorn whose origin as a Hellenic word the simple Koinars appeared not to realize. With their habitually careless capriciousness, however, the Olympians of Arkadia made no effort to apprise the Koinars of what seemed to be their ignorance. Instead, emulating their adoring Megars and Riders, the Olympians left these apparently asinine common folk to themselves. And with that decision was planted the seed of the tragedy that eventually doomed the Arkadian gods for as time passed in its generations the Koinars left to themselves grew into a virtually independent state within Arkadia. Koinars came to control not only their own wealth and culture but also much that had belonged to their aristocratic masters.

Although still socially inferior to the Megars and Riders the Koinars, acting freely and, it had to be admitted, benignly, became indispensable to the continuing prosperity of a docile Arkadian aristocracy. Although many Koinars lived and worked on the estates of the aristocrats many more began to live and work in separate Koinar settlements and many became dominant in financial affairs, medicine, and above all as managers and as drivers of innovation. So necessary did the Koinars become to Arkadian life that their power at once salutary and subtle was readily accepted as natural. Still the Olympian gods of Arkadia mocked them.

Eventually the time arrived when the Arkadian aristocracy ceased thinking of themselves as Hellenes; they had become Arkadians. Megars and Riders, now many generations removed from their homeland, had come to think of Hellas as a more or less mythical country, a place of story, not history. It was Arkadian history, much of it in fact Koinar history that young Arkadians were learning now. Even the old language of the Hellenes was neglected for it was much more convenient to speak the ever-changing "new language" of the Koinars with its contemporary idioms than to struggle with the creakily inflected forms of the ancient Hellenic tongue whether spoken or written. Even the Hellenic *alpha-beta* fell into disuse until only place names firmly rooted in the Hellenic past remained though the actual meaning of traditional names such as "Bradys", "Tachys", and "Pelorys", for the rivers, and "Plousios", "Chion", and "Hierys" for mountains, had been long forgotten.

The Olympian gods of Arkadia only began to perceive the perilous diminution of Faith in them when the Hegemony of Arkadia, recognizing that virtually all its citizens including Megars and Rider had by now embraced the moral principles of the Logos, established on Mt. Hierys a grand shrine called the "Logofane". At last realizing that their immortality, their power—their very existence—depended upon the faith of their mortal worshippers, the Olympians of Arkadia tried to save themselves by reversing the tide.

In the mistaken hope that changes in style might regain the worshippers they needed the old gods attempted to adapt to the changing society often in ludicrous ways. Father Zeus, for example, shaved his beard and renounced his characteristic lechery. Aphrodite covered her glorious nakedness with the veil-dresses fashionable in Arkadia. Apollo ceased his riddling oracles in favor of direct speech. Even Ares, bloody God of War and once the passionate lover of Eris herself, rumbled tripe in a misguided attempt to pose as a pacifist. The gods even attempted to speak in the new tongue which in private they cursed as "a barbarous dialect." Only Eris managed to learn, though imperfectly, the "Language of the Logos."

Thus did the Hellenic gods of Arkadia continue to fail, their temples deserted, their shrines empty, and such holy places were soon torn down, their stones scavenged for use in building roads and walls. The statues of the gods were removed to the recesses of the enormous hollow halls within the caverns of Mt. Kryptys. Even the few remaining priests eventually abandoned the gods and retreated to the Logofane to "study the Logos." The gods, already attenuated in body and spirit, were finished, abandoned.

One by one—with the exception of mad Dionysus and Eris herself—the gods found themselves banished, somehow transported by unknown but irresistible forces to the fiery halls within Mt. Kryptys where time had taken on dimensions and qualities unknown to them. Pale and bewildered the discarded deities, cursing the Logos, at first had clung to one another in the gloom of the caves which Eris knew as the Meta-chron caverns. Growing ever more tenuous in body and spirit the banished immortals played at dice, argued, blamed each other for their condition and hatched implausible schemes to re-establish themselves.

One by one, however, they fell into silence and surrendered to Fate.

One by one they withdrew from one another to wander in the corridors of stone to meditate in the dust until—grateful for the inner silence that descended on them—they abandoned awareness itself, becoming mere shreds of membrane, their tragedy almost complete.

Eventually, they would disappear entirely for the melancholy narrative whose end a grieving Eris had now reached allowed for no possibility that the old gods could be resurrected not by Eris or any other. Nevertheless, Eris now told herself, she could avenge them. Was she not still the Goddess of Strife, lover of havoc, drinker of blood? She would have vengeance. Eris would see this alien Arkadia extinguished, this Logos fetish destroyed along with its Koinar idolaters.

Eris thought of the unknown mortal she had detected wandering in the world beyond her prison. Had he not pledged himself to Eris' own purpose? Thus it was essential that she succeed in drawing that wrathful spirit to her for his advent at the Meta-chron caverns was necessary; he must not only become the instrument of her revenge, he must also believe in her for the sake of her own continued existence. He must come to her. He must. For both she and the mortal had the same destiny to fulfill: to destroy Arkadia.

NINE

Seraph and the Bem woman, Rin, had been making good progress for several nights now. In fact, Seraph reckoned that the river he sought probably lay no more than another night or two away from the place where they now meant to hide and rest for the day—the first light of which was already appearing behind the eastern mountains. Without having to be told, Rin helped Seraph from his mount and then went about concealing the pony in the high grass. She took a ragged swatch of sheepskin from a bundle she had prepared without Seraph's noticing it upon their departure from their last daylight camp. She spread the sheepskin on a small open space beneath an arch of thorn bush. From the same bundle she extracted a gourd that contained tunnik-flavored water. She placed the gourd on the sheepskin along with a small piece of half-spoiled meat stolen from the leavings of a dire-cat. Then Rin gestured for Seraph to make himself comfortable in the place she had readied for him. He obeyed her signal and stretched out. Softly she spoke.

"We will be safe here I think. The hunters seldom come this far eastward on the Bemgrass. Later, when the daylight chases off the big cats I will fetch water from the stream we saw and find some more tunnik berries, and some bones if the cats have left any. You may rest at ease." With this she stretched herself at his feet on the hard ground.

Although he refrained from saying so lest she regard him as a lesser man than the harsh masters she was accustomed to obeying, Seraph felt extremely pleased to have Rin with him. Could he have gotten this far without her help? Probably not. Nor would the pony have survived without her care.

"Rin," he said abruptly.

She lifted her head to look at him.

"Come lie with me."

She crawled to him at once.

Without speaking Rin lay on her back at his left side. Though they were not touching, Seraph was acutely aware of her presence. He found himself visualizing the Arkie harlots he had watched—was it two years ago now?—at the Komai of the soldiers. Rin possessed none of the aggressively flamboyant "charms" of those loathsome whores, but she was a woman and she had surprisingly aroused long-dormant desire in his maimed body.

Seraph had been schooled in the mechanics of sex by his shaman master even though Darst, as was his custom, had accompanied his instructions with sardonic laughter at Seraph's obvious aversion to the sexual act as well as his clumsy efforts to practice it. Still, Seraph knew what to do. The question now was whether or not to slake his unwonted desire in the body of the subservient Rin. Would it be wise to do so? His own undeniable need, however, decided the matter. He took Rin into his arms. She responded as she had been taught. Despite a mutual awkwardness, they engaged each other and brought the business to a satisfactory climax.

In the aftermath Seraph and Rin remained in their embrace. Had it been a good thing or a bad, Seraph asked himself, this coming together with the Bem woman? He could not answer. Nor, as he considered the question, did it seem to matter much after the event.

"I will sleep now," Seraph said. "When I wake in the dusk, will you still be here, Rin, or will you have run away?"

"I will be here."

"I am glad," he said, meaning his words.

When Seraph woke the setting sun had slid across the sky and was resting on the peaks of the western mountains. He had dreamed again as he had for many sleeps recently of a voice calling him, surely the voice of a divine being, and he knew that he must soon find the caller, lest the calling cease, causing him to miss whatever Fate had ordained for him. Still, he must wait for the full night before traveling on or risk blundering into a hunting party and never reach his summoner at all. And where was Rin?

Seraph sat up. Had she thought better of her promise and left him after all?

Rin appeared, bearing food and drink. Seating herself at his side Rin fed Seraph tunnik berries, nuts, and wild onions, as well as raw shreds of a frog. All this, Seraph surmised, was the bounty of her foraging while he had slept. Thanks to Rin, he acknowledged, he was no longer suffering the debilitating pains of demonic hunger.

Seraph drank some of the sweet water from the gourd that Rin had placed at his side. *Nor was demon thirst torturing him either,* he thought. Only a growing exhaustion plagued him. How much longer before his body and spirit gave out? Still he had to go on.

When Seraph had finished eating and drinking, it was Rin who broke the silence between them with an unexpected whispered question.

"How were you maimed? Your leg and eye?"

Rin looked away as if ashamed to have presumed with such a query and she hung her head as if she feared a blow as well for her temerity.

Seraph answered her with the truth.

"I was a throw-away child."

With undisguised bitterness Seraph told of his mother's mad hatred for him, her cruelty to him.

"She left me for dead on the grass."

Rin seemed entranced by Seraph's tale.

"Yet you survived," she said now daring to look at him directly. "How?"

As if relieved to lay down even for a short time a memory that was too heavy to bear in endless silence Seraph now told the Bem woman—*his* Bem woman—how the old Koinar couple had "rescued" him, how he had aided them to make slaves of throw-away Bem girls, how out of pure hatred—both of himself and the Koinars—he had slain the old couple, and fled.

Rin's curiosity—no, her interest in his life—was not yet satisfied.

"And so you returned to our people, to the Bem Colors?"

"I had no place else to go," Seraph replied with a grimace of disgust, "but now I have run away again for I have learned to detest the Bem."

After a brief hesitation Seraph elaborated as much to give shape to his own thoughts, as to inform her.

"I have recognized that the Bem are as ignorant as the wild ox they hunt. I have seen that they embrace the misery they bring on themselves. I have rejected their subservience not only to the Arkies but also to their impotent fool of a god, Dis."

Rin listened large-eyed with alarm. Surely, her big-eyed fear seemed to say, Dis would strike them both down with his fierce lightning, Seraph for speaking blasphemy, her for hearing it. Yet what else could she, a woman, do but listen? She did not dare to attempt to halt Seraph's impiety even if she had any idea how to do so. When Seraph finished, however, Rin tried with timid words to rebuke his blasphemy and in this way, perhaps, soften Dis' anger at both of them.

"Yet, despite what you say about Great Dis," she pointed out in a nervous murmur, "he chose you to become one of his priesthood did he not?"

Seraph frowned at her, his good eye red with fury.

"How do you know that?"

Rin had no choice but to answer as best and as humbly as she could.

"I saw you often among the people. You were always in the company of the Shaman Darst. It was said by all that Darst had made you his apprentice. That was the talk of the men. I only heard it. I never spoke of such matters; they were beyond my understanding."

"Were they?"

Seraph's wrath seemed to ebb.

"Darst was a cruel and ignorant Master much in the mold of the so-called 'God of Chaos' himself. The Bem are fools to appease this Dis who is of no-account in the cosmos but only an instrument to keep the Bem in everlasting sorrow. I challenge your Dis to punish me, Rin! He has no power, except over you ignorant Bem!"

Here Seraph halted his denunciation of the meaningless Dis for he could see that his words were only adding to Rin's alarmed confusion. Instead, speaking in a soothing tone, Seraph told her that he was journeying eastward to the River Pelorys in response to a call from afar, perhaps a summons from a new divine source.

Rin listened in submissive silence. Her whole being was filled with awe and admiration for Seraph. With his ravaged face and crippled leg, she told herself, he must surely be a chosen son of Dis, let him deny the god of the Bem as he would.

Or might Seraph be, after all, the prophet of this new deity he heard calling to him? How could she ever know? Of only one thing was Rin absolutely certain: this broken man disposed of powerful magic. That he had plucked her from the horrors of the Bemgrass was a sure sign that she was meant to serve him in whatever way he required. If needed, she would die for him. In the meantime she would lead him eastward and help him to take up whatever great task awaited him.

As if he could read her thoughts as he probably could Seraph began to speak to her of what he called his quest.

"I have resolved to destroy the Arkies," he said. "I have resolved to erase them from their delusional universe."

Thrilled at the prospect of being associated however humbly with so grand an enterprise, Rin wondered how he would do it.

By magic? Spells and curses?

Again Seraph seemed to have ascertained her thoughts.

"I will begin by learning all there is to know about the Arkie enemy."

This time Rin spoke aloud, in wonder. "How will you do that?"

Seraph frowned, apparently because of the weight of his thought. "I do not know yet. But I know that all this—my Bemgrass wanderings, you, the nights, the pony, the need to cross the Pelorys—all of these are pieces of my destiny."

By now a thin moon was rising.

Time to go.

Rin fetched the pony and helped Seraph mount. Then, using the thick cords that had once bound her ankles, she fastened on the pony's broad back the worn leather bag that contained their scant provisions. Finally, leading the patient pony by its bridle, Rin set off eastward toward the river, proud to assist the precious being she now meant to serve with all her heart forever. How free she felt! How miraculous were her feet! How marvelous to move unencumbered through the grass after a life spent in fetters! How glorious the night and the cool air of liberty!

May Dis forgive me, she whispered, but I will die before I will ever return to hobbles!

Seraph had conferred this glory upon her at a stroke! *What other glories might she experience in his service? Might he not make her fly as the birds fly or as the spirits are said to do? Oh, how she longed to soar! And why not? Was she not in service to one blessed, a maker of marvels?*

Rin glanced back and saw that Seraph had entered into a state of contemplation.

What wonders he must be pondering! How happily she would strive to please him in every way!

I am alive at last, she told herself, feeling the luxurious wet grass under her unfettered feet.

With the pale mountain sun at its zenith, Phylax, wearing trail garb of rough leather leggings and tunic, reined up his favorite warhorse "Driver" to afford the powerful animal, as well as the accompanying packhorse, a much-needed breather before resuming the climb to their destination.

Dismounting, Phylax led both horses to drink from a stream that ran in a trickle alongside the steep and rocky and thus seldom traveled trail. He also gave both Driver and the packhorse a supply of oats. Only then did Phylax reach into Driver's saddlebag and extract the sweat-stained map that he'd been using as a guide since setting out from the Logofane fifteen days earlier. The purpose of his journey, undertaken with the permission of the Logofant Megistes, was, ostensibly anyway, to take a brief furlough from his often boring exile at the Logofane, an exile imposed on him by Megistes himself.

When he had first arrived at the Logofane, Phylax—a half-Koinar and thus imbued with a Koinar's reverence for the Logos housed in the magnificent shrine on Mt. Hierys—had been awed by the splendor he encountered there. No longer did the Logofane resemble in any way the simple wooden shelter of Early Arkadia which Phylax in his ignorance of such matters had expected to still exist. Instead, over the generations, the shrine of the Logos had grown into a truly opulent establishment.

A domed temple of white marble encompassed by terraced towers, monuments, and clusters of gleaming outbuildings was set in the midst of formal gardens and a maze of carefully tended pathways. Most of these pathways led to the "Logofane Academy" another impressive marble edifice, this one devoted to researching and teaching "the nature and history of the Logos." The Academy was also surrounded by the dwellings of students and researchers as well as a number of "Meditation Houses" given over to "spiritual renewal" for those in need. Megistes had assigned Phylax to a Meditation House of his own.

Try as he would, however, Phylax had found himself unable to confront much less soothe his inadmissible but still raging passion for Kala Aristaia in the atmosphere of the Logofane which he found more than a little oppressive. Hoping to clear his mind sufficiently to face up to the turmoil in his heart Phylax had tried going for solitary walks in the woods of Mt. Hierys. The walks, however, were never truly solitary for other walkers were everywhere and his walks did little good.

The wily and wise Megistes had then suggested that Phylax undertake by himself a journey of his own choosing. Its purpose, supposedly, was to free him from the "oppressive atmosphere" of the Logofane though Phylax understood that its real purpose was to purge his troubled soul of its yearning for an impossible love.

Phylax had agreed with alacrity not to mention relief to go on the suggested trip. And so, over the previous fifteen days he had allowed deep draughts of mountain air and long days of profound silence to cleanse his heart of the passion that had been devouring it and that was certainly wrong both for him and for her whom he had coveted with an ardor so baleful that it threatened to annihilate all else in his life even honor and the rule of duty.

Put simply, since fleeing the Logofane, Phylax had at last recognized clear and whole the truth that he had surely known from the beginning of his collision with pernicious desire but had been unable to accept heretofore: Unless he was ready to betray all he honored in life Phylax had no choice but to abandon all hope of an honest love between Kala Aristaia and himself. Phylax knew he would love her forever; that would never alter.

Now, however, with the healing that his solitary journeying had engendered he finally had found the strength to renounce in the privacy of his own thoughts his unworthy longing for Kala Aristaia. Henceforth he was resolved to love her in silence from afar and to betray neither by word nor gesture the intractable pain of loss which he would now have to bear and hide for the rest of his life.

To pursue any other course Phylax had realized at last would not only destroy him it would also ruin both Kala and Milo. For Phylax had now perceived as no other could have that his *del* had stumbled into some mysterious spiritual crisis of his own from which he required rescue if he was to rule Arkadia someday.

In fact, Phylax had come to see that it might fall to him somehow to salvage Milo from his unknown malady. The task might even require Kala's participation. *Perhaps,* he thought, *such a dual effort would help to establish a suitable future relationship between himself and Kala.*

In any event, Phylax told himself, feeling a flush of genuine contentment for the first time since he had glimpsed the beautiful Kala Aristaia in her coach on her way to Ten Turrets, these past fifteen days on the trail had restored to him a proper perspective on the requirements of honor and duty. For the remainder of his journey, therefore, Phylax promised himself that, free from his burden at last, he would only focus on and enjoy the trail ahead. With this in mind and allowing Driver and the packhorse to continue to crop the sparse grass nearby Phylax returned to studying his map. So far the trip had unfolded just as Phylax had planned it.

The first leg had taken Phylax down the north slope of Mt. Hierys to the Katoran hills, then westward to the valley of the modest stream known as the "Upper Tachys River." Phylax had then followed the valley of the Upper Tachys northwest to the steep western slope of snow-capped Mt. Chion. At thirteen thousand feet, Mt. Chion was the highest of the "Arkadian Ring" of mountains. With its year-round snowcap and long glaciers it abounded in rushing snow-melt streams that flowed into a great lake located at an altitude of six thousand feet. This body of water was called "The Lake of the Moon" and was the final goal Phylax meant to reach on this journey. Counting the thirty miles already covered on the upward trail where he now found himself Phylax reckoned that he and the horses had already traveled about one hundred and eighty miles in fifteen days. Not bad at all he reflected especially considering the rough terrain the horses had had to struggle over.

Judging from the map Phylax also estimated that the Lake of the Moon lay no more than three or four hours further up the trail ahead. With the sun still high he felt confident of reaching that enchanted body of fresh water in plenty of time to set up camp and then climb to one of the nearby crags to observe the phenomenon, which he had never seen, famed all over Arkadia and called "The Sky in the Lake."

According to all reports that Phylax had heard on certain nights when the moon was full (this night was one of them) the black and placid surface of the lake reflected the rising moon with an eerie beauty so precise that the onlooker gazing down from the surrounding heights into the mirror of the great water soon lost the ability to distinguish the moon in the dark waters of the lake from the moon in the night sky. So much was this so it was said that some watchers, bewitched, would attempt to "swim to the moon" by flinging themselves "upward" from the heights. Of course these enraptured gazers would only fall to their death on the rocks below. Phylax meant to observe for himself this phenomenon of The Sky in the Lake.

Still another reason why Phylax was determined to reach the lake as soon as possible was the fact that he hoped to encounter a particular snow bear while camped in the vicinity of the lake. This creature described by the few mountain-people who had seen him as "gigantic and vicious" and "as big as a warhorse" and bearing "a shaggy coat of silky white fur" was said to descend fairly often from his natural habitat in the glacial snows in order to hunt human prey along the shores of the Lake of the Moon. Given the fact that the lake by far the largest body of standing water in Arkadia was thirty miles long from east to west and eighteen miles across at its widest part from north to south the rogue bear had an enormous territory over which to range. It was no wonder then that the rogue had so far escaped his hunters. In fact, Phylax reflected, no snow bear had ever been hunted successfully though generations of Megar and Rider young men had tried. Phylax, however, hoped to have better luck than his predecessors for reports had reached the Logofane while he was still in residence there that the rogue had been active recently on the very sector of the lakeshore where Phylax planned to camp.

According to those reports to the Logofane which Megistes dutifully sent on to the Hegemony at Ten Turrets though he considered it unlikely that any help would be forthcoming from that quarter, the bear in question had killed and devoured a dozen women and children most of whom had come to the Lake with camping parties to observe the full moon in the lake. It was Phylax's hope, therefore, that the rogue, having grown careless as a result of the ease with which he could fill his belly on human prey, would be attracted to his baited campsite whereupon Phylax, lying in wait, would put four or five swift javelins into the startled beast enough to kill even a snow bear. If successful, Phylax had it in mind to consecrate the destruction of the beast to his own re-born honor in this way marking his return to duty as achieved on this pilgrimage to the Lake of the Moon. In addition, Phylax planned to present the trophy-pelt of the rogue bear to the Logofane as a token of his triumph over his own savage self and the brute passions that had almost unmanned him. Only then would he feel free to beg Megistes' permission to return to Ten Turrets in order to take up again the life of service ordained for him.

Surging with renewed confidence in himself and in what awaited him ahead Phylax mounted Driver once more. With the patient packhorse in tow and Driver already *chuffing* with the effort of the climb Phylax found himself laughing aloud with happiness at the outpouring of the day's sunlight, at the power of Driver's stride, at the coolness of the air, and the pure joy of being fully alive once more. Then, as Driver crested a rocky outcrop onto a grassy plateau of no significant size Phylax suddenly heard a sound that stopped his carefree laughter at once.

It was the unmistakable hissing-growl of a dire-cat. Could such a thing actually be? He reined in Driver and stood up in the stirrups, a javelin at the ready. Another growl emanated from a nearby thicket. The packhorse whinnied in fear; Driver, trained to combat, snorted and stood fast. And there, crouched but not hidden in the bushes an astonished Phylax beheld the agent of his astonishment: a fully-grown male dire-cat, huge, and ferocious. With the superb nonchalance of a champion killer in full possession of his strength, the great cat emerged from the sparse undergrowth onto the trail itself at a point no more than a hundred feet further up from Phylax's position. As if posing to show himself off the beast halted and gazed with impassive yellow eyes at the human who had disturbed his afternoon rest.

Phylax returned the stare with unabashed amazement at the remarkable creature ahead whose natural habitat he knew lay in the

Bemgrass hundreds of miles away from the frigid heights of Mt. Chion. It was against all probability yet Phylax could not doubt that he was looking at a veritable dire-cat and a splendid specimen as well. The majestic animal, standing more than half as tall as Driver, and twice the size of other lesser predator cats, possessed a sleek pelt as black as night. A neck ruff of thick gray fur—the badge of the male—fell to his chest. A wide stripe of gray ran along his spine culminating in a gray tail, tufted in black. Each of his lethally powerful paws was booted with gray fur as well. The cat was still stopped, its yellow eyes fixed on Phylax.

"You are beautiful", Phylax found himself whispering, as if addressing the cat. "But are you planning to attack me? Please don't, or I shall be forced to kill you and I'd rather solve your mysterious presence here than destroy you."

Phylax lifted the javelin higher as if to show the dire-cat what it faced should it make any aggressive move.

The packhorse began to thrash, trying to run away but Driver, brave enough to charge into any conflict, held his ground. The cat, born with no capacity to feel fear some said, yawned, displaying dagger teeth. Then the cat turned, and slowly padded off up the trail as if resuming an interrupted jaunt toward some inscrutable destination.

Phylax, emitting a sigh of relief at having thus been spared conflict with the cat, subsided onto his saddle. He did not immediately return to his own journey, however, for he considered it only good sense to allow the great cat to get well ahead of him if indeed the creature was actually following this relatively easy (for him) trail instead of plunging cross country in the steep bush. Phylax and his horses, of course, had no alternative but to stick to the trail, the countryside being too sheer and brushy for their passage.

Phylax dismounted and again allowed Driver and the packhorse, calmer now, to nibble whatever grass they could find near the trail. Reflecting on his encounter with the cat, Phylax couldn't help but wonder again what a dire-cat, the nocturnal king of the far off Bemgrass after all, was doing in harsh daylight six thousand feet up the cold and rocky northwest face of an almost uninhabited mountain. Hunting? But game here was scarce surely insufficient to feed a royal predator. Unless this particular fierce hunter like the storied snow-bear had learned to feast on the tasty flesh of human pilgrims at the Lake of the Moon. *Yes*, thought Phylax, *that had to be the case*. Still, if one mystery was solved another remained: How had the dire-cat come to Mt. Chion in the first place? That part of the puzzle might go unanswered forever. But what did it matter? After all, the world was full of unanswerables.

A breath of cooling air reminded Phylax that the day was waning, time to move on if he meant to be camped by the lake when the full moon rose tonight. Phylax mounted Driver again and leading the packhorse, returned to the trail, confident that he had given the dire-cat more than enough time to get far enough ahead to ensure that he and the horses were now out of reach of the cat's knife-blade fangs.

As he often did when traveling in country new to him Phylax envisioned the last segments of the trail ahead as delineated on his map. As he recollected from the chart and notes Megistes had provided to him at the outset of the journey the mountain track continued steep and rugged for another two or three miles until it reached the relatively level surface of the "heights" that looked precipitously down on the lake some two hundred feet below. When he arrived at the heights, Megistes' instructions cautioned, he would have to "look sharp" to find the path, a series of traverses, that would lead him down to the lake shore. The rest of the journey, it seemed, would be quite simple once Phylax managed to get to the high ground and provided that sufficient daylight remained to make the descent to the lake.

All at once Driver came to an abrupt halt that shook Phylax out of his reverie and almost out of the saddle. The reason for Driver's ill-timed stop was immediately manifest: no more than fifty yards away the dire-cat had reappeared on the path. As he had earlier, the beautiful beast, motionless as a statue hewn from obsidian, kept his yellow eyes fixed on Phylax for several moments. Then he threw back his fierce ruffed head and roared. The gigantic bellowing reverberated across the rocky slopes and the scarred seams of the mountain. Phylax was struck by a singular impression: that the ferocious cat was challenging him to combat. Driver must have sensed the challenge too for he reared and pawed the air seeming to respond to the cat's roared summons. Standing in the stirrups, Phylax drew a javelin from its holder on the saddle and cocked his arm in readiness to hurl it when the cat charged as he seemed about to do. The enormous creature did not attack, however. Instead he turned and loped up the pathway, stopping once as if inviting Phylax to come after him then going on.

"Should I follow?" Phylax asked himself aloud.

Driver trembled ready for a fight at any signal from his rider. Phylax thought of the praise and glory that would come to him and to his White Angel comrades in arms if he killed the beast. But what if the creature turned out to be a "were-cat" of some kind and so immune to his weapons? Well, wouldn't it be even more glorious then to bring down such an adversary? In any case, whether he killed a were-cat or a natural being the ferocious beast would make a magnificent trophy. Phylax pictured himself bringing its pelt to the Logofane along with the pelt of the snow-bear that he meant to kill as well. In that event, two man-eaters would have met their just doom at his hands for the dire-cat too he now decided must also be a devourer of human flesh otherwise how could it feed itself in this mountain world so inimical to its natural bent? Truly, Phylax exulted, Fate was at work here on Mt. Chion.

Then as swiftly as it had flooded into him Phylax's enthusiasm for hunting the beautiful and somehow noble cat flooded out again. "Who are you and I, Driver," he wondered aloud, "to condemn this wild being out of hand and then kill him for no worthier reason than glory? Better to honor its mystery than steal its life in selfish ignorance, eh?" Phylax leaned forward and patted Driver's powerful neck to cool the horse's spirit still high from the near-confrontation with the dire-cat.

"Never worry, old warhorse," said Phylax to the stallion, "We still have a killer snow-bear to remove from the world. That beast is already condemned as an eater of children. So at least he will deserve the fate we are taking to him." With this Phylax clicked his tongue at Driver and rode on.

After another climb of an hour more or less Phylax and his tiring horses at last gained the level more or less high ground that overlooked the Lake of the Moon. Phylax was now having second thoughts about continuing down to the lake shore in order to make camp there tonight. Several forceful realities argued against going on.

First, thanks to the delays occasioned by his encounters with the dire-cat he had reached this high ground later than planned; the sun was already lowering in the sky and darkness would certainly fall before Phylax could reach his original destination.

Second, the obvious fatigue of the horses would greatly hamper their progress while at the same time augmenting the danger of going astray or falling in the dark on an unfamiliar road.

Third, though the dire-cat was no longer in evidence, the beast's apparent reluctance to act aggressively in daylight would surely evaporate in the dark hours when he was most at home as a hunter.

Clearly then to wander further on the strange trail ahead when darkness fell would be to invite the cat to press home what might become a calamitous night attack. *Besides,* thought Phylax as he examined the terrain of the high ground, *the view of the full moon in the lake below surely would be far more spectacular from this high vantage point than from the lake shore.* As for his planned hunt for the rogue snow-bear that could wait for another day. In fact the prospects of success against the bear would improve greatly with the rising of the next sun. Given all the variables Phylax made up his mind to find a suitable place to make his camp on the heights.

Dismounting to lead both Driver and the packhorse on foot Phylax set out to locate a site that pleased him and to do it before the oncoming dusk precluded a proper search. All at once, however, a high-pitched sound both piercing and sweet brought him to a halt. To his astonishment Phylax recognized the sound as a feminine voice making a wordless music as sharp and clear as the mountain air and as melodious as a stream foaming over rocks. *Was it a summoning call? Was some sorceress of the mountain commanding her sisters to attend one of their unspeakable full-moon ceremonies?*

Like virtually all Arkadians Phylax had heard stories about the supposed secret cult of enchanted women who came together every month on Mt. Chion to perform blood rites forbidden under the rule of the Logos. Phylax had always scoffed at such tales until now when a wordless anthem sung into a gathering dusk seemed to suggest there might be some truth in them after all. Of course, it was all nonsense Phylax admonished himself. And yet here was the song, the dusk, and Mt. Chion.

With curiosity impelling him Phylax could see no other course open to him except to put aside all else in favor of searching out the source of the music which he had to admit soared and swooped in a most engaging way. Phylax mounted Driver yet again for experience had taught him that it was always better to be in the saddle and armed when facing the unknown even if that unknown sounded like the voice of the Moon herself. Warily, a javelin in hand, Phylax nudged Driver ahead letting the gorgeous song draw him to the singer. He soon found her and he drew up astounded at what he beheld.

A woman naked except for calf-length boots of soft blue leather stood on the flattened top of a sunstone boulder facing out to the valley that held the Lake of the Moon. Stealthily, Phylax slid from Driver's back lest he seem too threatening, too much the mounted warrior, if the singer should turn and see him. Phylax kept his javelin in hand, however,

With her slim back still turned to him the woman singer remained unaware of Phylax's presence behind her for she went on with her song lofting it into the reddening sky as a bird does to satisfy some innate urge. Nor did she alter her stance as she sang. Her legs apart to maintain balance, her arms spread wide as if to embrace the world, the singer held her head tilted back as if directing her paean to heaven itself. In this posture, Phylax noted, the woman's hair, a mix of auburn and gold, hung down her back in a thick braid.

Unwilling to interrupt, Phylax held his peace waiting for the song to finish. He could not help reflecting, however, that this day had surely been one for wondrous events.

When the song trailed off into silence, the singer turned about and saw Phylax for the first time. Surprisingly, she betrayed no shock or even a flutter of unease at finding him there. For his part, Phylax's eyes confirmed that the woman was indeed completely—unashamedly—naked. His eyes also told him that she was a mere girl, probably about the same age as Kala Aristaia—but this girl was of a type altogether different from Kala for her small face was not "pretty" but "arresting" and her gray eyes seemed to dance with mischief. Her well-formed body revealed as it was now was also small but unusually athletic, the muscles visible under skin darkened by much time spent under the sun. This girl or sorceress possessed none of Kala's elegant beauty, nor even a conventional comeliness yet Phylax could see that she possessed a unique beauty all her own which Phylax found most appealing or was she using her magical-wiles to entrance him?

At last, apparently satisfied that she had allowed the stranger to look upon her naked body long enough, the girl smiled and spoke in a voice bubbling with merriment.

"So you have finally arrived! We have been expecting you for hours!"

With this the girl leaped from the rock to the ground a jump that the finest dancers of Ten Turrets would have envied. Now, with her on the same level as he, Phylax realized how small she really was for she came only to his shoulder a circumstance that only seemed to enhance her attractiveness. *Scintillating* that was the word that came most readily to Phylax's mind as he looked at her.

The girl suddenly emitted a boisterous laugh.

"You want to know how I knew you were on the trail today. Of course you do! After all you are still worrying that I might be a sorceress! Little me, the sorceress! Well you needn't fret. I learned you were coming from a doe you spooked in your clumsy way and she was quite indignant about it I can tell you!"

Phylax shook his head in confusion.

"Are you saying you speak to animals?"

Another robust explosion of mirth.

"No, no, they speak to me. They are better linguists than I."

Phylax decided to ignore the subject of talking animals. Instead, despite a certain gentlemanly reticence on the subject he asked if her absence of wardrobe might be making her feel a trifle chilly.

The girl seemed perplexed at his concern.

"Chilly? Why no, I'm quite comfortable. Why do you ask?"

Following Phylax's gaze that was now resting on her breasts where two bold little raspberries had formed, she cried with delight.

"Oh, I see. Why is it I wonder that young men find so much to fascinate them about a woman's unclothed body?"

Red-faced, Phylax could think of nothing the least bit clever to say in explanation.

Again, peals of laughter.

Like a merry bell, thought Phylax.

"Ah, well," the girl said, "I suppose I'd better respect your silly probity since you are my guest."

Phylax watched feeling clumsy and abashed as the girl strode, with a sauciness that reminded Phylax of a filly in her first spring, fling over to a modest camp that he had not noticed before. He noticed it with much interest now, however, because a proud gray warhorse a steed even taller than his own massive Driver stood there complacently chewing oats from a feed bag. Phylax, to his chagrin, felt a pang of unworthy envy at the sight of the horse for he would give much to own such a fine charger.

After rummaging in saddlebags lying about the camp's burnt out fire the girl donned a blue woolen cloak belted about the waist and returned to Phylax. She executed a mocking pirouette for him.

"Better now? Less terrifying?"

Phylax thought it best to change the subject at once.

"Does that fine horse belong to your man?"

The girl looked aghast as if she found Phylax's query incredibly stupid or insulting.

"My man? I have no man nor do I want one, not yet anyhow. The horse is mine. I raised him from a foal. His name is Thunder and if you think I can't ride him, I'm ready to bet I can ride him better than you can ride that fine horse of yours. A race. Thunder against your horse, the winner gets to keep both animals. What do you say?"

The girl lifted her chin toward him her face bright with belligerence.

Phylax only smiled for an answer for he knew better than to make a bet with a stranger even if she was a slip of a thing who liked to go around naked in the cold mountain air.

Spontaneously, the girl and Phylax burst into simultaneous laughter as both recognized the ridiculous nature of the proposed wager.

The girl's laughter, Phylax thought, made her radiant; it was a beautiful laugh. She was certainly not a sorceress, he concluded. For one thing, no sorceress ever enjoyed herself as much as this girl did. For a second thing, no sorceress could ever speak with such an unmistakably cultivated Megar accent. But if she was a Megar girl as Phylax now believed what was she doing gamboling about on her magnificent horse high up on Mt. Chion's freezing slopes? Had she run away from her family, a headstrong daughter, so spoiled she couldn't imagine that any peril could ever threaten her? And—by the Logos!—what possessed her to sing naked from the top of a boulder as if she was one of those wild women said to roam this mountain? Though burning with curiosity about these matters, Phylax was also well aware of the discourtesy involved in bringing them up and so he did not. He did, however, dare to nudge around the edges.

"You have a beautiful voice," he said, "but I didn't quite catch the words."

The girl smiled gently now.

"There were no words. I was just warbling, you see, like the larks. I was exulting, singing good-night to the sun and wake-up to the visiting Moon. That's all."

"It was beautiful," said Phylax meaning it.

Suddenly, the roar of the dire-cat like the first thunder of Doom resounded in the oncoming dusk. Phylax, furious with himself for having somehow forgotten the propinquity of that danger reflexively threw his arm around the girl and raised his javelin to defend her and himself.

"I should have warned you before this," Phylax declared, his eyes peering into the sparse bush nearby in search of the beast. "A dire-cat has somehow found his way onto the mountain. I saw him twice earlier today."

Again the cat roared, nearer than before. Phylax pulled the girl closer and held his javelin in position to hurl it and he'd better not miss for his other javelins were still in Driver's saddle-socket.

Unaccountably, Phylax felt the girl pushing him away as if to free herself from his protective grasp. Moreover, she was smiling up at him in the most inane way. *Was she so stupidly confident that she could not recognize the impending danger?* Using her quite remarkable strength to wrench free of Phylax's grip the girl broke into a completely mad fit of giggling.

"It's only Rumbles that you hear. He's pretending to be a big old fierce dire-cat when he's really just a sweet kitten at heart despite all his posturing."

Lost in near-infinite confusion Phylax could only look at her.

"Rumbles?"

"Yes. An associate of my father gave him to me when I was a little girl. As a kitten he was far from dire. The nearest thing to a roar that he could produce then, poor thing, was a sort of rumbling sound so I named him 'Rumbles'. Come out, Rumbles, don't be afraid." She slapped her hand against her knee. "Come on, Rumbles, come out. There's my big boy."

In obedience to her summons half a ton of black ferocity galumphed playfully out of some nearby bushes and thumped himself down at the blue-booted feet of his mistress where he proceeded to lick burrs from his paws with a tongue that rasped like a metal file.

Driver, unsure how to behave toward the cat without his rider on his back to direct him, backed away, snorting, tossing his head, whinnying, and trying to turn about until Phylax managed to calm him with a few soft words.

Overcoming his initial shock at seeing the small girl so cozy with the enormous beast Phylax managed to choke out, "This creature, your Rumbles, accosted us on the trail this afternoon. He wasn't so friendly then, and honestly, I can't believe you're quite safe with him now. He's a wild animal after all. Aren't you afraid he'll turn on you?"

"Rumbles? Never! It was I who sent him to find you this afternoon and to lure you to me. And he did a fine job, didn't you, my big, big boy."

The girl commenced to pet the creature's ruff eliciting a loud purring that started Driver whinnying again and caused Phylax to tighten his grip on his javelin.

"But I do understand your nervousness," said the girl halting her petting of the cat and turning a face full of sympathy to Phylax. "So I'll send him off to hunt his supper, though dusk is still a little too bright for him."

"Supper?" Was there no end to this girl's strange personality?

"Oh, yes. He enjoys catching two or three rabbits and a half-dozen of those flightless birds that abound on this mountain. Makes a good meal for him it seems." She turned her attention to the cat again. "Alright Rumbles go do your hunting now." She nudged him with a boot. "Go. Go on now. Go!"

The beast rose, stretched and galumphed off obediently.

"He will not return until daylight," the girl said.

Both Phylax and Driver heaved a sigh of relief at his going. The packhorse seemed oblivious as if terror had already overwhelmed his senses.

"The moon will not rise over the mountain for more than an hour," the girl said. "Will you share my supper with me?"

"Gladly."

She smiled warmly, a smile that Phylax found most beguiling.

"In that case," she said, "perhaps we ought to introduce ourselves. I am Nika Doraia only daughter of the family Dorides of the Katoran."

Phylax immediately recognized the name for Nika belonged to one of the most illustrious of the Megar families of Arkadia. Her father was a Chief Councilor to the Hegemon. *Why*, he wondered, *was this beautiful aristocrat going about naked, singing to the setting sun, and cavorting with a displaced dire-cat? Was she mad, perhaps, the family lunatic?* Of course he voiced none of these questions but introduced himself with a somewhat ambiguous modesty, simply as "Phylax" a minor aide attached to the Hegemon's Household.

"Now we shall get to know each other," she said. "I shall call you Phylax and you must call me Nika. Agreed?"

"Agreed most eagerly."

Lunatic she might be, but Phylax had to concede that in Nika's presence he felt a peculiar but most pleasant, happiness.

Following their meal of roasted fowl accompanied by bread and a flagon of strong red wine provided by Phylax, Nika and Phylax took their ease around the fire while waiting for the moon to appear over the mountain peaks. To Phylax's delight they quickly fell into relaxed conversation on this and that during which he could not help but recognize the intelligence that accompanied Nika's bold spirit. She was like no other girl he had ever met and he would be sorry to see tonight's moon-watch put an end to their too brief acquaintance.

At one point in their conversation Phylax remarked on her obvious enjoyment of the wine for she was then imbibing her third cup. Smiling, he said, "Most Megar families don't allow their girls to drink strong wine."

"No? I wouldn't know about that. I do a lot of things not allowed."

To emphasize her claim she drained her cup and grinned defiantly across the fire at him.

"Such as roaming about this mountain, eh?" said Phylax.

"Not just roaming, Phylax. Among other pursuits which you have already observed for yourself, I came up here to do some hunting."

Phylax was not surprised but as far as he could tell Mt. Chion didn't seem to offer much game worthy of her.

"What quarry are you after?"

Nika poured more wine and held the cup to her lips. "Snow-bear," she said and drank. "A certain rogue bear down from the high ice."

Phylax, filled with admiration for her courage, exclaimed, "But I am after him too! Maybe we can track him together!"

She shook her head, a sly smile on her wine-red lips.

"Too late, Phylax. Sorry."

Nika rose and pulled a yellow-white pelt out from under a disorderly pile of various supplies. Displaying it to Phylax she could not forbear a touch of hunter's bravado.

"I got him about a week ago. Had to follow him onto the glacier and I had to do it without Thunder who hates ice. He was a big bear alright but he turned out to be an old codger with broken teeth, who became a man-eater because he could no longer catch his normal prey. Poor old fellow. He went without much of a fight; it took only two javelins." She emitted a satisfied laugh. "But there'll be no more man-eating and I will be a heroine for my feat!" She tossed the pelt onto the pile and rejoined Phylax at the fire.

"You are remarkable," said Phylax. "Truly, I'm much impressed."

Nika shrugged. "I only wish that my father would be impressed."

"He doesn't approve of your, er, activities?

Nika grinned.

"He absolutely abominates the way I want to live. That's why he's sending me to Ten Turrets next month. By the Logos! Can you imagine it? I am to serve as handmaiden to the Betrothed of the Heir—what's his name? Milo?"

"Yes. Milo. It's a great honor to be chosen as a handmaiden and the Betrothed is a fine lady."

"Oh, I'm sure she is and Milo is a paragon no doubt. But it will kill me to be there in Ten Turrets, when I want to be here on the mountain to ride Thunder and play with Rumbles. Oh how I despise the way women must live in Arkadia!" She paused, looked Phylax in the eye, and said, "I have a secret ambition, Phy. Shall I tell you? You must never breathe a word. Swear by the Logos you will never tell anyone else."

"I swear by the Logos."

He could sense the pain that her obviously thwarted ambition caused her.

"I want to become a Rider." She paused and blushed. "Now you think me an idiot."

"Not at all."

In fact, from what he'd seen of her so far Phylax thought she would probably make a fine Rider.

"Thank you, Phy, but I know you're just being nice."

"No," he said emphatically. "When it comes to the Riders, I'm anything but nice. And, Nika, I happen to know that Rider regulations do not prohibit a woman from joining the Regiments as long as she is physically capable and can get through the rigors of the training."

She frowned in puzzlement. "Is that true? How do you know?"

Trying to keep his pride under control Phylax answered modestly, "I happen to be the Cadet Colonel of the White Angels Regiment."

Nika was incredulous.

"You? But you don't look like a Megar. The Riders are all Megars aren't they?"

"Used to be. But that's changing these days. I'm part-Megar. My mother was a Koinar but my father was a Megar. That's why the Hegemon Agathon took me into his Household."

"So you could get me into the White Angels?"

Nika was still incredulous though a hopeful gleam was shining in her eyes.

"Whoa," cried Phylax. "I never said I could get you into a Regiment. I only said the Regulations do permit girls to try for an appointment. You must first apply and then prove yourself."

"Then why are there no women in the Regiments now? Is it because it's all rigged against women?"

Phylax sensed her suspicion, her readiness to be disappointed. Her prickliness reminded him of something Megistes had said long ago: "Justice is very hard to define, but injustice is plain to see because it's visible in all who feel its sting."

Phylax was beginning to understand what the old man meant for Nika must have been feeling the sting of injustice for much of her young life. The realization lit in Phylax a determination to make sure that Nika received fair treatment should she actually apply to a Rider regiment. With this in mind he tried to answer her earlier query about the absence of women among the Riders.

"I don't know whether the standards are skewed against women. I know that very few women have ever applied in the past and certainly none of them have been like you, Nika. But I promise you this: if you do apply, I'll endorse your application. I'm only a Cadet Colonel you understand—a tyro still—but I do carry a little weight, I think."

When she looked at him he could have sworn there were tears in her eyes.

"Thank you, Phy," she said, "but I'm afraid it's hopeless. My father would never allow it." She paused then spoke again in a voice choked with grief over what she considered a lost dream. "To tell you the truth, Phy, I dread being a Ten Turrets handmaiden so much that I'm thinking seriously about running away, never going home again, just becoming a wild woman in these mountains, maybe joining up with the other wild women if they really exist. At least then I'll have some kind of real life."

Phylax said, "And what about duty?"

The answer to that question, Phylax now knew would direct his own life from now on and so the query had sprung readily to his lips. Nika, however, did not respond. Instead she pointed into the night where the full moon was now silently hovering in its pale glory.

Nika and Phylax, as silent as the moon itself, went together to stand at the edge of the precipice that overhung the lake. Without speaking, they gazed down at the reflection in the still, deep, and dark waters of the lake. The lake, now transformed into The Eye of the Moon, stared up at the night sky. Phylax thought how easily the viewer might lose the sense of what was up and what was down. It seemed quite obvious that you could swim to the moon, if you'd a mind to do it. But how were you to dive in? Up or down? Or did it matter, really? He found himself imagining how pleasant it might be to swim to the moon with Nika. Then it came to him that it surely would be even more pleasant to have Nika at Ten Turrets. She was half a goddess already, he mused. How much more she might become in Ten Turrets! Before he could stop himself, he murmured a plea for her to hear. "I hope you will come to Ten Turrets, Nika."

She did not respond.

"I shall be there," he added.

Still she made no reply, but he felt her warm hand so small for so formidable a huntress fold into his.

Phylax experienced a surge of feeling he could not identify at once.

Surely, it was joy he felt.

TEN

Seraph and Rin reached the long-sought Pelorys just at dawn
after still another night of hard travel that finally delivered them
from the high grass to the marshy verge of the great river's west
bank. As Seraph stared at the stream, stunned at the rare personal
success it represented for him, it came to him that the river's flow
seemed far less turbulent than his child's-eye memory would have it.
Nevertheless, he reckoned it far deeper and rougher than the placid
Bradys and so impassable at least in this place where he and Rin
had come upon it. Still he needed to cross to the other side where
the summoning fire was to be found. *But at least,* thought Seraph
exultantly, *from now on there would be no need to hide during the
hours of daylight for he knew that neither the Bemgrass beasts nor their
Bem hunters frequented the exposed banks of the Pelorys but only the
occasional Bem wishing to sell this or that to the Pious Koinar outlaw
merchants based on the far banks.* This Seraph remembered well from
his days of servitude to the aged Koinar slavers.

Seraph, still mounted, gazed across the river in near-rapture as
the rising sun turned the wide water to a plane of molten copper.
At this spot on the bank Seraph estimated the breadth of the river
at perhaps five hundred feet. Accordingly, he knew that despite the
absence of rough "white water" as the Koinars called it the current
here was probably—if deceptively—powerful, too strong anyway for
one of the Pious Koinars' rope-and-pulley ferry operations. His time
with the Koinars had taught Seraph that the Pelorys could be crossed
only in a very few places and this was not one of them. In fact the
crossing place that he now must seek probably lay further upstream
at some wide place where the river flowed with a manageable current.
Only in such a location, he knew, would the illicit Koinar traders have

rigged a raft-and-rope system to ferry themselves, their animals, and their merchandise back and forth. It had been by means of such a ferry system that Seraph himself had fled back to the Bem folk after taking his vengeance on his Koinar owners. And it was just such a ferry he must find now to take him, Rin, and the pony to the opposite bank. *Best to start looking for it at once.*

Feeling his heart racing with anticipation of a triumphal final end to his seemingly-endless journey Seraph leaned forward and tapped Rin on her shoulder breaking the trance that seemed to have seized her from the instant she had laid eyes on the fabled River Pelorys that all Bem had heard of but few had dared to look upon.

"Upstream now, Rin," Seraph instructed her, "and hurry. There must be a crossing and not too far away I warrant. I must cross to what awaits on the other side."

Obediently Rin though deeply fatigued set off leading the pony in a stumbling half-trot along the bank of the watercourse that seemed to her to presage both danger and deliverance for her as well as for the great prophet she now so willingly served.

As the morning ripened bringing with it a cloudless sky and a heat that quickly sucked the early dew from the grass, Seraph and Rin continued to make their way in silence along the western bank of the river. Although Seraph anxiously scanned the opposite bank for signs of habitation he saw nothing there but an apron of grass that gradually rose to become the forested foothills of gloomy mountains. Nor were there indications of any human activity on his own side of the stream except for the bleached skull and scattered bones of a child who must have fallen prey at least a year earlier to a dire-cat.

The unbroken silence was beginning to oppress Seraph. *Was it possible,* he asked himself, *that he was heading in the wrong direction or that a Koinar ferry was no longer to be found along this western bank? And what would he do if the Pious Koinars had abandoned their settlements on the other side?* Then, with a start of both relief and excitement he descried a feather of smoke on the opposite bank and he knew at last that he was on the right path.

"Keep going, Rin," he muttered. "We're almost there."

Minutes later, much to his satisfaction, Seraph spotted a cluster of huts across the river. These had to be a trading station of renegade Pious Koinars, who no doubt still trafficked with desperate Bem who were eager to sell their children, who would give an ox-hide or two for a half-dozen lengths of the wood that was so scarce in the Bem lands. Seraph noted too that the river had widened greatly here, was perhaps a thousand feet across and thus was far more tranquil than elsewhere on its course. *A good location for a ferry*, he thought. All at once before his straining eye he spied the ropes of a Koinar ferry.

"Stop, Rin."

Rin obeyed. But clearly she was uneasy at the sight of the unfamiliar apparatus and the huts across the river for she was trembling as she helped Seraph dismount. Seraph tried to reassure her with gruff words.

"There's nothing to fear, woman. Trust me."

Limping over to the sturdy piling and turntable around which the ferry's stout rope-cable was wound Seraph took hold of the thick cable and pulled with all his strength. This action he remembered would ring a bell on the other side as a signal to the Koinar traders of his presence. He pulled several more times with growing impatience.

Feeling disoriented by the strangeness of the great water, the intricacy of the rope-thing on its spool, and above all by Seraph's apparent confidence in this unfamiliar world that seemed to her so threatening, Rin let the pony crop the grass that was too bright and green here for her to look at and she sat herself down on the wet ground. Then, as she always did when faced with the incomprehensible Rin closed her eyes and tried to think of nothing. Only when she heard Seraph's shouting—followed by another masculine voice shouting in return—did she open her eyes again and then she wished she had not for the scene she now beheld only worsened her unsettled state.

An enormous man with a black Koinar beard that covered half his face and curled down his naked chest stood in what looked to Rin like a large wicker-work wagon—or a basket—with sides like a cart which was somehow resting on the water. Rin immediately thought that the wicker-wagon might be this "raft thing" that Seraph had often talked of. *The man in the raft,* thought Rin reflexively trying to shrink inside herself, *looked as big and mighty as a wild-ox.* She saw that he was hanging onto the thick ropes with both hands apparently to keep his "raft" steady but also to keep it away from the water's edge where

Seraph was now standing in mud up to his ankles. *Did the ox-man, this Koinar giant, fear the prophet she served? Did the ox-man perhaps sense and fear her master's power as she did?* All at once the ox-man bellowed to Seraph words that Rin understood for they were in the Bem tongue though poorly put together.

"You come for buy? For sell?"

"For business," Seraph shouted in reply. "Come, take us across."

The Koinar ox-man ignored Seraph's demand.

"What you sell? What you buy?"

"Take us across," Seraph cried in answer, "and I will show you."

The ox-man shook his shaggy head and made as if to pull himself and his "raft" back to the far bank. At this Seraph, suddenly speaking in a language that Rin did not recognize but that the Koinar ox-man seemed to know well began a new round of shouting and gesturing. They appeared to be communicating information that the ox-man found persuasive for the giant now pulled himself and his raft-wagon onto the soggy muck of the riverbank.

Seraph and the ox-man again fell to speaking together in what Rin now assumed was the Koinar tongue and once more Rin could not help but feel awe at how much her master knew of the strangeness that terrified her.

Seraph and the ox-man, both frowning and somehow urgent, continued their talk, resorting to many gestures, more than a few of them frighteningly directed toward her and the oblivious pony filling his belly nearby. The hand motions that the ox-man made toward her made Rin think that he did not wish to take her and the pony across, while Seraph was demanding that he do so. In the end it was plain to Rin that Seraph had prevailed for the heated palaver abruptly ceased and Seraph and the ox-man clasped hands in what even Rin recognized as a universal sign of agreement. *Good*, thought Rin. But then she was not so sure that she was glad after all that Seraph had succeeded in the argument, for she saw that it meant she would now have to enter the terrifying raft-thing and cross the even more terrifying water. *Could she endure such an ordeal?* Then she remembered that Seraph would be with her. Seraph would keep her safe. *This was a test*, she told herself. *When it was over*, she told herself, *Seraph would keep her with him forever and she, grateful for his protection, would serve him gladly whatever he required of her.*

Seraph watched with interest as the giant Koinar merchant pulled the pony by the bridle in order to bring him aboard the raft. When the beast balked, the Koinar, who said his name was Leo, laughed, and grunted to Seraph in the Koinar tongue.

"Good, good, the creature still has some spirit left, eh?"

With this the bluff trader, whom Seraph greatly mistrusted despite the bargain they had struck, produced a greasy cloth and fastened it over the pony's eyes. Deprived of threatening sights, the tough little animal calmed down at once. The Koinar, Leo, laughed heartily and led the pony easily aboard the raft.

"Hah! What they can't see they don't fear. Shall I tie something over the woman's eyes as well?"

Seraph translated the Koinar's question into the Bem dialect for Rin. She shook her head. In defiance of her own dread, Rin managed to haul herself up on the raft and sat with her head bowed and her eyes closed. The cold water of the river that was seeping into the raft soon wet her bottom. The raft began to move, the rope creaking in its spool as the Koinar pulled on it. Rin resolved to think of nothing other than the wet chill on her behind.

Though every motion of the Koinar raft caused his gut to slosh uncomfortably, Seraph forced himself to stand as the gigantic Leo pulled the raft across the smooth water. During the ordeal Seraph kept his eye fixed on Rin. Her continuing aura of dread reminded him of a threatened animal's fear-stink. *Of course,* he reflected, *in most ways Rin was an animal, stupid as the pony, but lacking the pony's docile dignity.* Watching her, Seraph experienced a disgust for her that bordered on fury. He was tempted to slap her doltish face to make her wake to what was happening. He refrained, however, for he knew she was too thick of mind to understand his purpose.

The crossing ended with a thump as the raft came to rest on the Koinar side of the river. Leo led the pony ashore.

Seraph, seizing Rin's thin wrist, yanked her roughly to her feet, saying, "Open your stupid eyes, woman."

Rin obeyed at once and Seraph pulled her by her wrist through the muck to the grassy verge.

"We shall drink a cup of tunnik together, hey?" said Leo the Pious Koinar whose religion, Seraph recalled forbade such strong drink though the Pious usually ignored the rule.

"Come then," said Leo.

Leo led Seraph, still towing Rin, who now held the pony's bridle, to a place where benches were arranged around a burnt-out stone hearth in the shade of a tree with drooping limbs. When they were seated, Seraph asked the question that had been troubling him since the raft had neared what looked to him like a deserted riverbank.

"Are there no others, or are you alone here?"

It was best to find out just what the situation was, for Seraph's mistrust of the Koinar remained unabated despite their agreement, and despite the Koinar reputation for honoring bargains as long as it pleased them.

The black-bearded merchant gave another burst of his hearty laughter.

"The station belongs to my six brothers and me. We do good business here trading in this and that." Leo paused showing yellow teeth in the midst of his curly black beard. "My brothers are around somewhere, I assure you. But you are safe with me."

Seraph observed a Bem girl of about ten or eleven and wearing a filthy smock approaching with a tray on which rested two large cups. Without a word, or even a glance at Leo or Seraph, the girl placed the cups on a bench before the two men then fled as fast as her skinny legs would take her back toward the nearest hut.

"We drink tunnik now, hey?" Leo took a substantial mouthful. "Business is thirsty work, hey?"

Seraph nodded agreement. He tasted the tunnik, aware that Rin was gazing at him, and longing for a drink. Of course she had not understood any of the talk between him and the Koinar and Seraph had no intention of enlightening her. *Rin could wait for her drink and when it came it wouldn't be tunnik juice.*

Leo stretched his thick legs out before him.

"It is good, I find, to rest and talk when business is done. It is good to exchange thoughts."

When Seraph nodded agreement, the merchant said, "So you will perhaps now say if you have any other business on this side of the river for I sense that you are not an ordinary man of the Bem. You did not cross the river just to return to the Bemgrass when we are done here, so I wonder if you might be an outcast from your people. If so, my brothers and I might be able to help you in one way or another for a price, of course."

Seraph said, "I am a man on a quest."

The Koinar raised his bushy eyebrows inquisitively, and Seraph explained.

"I have been summoned across the river, or so I believe, by a light I have seen by night. I wish to go to that light. Do you know of it?"

The Koinar rumbled in his chest and spat a gob of mucus onto the grass.

"No doubt you are speaking of what we true Koinars call 'the mountain fire'. It burns from inside caverns that lie within the mountains south of here."

Leo paused, spat again as if performing a ritual, and continued. "I can tell you nothing about that fire or the caverns for there is something unclean within that mountain, something that wishes to destroy the Logos of the true Koinars."

Leo paused, spat again, and continued. "As all men know, we true Koinars, whom others call "The Pious" are above all else loyal to the Logos as it was originally conceived. For this reason we choose to live apart from our fellow Koinars in Arkadia. And we are satisfied to live in our poor settlements in this neglected region. We do this because we revere the Logos as we think proper. Our laws forbid all Pious Koinars to go to that mountain where the unclean fires burn. Nor may we help others to go there. So I counsel you, foolish Bem: abandon your false quest, and go home."

"But I must go to that light," Seraph insisted.

The Koinar growled.

"Had I known your destination, I would not have done business with you, but since we do have an agreement, let us conclude our bargain quickly now and then you must be on your way for I begin to suspect that you may be unclean yourself."

With this the Koinar merchant rose and strode swiftly toward the nearby collection of huts.

Seraph sat in perplexed silence. *Unclean? A filthy renegade Koinar trader dared to speak of him as "unclean"?*

Seraph glanced at Rin, who was staring at him as stupid and uncomprehending as ever.

Leo the Koinar, returned leading an Arkadian-bred horse, a white mare, already saddled with a thick Arkadian blanket and hung with the "foot-holders" as Seraph thought of them that gave Arkadian Riders their sure balance as they rode. The mare also wore a set of Arkadian reins and a bridle.

"Here is the horse, as we agreed," said Leo with a scowl. "This mare is in her prime, gentle and willing. Her tack is the best I can do. With those stirrups, even you should have no trouble guiding her and keeping your seat."

In fact Seraph was suddenly feeling quite nervous at the prospect of mounting and riding this creature that, however gentle and willing she might be also seemed enormous in comparison to the Bem pony, the only mount he had experienced heretofore. Still, Seraph recognized that he needed such a steed in order to carry out his mission. Only with the Arkadian horse and the foot-holders, he was convinced, would he be able to travel fast, far, and free of the clumsiness occasioned by his lame leg. Hence Seraph tried to reassure himself that he would soon overcome his initial nervousness about riding the mare but he only half-believed it.

The Koinar, scowling at Seraph as if now revulsed by his Bem customer, threw a pair of large leather bags over the mare's withers.

"Grain and a feed bag for the horse, hard bread for you."

Leo wiped his hands on his shirt.

"And so we are finished, Bem. I shall take the woman and the pony according to our bargain and you will ride away on the mare and never return. Understand?"

Seraph nodded. Limping, he led the mare, certainly docile enough, over to an unused bench. Using the bench as a step, Seraph struggled onto the back of his new mount. *It will work*, he told himself. *Yes, it will work.* Seraph then looked down at Rin. Her eyes were big with confusion and what was clearly a growing alarm.

Seraph looked at the Koinar trader. "The woman is yours," he said in the Koinar dialect, "and the pony too."

At this the Koinar seized Rin by her upper arm. She understood at once. Seraph had sold her to the Koinar in exchange for the white mare. As she saw him riding away from her, Rin commenced to scream in horror of his betrayal. The Koinar brute started dragging her away. Still she howled after the mounted figure of the prophet whom she had only wished to serve with all her soul.

"Do not leave me, Master! I beg you! Lord Seraph! Take your Rin with you! Bind me again, if you wish! Take pity, Master! Pity your Rin! If I have offended, forgive me!"

Only when the Koinar struck her face with his huge fist, did Rin cease howling her pleas. She continued screaming wordlessly, however, until the Koinar pushed her into a dark shed and then into a stinking cage with other slaves, some of whom sniggered at her plight. Only then did Rin's screaming turn into bitter tears.

Deep within hollow halls of the Meta-chron caverns the goddess Eris raged. When would the mortal, her instrument of vengeance, her only hope for continued existence, finally reach her? She could still feel his approach, but was unable to judge his progress—if any. This inability, she fumed, no doubt resulted from the distortions in perception induced by the unnatural Meta-time that prevailed within the underworld that imprisoned her. Still, Eris reminded herself, despite her fury this Hades preserved her alive even as it inexorably absorbed the dimming shades of the deceased Olympians of Arkadia. Though well aware that her existence within these caverns was being preserved by the vagaries of Meta-time, Eris found them maddening nevertheless. And so it was that in a constant storm of wrath she continued to wander from one vast chamber to another as if in search for some "thing" that she could relate to herself.

Eris' meanderings, however, had turned up only some additional disheartening artifacts that were in effect further commentaries on the demise of the gods. For example, under one soaring dome illuminated by the red light of fire bowls, she came upon an ossuary of marble statuary much of it consisting of remnants from the toppled Arkadian gods dragged from their temples to this dusty boneyard after their overthrow. These gleaming fragments, many of them still ravishingly sensual specimens of the sculptor's art must have been dumped with indecorous contumely into this sooty eternity for broken marble legs, arms, and even heads, lay randomly about in the gloom.

After closely examining the debris of scattered limbs and battered torsos Eris satisfied herself that no sculpture of her lay among the pale remains of her once divine sisters and brothers a circumstance that only made her wonder yet again how she had been spared and for what purpose. Bent on finding some explanation for her good fortune if "good" it was, Eris undertook a further exploration of the branching caverns. In one of these, she began to sense the presence of another in the blackness. She halted, trying to locate the whereabouts of the other. Yes, she certainly detected the faintest susurrus, as if this unknown being—or thing—intended her to know of its proximity but not its identity or even its nature. Moved by a new surge of rage, Eris challenged the hidden one. "Come. Show yourself if you dare!" There was no response other than an unintelligible whisper as if the intruding presence was murmuring to itself. Eris cried into the darkness: "I am Immortal Strife! I fear nothing! I am cowed by nothing!"

Again the thing, surely a denizen of these Meta-chron caverns, clung to its not-quite silence. Eris emitted a sharply derisive cackle of laughter to register her disdain for this coward something that swaddled itself in a darkness blacker than night.

Eris resumed her furious foray boldly advancing further into the cavern. She sensed the other still dogging her steps. Was it, perhaps, some form of beast stalking her as prey? If so, why hadn't it attacked already as any simple dire-cat or wolven-beast would have done?

Again she called to it.

"Fool, I shall soon destroy you with my rage."

Ahead Eris spotted a red glow where a new array of fire bowls illumined another side-section of the cavern. There, in the inconstant light the nature of her stalker would be revealed she told herself with satisfaction unless the coward fled beforehand. But when, having reached the light, she twisted about to catch her pursuer exposed Eris could only make out what appeared to be a cloud of blackness that screened her stalker from her sight. Although the fire-bowls even in this dim precinct of Hell certainly sufficed to dispel any nearby darkness, the inky nimbus following her as if obedient to a Meta-physical power forever opaque to lesser divinities like herself remained in place to shield her pursuer from her eyes.

Eris felt her wrath displaced by a shudder of dread passing through her. It came to her then that the opacity not only hid her tracker, it was the very essence of that other, the very atmosphere in which it existed. Gods and mortals might be ruled by nature, Eris realized, but this, this inscrutable blur of menace, she sensed was free from all known bonds for it certainly had to be of an order beyond mere nature and was surely then incomprehensible to living things.

Still, what did it desire from the Goddess of Strife? Was it perhaps the "Maker" of these caverns, their "Ruler," perhaps, but far more puissant than any Hellenic King of the Underworld? Had her wandering in these depths offended their Lord? On the edge of panic, Eris whispered the question that came unbidden to her mind: "What do you want of me, Dread Sovereign?"

There was no response, no movement within the ebon cloud. Yet Eris somehow understood beyond any doubt that this "shape" was indeed the "Ruler of this Underworld." So far it had spared her from the fate of the other Olympians of Arkadia. Why? Perhaps it had done so for some purpose that would only come clear to her when the Lord of her prison wished her to know. In any case Eris reckoned that she would survive in her dungeon after all, at least until the mortal, her instrument of vengeance, arrived in answer to her summons. Would she and the mortal then become subjects of this Dread Sovereign? She could not know. She could only wait and submit. With this resignation of her will the opaque blur evaporated as if sucked into itself. Subdued, the Goddess of Strife set off to find her way back to her place of waiting.

On a cool afternoon when the sun looked like a silver disk behind a veil of gray clouds and a chill wind blew intermittently from the eastern mountains, Kala Aristaia wrapped herself in a woolen cloak and repaired as she often did to the roof garden of the Hegemon's Residence. There she knew she could enjoy an hour or two of much-needed solitude thanks to the vexatious weather which she was sure would certainly have kept most potential visitors comfortably indoors. And so it proved. Only three or four other sturdy souls were to be seen in the garden and these, obviously valuing their own solitary state diligently ignored Kala's arrival among them.

Glad of the silence disturbed only by the irregular gusts of wind that rattled the dry leaves Kala seated herself on a marble bench. She gazed dreamily out toward the eastern mountain peaks many of them obscured today behind gray mist. She tried to locate Mt. Chion's snowcap out there but could not.

Kala had been reading about Mt. Chion, its odd animal inhabitants and its even more peculiar human denizens such as the female cultists alleged to practice certain ancient rites on the mountain's snowy heights and she would have liked to look upon it, even though from a distance, with her own eyes. This was especially so because Mina had learned only this morning from a gossipy steward named Aleph that one of the young women the Hegemon had "invited" to serve as Kala's Handmaiden was the eccentric, and Kala supposed, "scandalous" daughter of a prominent Councilor of the realm. This girl whose name and family Mina had not been able to pry from her informant was rumored to spend more time riding her horse on Mt. Chion than dancing the night away with handsome young men. Kala hoped that for once the Residence chatter turned out to be true for however odd this unnamed young woman might be she would at least be a welcome change from the simpering sycophants Kala usually had to endure among the female population of the Residence.

At this moment a male voice encroached on her wandering thoughts. Kala looked up to find Megistes standing over her.

"Forgive my intrusion, Kala Aristaia," Megistes said. "But I must discuss an urgent matter with you."

Suppressing an irked sigh for it would not do to show the venerable Sage even this slight discourtesy Kala gestured for Megistes to seat himself beside her on the bench.

The old man whose white beard made a sharp contrast with his cold-reddened face did so and launched at once into the "urgent matter" that had impelled him to seek her out.

Listening with her full attention and with growing astonishment Kala soon gathered from the old man's blunt speech that in defiance of all protocol and all precedent governing a Betrothed Pair, Megistes had arranged, never mind how, he said, a secret late-night meeting between Kala and her Betrothed to take place in Milo's private quarters.

Bad enough, thought Kala, *that the patriarch had failed to consult her before contriving such a genuinely scandalous affair at which no one else, not even Mina or Megistes himself was to be present, it was even worse that the devious Sage, like some cheap sorcerer, apparently believed he could gull her with ingenious words into so readily discarding the codes that guided her life. Surely Megistes understood full well that as a Megar virgin Kala was forbidden by iron custom to associate in private with any man or boy, even her Betrothed, except males of her own immediate family until after her marriage. And the stricture applied to all circumstances even the most innocent. Was it possible that the aged scholar had forgotten that she was bound by that immutable rule?* If so, she now reminded him in plain words.

"I am still a virgin, Master. I have never been alone with any male outside my family."

Megistes growled with what seemed irritation as if her principles were nothing to him.

"By the Logos, girl, you are alone with me right now! Have we not had private conversations in the past?"

"But you are exempt, Master, as my teacher."

"What nonsense this is," Megistes muttered. "Now understand this, Kala Aristaia: Your Betrothed has become unsettled in his mind. Only you possess the power to restore him to equilibrium."

Kala could not help exclaiming in sudden fright and confusion.

"I? I have no power, Master!"

Megistes grimaced at her outburst.

"You must put aside your nonsensical 'iron rule', girl, and go to Milo as already arranged. Then you must listen to him no matter how confused his thoughts might seem to you. Let him talk and then you must act boldly."

Megistes' vehemence with regard to this matter which still eluded her understanding left her appalled.

"Act boldly? Me?"

Kala was near to tears. Abruptly she found herself longing to be back with her mother at Richland Hall the two of them strolling contentedly in the gardens where she had never needed to "act boldly."

With inexorable single-mindedness Megistes pressed her further but more kindly now. "Dear Kala," he said taking her warm young hand in his frigid claw, "try to believe me. Our beloved Arkadia is in crisis. I alone know it as yet though presently I hope you will know it also."

"Crisis, Master? I know nothing of any crisis."

The gathering tears were beginning to cloud her vision.

Again the ancient face knotted into a grimace.

"Listen to me girl: Our next Hegemon, your husband-to-be, is being devoured by evil forces—demons if you like—that he himself has created in his mind. That is the crisis, girl!"

Megistes paused for a breath as if ordering his thoughts and then went on with a less strident voice.

"Although it is admittedly a weakness in our system the fact is that our Arkadia places most responsibility for our government in the hands of our Hegemon. Thus Arkadia requires a Hegemon of vigorous mind and excellent character in order to function well. In his present state Milo seems lacking in both. The future of Arkadia is, therefore, at risk. After much thought I have concluded that only you, Kala Aristaia, can save our future Hegemon. In this unprecedented situation Arkadia does not need a custom-bound virginal girl but a woman possessed of the courage to act with the necessary boldness."

To her chagrin Kala felt her tears begin to fall.

"I don't know how to be bold, Master."

Megistes replied with unremitting severity.

"Let your heart instruct you then."

Megistes rose from the bench.

"Perhaps you wish to consult with your Mina about this matter. Very well, do so then, but time is short, Kala Aristaia, and remember: your fate, too, hangs on your answer."

With this, Megistes, stiff from the cold and from sitting for too long on the hard bench, limped away.

Pulling her cloak tighter against her body Kala watched the old man go. She was furious with herself for having given into tears while the Sage looked on. The truth was that she still was the "custom-bound virgin girl" that Megistes had described with such obvious scorn. Kala's principles had meaning for her. She could not change to something else, some alien "other self", simply because the great Megistes ordered her to do so. This reflection generated a flush of resentment in her which soon elided into a shudder of shame. In one particular, however, she realized that Megistes had spoken rightly:

She did need to hear Mina's advice. Mina loved her and she trusted Mina.

Later, when a still-distraught Kala informed Mina of her encounter with Megistes the nurse only nodded and said, "He is a wise fellow, old Megistes." Kala was shocked at Mina's mild reaction.

"Dear Mina, the man wants me to agree to an assignation with Milo—alone—in his private quarters!"

Again Mina only nodded and it dawned on Kala that Mina already knew about and had consented to Megistes' stratagem. *Probably,* she thought, *Mina and Megistes had devised the scheme together.*

"I can't do it, Mina," Kala murmured.

"Humph," replied the nurse, "Of course you can do it. You must do it—and you will."

"And what of our custom?"

"Humph. When custom fails to serve us, then we must cease to serve custom."

"Then you actually approve of my going alone to Milo?"

"I approve of your rescuing your Betrothed from his torment."

"But I don't know how!"

Kala's voice sounded like a shrill whine in her own ears.

Mina smiled.

"You will know what to do when the time comes."

Seeing the tears gathering again in Kala's extraordinary eyes, Mina added, "Now, now, no more bawling, darling girl. You must save that poor weak boy from danger and that is that."

Kala, remembering how much her sketched portrait of Milo had disquieted her, reached for a final straw.

"I do not love him, Mina."

"Tush. You speak as a child. You do not know this Milo yet. There are many kinds of love; you will find the kind fitting for you and him. Never fear."

Kala and Mina both fell silent for both knew that Kala's struggle was over.

So it was that on the appointed night Kala Aristaia, attired in a plain robe of white linen, hair not dressed but loose, followed Mina out into the chill corridors of the Residence deserted at this post-midnight hour when all honest hearts in the Hegemon's service were abed.

As Kala and Mina stole toward Milo's chambers as arranged, Mina holding a single candle to light their way, Kala heard her beloved nurse whisper: "Darling girl, tonight you look like the golden child you once were."

Kala made no answer. By now she had resolved that she would make herself dare anything tonight. She would steel herself to the required action whatever form it took.

When they arrived at the designated door Mina knocked lightly. There was no response. Mina pushed the door open for Kala who hesitated at the threshold.

"Go on," murmured the nurse. "Go in—and remember: No artifice. Be simple."

Kala entered. Mina withdrew, closing the door softly behind her.

Kala found herself alone and shivering. Never had she felt so alone. Never had she felt so inadequate or so wicked.

The expansive chamber lit only by a single lamp its walls hung with heavy black drapes seemed in disarray. Discarded clothing including muddy military boots lay scattered about along with used dishes and half-empty wine cups. A heavy odor compounded of stale air and uneaten food hung in the room. It took Kala a few panicky moments to locate Milo in the gloom.

Wearing only a pair of ragged breeches and an open shirt, both articles of clothing much stained, Milo was sitting hunched up on a large cushioned chair. He was staring at Kala with eyes that reminded her of a trapped animal. His unkempt blond hair and stubble of beard gave her the impression that he had not slept for days. Since there seemed to be no other place for her to sit, not that he'd invited her to do so, Kala made her way over to the vast bed, unmade, and seated herself primly on its soft edge. Kala looked at her Betrothed expectantly. *Surely he must speak first to initiate matters.*

Moments passed. Then Milo spoke in a voice that she heard as a harsh whisper as if he was speaking under his breath to himself. "She doesn't want to marry you, fool."

Kala was not greatly surprised to hear her Betrothed greet her so strangely for hadn't Megistes warned her that his mind was unsettled? But how was she to respond to him?

Before she could think of a reply, however, Milo spoke again in his rough whisper this time speaking to her unambiguously.

"Of course you don't wish to wed me. I know that. How could a girl like you want me? I understand your distaste for me and I don't blame you. I know I'm disgusting."

These distraught sentiments Kala realized were the first he had ever expressed directly to her.

But how was she to interpret them? Was Milo under the impression that Megistes had brought about their secret meeting so that she could declare her unwillingness to marry him? Given Milo's apparent inclination to accede to such a proposition might she not with a clear conscience now seize upon his words as an opportunity to withdraw from their Betrothal? But would her sense of honor allow her to do so? Clearly, her Betrothed had stumbled somehow into a mental morass. He needed her, yes, but did she dare try to penetrate the maze of his mind and how was she to do it? Could it be done?

Suddenly Milo began muttering again a rapid flow of confessional whisperings in the third person apparently meant as a demented denunciation of himself.

"Milo to be Hegemon? No. Never. Milo, the weak? He hates himself, yes he does, for he knows better than any how cowardly his heart is, yes and how petty, and unworthy. Milo, you see, wants to follow the great Agathon, to bring peace to all Arkadia. Oh, yes, that is what he wants but he knows he will fail. He would run away, Milo would, if he dared, the fool. He shakes with terror of being made to mount the High Bench. And so he suffers with the Dims and Darkenings, witless, you see, incapable of great things. Oh, stupid Milo must live in pain. Forever and ever!"

As Milo went on in this manner, repeating himself, citing still again his weaknesses and his unworthy soul, his disgust with himself, Kala could only listen. At sea in a storm of confusion Kala did not dare to speak lest she inadvertently upset him further. Yet she was sure that despite the tempest of mad images he was spewing forth she grasped the underlying cause of his agony: he knew himself unsuitable for the role that Destiny had chosen for him, a role that required him to wield power, to make life and death judgments, and no doubt worst of all for an unwilling Hegemon to take responsibility for the lives of others by formulating for them a vision of the Arkadia in which they would have to live. Kala could understand how dwelling on one's shortcomings, real and imagined, in the face of overwhelming exigency can unbalance the sensitive mind, could bring about—what was it Milo called them?—the "Dims" and the "Darkenings" which she took to be his code for depression of the spirit, even despair. Clearly her Betrothed was in crisis as Megistes had so cogently put it. Clearly, too, she had to try to help him for she knew as one of the Arkadian elite that despair was a crime in one chosen to lead.

To Kala's consternation the deluge of self-censure unexpectedly ceased. She looked over at Milo, now silent in his great chair, his head bowed to his chest, his mop of greasy blond hair hanging over his eyes. *Was he waiting for her to respond to his sorrowful soliloquy? He would have to wait long then,* she thought, *for she had nothing to offer him—not yet in any case.*

Milo raised his head, his disturbingly watery eyes searching her face. He whispered to her again apparently once more aware of himself and of her as well for he spoke to her by name.

"Kala, please never call me 'Strategat'. I cringe when people call me by that title. I don't deserve it. Promise you will never say 'Strategat' to me."

Kala nodded her agreement although his request struck her as every bit unhinged as his third-person monologue.

Strategat. Might Milo's apparent distaste for that word provide a portal through his erratic verbiage to some common ground of communication? It was worth a try Kala told herself for she was discovering in herself an unanticipated upwelling of tenderness for the agonized young man opposite her. Accordingly, she felt it necessary to express her sympathy for him.

"I shall never call you Strategat," she said in a voice that seemed to her surprisingly composed. "To me you will always be 'Milo,'" she added.

"Thank you," Milo replied, his rasping voice tremulous. Then, his eyes wandering as if he was addressing an invisible auditor, he said, "How kind she is to poor Milo. No, she doesn't laugh at miserable Milo, does she?'

Attempting to pass through the narrow gateway of his eccentric language to establish herself as a presence in his battered mental world, Kala, evincing a calm she did not actually feel but the impersonation of which she hoped might allay some part of the bizarre self-loathing that seemed to be infesting Milo's soul declared, "I will never laugh at you, Milo."

Adjusting her perch at the edge of the bed in order to confront him more head-on, Kala elaborated.

"I will not laugh, Milo, because I see that your life and mine are now intertwined. Where you are, I must also be. What you feel, I too must feel. My destiny is to share yours and to help you carry your Destiny's burdens. I beg you not to leave me alone in this for I cannot leave you alone."

Kala halted, sensing that she had said enough but, more important, recognizing, to her own astonishment, that what she had just disclosed to Milo was irrevocably true. More, she realized all at once, that in conveying her assurances to her Betrothed she had also committed herself fully to the task of salvaging him from his demonic "Dims and Darkenings" just as wise old Megistes had foreseen that she would. Now, having delivered her life to that mission she could only trust that, somehow, she could find the means to accomplish it.

Again Milo was hanging his head. Again his voice reached Kala as a harsh muttering.

"Milo plays at a shameful game, he does."

"Shameful?" Kala sensed some revelation accumulating in the offing like a storm. She resolved to press toward it for her sake as well as Milo's.

"There is nothing shameful between us two, Milo. Nothing. I promise you."

Milo seemed not to have heard her. Or perhaps he was ignoring her.

"Poor Milo," he muttered, "poor Milo has tried to stop playing his shameful game, you see. But he can't. He is too weak."

Kala hurled a shaft into the dark. "Perhaps I should play Milo's game too," she suggested.

At this Milo looked up at her, feral alarm in his eyes.

"Oh, no, no, no! Kala must not play!"

"Then, of course, I won't play, if you say so. But can you just tell me a little about the game? Dear Milo, can you not share with me please? For I am in the dark."

A silence followed her plea. Kala realized that she had called him "Dear" Milo. The fond expression had tumbled naturally from her lips surely an unmistakable mark of her expanding attachment.

Milo, however, only lowered his head once more. Kala interpreted this behavior as a sign that he longed to unburden himself to her but feared her reaction. She thought to encourage him with another murmur of affection. "Dear Milo...."

She got no further, however, for Milo, abruptly lifting his head, stared at her for several moments and then spoke to her in a voice uncommonly shrill for him.

"Do you know that Milo owns the Eye of Isis? It is his Darling. He plays with it you see and he hides it away from all who wish to call him Strategat."

Milo gave Kala what she could only regard as a "sly" look then continued with his peculiar form of speech.

"Shall Milo show the Eye to Kala? Shall he? So beautiful Kala is! Shall Milo show his Darling to beautiful Kala?"

Though Kala certainly wished to view her Betrothed's "Darling" she dared not say so aloud lest she inadvertently disturb some moment of revelation that seemed to be approaching and so shut once more the delicate gate of communication with him which had somehow opened. And so she only gave a quick bob of her golden head to signify that she did want to see his Darling Eye of Isis—whatever it might be—even if, as she suspected, it turned out to be no more than a "good luck" talisman such as boys were wont to collect and value.

At her nod, Milo ejected a heart-stunning whoop, then leaped from his chair and snatched up a small, highly-polished wooden chest which reposed on a nearby shelf. Proceeding with reverential care, Milo opened the box, that Kala noted was lined with dark blue or black velvet and extracted what appeared to be a transparent glass ball of some kind. The Eye of Isis, she presumed.

Holding the glass sphere carefully in both palms, Milo carried it to where Kala sat on the edge of the bed. He held it out for her to look at.

"Don't touch it," he whispered, as if fearful she might cause it some injury.

Obediently, Kala bent forward to examine the glass ball without touching it. In spite of the semi-darkness of the chamber Kala could now see that the globe was not transparent at all but filled with a gray swirling that resembled nothing so much as smoke. Puzzled, she wanted to take it into her own hands but she didn't dare ask him for it.

Instead, she bent to look more closely and possibly determine what, if anything, lay within the ball under the obscuring smoke.

As Kala examined the glass of his Darling, Milo found himself examining her. How gentle and how kind she was! And beautiful too, of course, but everyone exclaimed over her beauty; it was the kindness of her spirit that stirred Milo. She made him feel peaceful. Milo was suddenly certain that Kala would never hurt him. Megistes had promised that this would be the case when he had urged Milo to agree to this private encounter with his Betrothed though it was against all the rules. Milo had agreed because he trusted the old man whom he loved far more than his father in fact. And so Kala Aristaia was here, with him, in the darkest hours of the night, and Milo was showing her, with hands that did not tremble for once, his Darling Eye of Isis, his precious treasure for he now realized that he trusted Kala as well.

"Do you wish to hold it in your hands?"

The question escaped Milo with no forethought and left him astounded at his temerity. Gently, as he held the glass toward her, Kala took the Eye into her own palms. She looked up at him in surprise, her sapphire eyes reflecting the candle-light and Milo knew that she too perceived the Eye's power. Cupping the glass in her hands, Kala felt what seemed to a be a miniscule vibration from within the globe, as if some tiny creature, perhaps a captive djinn from one of Mina's tales of her strange far-off homeland, was hiding in the swirling smoke inside.

The tiny throbbing of the globe reminded Kala of books she had read by certain scholars of the Logos who reported a somewhat similar sensation as one of the effects of the Venerated Object when handled with proper reverence. Of course Kala, not being a scholar, had never been privileged to view the Logos up close much less to touch it. Still, she couldn't help but wonder if Milo's Darling might share to a far lesser degree of course some of the mysterious qualities of the Logos. But of course the mysterious qualities of the globe would be of a perverted nature, would have to be for it was obvious that, unlike the beneficent effects associated with the Logos Milo's Eye of Isis had only wrought evil on him such as delusional behavior and loss of confidence to mention only the two most prominently on display in her sight.

All at once Kala found herself wishing fervently that she had the power to disperse the eddying fumes within the globe and reveal whatever lay hidden there. To her astonished delight, no sooner did this ardent desire enter Kala's mind, than the swirls of smoke began to disappear from the glass ball like sooty water draining from a tub leaving the glass perfectly clear—and perfectly empty. Her lovely face filled with amazement, Kala looked up at Milo as if for an explanation. In response he only shrugged and smiled shyly but proudly too. *Was the smoke a trick*, she wondered, *or did the thing, which though now smokeless continued to pulsate in her hands, possess additional capabilities?*

"What else can it do?" Kala asked.

Surely, she thought, there was more to the device than a knack for emptying and presumably filling itself with a cloud of smoke for had it not also proven its capacity to unsettle the balance of her Betrothed's mind?

In response to her query about what other tricks his "Darling" could do, Milo surprised Kala by abruptly sitting down next to her on the edge of the bed. He then surprised her even more by commencing to tell her, softly and unhurriedly, and above all in coherent language, what else the Eye could do, and had done, in the shameless games he had played with his "treasure". He began by relating to her how he had discovered the Eye in a magic shop in Northfair and how he had purchased it—on a whim—from its gnome-like proprietor, although he did not at first credit any of the powers that the gnome had claimed for it.

Kala interrupted. "What powers?"

Milo went on as if he had not heard her relating how he had soon learned that merely holding the Eye in his hands ameliorated the Dims and lightened the Darkenings until he soon came to love the Eye as his Darling, the instrument that soothed his troubled soul.

Continuing his confessional tale without constraint, Milo recounted how he had discovered that he could use his own sexual ardor to summon or perhaps create, he knew not which miniature figures always completely naked, of women he had seen in reality (they were never naked then, of course) and whom he had desired. With them displayed within the Eye according to his whim, Milo declared, he had become adept at manipulating them for his own "shameful pleasures", causing them to dance and show themselves lustfully while he "pleasured" himself as he gazed on the lewd images within the glass. Milo halted.

"Do you understand what I mean when I say I "pleasured" myself?"

Kala nodded. She had grown up among three older brothers. How could she have remained ignorant of the virtually universal practice of young men?

Returning to his tale, Milo said, "Of course, the women who frequented my beloved Eye never knew what use I made of their beauty. Time and again, overcome by shame, I would try to break my habit for I was always aware of its demeaning aspects, especially for one meant to become Hegemon of Arkadia. I was also aware that my shameful behavior maligned the innocent women I used for my wanton game. Oh, the contempt I felt for myself! The shame that ate at me! But I couldn't stop. I couldn't!"

Kala, all at once sensing an increase in the vibrations given off by the globe in her hands, found herself wondering if the glass was about to produce one of Milo's miniature women. Instead the globe filled with smoke and its vibrato ceased as a disturbing question induced by the Eye made its way into Kala's consciousness. She immediately directed the query to Milo. "Was I one of them?"

"One of whom?"

"The miniature harlots of your imagination."

Milo lowered his head in mortification.

"Yes. I wanted to see you naked."

"And did you see what you wanted to see?"

The very idea of his reducing her to an image in his Darling globe made her stomach queasy.

"Yes," he answered, keeping his face averted from her.

"And my tiny image gave you satisfaction?"

"Oh, Kala, I am so sorry!"

Milo was, Kala saw, near to weeping. With that realization she comprehended the extent of the evil already wrought on her Betrothed by his infernal "Darling". Delusion, addiction, despair (which is a great crime in one fated to rule) these were the fruits of his abject submission to his "Treasure".

Though Kala did not yet grasp the full extent of Milo's corruption by the Eye of Isis one overarching truth she understood full well:

By one foul means or another her husband-to-be had lost himself and it was essential that he be restored to himself again for the sake of Arkadia, the blessed land, the Logos, and the people—yes, even for the sake of the wretched Bem. Kala could see with undeniable clarity, however, that having lost himself in a dark forest of his own making Milo was incapable of finding himself again by his own efforts however willing he might be to try. And so it must be her business now to bring about his restoration. Moreover, guided by the instinctive wisdom of her gentle heart Kala understood how to rescue him from his corruption. She had to love him with all her soul not in spite of his weak and demented state but because of it. His restoration and all of Arkadia depended upon her loving him. Was this not the highest form of love, the kindness that evokes love in the other? In that fact she knew lay Milo's salvation and her own. And hadn't Mina said it herself? There are many kinds of love.

By now Milo was sobbing out his remorse.

"I'm so sorry I dishonored you, Kala. I do so love you. Truly!"

Kala embraced Milo keeping silence and soothing him in her arms until he was more or less calm again. Only then did she loosen her embrace and speak to him. Holding up the smoke-filled glass for him to see she said, "I shall keep this thing, this so-called Eye of Isis, for you, Milo."

Kala detected the rush of panic Milo felt at her announcement for his eyes revealed it.

"You needn't fear, dear Milo. I'll keep it safe for you. Should you ever want it again you may have it. I can promise you this Milo for I know that from now on you will have no need of the miniature delusions it provides."

Kala saw the distrust that still clouded his eyes.

"Rely on me," she added.

Milo said, "How can you know I won't need it again?"

"I know."

With this Kala rose from the edge of the bed, replaced the globe in its velvet-lined chest, and then turned back to him.

"You won't need that engine of corruption ever again Milo for you will have me."

Kala removed her gown, and stood before him naked. Milo gasped as if stunned at the vision she had turned to reality for him.

"Oh, Kala, I do so want you!"

They made love with a passion that astonished both of them and left both of them with no capacity for further talk. In the aftermath they lay together, silently entwined, deeply aware that together they had begun a journey to the unknown but one that promised joy to each of them.

As he lay at peace with his Betrothed Milo marveled at her blood, not because it meant she had been a virgin, he had already known that much about her but because it meant that Kala, splendid Kala, his Kala now, had allowed poor feeble Milo Agathonson to have the honor of her virgin blood. With this thought in his mind Milo fell into a profound sleep—the first he had experienced in months.

Kala watched at Milo's side until she was certain that no careful movement of hers would wake him. Only then did she slip out of the bed, pull on her gown, and retrieve the chest that contained the spiritually putrid Eye of Isis. Kala took a final, fond look at her sleeping Betrothed, barely visible in the last gasp of a candle. Was he dreaming? She hoped so and that he was dreaming of her. Noiselessly, she let herself into the corridor where only the very first gray fingers of dawn had appeared. She began to make her way back to her own quarters when a harsh laugh from somewhere caused her to start with alarm.

"You squeal like a sow in her pen when you fuck, sweet Kala Aristaia. Did you know that about yourself?"

Darden.

A trifle unsteady as if he'd been drinking the night away, Darden stepped out from the dark enclave where he'd concealed himself.

"You were very amusing you and my mad brother with all your squawking and grunting and squealing. I thought it would never end so I could finally get to sleep. Who'd have thought mad Milo had it in him to actually fuck a real girl? Usually he's content with his reliable right hand. Or didn't he tell you that?" Darden lurched forward a step or two. "And you, Kala Aristaia, the virgin Betrothed, playing the whore in the wee hours! Surely you can do better than my brother. Who else do you fuck, Kala? Surely mad Milo's not enough man for you."

Kala made no reply but only stared with cold disdain at Darden. The young man certainly possessed a ravenous malevolence that both infuriated Kala and aroused her disgust.

"You surely realize that brother Milo is crazed," chortled Darden. "Or maybe you dream of ruling through him, hey?"

Judging wrongly that Kala's silence signaled that he had intimidated her Darden continued with the precocious sarcasm in which he took such delight:

"Sooner or later a mad husband will prove a trial for you, never mind how much he makes you squeal in bed. But a mad Anax or Hegemon will prove a tragedy for our precious country."

Finally Kala replied.

"What a snot-face you are little Darden, struggling so hard to show me your cleverness. But take care for if you make me your enemy, I will make you so sorry you will piss in your pants every hour of the day. So beware of me, wet britches."

Kala swept past him without another word or even a brief glance.

Back in her own suite Kala put the Eye of Isis away in a cabinet where she kept those pencil portraits which for one reason or another had displeased her. She took the picture of Milo—the one that had upset her so much at first—out of the cabinet. Without looking at it again she tore it to bits and threw the pieces into the fireplace. The portraits of Milo that she would make in the future she was sure would please her as the other had not. Kala locked the cabinet leaving the box containing the Eye sequestered in the back of the top shelf. And there it would remain, she vowed to herself, for as long as she lived for she was now determined that she would love Milo, and that her love would endure for at least as long as her life.

Responding to a cryptic invitation, or was it more of a summons, from Mina, the beloved maid and companion to Kala Aristaia, a wary Phylax presented himself at the woman's private living quarters on the afternoon and at the hour stipulated. Phylax was immediately admitted by Mina herself to the small but well-appointed suite of rooms which the Chief Steward of the Hegemon's Residence had provided at Kala Aristaia's request as lodgings for this Mina who was clearly an important figure in the household of the Heir's betrothed.

After a polite but terse greeting Mina without offering her visitor the customary cup of watered Megar wine ushered Phylax down a well-lit hallway to a sun-filled little room where to his astonishment he found Kala Aristaia seated on a divan as if waiting for him. At the sight of her Phylax's heart swooped like a hunting hawk. As was always the case whenever he encountered Kala's glorious presence he was so enthralled by her beauty that he stood before her in stunned silence.

Unlike the elaborately-dressed hair and fashionable costumes she wore on more formal occasions on this afternoon Kala's long platinum hair was bound in two gleaming plaits arranged around her head like a crown. She wore a loose ankle-length gown of undyed linen cinched around the waist with a golden cord. Her feet were shod in leather sandals. Even arrayed in this simple style, which suited her very well indeed, Phylax thought she could not help looking like the royal personage she was.

For his own part Phylax, who had not known what or whom he might find at Mina's lodgings, was clad in a white leather jerkin and trousers, as well as low boots—the ensemble which comprised the dress uniform of the "White Angel" Regiment of the Riders of Arkadia. Though Phylax always found his "whites" uncomfortable, he was exceedingly glad that he had donned them this afternoon especially now that he saw that Kala and he were to be Mina's only guests. In truth, he rather hoped that Kala would surmise that he had worn the uniform to please her.

At this moment Mina, who looked to Phylax even grimmer than usual today, silently withdrew like a retreating ghost. Kala and Phylax were left alone with each other for the only time since they'd been introduced, a circumstance that Phylax took as Mina's devious purpose in inviting him to her quarters. With Mina's departure an unsmiling Kala rose from the divan and met Phylax's eyes with her own as if she was studying him.

To Phylax Kala's eyes looked like sapphire pools—placid and depthless—and hypnotic. As he looked into those eyes he sensed something new about Kala not just in her magnificent eyes but about her whole person. Kala seemed somehow "serene" in a way he hadn't detected before. It was as if some "repose of spirit" had descended on her. *Had something happened,* he wondered, *to bring about this change in her? Then, with a thrill of joy, it struck him that she must have discovered that she loved him as much as he loved her. Let it be so,* he thought and at once longing for her swept aside all previous considerations of honor and duty. Phylax's earlier determination to love Kala in silence and from afar dissolved in the reborn hope that he read in the eyes she kept fixed on him. Phylax saw in those eyes a desire to match his own. *Was it possible after all that they could love each other perhaps in secret?* No matter what the cost, he was ready to abjure honor—hers as well as his—for the chance to make real the aspirations of his heart and hers as well.

When Kala held out her right hand toward him Phylax interpreted the graceful gesture as a signal to enfold her in his arms something he had yearned to do since he'd first laid eyes upon her through the glass of the coach that was carrying her to her Betrothal at Ten Turrets. Now, he told himself, yearning was about to become reality. But when, with thundering heart, he moved to embrace her, she recoiled. "Not now," she murmured, as if uttering a plea.

Phylax halted in confusion. *Not now? Did those words mean that she wished to defer their first bodily contact? But why delay further the sweetness both of them wanted? Had they not been left alone precisely to allow each of them—at last—to express love for the other?* Despite his perplexity, Phylax acceded to her whim, if whim it was, though desire for her was burning in him body and soul. Still, he could not refrain from at least trying to speak his love to her.

"Kala", he murmured, "You must know how much I..."

She silenced him immediately by pressing the index finger of her right hand against his lips.

Astounded, Phylax stared at her adorable face as she whispered a heart-crushing appeal.

"No, no. Use no words of love to me, Phylax. We two must never say 'love' to each other. Promise me that, I beg you."

Consternation raged in Phylax's heart and brain. *No word of love for Kala Aristaia? No sounds of love for the only being he would ever adore in this life? He could promise no such thing unless she was willing to silence him for eternity with her cool finger against his lips.*

Kala's sapphire eyes fixed on his, she murmured again. "Promise me Phylax. Honor me in this for I am terrified that if I once hear you say you love me my soul will crack as will yours and we two will be lost. Lost."

Though he would rather have swallowed serpent's venom than obey her Phylax finally nodded agreement for it came to him as revelation that to refuse her entreaty in any particular would destroy her, would truly destroy her.

Removing her silencing finger Kala breathed her deliverance.

"Thank you, Phylax; you have saved me from myself and I think you have saved yourself as well."

Phylax found he was unable to speak for suddenly his mouth was full of the ashes of his hopes. He recognized that at this moment he understood nothing, except that, for reasons he could not yet fathom, the bright dream of making Kala his had flared briefly and then died. The world, Phylax felt, had returned to its prescribed orbit and Kala Aristaia would never be his. He almost cried out for the agony of it. At the same time some emotional instinct told him that to protest his fate in any way would not only fail to remedy his own pain it would also earn him the contempt of the woman he still loved and would always love. Hence he clung to silence as Kala, in an almost inaudible voice, revealed her own bewilderment at the re-alignment of her life.

"A week ago," Kala breathed, "though I could not then acknowledge it even to myself, I am sure that I would have found myself rejoicing to be here like this with you, Phylax. A week ago, I think, I would have chosen to be Phylax's thing, rather than become a Hegemon's Lady. But all that is now gone."

Phylax continued mute for he knew that what was gone to use Kala's phrase was gone forever. Only grief remained to be stored in the deepest chamber of his heart until time devoured not only the grief but him who grieved as well. Of that Phylax was certain. And he knew one other truth with the certainty of the mortally wounded: Kala needed him now; she would not love him, but she required him to stand with her now. Whatever had happened to shatter his brief and unworthy dream of her, he must not allow it to shatter her as well.

All at once, letting a sob break from her, Kala turned her back to Phylax as if she could not trust herself to look into his face. She began to speak again, her voice trembling as if straining with the effort to frame her thoughts in spite of the tempest roiling her breast:

"I have resolved to be the Hegemon's Lady with all my heart because I know that I must." She paused for a deep breath then continued. "I have resolved to do the thing that only I can do: restore Milo. It is a thing much bigger than I, even bigger than you, Phylax. But it will not be bigger than the two of us together. It must be done, though it means that I cannot, ever, be Phylax's thing." She turned to face him now. "Help me in this, Phylax. There is good in Milo. Together, renouncing all that might have been, all that will from now on remain unsaid between us, we two can provide the strength Milo needs. Will you help me prepare Milo to be the ruler of Arkadia?"

At last Phylax found a voice though it amounted to little more than a croak. "I will, Lady."

Bracing himself to attention, he delivered the salute that his Regiment ordained for the Hegemon's Lady. Then, acknowledging that a reborn duty and therefore honor had reclaimed him, Phylax strode away from love and the woman he would always worship in silence from afar. As he did so he heard Kala whisper from behind his back or was it only that he wished to hear it, "Thank you, Phylax."

Megistes having listened undetected to the colloquy between the young man and woman he cared for most in the world, stepped out from the shadowed alcove where he had secreted himself. He sighed glad to find himself alone.

"And so," Megistes muttered, reflecting on the pledge made by the two young people, "this is how hearts are broken, but souls are saved, and how lives are shaped among the good.

ELEVEN

As he guided the white mare for a second day southward along the wide and grassy east bank of the river Seraph continued to congratulate himself on the bargain he had made with the Pious Koinar, Leo. Never before had he felt so comfortably mounted. He attributed this welcome circumstance not only to the mare's easy gait but even more to the fact that the miraculous "stirrups" still unknown to the benighted Bem allowed him to ride with his lame right leg stretched out at rest instead of having to clamp it painfully against his horse's side in order to keep his seat. *Surely,* he reflected, *he had been justified in giving Rin to the slaver Leo in exchange for the mare.*

According to the Koinar, Rin would now join his menagerie of Bem female slaves all to be taken eventually to the Northfair slave mart for sale at a "very decent profit." More than likely Seraph supposed the Bem woman would finish her life's journey as an inmate of a brothel in one of those immense port cities said to exist on the farther shores of the Onyx Sea. *Would such a life not suit her?* Surely, as time passed, Seraph told himself, she would recognize that her whore's life even as a slave was superior to her previous existence as a worthless woman among the ignorant and brutal Bem. *And if Fate treated her harshly? Well, so be it.*

Seraph could permit himself no remorse for having sold the Bem woman. It had been a necessary act for he required a proper mount and sufficient supplies if he was to continue his search for what Leo had called "the mountain fire" and what he himself knew was in truth a mystical beacon calling to him.

All that had happened so far, as well as all that was yet to happen, he told himself, *was essential to his quest to bring down the Arkie state and all it represented. Surely his holy mission outweighed by far the insignificant life of the Bem woman. Rin had served her purpose and that was enough. He vowed to think of her no more.*

Seraph went on southward along the river's edge pausing only for brief intervals to allow the mare to drink from the river and crop the grass while he stayed mounted on her back. He did not dare to dismount or dally any longer than a fraction of an hour for he feared that the perfidious Leo truer to his acquisitive cult than to his bargain with an ugly and crippled Bem might be trailing him even now in order to re-take the mare.

Therefore, despite the weariness that had invaded his body even to the marrow of his bones, Seraph was determined to continue on southward until he could go no further. This second day of his journey he reckoned had about three more hours of daylight left to it. He had to take advantage of them. Perhaps he thought he might even reach the "unclean" precincts of Leo's "mountain of fire" before the fall of darkness. Certainly the Koinar would not dare to seek him there, especially in the dark.

Soon Seraph noted that the nature of the land to his left was beginning to alter as he went on, changing into a region of wooded hills at the foot of a range of sharply sloping mountains. Surely his sighting of mountains meant that he was nearing his goal.

As dusk gathered over the river to his right and in the steadily-steepening wooded hills to his left Seraph, lulled by the even gait of the mare, slipped into a doze until the squeaking of wooden wheels on the marshy ground of the riverbank jarred him back to wakefulness. Seraph recognized the squeaking as the sound that a heavily-laden cart makes. Though he could not tell from which direction the unpleasant noise was coming he knew that it could only mean trouble for him if he was seen by the carters whoever they might be. Accordingly, panic rising in his chest Seraph urged the mare away from the river and into a stand of tall trees and heavy underbrush. Here, Seraph thought, he and the mare could hide from anyone passing along the riverbank.

As it turned out the squeaking—very loud now—came from a caravan of four ox-driven carts heading north along the river. From his sheltered position in the wood, Seraph observed that the drivers of the carts were sturdy Koinar men each resembling the slaver Leo right down to their flowing black beards. *Were these Leo's six brothers returning from some commercial enterprise in the south and now bound north back to their trading station where Leo awaited them with his contingent of slaves?*

It was plain to see that the carts were heavily laden with logwood, bales of cloth, and tall earthenware jars which probably contained Arkadian wine. All such goods Seraph knew were unavailable in the sparsely-populated Pelorys settlements of the dissident Koinar sect who refused to recognize the authority of the so-called "Hegemony" of Arkadia. And so, Seraph reasoned, the goods in the carts must have been obtained, probably in some illicit fashion, from sources within Arkadia proper and were now on their way to the trading station where Leo was surely waiting to receive them. Seraph found this conclusion comforting for it implied that he need not worry any longer about Leo trailing him. With an acerbic smile Seraph realized that the carts on their trip south to Arkadia proper and now heading back north must have passed twice through the "unclean territory" that Leo had mentioned with such disgust. Apparently then, the "unclean territory" was not too unclean to thwart the Koinars' lust for business.

Seraph watched from his station in the woods until the passing carts melted into the deepening dusk and the sounds of their wooden wheels no longer impinged on his acute hearing. Then, acknowledging that he could no longer fight off exhaustion (he calculated that he had gone without sleep for a day and a night, probably more than twenty hours by now) Seraph decided that he had better try to sleep for two or three hours right where he was in the wood despite the insects buzzing about. His decision he told himself would not only provide him with essential rest it would also allow the Koinar carts time to put a safe distance between themselves and him. *Perhaps,* he thought, *when he woke again, he might resume his journey by moonlight.*

Having made his decision, Seraph slid clumsily from his horse landing heavily on his behind. Clearly, the struggle to mount and dismount would always prove an ordeal for him. Fighting to stay awake, Seraph tied the mare's reins to a sapling and put grain in her feed bag. He calculated that he had fixed the reins sufficiently loose and low on the sapling to permit the mare to crop the tufts of rough grass that grew under the trees. He probably should bring her again to drink at the river but Seraph felt much too worn to undertake the irksome task. He would water her in a couple of hours when he woke again. For now it was sleep he required.

Seraph lay the heavy horse blanket on the ground and stretched out on it. At first sleep eluded him for he kept recalling Rin's screams as Leo had dragged her away. Rin's remembered cries, disturbing as they were, ceased after a while however as Seraph descended into the welcome darkness of sleep.

Seraph woke cold and wet in a world gone gray. He sensed at once that it was dawn though on this dull and damp morning no exultant birdsong was announcing that fact. Seraph realized that he had slept through the night.

Shivering, Seraph sat up on the blanket and looked around. The heavy fog as impenetrable as soaked wool obscured everything except the nearest tree-trunks slick with cold condensation. He was hungry and thirsty after his long sleep.

Groaning with the stiffness in his joints Seraph struggled to his feet to fetch the bags of bread and water that he had stowed on the mare. But where was the mare? Astonished, he looked around in a circle. Seraph recognized the sapling to which he had tethered the mare. She was no longer there. His blood began to pulse with alarm. *Had the mare been stolen? No, no, that was impossible. No thief could have seen her hidden in the wood. She must have somehow loosened her tether and wandered away. But where?*

Shuddering with apprehension Seraph thought how imperative it was to find her.

The mare carried the supplies they both needed. Even his flint knife was stored with the mare. Only on her back could he continue his grand mission. Was his quest to fail now after so much suffering on the Bemgrass, after he had finally come in such close proximity to his goal? No, no, he must not lose control now.

Hold and think calmly he admonished himself.

Seraph reasoned that it was likely that the mare had merely wandered off. If so, she could not have gone very far in the dismal obscurity of the fog. Even now she might be standing unseeing and befuddled only a few yards away. He had to look for her without delay however lest she begin crashing about blindly and injure herself. It then occurred to Seraph that, thirsty, she might have found her way to the river earlier—before the mist had thickened—and was now halted nearby awaiting rescue. As he considered this possibility it took on the lineaments of certainty. Of course, the mare, guided by instinct, had gone to the river to drink. And the odds were that she was still there contentedly cropping the wet grass of the riverbank. Seraph would find her easily once he got himself out of this maze of trees. He set off at once in the direction that he hoped would take him to the river.

Struggling through the dripping underbrush, Seraph found the going much harder than he had anticipated. His breath became labored. His lame leg soon felt as heavy as Arkie iron. He pushed on nevertheless. *But would this obstacle course of woods and fog never end? Was he perhaps going in the wrong direction losing himself irrevocably in the gray wet?*

Suddenly a rat-like little creature, startled by Seraph's clumsily thunderous approach scurried from under a bush and raced away into the mist. Seraph had some vague recollection that such rat-creatures usually lived at the water's edge. If so he told himself he had only to keep to the same path as that taken by the scared rat and he must eventually come out near the river bank. And so it proved as he soon emerged from the wood onto a flat area of mud and grass that could only be the marshy edge of the Pelorys.

Though thankful to have escaped the woods Seraph was dismayed to find the swirling mist here by the river even denser than the forest variety. He knew that he would never find his mare in this gray stew. Still, he clung to the desperate hope that the mare had indeed found her way to the river, would stay wherever she was now, and that somehow he would catch her when this filthy fog finally lifted—if it ever did. Beyond that, he had no idea what more he could do.

In near despair Seraph limped across the muck, knelt, and cupped river water in his hands and drank. His leg was stiff with cold and exertion. *Seraph the gimp,* he reflected bitterly, *was he always to be no more than "Seraph the gimp"?* He struggled to his feet and made his way back to the grassy verge.

There unless his straining eye deceived him Seraph suddenly discerned a shadowy figure standing in the leaden shrouds of mist.

He felt terror like a frozen fist seize his heart. *Had Leo or one of his brothers trailed him to this gray nothingness after all? Was his grand quest to end in this void at the ignominious hands of a devout killer?*

Seraph now deduced from the fact that the other was not moving that his would-be killer had not detected him in the fog, that his potential assassin was probably as blind in the soup as Seraph was himself. Seraph also concluded that unarmed as he was and handicapped by a sightless eye as well as an all-but-useless leg any attempt to hide himself in the mist would only be to postpone the inevitable fate that awaited him at the Koinar's hands when the fog lifted. No, Seraph decided, he had only one chance to save himself: he had to attack his potential murderer at once and try to strangle him before the creature knew what had hit him. It was, admittedly, unlikely that he would succeed but with the element of surprise on his side he might bring it off despite the odds. In any case, he could think of nothing else to do to save himself.

Seraph moved closer readying himself to pounce on his quarry. He realized that the other no doubt also confused in the dense atmosphere had now turned his back in this way improving somewhat Seraph's gamble. *Do it now,* he told himself. *Now!*

Seraph flung himself as best he could on the other's back and bore him to the ground. The other, smaller and weaker than expected fought back with fury as Seraph sought to seize his slim throat. Only when the other began to scream with terror and rage did Seraph recognize his squirming, kicking, and fierce antagonist. Rin!

Bent on vengeance Rin meant to kill him that much was clear, nor could he blame her. Soon, as his grip weakened, she tore his hands from her throat and twisted away, gasping. Seraph's attack had failed. Now it would be Rin's turn and he doubted that he still possessed the strength to resist the furious onslaught he anticipated. But, instead of assailing him, Rin spoke to him in a voice heavy with import.

"I am here, Master, your servant Rin, come to help you."

Seraph, bowled over with both astonishment and gratitude, fell back speechless onto the soaked grass.

At once Rin rose to her feet and disappeared into the mist. She returned moments later leading Seraph's "lost" mare and the Bem pony now loaded with strange baggage. Without a word Rin helped Seraph to his feet. Taking his hand she helped him mount the mare and then led the two laden horses back into the woods where the fog was less dense.

After helping Seraph to dismount she tethered the horses without removing their loads. Only then did Rin come and sit on a fallen log opposite Seraph who had taken a seat on the ground his back propped against a tree. Neither of them spoke, Seraph because for once he could think of nothing to say, Rin out of shyness in her master's presence and gratitude at having found him again.

As the mist slowly thinned under the goad of daylight Seraph saw that Rin was wearing a rough-wool shift under an undyed shawl and that both garments were covered in bloodstains. Seraph finally spoke.

"Blood, Rin? Are you wounded?"

Rin shook her head, sending drops of water flying from her shaggy hair.

"No. You see his blood, master. The Koinar's blood."

Rin took a torn piece of Koinar flatbread from somewhere under her shift. She offered it to Seraph. "Hungry, master?"

"No."

The weight of his mission had taken away all desire for food. Instead Seraph watched Rin devour her bread. Rin's return, Seraph told himself, was surely more proof of the validity of his quest. How had she accomplished it? He did not ask her for he expected that in her simpleminded way, she would tell him when ready. He must not press her too soon lest, to evade further pain from the still-raw recollection of her experience with Leo, she repress its memory altogether.

Mist, along with an icy if intermittent drizzle, had engulfed Mt. Chion all day as it had for the previous four days as well. Mounted on her favorite horse, the magnificent charger Thunder, a downcast Nika Doraia reined up on one of the steep mountain trails that she knew so well in order to assess what she called her "situation" which was to put it bluntly, miserably disappointing.

Four days earlier she had set out on this latest of her many solitary jaunts up the rugged slopes of Mt. Chion. Nika's main objective had been to view once more the full moon as it swam in the flawless mirror of its famous lake. Nika had also intended to calm her spirit by doing some hunting of small game from the saddle. The wretched weather, however, had balked her on both counts. She had seen no sign of any game worthy of her javelins. Even worse, unlike last month's moon whose brilliance she had shared with the young man, Phylax, this night's Eye would languish, unseeing and unseen, behind a ceiling of obscuring clouds. And so the entire trip, probably the last Nika would ever experience with the freedom of youth, would have proven itself a gloomy disappointment when she headed home as she would tomorrow in accordance with her solemn promise to her father.

Reckoning that no more than two hours of gray light were left in the melancholy day, certainly insufficient time to continue a fruitless search for game, Nika decided her best course was to descend from the heights to the Lake shore below and make camp where she could light a decent fire to keep her warm for the long, and no doubt depressing, night ahead.

Nika also hoped that Rumbles, who had gone out on his own at the start of their trip and had not shown himself since, would spot her fire and come forth again. In truth Nika was beginning to worry about Rumbles for he seemed to be sinking more and more into his true dire-cat nature. *Maybe,* she thought not for the first time, *Rumbles was reaching the age when he needed to return to the wild.*

Dismounting from Thunder whose unusually morose attitude seemed to express an equine disappointment at the failure of the hunt Nika began to lead the mighty horse cautiously down the nearest path strewn with slippery rocks toward the lake shore. As she did so Nika's mind returned to the problem of Rumbles if problem it really was.

Nika had already accepted the hard fact that she could not take Rumbles with her when she departed in a few days to take up her post as handmaiden at Ten Turrets. At the same time she refused to countenance any idea of keeping Rumbles caged at the Hegemon's fortress-capital. Further, Nika did not dare entrust Rumbles to her father's gamekeepers for whom a dire-cat, even one as beautiful as Rumbles, was no more than a vicious beast to be destroyed. On the other hand she knew that if left to roam on her father's estate her great beast would soon begin taking and devouring any prey he found including humans. Rumbles was, after all, a dire-cat adapted to murdering his meat. Given all the negative contingencies, Nika had finally devised a plan that she hoped would grant Rumbles freedom and at the same time ensure the safety of the defenseless human beings in her father's employ.

Briefly, Nika intended as she traveled to Ten Turrets to make a detour across the River Bradys to the edge of the vast Bemgrass and there urge Rumbles to take the freedom he needed and probably wanted. At least in the Bemgrass he could live as his nature inclined him. Nor did Nika doubt that Rumbles would seize the chance to run at liberty on the Bemgrass for his absence over these last four days seemed to confirm a growing surmise that her beautiful Rumbles was ready to claim his dire-cat birthright. Of course she had to face the possibility that Rumbles' prolonged absence on this current excursion might indicate that hunters had captured or killed him already for she had heard dim hunting horns and what sounded like human cries from time to time today in the misty valleys on the mountain. Still, Nika could not seriously entertain the notion that her fierce great cat had collided with calamity for if Rumbles had suffered disaster at the hands of hunters, she was sure she would have sensed it in her bones and blood.

Besides, she told herself, *no ordinary hunting party could ever subdue her Rumbles.* Nika felt confident that sometime tonight her naughty beast would join her and Thunder in their rough bivouac.

With her camp—ground-sheet, tent, stores-pack and saddlebags—set up at the edge of the lake in a copse of hemlocks which dripped rain from every branch Nika covered Thunder with the heavy blanket he favored and prepared his feedbag as well. Only then did she build a fire. Nika had intended to catch a few fish for her supper but the continuous drizzle as well as her own lack of appetite discouraged her from making the effort. Instead, after calling fruitlessly for Rumbles— *"Come out, Rumbles, come out my big boy!"*—she fetched a leather flagon of unmixed wine from her storage pack and huddled around the fire in her long cloak. Drinking the wine directly from the flagon Nika watched the coming night add its damp shadows to the gloom of the outgoing day.

Nika found herself reflecting on how much the damp and mists which had oppressed her for these past days matched the dark state of her mind. She even considered the possibility though she did not really believe in such things that the gloomy weather was an omen, a foretelling of the miserable future that awaited her when she returned, as she must, to Golden Walls, the grand estate of Typhon Doridis, Chief Councilor to the Hegemon and her father.

Nika harbored no doubt whatsoever that when she got back to Golden Walls, her father, "Typhon the Ready" as he was known to his fellow Megar lords of the Katoran, would have all her baggage and belongings packed and waiting along with a grand coach and servants to accompany her to Ten Turrets where she was to languish for a term of three years as one of the mincing Handmaidens to the Betrothed.

"A great honor, dear Nika," her father insisted when the Hegemon had announced Nika's appointment.

Despite his daughter's furious rejection of the "honor" being bestowed on her, Typhon the Ready, smiling buoyantly, had persisted in his argument.

"I am sure you will enjoy your duties, my child, if you give it a chance."

Of course Nika had known full well that her father, no more than she, had the slightest idea what a Handmaiden's "duties" might be.

Suddenly, Nika's dark reflections were interrupted by a blast of hunting horns accompanied by baying hounds and all sounding too close for comfort. Jumping to her feet Nika gripped one of her hunting javelins and scanned the cliffs, their bulk alone still visible, that loomed over the Lake of the Moon. Though it seemed to Nika that the wild sounds of horns and dogs had probably originated from those heights nothing was to be seen or heard up there now.

Seating herself once more at the fire Nika continued to look up at the sheer stone face directly above her. It was only a month ago on a ledge of that very precipice that she had encountered the young man, Phylax, who had intrigued her so. On that night, she remembered, Phylax and she had observed a splendid display of the great White Eye in the lake and Nika had enjoyed a kind of relaxed happiness with another that she had never experienced before and which she now thought gloomily she would probably never experience again. *How cheerful that night's festival had been!*

Drawn by the Eye, how happily the numerous Arkadian folk— families, lovers, and wonder-filled children—had walked the lakeshore to absorb the blessings of the moon's light. Tonight, however, with the

White Eye hidden the woods and the lakeshore were bereft of visitors, and—except for the intermittent baying of dogs and the sounding of the inexplicable horns—silent.

Pulling herself closer to the hissing fire, Nika drank again from the leather flagon now almost half empty. She tried to empty her mind of nagging thoughts about what lay ahead for her. The effort, however, only exacerbated the painful truth: She would detest her incarceration in Ten Turrets no matter what her "duties" as handmaiden turned out to be. She might very well die in such captivity. And this seemed all the more likely now that her father had at last seen fit to reveal to her whom she was to serve as Handmaiden: Kala Aristaia, of all people!

Nika and Kala had known each other briefly as children. Nika had not liked Kala then, had in fact been childishly mean to her. Nika could not help but suspect that Kala, now risen so high in the Hegemony, meant to exact some kind of revenge for Nika's ill-treatment of her as a child. Why else would Kala Aristaia, the Betrothed, accept "wild Nika" as her servant?

The fact was that all her life Nika had despised the bland and spiteful females of her own Megar class who thronged like flocks of fat pigeons forever waddling and pecking after morsels of gossip. And those women despised Nika in return. Surely the other girls chosen to serve as handmaidens would hate the wildflower among them!

As much as she disliked Megar females, however, Nika disdained even more their dainty "men" who twittered with other nonentities and, as she had long surmised, only played at soldiering in the Hegemon's fortress-capital. Such creatures it seemed to Nika, though in fairness she had had no direct experience of them, were better suited for dancing at the Residence than for running down Bem terrorists in the Forbidden Zone.

Of course, Nika had to admit recalling her encounter with the young half-Koinar, Phylax, her harsh judgment could not be true of all the male inhabitants of Ten Turrets. Still, she would bet that it was true of most of them. In any case she thought Phylax was most probably an exceptional young fellow as he had demonstrated in a recent letter he had sent her and which she carried in the saddlebag she reserved for her most important personal possessions.

With the exception of Phylax and perhaps some others she had yet to meet Nika expected to be revolted by almost all the denizens who buzzed like nasty hornets within the aureate brick hive called Ten Turrets for it was liberty and solitude that she cherished and which she now knew she had to give up. *For most of her life,* Nika reflected, *she had warred with Typhon the Ready for license to live pretty much as she pleased.* And she had emerged victorious from most of their battles for Nika had learned early on that Typhon the Ready was seldom prepared to deny his motherless little girl (her mother having died when Nika was only three) even her most outrageous importunities such as her demand to be permitted to ride Thunder without escort. Nor did Nika's father wish to expend large segments of his valuable time in wrangling with his only child, the daughter he adored.

Moreover, Nika had realized as she grew older that in his secret heart her father considered her a singularly gifted girl and so almost invariably gave into her unorthodox style of living lest he inadvertently stifle a spirit which might one day astound Arkadia's more ordinary run of men and women.

Yet, despite all her victorious struggles with her father, Nika had also come to realize that for all his malleability, if Typhon the Ready truly set his mind on any matter of importance concerning her, then no form of combat not even tears could move him. Nor would he compromise on such matters. In these instances that luckily were few Nika had eventually recognized that she had to capitulate or break her father's heart—and that was something she simply could not bring herself to do. There were two such capitulations to her father's will that came readily to her mind.

In the first such she had acceded at the age of seven to her father's requirement that she submit to a course of studies with a series of private and prominent tutors. In retrospect she had been grateful for her father's unyielding insistence on educating his extraordinary daughter. Without that education, Nika had since acknowledged, she would now be as ignorant as one of those Pious Koinar women and just as ill-equipped to shape a unique life for herself.

The second of her major capitulations to Typhon the Ready was, of course, the most recent and most troubling one: her agreement after long resistance to serve as Handmaiden at Ten Turrets. Nika had given in to her father's adamantine persistence on that score when at last she perceived that her obedience had become for him a question of honor.

The Hegemon himself had asked that Typhon send his only daughter to attend on the Heir's Betrothed. As a First Counselor to the Hegemony, Typhon could not refuse the request without bringing disgrace on himself and the family name. If he was unable to comply with Strategat Agathon's wish, Typhon the Ready would no longer be willing to show himself at Ten Turrets. He might as well go into seclusion for the rest of his life and all because his obstinate and selfish daughter had no stomach for life at Ten Turrets nor any true sense of duty either.

And so, despite her apprehension about Kala Aristaia's attitude toward her, Nika was unwilling to break her father's heart or see him disgraced. And so she had yielded. She would travel to Ten Turrets at the end of this current unsatisfactory visit to Mt. Chion and she would stick it out for the full three years. To this she was now resigned even though she would no doubt have to suffer petty humiliations at the hands of a vengeful and shallow-minded Kala Aristaia.

In addition to the need to preserve her father's honor Nika secretly harbored another, more selfish, reason for assenting to service as the Betrothed's companion: She still hoped for an opportunity to become the first woman to win appointment to a Rider Regiment preferably the White Angels. Nika knew that she could only make that dream a reality if she was physically present at Ten Turrets. And what honors she might reap for her father if she succeeded in that ambition!

Of course she realized that the odds against her gaining her objective were slim at best. And so she had kept from her father any inkling of her singular aspiration at least until she could make some realistic assessment of her prospects. All that she actually knew right now was contained in the letter that Phylax as promised had sent to her and which she had received two weeks ago. As if to counteract the gloom of these last few days Nika quickly retrieved the letter from her personal bag, and opened it for what was probably the hundredth time. The missive was to the point, business-like, and written in the standard calligraphy taught to cadets in Regimental Schools to ensure clarity in the transmission of orders and information. Though she knew the letter by heart by now, Nika read it again:

*From Cadet Commander White Angel Regiment, to Lady
Nika Doraia at Golden Walls, The Katoran*

Greetings

*Regarding the matter we discussed on the night of the full
moon at the Lake of the Moon, I have now consulted with the
Chief of Enrollment for the Array of Arkadia and with the
Commandant of my own regiment. I received the following
information from these sources:*

1. *There is no specific regulation that would bar a woman
   from service with any Rider Regiment.*
2. *It is true that women have not yet served with the
   Riders. It is also the fact that no female has ever made
   application to do so.*
3. *Any candidate for the Service, female or male, must
   pass through stringent tests of physical capacity,
   horsemanship, and weapons skills. Only those who
   demonstrate the highest abilities in these areas as well
   as the will to endure rigorous field trials will be admitted
   as Regimental Cadets. There are no exceptions to these
   rules.*
4. *Once admitted to a regiment as a cadet, the candidate,
   female or male, must live in barracks with other cadets,
   sharing food, communal sanitary facilities, sleeping
   quarters, and all other aspects of a vigorous course
   of training exercises. No cadet, male or female, is
   permitted any special treatment of <u>any</u> kind during his
   (or her) cadet career.*
5. *The Chiefs to whom I spoke made it clear to me that
   they believe it virtually impossible for any woman to
   achieve full membership in any Rider Regiment though
   they would see to it that all trials and tests were applied
   fairly and they would welcome with open arms any
   woman who could make a place for herself among the
   Riders of the Realm. (You may take <u>that</u> with a grain
   of salt.)*

> 6.   *The Chiefs were also keen to point out to me that fewer
> than one out of three male candidates, many of them
> fine athletes, actually achieve places among the Riders.*

> *This is the best information I could discover for you Nika
> Doraia. I suppose that the task you have set for yourself must
> seem daunting and if you decide you would rather pursue
> some other goal I for one would not blame you. Whatever
> you decide, however, I trust that you will still come to Ten
> Turrets and that you will accept me as your friend there.
> May it be so. Phylax.*

Judging by what Phylax had written Nika reckoned that the Rider chieftains probably would treat her with fairness as a Rider candidate. But even so, she could not help wondering if she could survive barracks life with forty or so lusty young men. Nika also had to acknowledge that she might find in the end that she wasn't good enough to win a place in the Riders. *How could she endure such a verdict? Perhaps,* she thought, *it was really fear of failure, not the loss of her freedom that had made her so reluctant to face whatever was awaiting her in Ten Turrets.*

"By the dust of the Logos!" she muttered echoing a favorite epithet of her father's, "I wish I could see clearly the path ahead! Why does life always twist and turn so?"

The fret-filled question reminded her of the other letter she had received in the last mail packet from Ten Turrets along with the one from Phylax. This second missive, completely unexpected, also troubled her. Extracting it from her bag, Nika re-read it yet again. As on earlier readings she sensed a dark meaning lurking beneath the outwardly amiable sentiments the letter expressed:

> *From Kala Aristaia, Betrothed of the Heir Milo Agathonson,
> to Nika Doraia, her friend.*

> *Greetings!*

> *I have at last been told the names of the women who are to
> be my "handmaidens" here at Ten Turrets. Imagine my joy,*

Nika, to find that you will be one of my companions. I hope that we shall ride together as we did as children! How much I will enjoy having you as my guest this time! Come to me soon! I am waiting! Kala A.

That was all. The arrival of this letter not only seemed to validate Nika's generalized anxiety about serving as handmaiden to the Betrothed it also brought back specific memories of her previous experiences with the beauteous Kala. In fact, the more she thought about it, the more she re-read the note, the more certain Nika felt that Kala's words contained veiled references to a particular encounter that had taken place one summer when Kala and her haughty mother had spent an interlude at Golden Walls.

During that visit Nika recalled that, though only seven years of age herself, she had delighted in tormenting seven year old Kala Aristaia, her then-helpless guest.

"We shall ride together as we did as children! How much I will enjoy having you as my guest this time!"

Surely these words in the letter implied a hangover of ill-will from that long ago summer.

Nika sighed.

Although Nika recollected relatively few details of Kala's stay at Golden Walls she did still carry in her mind a luminous picture of the girl herself as she had been then. Even at seven Kala had been a perfect girl-child, golden, sweet, compliant—unwilling to entertain at least openly any mean thought.

On the other hand Nika herself had been burnt brown from the sun that summer and professed only contempt for "prettiness and stuff."

Further, though claiming to be indifferent to her own looks because she so much preferred adventure, the truth was that Nika had been consumed that summer with a furious and secret jealousy of "Little Lady Perfect" whom everyone at Golden Walls seemed to love and admire so much more than their own wild little Nika.

During that summer visit, therefore, Nika had often led Little Lady Perfect into risky behavior that the girl had insisted she enjoyed despite the grime such behavior entailed and despite the rebukes Kala earned from her mother as a result.

"We shall ride together as we did as children!"

Surely that phrase in Kala's letter could only refer to the infamous day when Nika had climaxed her jealous anger at her guest by commandeering one of her father's horses and galloping the beast bare-back, poor Kala forced to ride pillion across the meadows and fallow fields of the estate.

Naturally in the course of the ride Kala to Nika's delight had taken a tumble into a drainage ditch from which she had emerged with scrapes and bruises and covered with muck. Instead of bawling as Nika had expected, however, Little Lady Perfect had professed herself "inspired" by her adventure as well as "thrilled" to find herself sheathed in slime.

Needless to say Nika had been seriously reprimanded by her father despite Kala's declaration that she, Kala, was at fault for having "begged the ride" with Nika.

The summer visit had ended soon after, Kala thanking Nika for "all the fun" surely to be recognized now as sarcasm! and Nika grudgingly admitting to herself at least that once you got past her perfect hair, eyes, and skin, Kala might not be "entirely stupid."

In subsequent years, Nika and Kala had had no occasion to meet again. Yet now Kala Aristaia had written that it *pleased* her that Nika was to be her "companion". How could Nika doubt that Kala, despite her sweet words, was planning to take her vengeance at Ten Turrets? "Why," Nika groused folding Kala's note and putting it away, "is mere living suddenly turning into such a complex business?"

As the wet dusk at her lake shore camp steadily morphed into a wet night Nika again was startled by a blast of hunting horns this time followed by a muffled roar. *Rumbles?*

In the ensuing silence Nika couldn't help thinking that the sounds probably did have to do with her wayward dire-cat. *If so, she reflected, there was no remedy for it. Rumbles, after all, had little to fear from hunters be they ever so determined. Besides, Rumbles would return to her if and when he had a mind to do so, hunters, horns, and dogs be damned.*

In the meantime with her fire rapidly dying into a handful of glowing embers Nika was feeling an irresistible urge to take refuge in sleep from the dripping night. She finished the little wine left in her flagon and settled herself to receive the benefaction of slumber.

As she descended into the hypnotic state that lies between the wakeful world and the realms of reverie, two simultaneous thoughts floated into Nika's drifting mind.

In some fashion every aspect of her life seemed to have come loose from its moorings. She was adrift, disjointed and as torn as ever between obligation, to her father, ambition, to make a life with the Riders, and trepidation, about a future more and more beyond her control. It came to her that if any honorable course lay open for her to slip through the closing gates of Destiny she would take it.

"But there is such a course open to you, Nika Doraia."

It was a woman's voice, the accent unknown to Nika. *Am I dreaming already?* she wondered.

"Not exactly, Nika" said the odd voice. "But you are in a state much like a dream."

The owner of the voice appeared from somewhere. She was a tall woman. To Nika's consternation she seemed to be wearing the guise of a great owl: masked and garbed in a cloak and leggings of tawny feathers. Her feathered robe fell to her sandaled feet and glittered with an iridescence not found in the natural world. Nika at once concluded that this "owl" had to be one of the wild women said to roam the cold slopes of Mt. Chion.

The owl-woman spoke again.

"I am called 'Maenad', which is both my name and the name of the sacred band of women whom I lead."

"Lead? Lead where?"

Nika was not sure if she had spoken her question aloud or only formulated it in her mind. But it seemed to make no difference to the Owl-woman for she answered aloud with no hesitation.

"My women and I go in search of the god Dionysus whom we Maenads have served throughout the ages. Each month when the Goddess Moon is full we hunt the god on this mountain through valleys and mists and snows as well."

Nika recollected the hunting horns which had haunted her all day.

"To what purpose do you hunt this god of yours?"

"For worship and sacrifice, to achieve the ecstasy he brings to us. The Dionysus we captured this month is especially beautiful. Come see for yourself Nika Doraia. Come."

In response to the command Nika felt her body rise from its sleep pallet. The Priestess Maenad took Nika's elbow with a hand that was warm and certainly human. Together, not touching the ground or so it seemed to Nika, the Owl-woman guided Nika into a circular grove of pines within which stood a ring of noble oblong rocks each raised on its end as if looking like sentient beings into the center of the circle where a massive flat stone like an altar reposed. Nika saw that from this place which she had never noticed before and which was so obviously dedicated to rites unknown to her she could look out to the surface of the lake sleek as black silk on this night of a hidden moon.

The Owl-woman, the Priestess, held out a goblet to Nika.

"Drink the wine of the god Dionysus. It is like no wine from the vines of men."

Nika drank from the cup. It seemed to contain sweet air mixed with some live elixir whose origin was surely not of the world she knew. And then she drank again. Nika felt as if she was emptying light into her soul.

"Look on this moon's Dionysus."

The Owl-priestess gestured and Nika, following her motion, saw a young man sprawled naked on a central *lithos*. His chest was heaving, perhaps from ecstasy or dread. Though unbound the youth seemed unwilling—or it might be that he had been rendered unable—to flee whatever was to come to him. The Owl-priestess clapped her hands sharply.

At the sound, women clearly the Maenads of this strange god called Dionysus appeared. Many of them were bearing torches. Seeming to emerge from every cove, tree, and den, these women of the god, all of them clothed in animal skins of wolves, leopards, and the tribe of black panthers long gone from the world swayed into the grove. The Maenads took up positions within the standing circle of sentient rocks. There they stood hips swaying as a sinuous music of flutes, tambourines, and reeds pervaded the torch-lit grove. It seemed to Nika that the eyes of the women were fixed with lustful hunger on the naked god spread upon the central altar.

Upon a signal from the Owl-priestess unseen trumpets burst out and to Nika's amazement the clouds blackening the moon immediately parted whereupon a silver luminescence enveloped the sacrificial *lithos* and the placid water of the lake. Figures of women, garbed in white, rose from the water, their soaked gowns clinging to their bodies. These risen Maenads appearing to float in air joined their sisters within the ring that surrounded their sprawled god. Concealed drums joined their powerfully insistent rhythms to the music of the flutes and tambourines. The Maenads danced, their movements wild and growing wilder as the drumming compelled the dancers to reach climax upon climax.

"Come join us, Nika," murmured the Owl-priestess. "Dance for the god."

Nika did. She became one with her sister Maenads. She found she could not stop her whirling body in thrall to impulses alien to the Land of the Logos.

Suddenly, the mad drumming ceased.

Bathed in sweat, Nika collapsed onto the pine needles that covered the ground. She watched at first not sure whether the scene she was beholding was genuine or a pantomime as the Maenads fell on the god-boy and commenced to tear him apart.

Fighting with each other like ravenous lionesses at a kill the women rent the god-boy's surrendered flesh with their teeth all the while howling and screaming for a place at the carcass. From time to time one of the women would run off with a half-gnawed bone—an arm, a rib, a hand—in order to feed alone in the woods. Some fled with their portion and sank down into the lake to devour the holy flesh.

By degrees the frenzy diminished as the Maenads, satiated, withdrew one by one. At the end, Nika, exhausted from the dancing, lay alone on the pine-needle carpet. She gazed in stunned silence at what was left of the god: only bloodstains, not a speck of flesh, not a sliver of bone.

The Owl-priestess, her feathered mask stiff with dried blood from her own participation in the mindless feast, reappeared. She held out a gobbet of raw flesh indicating that Nika should take it.

"Here is the escape you wished for, Nika Doraia. Eat of the god's body and become one of us. Become one of us and without remorse defy the tyranny of men."

As Nika looked at the crushed cube that once was part of the boy, for surely he had been no god, Nika seemed to hear again the question Phylax had posed to her at that last full moon when she had talked about running away to join these same wild women who, it turned out, actually existed!.

"And what about duty?" Phylax had asked.

A difficult question, but after this night's blasphemous assault on the Logos and all it stood for, it was one Nika felt she could now answer.

Duty is that which requires you to stand and fight the never-ending battle that is the world.

Nika knew now that she was not made for mindless worship. She knew also that flight could never assuage her soul; it could only obliterate it.

Aloud, Nika said to the Owl-priestess, "I think you have taught me without intending it that it is better to fail with honor than run away from what one ought to do."

The Owl-priestess popped the gobbet of her god's body into her mouth, chewed, and swallowed it. Then she called out: "Come forth now!"

Nika rose to greet the creature that appeared from the bush beyond the grove. It was Rumbles. The great beast padded forward and flopped at the feet of the Owl-priestess. Then, staring with yellow-eyed contentment, he switched his tail making it plain to Nika that he had found a new mistress. Am I not an enchantment too? he seemed to say. *Is it not best then that I remain with others who share enchantment with me?*

The Owl-woman said, "I shall be watching you, Nika Doraia, though you will not know it."

Silently, she walked off into the forest. Rumbles rose and followed.

"Farewell, Rumbles," Nika murmured.

Nika woke at dawn refreshed. *Had it been real?*

As real as such things can be she told herself. And besides, she found that she did not care. Real or a dream it did not matter. What mattered now was to live as honor required.

Mounted on Thunder, Nika descended in the pale sun's light from the mountain to the authentic life that she now meant to pursue whatever the cost, whatever the risk.

As Thunder carried her down to the foothills of Mt. Chion Nika experienced a surge of joy inexplicable except as a reward for right action. Nika also decided that she would not travel to Ten Turrets in a splendid coach as her father wished. Nor would she countenance an escort of any kind. No, she would make her journey to Ten Turrets, and whatever awaited her there, riding on Thunder. They might as well know from the start what she was made of.

TWELVE

As Rin made camp on what surely would be the final night of her journey with her master for they were now within sight and sound of the fire-cave her lord had been seeking she gave way to the terror which she had been suppressing since her reunion with the prophet she revered more than her own life.

What Rin dreaded was that tomorrow when her lord Seraph at last reached his destination he would abandon her again. If that happened, she knew, she would surely choose to die. She would burn herself alive in the fire from the cave mouth or she would fling herself into the Pelorys to drown.

Since her reunion with her master on that morning of the fog, Seraph had not spoken to her. Rin understood that he was much distressed, that as he neared the fire his mind was necessarily fixed on the enormous thoughts that occupied him, thoughts that she could never comprehend. Rin knew she was of little importance to him, that her role was to serve and accept. And she was content with that.

And yet Rin could not help craving his re-assurance that after they reached the fire he would keep her with him, to serve him in any way he wished. Rin did not dare to ask him for the re-assurance she yearned for. She feared that if she did, he would rebuke her and then order her to leave him. That command, she knew, would not only break her heart, it would destroy her.

Yet, she thought, *his silence troubled her. After asking her only once to tell how she had fled from the giant Leo, her master had seemed to lose interest in the tale. But why? Was her master's silence a sign of his displeasure because she had not told the story when asked?*

In truth, Rin had refrained from recounting her escape not because she did not wish to do so but because her memory of it was a disjointed tangle beyond her ability to unravel. Yet it seemed that she must try or risk sinking to nothing in her master's eyes. So, on this final night of their journey after they had eaten and their campfire had diminished enough to cast only a red light on her master's torn face, Rin, picking cautiously through the rubbish heap of events that cluttered her memory began the struggle to set forth her tale.

Opposite her in the fire's glow, Seraph, who, unknown to Rin, had been silent for all these days in order to avoid thinking too much of what horror might be lying in wait for him at the cave listened glad of the distraction.

Why, he wondered, *was Rin speaking now after so much reluctance?* Rin alone knew why.

Seraph was all attention, therefore, as Rin commenced a rambling recital that required him to interrupt her many times for clarifications. The account that finally emerged, however, engulfed him entirely.

When the Pious Koinar, Leo the Giant, threw Rin into the cage with the other slaves, they were all young Bem girls, eight of them, the oldest no more than twelve, the Bem woman sank down and wept until she emptied herself of tears. Rin did not blame Seraph for her wretched plight but only herself. In some manner, she decided, she must have displeased her master, must have failed him in some way. Otherwise why would he sell her to the Koinar beast?

For reasons that confounded Rin the captive girl children in the cage found her tears a matter for laughter and mockery. *Probably,* thought Rin, *this was because they had already accepted their bondage. Perhaps, unlike her, these girls considered their enslavement an improvement over their previous condition as Bem females.*

At some point the giant Leo came to the cage with bread and a kind of gruel for the inmates. While the little girls fought with one another for the food, Leo entered the cage and pulled Rin out. Of course she understood what he wanted of her and she offered no resistance for she was used to giving her body to men without feeling anything. Only with Seraph, her true master, did she allow herself feelings.

Rin did not resist when Leo pulled her into a dark room within his house, his sleeping place, and ordered her to open her legs to him.

Afterwards he lit a candle and apparently unsatisfied with her he looked for a long time into her face as if studying it for some meaning.

Leo could speak a little of the Bem tongue and told Rin to don a woolen shift that was hanging in the room. She did so. Then, saying he wanted her to stay in the house with him until his brothers returned for their share of her body, Leo warned her to obey him without hesitation or he would cut her throat with no scruple at all. To drive home the point Leo drew a long metal knife from his belt and brandished it at her.

Rin cringed for the knife of Arkadian origin frightened her as the massive Koinar knew it would. Then he ordered her to lie still on the bedstead and extend her legs toward him. She did so thinking he wanted her again. But it was not her body he wanted it was something now far more dear to her, though at that moment she did not suspect what it was. Then she saw that Leo was kneeling on the bed with a length of rope and ankle cuffs in his hands and Rin realized, with a stab of horror that he was preparing to hobble her, to bind her again as she had been bound for so many years before the coming of Seraph. Rin could not bear it. Leo could kill her she told herself but not bind her.

With no thought other than her refusal to submit to binding she found the strength to tear the metal knife from Leo's belt and drive it under his thick beard, burying it up to the hilt in his throat. Rin saw Leo's eyes roll up with astonishment. His blood, a hot and sticky flood, spurted over Rin's new shift. Leo collapsed on top of her.

Soaked in his blood Rin wriggled out from under his weight. *What now? Might she escape? She had to try, at least that.* Carrying Leo's candle and the bloody knife, Rin went out of the room.

In the kitchen Rin found an old Koinar woman and a young Bem girl, the same child who earlier that day had served Seraph and Leo with tunnik. The old woman was shaking with dread of the bloody blade in Rin's hand. The big-eyed little girl, when asked, whispered to Rin that Leo had been left alone to guard the station but was expecting his brothers to rejoin him soon.

Rin recognized that Fate was granting her a chance to save herself but she also realized that she had to act without delay. Driven by her need to get away as fast as possible Rin flew about the Koinar house gathering what provisions she could find easily: bread, leather drinking containers filled with tunnik, dry meat, lentils, cheese, and whatever else she could lay her hands on. She tied this booty on the Bem pony which she found stabled in a shed.

Rin also discovered in Leo's room a metal-tipped javelin and another knife. These she also added to the pony's load. She then took a shawl to protect her against the cold of the moonless night. Finally, using one of the keys she discovered on Leo's stiffening body she unlocked the slave cage told the little girls that she was fleeing, and they were now free too. Did any of them wish to join her? They made no answer but only stared at her in dumb confusion or perhaps it was hostility she saw in their eyes.

Knowing she must waste no time in useless argument with them Rin left the girls in their unlocked cage. *Let them escape on their own, if they decided they wanted their liberty.*

Rin then mounted the pony unmindful of the burden he was already carrying and rode into the darkness away from the Koinar station. Soon, somewhere at the river's edge, she halted. What now? Where now?

Rin knew of no way to re-cross the big river to the Bemgrass on the other side. She could not work the raft-ferry even if she dared to try. She knew that to the north past the Koinar station lay a hostile territory where other Koinars like Leo dwelt. And further north still at the limits of the Koinar land lay a place called Northfair where slave buyers purchased the Bem girls brought to them.

Rin could not go to the north then but neither could she remain where she was now. And so she elected to go southward as her master had done. Perhaps she would find him. If so she would beg him to receive her again. *And if he refused?* Then she would follow him at a distance unseen but always vigilant to come to him when he needed her.

Rin could not help but think that sooner or later Seraph would need her maimed as he was. Moreover, she knew his destination: the mountain of fire that he felt calling to him. And so, even if she somehow failed to overtake him, she would surely find him at the place of fire that he sought. With this resolve in her mind, Rin set off into the night of cold stars, the pony patiently bearing her and her loot.

As she and the pony plodded southward in the darkness Rin felt her heart soar like a lark rising into the dawn for she was suddenly filled with the great joy that comes with liberty. She had done what no other Bem woman had ever done: She had achieved her own freedom by finding the courage to strike down the oppressor who meant to take it from her and she had bathed in his blood. Surely her master, who knew so much that was too large for her own comprehension, would now recognize her worth. Surely he would.

As the new day dawned, Rin hid herself and the pony in the woods lest some passerby discover her with her loot from Leo's house and wearing a bloodstained shift. So it was, therefore, that she was able to watch in safety as Leo's brothers, for the men she beheld could be no other, drove their carts past her hiding place on their way to the Koinar post where (she exulted at the image in her head!) they would find their brother a stiffened corpse in his own bed.

When night fell again, Rin resumed her southward trek even as a heavy mist formed over the river. With the passing of the night hours the river mist thickened into a blinding fog that swelled to envelop the land along with the river.

At the next dawn the fog became an impenetrable whiteness. Still Rin traveled southward, trusting to the pony's instincts to keep to the right path. Then, in the blank whiteness, she came upon the mare that her master had obtained in exchange for her and she realized at once that her master had to be nearby, perhaps lost in the fog and that he needed her.

"And so I came back to you, Master," Rin said, humbly concluding her story. "Your Rin is ready to continue serving you in all ways if you will have me." She bowed her head. "Keep me with you on your great quest, Master," she pleaded with an irrepressible sob.

Seraph made no immediate reply. He had already decided to keep her with him, for her help, he recognized, would be of much value. At this moment, however, Seraph was contemplating a larger matter one that gave him much comfort.

The fact of Rin's survival and her presence here with him tonight had to be further proof that his mission was sanctioned by the mysterious Fates that control the cosmos. His quest to destroy the Arkie oppressors he saw would always transcend the lesser concerns of lesser people. And so he must never let himself falter out of foolish modesty of heart or head. Instead he must always cling to the cosmic role that had been thrust upon him.

Satisfied anew that he was destined for greatness the nature of which he would begin to learn tomorrow at the cave of fire Seraph now gave Rin the assurance she sought.

"We shall go together to the fire, Rin. And thereafter, whatever happens, you will be with me."

Weeping for simple joy, Rin knelt before him.

"I shall be honored to serve you in every way, Master."

Rin did not yet presume to utter the other, the surpassing truth rooted in her soul: *"I love you Master."* Perhaps a time would come when she would be able to speak those words. But not yet.

Seraph reached forward and wiped a tear from Rin's cheek.

It may be that some women do possess souls, he thought.

"Normally, as you know, I am not one to seek omens in dreams," said Agathon. "But recently I have been experiencing persistent nightmares of calamities and so vividly do they seize me that they induce a melancholy which carries over into wakefulness and darkens my days."

Agathon paused. He glanced sharply at Megistes, as if expecting an immediate expression of skepticism from the old man. When the anticipated comment was not forthcoming, however, Agathon continued.

"In spite of my rational doubts about presentiments and such these horrible night visions have recurred so often now that I have begun to wonder if they might actually be signals—warnings perhaps—from some abyss of my mind which detects the approach of danger and cataclysm and sets them forth symbolically in dreams while my higher mind sleeps. Might this be possible? What do you think, old friend?"

The Hegemon stared at Megistes, awaiting his reply.

Though a scoffer when it came to the notion of ominous nightmares, in this case Megistes not only sensed Agathon's agitation as a result of his sleeping visions he also found himself sympathizing with his friend's distress. Clearly, these nightly bouts with terrifying images had disturbed seriously the Hegemon's naturally tranquil and confident inner self. That being the case, Megistes reflected, *Agathon had done well to summon him for counsel even though it was the middle of a chilly night.*

Despite his own skepticism in these matters Megistes regarded Agathon's perturbed state as a grave business since in his view anything that unsettled the judgment or the spirit of the Ruler of Arkadia had to be treated by the Logofant of the Realm as problematic. Hence, Megistes probed further, but gently, avoiding any suggestion of his own skepticism.

"So, can you tell me about the content of these nightmares?"

Agathon frowned, as if the question irritated him.

"I don't recall them in detail only in general, in images."

"Then just give me what images you remember."

With an exasperated sigh, Agathon covered his eyes with his left hand apparently in an effort to visualize again what he had "seen" while asleep.

While he waited for his friend's reply Megistes examined by the dim light of the single lamp this room which Agathon always called his "study" and which seemed in some odd way reflective of the Hegemon's character. Here were the familiar walls of books, the work-table covered as always with a snowfall of notes and papers, and the two battered antique leather couches in one of which Agathon now sprawled while Megistes sat rheumatically stiff in the other. *This chamber which hadn't changed in any noticeable way since the first days of Agathon's reign revealed just how much a creature of habit this conscientious Hegemon was,* mused Megistes.

Above all, thought the Logofant, *Agathon prized order in his working life as well as in the other areas of his existence. He liked to keep regular hours, sleep well, and follow a schedule that allowed him to "get things done in a timely manner" as the man himself often put it.* That Agathon felt compelled to interrupt his life's routine to deal with his nightmares surely made it plain that they disturbed him even more than he was willing to admit. Moreover Megistes suspected that other concerns, less recondite than his nightmares but somehow connected to them, were also weighing on the Hegemon's mind. If so, Megistes felt sure they would reveal themselves during the discussion still to come.

At last Agathon lifting his hand from his eyes spoke.

"Well, I'm sorry but I don't think I have the words to convey the absolute dread these nightmares arouse in me. I can tell you that as I try to recreate them now I realize that there really have been only three of these terror-dreams though each has been repeated over and over again in slightly different form each time."

"But always focused on the same calamitous events?"

"Yes. In the one I'll call the first though by now the sequence has become rather mixed up in my mind I am riding alone in the Forbidden Zone trying to find Milo when I smell smoke. I try to rouse the Riders supposed to be on patrol in the Zone. But their outposts are empty. I then ride up the slope to the Bemgrass and I find the entire region in flames, smoke thick everywhere. It is a mad scene, Bem warriors slaughtering each other, dire-cats in flames roaring and devouring Bem children. I try to organize the maddened folk to fight the conflagration but I find I am dumb, try as I will, I cannot make myself heard and I ride off blaming myself for I know the flames will devour the Bem."

Agathon halted. He shook his long silver mane as if trying to shake off the memory of the Bemgrass aflame. Then, favoring Megistes with an apologetic almost embarrassed smile, he continued.

"I'm sorry I don't seem able to impart the utter anguish this nightmare creates in me." He took a breath. "The other two are equally horrific to me at least. I won't try to describe them in much detail trusting that your imagination can supply your own particulars. In the second dream or rather, the one I have designated as the second I am meditating alone in my little marble sanctuary in the roof garden of the Residence when I feel a tremendous shuddering of the building. It shakes me out of my trance. In panic I run out onto the roof. The world is convulsing. From the roof garden I stare as Ten Turrets crumbles before my eyes, the walls and towers crashing down. Above, on the heights of Mt. Hierys, I see the Logofane collapse. I weep for I know this is doom for Arkadia and I can do nothing.

"I shall tell you the third vision even more briefly. In it I am being driven in my chariot along the south bank of the River Bradys. The charioteer is my favorite, the stoic Karou. Without warning or any sound at all the Bradys, normally so placid, begins to swell over its banks. Karou and I simultaneously spot the cause of the flood: a great wall of water is rolling toward us, against the usual flow of the river. Karou turns the chariot and he tries to outrun the mountain of water. But we are engulfed. I am holding my breath, struggling to escape. But it's no use. I have to draw a breath. But I only inhale filthy water and I drown. Just as I die, I hear Karou shouting, "You did this, Agathon! You!"

Apparently finished with his recital Agathon looked at Megistes and then flashed a twisted smile as if abashed.

"Well, what do you think? Do you detect any meaning here, any validity?"

Megistes shrugged.

"Maybe. More to the point, however: what do you think your nightmares mean?"

Agathon frowned.

"As irrational as it must sound I can't help feeling that they presage something terrible gathering over us, some upheaval."

Now it was Megistes who frowned.

"Perhaps some part of you senses difficult days ahead." Megistes paused, as if to gather his thoughts, then resumed. "After all, haven't we often observed certain animals—our hunting dogs most notably—seem to feel in advance when an earth tremor is in the offing? They become restless even howling for what seems to us no reason. How do these animals sense the catastrophe ahead? The theory is that they detect small signs not discernible to humans a slight trembling of leaves when there is no wind, for example, or a wispy odor of escaping volcanic gas, a tiny change in air pressure, even a hissing in a well. Though such aberrations are of little consequence individually, when taken together they signal—at least to animals—that disaster is approaching."

Agathon grimaced good-naturedly. "So I am an earthquake-detecting dog?"

Megistes ignored the jibe.

"Well, you are not a dog but a highly perceptive man who occupies a critically important place in our world. My guess is that your disturbing dreams are the result of some internal agitation which your waking mind does not wish to contemplate."

"Hmm. You'll have to explain that further for me."

Megistes shrugged again.

"This is just speculation, you understand, but I am conjecturing that for some time now you have rather like our sensitive hunting dogs been aware on some level of untoward minor happenings in the Realm. While your intellect disregarded them and rightly so for the Hegemon must ignore small matters, these bits of troublesome information have accumulated in your deeper mind where dreams are born. Eventually when your mind could contain no more it boiled over into these terrifying nightmares of yours. I'm just guessing, of course."

Agathon, who had been stretched out listlessly on his aged couch, now sat up, his handsome face a mask of wonder.

"Of course you are right, Megistes! Of course! I thought none of it mattered, you see! I mean these small events, the little things that were not right somehow. I thought them too trivial to be taken seriously, too insubstantial to signify anything important. But, as usual, you are right my friend. Some abode of wisdom in my heart has been trying to alert me to a coming danger that I've been too obtuse to see for myself. Thank you, Megistes, for explaining me to myself. You cannot know how relieved I am to find that I am not going mad after all."

Megistes felt immensely pleased that his facile surmise, for he knew it was no more than that, about Agathon's frightful visions had in some manner relieved the Hegemon's worst anxiety about the soundness of his reason. Nevertheless the old Sage couldn't stem a surge of curiosity about the "small events" and "little things" which apparently had given rise to Agathon's disturbing dreams. And so Megistes, recalling some of the inexplicable "minor happenings" which had vexed his own activities recently, made an impertinent request of his dear friend.

"Will you tell me about some of those incidents that you thought too insubstantial for your attention?'

"Hard to remember all of them. Why do you want to know?"

"I may have overlooked similar occurrences in my own sphere of responsibility."

"I see," said Agathon at once thoughtful. "Well then, let me think. As I look back on the last months it seems to me that the first reality I failed to recognize was the fact that recently Bem terror has increased remarkably. This is especially so among those Bem boys who come across the Bradys at low water in order to murder picnicking families, lovers strolling the south bank, and even old women and hiking children. The number of such incidents has almost doubled recently. Unfortunately our reprisals by 'punishment squads' of Riders also seem to have been less successful than in previous months. Thus perhaps a quarter of these vicious young terrorists now manage to escape into the Bemgrass. Though our Riders do their best to capture the culprits alive the Bem murderers prefer to kill themselves—as they always have—rather than fall into our hands for interrogation. That much remains the same at least. But, as I look back now, even the quality of Bem rage seems to have deepened, if I can put it that way."

Megistes found Agathon's account puzzling as well as frightening. *Why*, he wondered, *had Agathon failed to consult him about all this?*

"What do you mean in practical terms when you say Bem rage has deepened?"

"The Bem terrorists," said Agathon, "have taken to kidnapping solitary and vulnerable Arkadians, people who might be on a nocturnal errand or maybe a couple of lovers oblivious to all but themselves. No ransom, of course, but the victims are then tortured to death and flung into the Bradys or left in the Forbidden Zone to be discovered by Riders. Even one of our Rider cadets lost on a night patrol fell into Bem hands to be tortured and murdered. Yes, the Bem have become more vicious than ever and far bolder than ever. My own Charioteer, Karou, was attacked on his way back from visiting his cadet son in the Zone. He managed to escape by whipping up his team. Since he speaks some of the Bem dialect he was able to report that as he fled his assailants he heard them shouting after him: 'Our Savior is coming, Arkie! Let all Arkies beware!'"

"By the Logos," Megistes found himself exclaiming. "These are not minor incidents, Strategat!"

More abashed than before, Agathon nodded. "As I look on them coldly now, I realize it, my friend, and I wonder how I was so blind that I disregarded their import. What was wrong with me?"

"You are a human being, subject to human failings. But, thanks be to the Logos you have recognized your error now." Megistes paused, then said, "Were there other disturbing signs that you can recall?"

The Hegemon rested his chin in his hand.

"As I think of it now, aside from the obvious acts of terror, there were numerous other indications of, what shall I call it, restlessness among the Bem."

"Such as?"

"At the most recent Passing, for example, I couldn't help but notice an increasingly sullen attitude among the Kapits and Shamans when they knelt to ask my permission to enter the Zone. Some of them even seemed to sneer at me. Others, including some warriors, wore insolent smiles and gabbled discourteously among themselves during the ceremony. It made me furious at the time but I decided to ignore it for the sake of amity. I think now that I was wrong to do so."

"Anything else?"

"Nothing I observed myself but Phylax has reported to me—unofficially—that he suspects the Bem have been secretly conducting sacrificial rites while camped in the Forbidden Zone. This is strictly prohibited as you know. The evidence? Burnt bones, some of them human. Phylax also reported that while on patrol, after that most recent Passing I mentioned, he and his lads wounded and then took prisoner a young Bem warrior who just before he died boasted that the mad oracle of the Bem—what do they call him?"

"The Vessel of Dis."

"Yes, the Vessel. Phylax said this maniac has apparently been predicting that a great mage is going to come from the sky soon to lead the Bem and reclaim their land from the evil Arkies. Incidentally, Phylax was reporting to me in private about these matters as part of his confidential oversight—at my instruction—of Milo's behavior as a White Angel cadet. I'm afraid I paid far more attention to Phylax's evaluation of Milo than I did to his reports about a potential Bem savior out of the blue. That was surely a short-sighted mistake."

Agathon fell silent but soon broke his silence again.

"You know, Megistes, a delegation of Northfair merchants came to Ten Turrets a couple of months ago seeking my permission to trade with our Pious Koinars. I granted it of course, why not encourage legitimate commerce out there along the Pelorys, but in the midst of our negotiations one of these shrewd Northfair traders asked me point-blank if there was any truth to the rumor rampant among the Pious Koinars that the Bem were planning an uprising and that some Bem warriors had even found a way to cross the Pelorys to raid. I assured him that the rumor was mere gossip. But now I wonder if the Pious Koinars know more than we do."

"I doubt it," Megistes replied. *But perhaps it was true that Bem warriors had found a way to cross the river,* he reflected, *recalling that his best agent among the Pious Koinars a huge ruffian known as Leo the Giant had been murdered in his own house not so long ago probably as he slept. Could that killing have been carried out by Bem warriors as a reprisal against Leo for his spying on behalf of Arkadians?*

Megistes now remembered as well that a pair of the ankle cuffs worn by Bem females had also been found with Leo's corpse as if meant as a warning to other potential spies among the Pious Koinars. Given all he had just heard from Agathon about the missed signs of a burgeoning restiveness among the usually-cowed Bem Colors Megistes reckoned that prudence required a resurgence of vigilance from the Arkadian Hegemony beginning with the Hegemon himself.

With this in mind, Megistes said, "Well, Strategat, despite an inexplicable lapse of watchfulness on our part nothing is really lost as long as we speedily adopt a program to guard Arkadia from any Bem uprising even if it means dealing a crushing blow to any suspicious Bem activity. In my view we need to be ready for anything. That much seems clear."

Agathon nodded agreement.

"Of course you're right, and I'll take some initial steps tomorrow. Still, I keep asking myself why I failed to recognize the import of the signs that were apparent to others. I can only think now that I did not want to see the evidence before me, that I was in a state of abjuration so profound that it took a course of terrifying dreams to chase me out of my mental hiding place."

He paused, his face twisted with an anguish that seemed to Megistes unwarranted. After all, the Hegemony had not yet suffered serious harm because of the Hegemon's lapse in judgment and Agathon himself was now resolved to act as he should have earlier. Surely this conscientious Hegemon was being too harsh in blaming himself for his tardiness especially now that the remedy was about to be applied.

Megistes was clearing his throat to voice these sentiments when Agathon in a single precipitate movement sprang from his couch and began stalking back and forth in obvious perturbation. Megistes observed the Hegemon's distress with astonishment. *Was his old friend working himself up to disclose something else? Something extremely painful to him?*

Agathon paused in his stumping about. He fixed Megistes with eyes swimming in unshed tears.

"I'm ashamed to admit what I now believe was the true reason for my blind state."

He sucked in air as if no ordinary lungful would suffice.

"My dereliction has to do with Milo," he said.

Megistes' astonishment swelled.

"Milo? What, in the name of wisdom does Milo have to do with any of this?"

"Everything probably."

Agathon abruptly dropped into the nearest chair.

"But first I have to reveal something which is for your ears only. You must never speak of it to another soul. Agreed?"

Mystified, as well as astonished, Megistes nodded.

Agathon, wringing his hands, leaned forward in his chair.

"I am mortally ill, Megistes. I have a wasting disease for which there is no cure." Another lungful inhaled. "I am told that my departure from this world is not exactly imminent, but I am definitely on the down slope. I should last another two or three years say the physicians whom I have threatened with dire punishment should they even whisper anything at all about my condition."

Agathon took another deep breath.

"I see I have shocked you, Megistes. Well, I am shocked too. It's no use trying to cheer me up about this, old friend. In fact I forbid you to utter any expression of sympathy, or sorrow, or any talk at all about this thing. In fact let us make a covenant between us—two honorable men—that from this moment on neither of us will speak of this thing to each other or to anyone else until I hear Mortal Necessity's implacable summons. Will you respect my wishes in this?'

Though profoundly shaken to learn of the Hegemon's atrocious lot, for silver-haired and action-prone Agathon looked as hale as ever Megistes said without hesitation, "Of course I will respect your wish, dear friend, though I cannot empty my heart of grief."

Agathon regarded his aged teacher with a smile perhaps of gratitude.

"So be it then. Believe me, Megistes, I've accepted what's happening to my body. I see it as my just fate. What I have not been able to accept—I realize this now—is the prospect of Milo as my successor. I think that's why I blinded myself to the signs of a coming upheaval among the Bem. I did not want to see, did not want to make the decisions I might need to make. Thus the nightmares: My interior ghost castigating me."

Agathon leaned back in his chair as if awaiting his old teacher's comment.

Willing his mind to sail where Agathon pointed, Megistes said. "What is it about Milo that disturbs you so?"

Megistes had had the impression that under Kala Aristaia's tutelage the Hegemon's Heir had been swiftly emerging from his period of dejection.

"His behavior disturbs me," said Agathon. "He continues to exhibit no maturity, no interest in his heritage and, I'm sorry to say, he makes it plain in many ways that he has little genuine concern about preparing himself for the responsibilities that await him. Yes, it's true that Kala Aristaia is a dear girl and she has done much to improve Milo's private life in the Residence. No more drunkenness at least and he no longer spends day after day burrowed like a mole in his quarters doing who-knows-what. That's all well and good. But when Milo's away from his Betrothed, taking part as he often must now in public matters, his actions and attitude leave much to be desired."

Megistes had heard none of this before.

"In what way does he fall short?"

"Well, these incidents taken singly can seem petty but in the aggregate they add up—at least in my view—to actual contempt for the Hegemony and for Milo's own place in it."

"Examples?"

"It gives me no pleasure to recount them." Another frustrated inhalation of breath. "Let me give you just some recent instances, shall I?"

"Certainly."

"At this recent Passing ceremony Milo made not the slightest effort even to appear involved. He spent most of the day yawning as if to underscore his boredom and grimacing as if unable to contain his contempt not only for the Bem but also for me, the Array, the entire rite. Even Darden behaved better than the Heir to the High Bench. I can tell you that Milo's public display deeply offended many of his fellow Riders. He must have been aware of it but made it plain that he didn't care.

"Nor did he even try to make amends at the annual Feast of the Array that traditionally follows the Passing. Instead of taking part in the festivities or at least pretending an interest in the games or the dancing, he took himself off to his tent without a word. Phylax told me later that the Troopers took this act as a slap in the face especially because it came from the young man who is to be their commander when named Anax in a short time.

"Phylax also reported to me with much reluctance I assure you that Milo, who used to take such pride in the White Angels Regiment, is now seldom present at musters and has stopped entirely playing any part in regimental maneuvers which is an unwritten duty of the next Anax. Phylax makes no secret of his concern for his old *del*, especially since Milo simply ignores all attempts to advise him.

"And I, too, have seen with my own eyes some even worse conduct at those public affairs he is expected to attend in order to prepare himself for his duties as Anax."

Agathon paused as if ashamed to reveal more of his elder son's shortcomings.

Megistes, however, prodded the Hegemon to continue. "You might as well get it all out so that I may fully understand."

"Yes, yes. Well, I have observed this young man who will be Hegemon actually fall asleep, and snore—head back mouth gaping—while the Council is in session. And he shows no inclination whatever to take part in debate. Members have complained to me about his lack of interest and his ignorance of Council protocol as if I am somehow able to change the boy. I am at my wit's end, Megistes. Is Milo slipping into some kind of madness? I just don't know. What I do know is that his bad deportment of which I've given you only some examples amounts to more than the usual adolescent grumps. Given the turbulent times that seem to lie ahead for the Hegemony I must ask myself: Can Milo cope especially after my illness takes me off?"

The Hegemon's question was one that Megistes did not wish to answer. And so he posed one of his own.

"Have you tried remonstrating with the boy?"

Boy, thought Megistes, *was the wrong word, for Milo, though still only sixteen, was no longer the Sage's eager student but a chosen young man on the brink of enormous responsibilities which he seemed unable, or unwilling, to shoulder.*

And so Megistes added a clarification to his query.

"I'm not talking about a gentle scolding of Milo I'm talking about a scorching dressing down, volleys of threats, punishments of one kind or another, but dire, really dire."

Agathon shook his head.

"Instinct tells me that Milo will never respond to that kind of reproof. Any form of scolding only drives him to silence, a kind of stubborn withdrawal. If he does deign to reply it's only to admit his failing, and promise to do better. Of course his promises are always in vain. Any advice for the unhappy Hegemon of Arkadia?"

"As a matter of fact I do. Admittedly, it's a rather odd strategy but one that in view of Milo's peculiar psychology might bring him around especially if Kala Aristaia plays her role as vigorously as I think she would."

"Well?"

A skeptical "well" from Agathon.

Said Megistes who recognized the odds against his proposal succeeding, "I would urge you to elevate Milo to Anax now. Don't wait. Do it as soon as possible. When it's done marry him at once to Kala Aristaia so that as his wife she will have every opportunity to advise him on all matters and even travel with him on maneuvers and bivouacs. She is a courageous girl and highly intelligent. She will become a great and beneficial influence. That's my advice, old friend: force the responsibility of the office of Anax on Milo. Make him do the job, rise to the demands of office. I think that, like many men with little natural liking for power, Milo will find the necessary fiber within him. Thrust the responsibility on him and watch him grow into it, eh? May I remind you Agathon that you shrank at first from the demands of office until the press of duty seized you."

Agathon aimed an incredulous sniff at his old tutor.

"I wish I could share your confidence in my son's character or your certainty about Kala Aristaia's potential ascendancy over him. But I find myself more than a little doubtful. Perhaps it's because I have had too much experience with the current Milo to believe he'll come around. I keep thinking how sad it is that we must seek the reform of my Heir's character as the chief hope for the Realm's future."

"It is a weakness of our state," Megistes remarked as he had so often in his career, "that so much of Arkadia's success depends on the quality of her rulers, but there it is, the reality. Of course, if you named Milo Anax as you probably will have to in the end you could employ a simple expedient to ameliorate the chances that his appointment would result in catastrophe."

Agathon sniffed again.

"And, what might that be, my wily friend?"

"You could appoint two or three experienced men from the ranks of the Council to act as deputies to the Anax, spread the responsibilities."

Agathon smiled as if he found the suggestion ridiculous but endearing.

"Spread confusion as well," he said. "Spread the political infighting, instigate a struggle for power. Not workable in practice Megistes."

"Then name Milo and be done with it. Take your chances."

"Or, instead of Milo, I could appoint another."

"Darden?"

"Logos preserve us! Darden has been on his good behavior but to quote him he still 'hates' me and he 'hates' Arkadia even more. That's why I've decided to accede to your request that he be sent to study with you at the Logofane. Perhaps, as you have suggested often before this, long exposure to the Logos and to you will calm his so-called hatred. I have ordered him to be ready to leave within the week."

"Thank you for giving me so much notice," said Megistes dryly wondering how Darden had developed his capacity for distilling his "hatred" into a contemptuous scorn that Megistes no longer had the stomach to rebut. A puzzle. In any case Megistes told himself sardonically having Darden under his charge at the Logofane would certainly enliven the place.

Agathon spoke again, interrupting Megistes' musing on Darden.

"Suppose, instead of appointing Milo, I break precedent and name a truly worthy Anax?"

Megistes had no difficulty guessing the identity of the Hegemon's probable choice.

"You mean Phylax, of course. There could be no one better. But he would not accept."

"He would if I pressed him for the good of Arkadia."

"Perhaps," said Megistes realizing that Agathon was entirely serious. *How worried the Hegemon must be about Milo's elevation to a seat of power if he was entertaining such a radical move!*

"There is precedent for a nomination outside the usual order," Agathon said. "When an Anax dies or is incapacitated the Hegemon has the power to appoint a qualified substitute. Past Hegemons have done just that when necessary."

"But no Hegemon has ever deposed a living Heir in good health."

"I can make the case that Milo is ill, unable to meet the obligations of the office of Anax. I know that the majority of the people would actually prefer Phylax over Milo."

"That may be but the people don't get to vote their approval of the appointed Anax that is the prerogative of the Council meaning the Megars who dominate it. And we both know that the Megars will balk at any action by any Hegemon if it seems to threaten hereditary rights in the slightest degree let alone to the enormous extent this idea surely does. After all, the fortunes and the stable powers of the Megars depend on their ability to pass property on to their heirs in the traditional way, to arrange marriages that strengthen alliances between families and clans, and to use those alliances to keep political power within their caste. The Megars would rise in protest if you were to nominate Phylax."

"I think many would support my choice."

"Maybe," said Megistes, "but many more would refuse to approve. Arkadia could erupt in civil war. Is that the legacy you wish to leave behind you in a time of growing instability among the Bem?"

Agathon fell silent as did Megistes for both men dreaded any outbreak of conflict among the various factions of the Hegemony. This was especially so because the lineaments of such an armed clash were already, if vaguely, presaged by the very existence of the varied factions to be found within the political and social structures of Arkadia.

The most powerful of the emergent factions within the Hegemony was composed of those Megars who finally having run out of patience with Bem terrorism wanted to use the armed might of the state to exterminate as many of the "bestial" Bem as feasible and then drive any surviving remnant into the western mountains far from the borders of Arkadia. In the process of eliminating the Bem "once and for all" this party of Megars also wanted to seize the salt beds of the Bemgrass, and, in passing, removal of the "illegal" Pious Koinar settlements along the east bank of the River Pelorys. Disturbingly, this Megar "Party of Just Revenge" was drawing more and more adherents to its program every year.

The other major font of discontent was to be found within the ranks of Arkadia's Koinar citizens. With the exception of their "Pious" sect who had an agenda of their own the Koinars of Arkadia were virtually unanimous in their demand for full voting representation in the Grand Council of the Hegemony. As matters stood now the Koinar representatives in the Council were allowed to debate freely those measures presented for the legislators' consideration and consent but were not permitted to vote on them.

Only recently in a public letter circulated throughout the Hegemony the Speaker of the Koinar contingent in the Grand Council, Rab Zebulon, had summarized the Koinar position on the matter with impressive economy.

Wrote Zebulon:

"Since the people of Arkadia have appropriated our Koinar tongue and much of our culture as well as our Logos, our enterprise, and even many of our laws, we think it only right that we Koinar folk be compensated for our contributions with full membership in the government of the nation that we so effectively helped to create. This can only be accomplished by awarding us the vote in Council. Few of us wish to return to being a state-within-a-state. Nor, unlike our minority of self-styled "Pious Koinars' do we want some "autonomous region" assigned to us. What we want, what we deserve, are the rights and privileges enjoyed by our fellow citizens."

Rab Zebulon's statement had created a stir making it virtually certain that "voting representation for Koinars" as the issue was generally formulated would be addressed relatively soon. But the question remained whether it could actually be accomplished under present circumstances without armed resistance from Megar and Rider families. The possibility of civil conflict over this issue, therefore, was also a source of the current pollution in the political atmosphere of Arkadia.

Clearly then at least in Megistes' judgment if Agathon was to disrupt the customary process of choosing an Anax even if he did so for the general good he might very well put so much additional strain on the foundations of the state that the Hegemony might collapse into the very conflict that all parties claimed they wished to avoid. The only winners then would be the Bem.

Both the Hegemon and his Logofant were very well aware of this present precarious state of affairs in Arkadia and so neither saw any reason to speak of it choosing instead to let it rest until one of them felt obliged to break what had become a lengthening silence between them.

It was Agathon who finally spoke.

"Ah, Megistes, my friend, I suppose that as usual I must accept my own limitations as Hegemon. Very well, then I shall not appoint Phylax. Milo will be named Anax and may the wisdom of the Logos protect us."

Megistes nodded. "The worst of our fears often never come to pass," he said.

"You think not?"

"I hope not."

Again they fell silent Megistes contemplating the impending death of his friend, the man he loved most in life. *Why,* he asked himself, *is the world always such a complex web and we inevitably caught in its tangles?*

Agathon, too, was contemplating the onrushing termination of all he was, had been, or might have been. *He had achieved little enough in his life,* he reflected. *How much more he could do if only he had more time! But he understood that yearning after the unobtainable was a sentimental absurdity. Fate was fate.*

"Dawn is breaking," he murmured to Megistes.

"Why so it is," the old man replied.

The fire Seraph had been seeking for so long roared out of a cave part way up the western slope of the mountain which he now realized was the one the Arkies called "Mount Kryptys".

The cave mouth belched flame and a dense yellow smoke that carried the stink of putrefaction and Sulphur as well as other subtler exudations that, even at a distance, were producing a "floating" sensation in Seraph as he approached the blaze.

The orifice of the cave was easily accessible if the visitor could overcome instinctual fear of uncontrolled combustion and revulsion at the smoke's stench for it lay at the terminus of a gently rising "meadow" composed of what looked like waves and whorls of polished black rock that might once have been liquid until somehow petrified in mid-flow.

There were those among the Bem shamans, Seraph recalled, who believed that the black-stone meadow had been formed somehow by the mountain itself in ages past.

Because he did not wish to risk injury to the invaluable mare and pony by forcing them to climb this meadow of slippery and often sharp rock Seraph chose to advance on foot with Rin's aid to the flaming cave mouth.

As he worked his way up leaning much on Rin's arm Seraph tried to avoid thinking about any terrifying entity that might be awaiting him at the fiery entrance to the cave. Instead he kept his attention focused on the extraordinary "high road" of rock that led to it.

No vegetation of any kind grew on the impermeable surface of the Blackstone whose width Seraph estimated at two hundred yards at least. Seraph also found himself speculating that in some dim long ago the "high road" or "meadow," as some Bem shamans named it, had somehow burned its way through a large segment of the forest that still covered most of these lower levels of the mountain. *Perhaps,* Seraph thought, *the Blackstone had once been a river of flame that had burned itself out, leaving this glossy residue.*

Scattered here and there on the hardened surface, Seraph noticed, were smaller stones many having a gem-like sheen. Seraph had already discovered that these stones had edges that seemed sharper than the keenest of the Arkie metal blades. He had filed this impression in the back of his mind to be considered in the future assuming he would have a future.

At last Seraph and Rin came to a level area like a terrace of the glossy stone that stretched for forty or fifty yards in front of the roaring entrance of the cave. Here Seraph and Rin halted as if to gather strength for the final leg to the fires and here they were staggered by a sudden blast of heat and sulphuric odor like the breath of the great mountain itself.

It struck Seraph how apt was the Pious Koinars' description of these precincts as "unclean" for the barren slope together with the unnatural fire and mephitic air were certainly inimical to living creatures despite the rather pleasant sensations he was experiencing whenever he could wrench his mind away from his fears.

Unclean, indeed.

Still, Seraph knew that something immense, some force not to be resisted, had surely summoned him to this foul place and now he must go forward and present himself to it.

Turning to Rin, he said, "You must go back now, while I go forward."

Rin started to protest, as he expected she would but fell silent when he held up his hand.

"This is my destiny, Rin. Do as I say."

With a knot of dread in his chest a circumstance that he considered unworthy of the new being that he hoped to become in the forge of the flames ahead, Seraph forced his battered body to limp forward until he came as close to the fiery entrance as he could without immolating himself. Here he halted and waited, for what, for he knew not. The bellowing of the blaze deafened him. He found himself swaying dizzily in the furnace blast. Engulfed in heat, smoke, and fumes, he had to struggle to breathe. He waited.

Despite the primordial chaos vomiting from the cave mouth, Seraph was by some unknown means able to detect cries and moans from within as of suffering creatures not wholly human. He continued to abide, swaying, choking. *Was he expected to force himself to pass somehow through the conflagration into the hell beyond?*

Seraph heard a voice, a sexless whisper that had gotten into his head though he knew it emanated from within the cave.

"Leave this place now, Mortal—and wait for me."

His will virtually absent Seraph turned away and reeled back toward Rin.

At Seraph's insistence, Rin set up their camp in the slope-forest adjacent to the black road to the cave. From this site she could see—and smell—and hear—the witch-fire as it ejected its tongues of baleful flame and its billows of vile smoke. Although Rin herself desperately wished to flee from this site that seemed to her evil in ways beyond her grasp, Seraph, exhausted after his mysterious interval at the cave-mouth made it plain that he intended to remain in the vicinity.

"You may depart, if you choose, Rin," Seraph declared in a rasping voice that seemed much weakened by his ordeal at the witch-fire, "but I shall stay here as I must. The business will soon be finished one way or another."

Rin said no more about fleeing for Seraph was master and she had to obey him. *Besides,* she reflected, *the truth was that this "unclean" mountain offered them the only sure safety from the vengeance of Leo the Giant's brothers for if those Pious Koinars were still seeking to avenge their dead brother they would certainly avoid contact with this evil-looking district of their domain.*

As soon as Rin finished establishing their rough camp, Seraph, refusing the bread and drink that Rin offered him, fell deeply asleep.

As Seraph lay stretched out on his back on her shawl, Rin sat up to watch over him as he slept. Seraph drew breath so seldom and made the movements of sleep only after such long intervals that she thought it prudent to listen to his slow heart from time to time to assure herself that he was still alive. *Something had surely happened to him up there at the cave-mouth* she thought. *Whatever it might have been—good or evil—she intended to guard him well until he came to himself again. Perhaps then, he would see how her love protected him.*

Behind the curtain of flame, Eris, Queen of Strife, paced in restless anxiety. *When was she to be loosed once more on the mortal world?* The question which was also an implied complaint was directed to the invisible lord of these infinite caverns.

In truth Eris was fretting lest her Dread Sovereign, by delaying her exit, force her to wait too long, and so cause her to miss the moment—which was now!

Eris had understood as soon as the mortal had presented himself at the entrance to her prison that he was the one she required. Even from behind the curtain of fire she had recognized that he would be the perfect instrument of her vengeance, that his faith would guarantee her resurrection.

But all this could only be if the Dread Sovereign of these cosmic caverns granted her license to mold the mortal's spirit, to enlarge his ambitions, and above all to plant in him a hunger to rule as a god in service to the true Overlord of Creation.

All this Eris had already promised to her unseen lord. Her pledge, she knew, was a desperate plea to her silent suzerain: *Free me to bring glory to your reign! Loosen my bonds that I may breathe in the hatred within this mortal's heart and so advance your designs. Free me, Lord!*

Suddenly, the imprisoning flames ceased, snuffed out like mere candles. Smoke no longer billowed forth but drifted in clouds into the black night. Cautiously Eris stepped from the cavernous underworld. She inhaled deeply in cool darkness. Here, she perceived exultingly, time flowed as mortals experienced it and space existed in a steady state which mortal men, ignorant of how space can expand and contract at whim as in these Meta-chron caverns, thought "natural".

Eris whirled about delighted to discover that instead of the grime-streaked rags she had been wearing while imprisoned she was once more garbed in the radiant white *chiton* and the draped gown suitable to her divinity. Whooping with the pleasure of it, Eris now embraced a passing night breeze to carry her to the mortal she sought.

As she flew Eris gloried in her flight. Weightless, limitless, all spirit no more than a membrane, she rejoiced, once more a goddess.

To reassure herself of her restoration to her proper condition she held up her hand before her goddess eyes and found a new access of rapture there—for she could once again look through a transparent hand and view the cataract of stars in the night sky.

Eris laughed to be herself again and laughed again because she understood what He who ruled the underworld wished her to do and she would do it she vowed with passionate zeal: She would attach herself to the mortal and she would show him how he must re-make himself in the image of the Dread Sovereign of Creation.

Eris soon located the place where the mortal slept dreaming his mortal visions under the watchful eyes of the fretful woman, his companion. Descending in a form too tenuous to register on bodily senses Eris laid an unseen finger lighter than thistle-down between the mortal woman's worried eyes.

Rin, who had been thinking how to persuade an awakened and refreshed Seraph to depart this place of evil desires, felt a brief cold spot between her eyes as if a drop of chill rain had fallen there.

Then a darkness engulfed her.

Rin slept at the bottom of the deepest dry well in the universe.

Eris satisfied that she could still wield her power with elegance hovered over the sleeping mortal whose name, she now divined, was "Seraph." Eager to practice once more the artistry that had once brought her bliss beyond compare Eris sent her mind into Seraph's dreaming.

Immediately she encountered a storm of images. As these gyrated about her some lingered long enough for her to identify them: the River Pelorys in churning brown flood, the gleaming skeleton of a child, a white mare singing to the moon, a swamp of cold fear and hot fury. Hunger in the grasslands, too.

Eris sent her thoughts through this thrashing storm in the mortal's mind and found the opaque silence at its center. Here, where the mortal's understanding lay inert and receptive, she began to thrust into him the first of the many lessons she intended for him as he grew capable of accepting them.

Real magic Eris disclosed mind to mind is not mere trickery to fool fools; it is possession of knowledge of the authentic forces of the Cosmos and how to use them.

Know this, mortal, the goddess made Seraph understand, *all the worlds in all the universes operate according to laws which differ in each world. I shall teach you the cosmic rules that apply in your world, this world. I shall show you how to achieve the power to bend those rules to your will. It shall be my joy to do this in order to avenge through you my destroyed brothers and sisters of Olympian Hellas. In time I shall teach you even the art of stealing souls. I shall come to you often from now on with such knowledge. Be always ready to receive me. To begin our journey together I leave you with the first truth you must learn: All Creation is governed by the Dread Sovereign, my lord and now yours as well. Expect me again.*

Eris withdrew from the mortal's dreaming. She flew on the wind into the night sky triumphant in her restored immortality.

Printed in the United States
By Bookmasters